Kinch Riley
&
Hickok & Cody

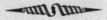

Kinch Riley

DEATH SHOT

McCluskie's knees buckled and he was suddenly gripped with the urgency of killing Anderson . . . He heard the gunfire and the terrified shrieks of dance-hall girls, sensed the crowd scattering. But it was all somehow distant, even a little unreal. Blinded, falling swiftly into darkness, he willed his hand to move. To finish what he had come here to do.

Another bullet smacked him in the ribs, but like a dead snake, operating on nerves alone, his hand reacted and came up with the Colt. That he couldn't see Anderson bothered him not at all. In his mind's eye he remembered exactly where the Texan was standing, and even as he pressed the trigger, he knew the shot had struck home . . .

"MATT BRAUN IS ONE OF THE BEST!"
> —Don Coldsmith, author of the Spanish Bit series

"HE TELLS IT STRAIGHT—AND HE TELLS IT WELL."
> —Jory Sherman, author of *Grass Kingdom*

Kinch Riley

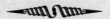

(Previously published as *Kinch*)

MATT BRAUN

St. Martin's Paperbacks

These novels are works of fiction. All of the characters, organizations, and events portrayed in them are either products of the author's imagination or are used fictitiously.

KINCH RILEY / HICKOK & CODY

Kinch Riley copyright © 1975 by Matthew Braun.
Hickok & Cody copyright © 2001 by Winchester Productions, Ltd.

All rights reserved.

For information address St. Martin's Press, 175 Fifth Avenue, New York, NY 10010.

ISBN: 978-1-250-29398-5

Our books may be purchased in bulk for promotional, educational, or business use. Please contact your local bookseller or the Macmillan Corporate and Premium Sales Department at 1-800-221-7945, ext. 5442, or by e-mail at MacmillanSpecialMarkets@macmillan.com.

Printed in the United States of America

Kinch Riley St. Martin's Paperbacks edition / June 2000
Hickok & Cody St. Martin's Paperbacks edition / May 2001

St. Martin's Paperbacks are published by St. Martin's Press, 175 Fifth Avenue, New York, NY 10010.

10 9 8 7 6 5 4 3 2 1

For

JTA

A Kindred Spirit
Who Was Always There

AUTHOR'S NOTE

THIS IS an epitaph for Kinch Riley.

Essentially it is a true story, gleaned from musty newspaper archives and the chronicles of men who were there. The place is Newton, Kansas, during the summer of 1871. On a sweltering August night a gunfight occurred which came to be known as "Newton's General Massacre." According to the *Topeka Daily Commonwealth*, six men died in the space of ninety seconds. Three more were wounded, one of whom was later killed under curious circumstances. Witnesses to the slaughter credited a young boy, known only as Riley, with having accounted for most of the dead.

Kinch Riley is the story of what led to that fateful night in Newton. More significantly, perhaps, it is a reasonably accurate account of how a bond of loyalty came to exist between a lawman and a consumptive youth of seventeen. Certain liberties have been taken with names and events, but *Kinch Riley* nonetheless explores one of the Old West's most enduring mysteries. While supporting details are available regarding events leading to the shootout, little is known of the boy named Riley.

After killing five men he simply vanished from the pages of history.

The enigma of Kinch Riley has confounded Western scholars for better than a hundred years. Though the story which follows is fiction based on facts, it provides one solution to a seemingly unfathomable riddle. Perhaps the only solution.

At last, it lays a ghost to rest.

CHAPTER 1

MCCLUSKIE SWUNG down off the caboose and stood for a moment surveying the depot. It was painted a dingy green, the same as all Santa Fe depots. Not unlike a hundred others he had seen, it had all the warmth of a freshly scrubbed privy. The only notable difference being that it was newer and bigger. Rails had been laid into Newton less than a week past, and the town had been designated division point. Otherwise, so far as McCluskie could see, there was nothing remarkable about the place. Just another fleabag cowtown that would serve as home base till the end of track shifted west a couple of hundred miles.

Hefting his war-bag, he walked to the end of the platform and paused for a look at Newton. The corners of his mouth quirked and he grunted with surprise. It wasn't Abilene, but it was damn sure more than he had expected. Especially out in the middle of nowhere, with the rails hardly a week old.

Newton was laid out much on the order of all cowtowns. Main Street spraddled the tracks, with the red-light district on the southside and most of the business establishments on the north. Side streets, none of which were more than a block long, branched off of the dusty main thoroughfare. Nearly every building had the high false-front that had become the trademark of Kansas railheads, and the structures looked as if they had been slapped together with spit and poster glue. What amazed McCluskie was not that Newton existed, but that it had sprung from the earth's bowels with such dizzying speed.

He dropped the war-bag at his feet and started rolling a smoke. The paper and tobacco took shape in his hands without thought, almost a mechanical ritual born of habit. Searching his vest, he found a sulphurhead and flicked it to life with his thumbnail. Touching flame to cigarette, he took a long draw and let his eyes wander along the street. His inspection was brief, for a well-chucked rock would have hit the town limits in any direction. But little escaped his gaze, and except for the hodge-podge of buildings, there wasn't much to stir his interest.

Whatever Newton had to offer wouldn't be all that different. He'd seen the elephant too many times to expect otherwise. Cards and shady ladies and railhead saloons were the same wherever a man hung his hat. Such things didn't change, they just shifted operations whenever the end of track changed. Most times it seemed they had even hauled along the same batch of customers.

McCluskie stuck the cigarette in his mouth, again hefted the war-bag, and started down the platform steps. Somewhere behind him he heard his name called and turned to find Newt Hansberry, the station master, bearing down on him. He didn't care much for Hansberry and had purposely avoided the depot for just that reason. But then, he was sort of standoffish about people in general, so it wasn't as if he had anything personal against the man.

"Mike, you ol' scutter!" Hansberry rushed up and commenced pumping his hand like he was trying to raise water. "Where the hell did you spring from?"

"Just pulled in on the cowtown express." McCluskie retrieved his hand and wiped it along the side of his pants.

The station master shot a puzzled glance at the cattle cars, then barfed up an oily chuckle. "Cowtown express! That's rich, Mike. Wait'll I try that on the boys." The laughter slacked off and his brow puckered in an owlish frown. "Say, what's a big mucka-muck like you doing in Newton, anyway? The head office didn't tell me you was comin' out here."

McCluskie's look was wooden, revealing nothing. "Why, Newt, you know how the brass are. They're so busy shufflin' people and trains they don't tell nobody nothin'."

"Yeh, but they don't send the top bull to end of track just for exercise." Hansberry cocked one eyebrow in a crafty smirk. "C'mon, Mike, 'fess up. They sent you out here on some kinda job, didn't they? Something hush-hush."

"Sorry to disappoint you, Newt. They just wanted me to have a looksee. Sorta make sure the division has got all the kinks ironed out. Y'know what I mean?"

Hansberry blinked and nodded, swallowing his next question. What with him being station master, that last part had struck a little close to home. "Sure, Mike. I get your drift. But don't worry, I run a tight operation. Always have."

"Never thought you didn't." McCluskie let it drop there and jerked his thumb back toward the main part of town. "What's the low-down on this dump? Anything happened I ought to know about?"

"Well I ain't seen Jesse James around town if that's what you mean. Course, I don't guess the likes of him would go in for robbin' cattle cars anyways."

"Not likely. That wasn't what I was drivin' at, though. Anybody tried to set himself up as the kingfish yet?"

"Hell, ain't nobody had time. They been too busy gettin' this place built. 'Sides, Newton's not rightly a town anyway. Wichita's the county seat and this here is just a township. Won't never be nothin' else, neither. Leastways till somebody proves it's on the map to stay."

"So I heard."

The station master gave him a guarded look. "Yeh, I guess you would've. Don't s'pose there's much that gets past you boys at the head office."

McCluskie let the question slip past. "What about law? They got anybody ridin' herd on the trailhands?"

"Oh, sure. Some of the sportin' crowd and a few of the storekeepers got themselves appointed to the town board and they pestered Wichita into sendin' a deputy up here permanent. Good thing they did, too. Otherwise them Texans would've hoorawed this place clean down to the ground."

"This lawdog, he anybody I know?"

"Sorta doubt it. Name's Tonk Hazeltine. Some folks says he's a breed, but he don't look like no Injun I ever saw. Queer kind o' bird, though. Acts like he just drunk some green rotgut and didn't care much for the taste."

"Don't think I ever heard of him. How's he handle himself? Been keepin' the drovers in line?"

"Yeh, what there is of 'em. Y'know the stockyards have only been built a couple of weeks. We're just now startin' to steal a few herds away from Abilene."

"They'll come, don't worry yourself about that. Before the summer's out we'll have the K&P stewin' in their own juice."

"I 'spect you're right. Leastways I ain't never known the Sante Fe to make no foolish bets."

McCluskie merely nodded, his eyes again drifting to the street. "Understand Belle Siddons is in town."

"Sure is. Got herself a house down on Third Street. I seem to recollect you and her was sorta thick in Abilene."

"You oughtn't to listen so good, Newt." McCluskie flicked his cigarette stub onto the tracks and started down the platform steps. When he reached the bottom, he stopped and looked back. "What's the best hotel in town?"

"Why, I guess that'd be the Newton House. Fanciest digs this side of Kansas City. Just turn north across the tracks and keep goin'. You can't miss it."

McCluskie turned south and headed down the street, walking toward a ramshackle affair that proclaimed itself the National Hotel.

Hansberry watched after him, cursing softly under his breath. There was something about McCluskie that rubbed a man the wrong way. Even if he was head of security for the line. But it wasn't the kind of thing a fellow could put into words. Not out loud anyway.

McCluskie had a certain Gaelic charm about him, with a square jaw and a humorous mouth that was about half covered with a brushy mustache. Yet he was also something of a lone wolf, and damn few men had ever gotten close enough to say they really knew him well. Not that he threw his weight around, or for that matter, even raised his voice. He didn't have to. Most folks just figured he preferred his own company, and they let it go at that.

Part of it, perhaps, had to do with his size. He was a tall man—over six feet—and compactly built. Sledge-shouldered and lean through the hips, he had the look of a prizefighter. Which he might have been at some time in the past. Little was known about him before he showed up in Abilene back in '69. There, working for the Kansas & Pacific, he had killed one man with his fists and a couple more with a gun. After that nobody felt the urge to ask questions.

Yet, as he thought on it, Hansberry was struck by something else entirely. The queer way the Irishman had of looking at a man. Not just cold and unfeeling, but the practiced eyes of a man who stayed alive by making quick estimates. It was sort of unsettling.

The station master watched McCluskie disappear

through the door of the hotel, then turned away, muttering to himself. Somehow the day didn't seem so bright any more, but a quick glance at the sky merely confirmed his misgivings. There wasn't a cloud in sight.

McCluskie came down the hall from his room and entered the lobby. He had shaved, changed to a fresh shirt, and brushed the dust from his suit. His face glowed with a ruddy, weathered vitality, and he was whistling a tuneless ditty to himself. Except for his size and bearing, and the bulge on his right hip, he might have been a spiffy drummer out to sweet-talk the local merchants. As he approached the desk, the room clerk brightened and gave him a flaccid smile.

"Yessir, Mr. McCluskie. What can we do for you? Hope that room met with your satisfaction. We don't often get folks like yourself in here. Railroad men, I mean. Mostly the rougher crowd. Y'know, trailhands and mule-skinners and the like."

McCluskie simply ignored the chatter. He took out the makings and started building a smoke. "Need some directions. Belle Siddons' house on Third Street."

The clerk's smile widened into a sly, dirty grin. "You sure know how to pick 'em, Mr. McCluskie. Belle's got the best sportin' house in town. Oughta warn you, though, it's awful expensive."

McCluskie nailed him with a flat, dull stare. "Something tickle your funny bone?"

The man blinked a couple of times and looked a little closer. What he saw was a face that sobered anyone with the savvy to read it. His grin dissolved into a waxen smile.

"No offense, Mr. McCluskie. Just tryin' to be friendly. Service of the house."

"Forget it. What about the directions?"

"Sure thing. Belle's house is just this side of Hide Park. Big yellow house right on the corner of Third. You won't have no trouble recognizing it."

"What's Hide Park?"

"Why, the—uh—y'know. The sportin' district. The parlor houses are on Third and down below that are the dancehalls and the cribs. That's why they call it Hide Park. Nothin' but bare skin and lots of it."

McCluskie just stared at him for a moment, then turned and walked from the hotel.

Striding down South Main, the Irishman found it about as he had expected. Within the first block there was a grocery, two hotels, a mercantile, and a hardware store. Then for the next couple of blocks both sides of the street were lined with saloons and gambling dens. Evidently everything below that was Hide Park.

The more he saw, the better he liked it. Plainly the townspeople had been at some pains to lay it out properly. Newton straddled the Chisholm Trail and was sixty-five miles south of Abilene. Which meant that its future as a cowtown was pretty well assured. At least for a couple of seasons, anyway. Once track was laid into Wichita, some twenty miles farther south, Newton's bubble would burst like a dead toad in a hot sun. But that was for him to know and them to find out. There was nothing to be gained in letting it get around that the Santa Fe had a finger in the pie. Right now it was enough to wean the Texans away from Abilene. The next step would come in its own good time.

Late afternoon shadows splayed over the town, and already the street was crowded with Texans. Watching them as he strolled along, McCluskie marveled again at the cowhands' childlike antics. Somehow they never seemed to change. After two months on the trail, eating dust and beans and working themselves to a frazzle, they couldn't wait to scatter their money to the winds. Painted women, watered-down whiskey, and rigged card games. That was about their speed. Almost as if they had some perverse craving to be flimflammed out of the dollar a day they earned wet-nursing longhorns. It just went to prove what most sensible folks already knew. Texans, give or take a handful, weren't much brighter than the cows they drove to railhead.

Still, a man had to give the devil his due. Without the Texans and their longhorns, the Santa Fe would be hard pushed to pull off the scheme that brought him to Newton. The thought triggered another, and he reminded himself to have a look at North Main before dark. Might even be well to introduce himself to some of the town fathers. Let them know he was around if they needed a hand with anything. Texans or otherwise. Never hurt to have a foot in the door with the uptown crowd. Especially the ones who fancied themselves as politicians.

Nearing Third, he spotted the yellow house on the northeast corner and angled across the street. Inspecting it closer, he decided the room clerk had been right after all. Upside the drab buildings surrounding it, the yellow house stuck out like a diamond in an ash heap.

McCluskie went through the door without bothering to knock and found himself in a small vestibule. The layout was as familiar as an old shoe and he proceeded immediately to the parlor. There he came on a black maid, humming softly to herself as she set things in order for the evening rush. She straightened up and gave him a toothy smile.

"Mistah, you're gonna hafta come back. I knows you got the misery jest from lookin' at you, but we ain't open till aftah suppahtime."

That was something he had always admired about

Belle. She taught the help how to diddle a man and make him like it. Even maids.

"Tell Miss Belle she's got a gentleman caller."

Apparently that was a new one on the black woman. Her sloe eyes batted furiously for a moment, then she hitched around and scurried from the room. As she went through a door to the back part of the house, she muttered something unintelligible. From the little he could make out, it was a fairly one-sided conversation.

Left to himself, McCluskie examined the parlor with a critical eye. It was nothing less than he would have expected of Belle Siddons. She had a reputation for running an elegant house. Not at all like the two-bit cribs and dollar-a-dance palaces down the street. Plainly, from the looks of the parlor, she hadn't lost her touch. Grunting, he silently gave the room his stamp of approval.

"Well as I live and breathe! If it's not the big Mick himself."

Turning, he saw Belle standing in the doorway, smiling that same soft smile he remembered so well. Outwardly she seemed to have changed not at all, though it was something over a year since he had last seen her.

She wasn't a small woman, yet there was a delicacy to her that somehow belied the shapely hips and full bust. Her hair was the color of a raven's wing, glinted through with specks of rust when the light struck it just right, and her eyes had always reminded him of an emerald stick-pin he once saw on a riverboat gambler. But it was her face that stopped most men. Not hard or worn, like what a fellow who frequented sporting houses would expect to find on a madam. It was an easy face to look at, pleasurable. Maybe something short of beautiful, but with a devilish witchery that made a man sit up and do tricks just so he could watch it smile.

"Belle, you look nifty as ever." McCluskie was hard put to keep from licking his mustache. "Appears life's been treatin' you with style."

"I can't complain." She walked toward him, airily waving her hand around the parlor. "What's the verdict? Think it'll pass muster?"

McCluskie caught a whiff of jasmine scent as she stopped before him, and for a moment he couldn't get his tongue untracked. "The house? Why, sure. Even classier than the place you had in Abilene."

"Yes, good old Abilene. Every now and then I think back on it and have myself a real laugh." A curious light flickered in her eyes. Somehow it put him in mind of a tiny flame bouncing off of alabaster. "But that's water under the bridge. Tell me about yourself, Mike. What have you been doing since the good old days?"

The way she was looking at him made him uncomfortable as hell. Almost as if he should be scuffling his toe in the dirt and apologizing for some fool thing he'd done.

"Nothin' much. Just pickin' up a dollar here and a dollar there."

"I do declare, a modest Irishman. Never thought I'd live to see the day."

"Well, you know me, Belle. I never was one to toot my own horn."

"Don't be bashful, honey. You're among friends. Why, everybody in Kansas has heard about Mike McCluskie. Some folks say the Santa Fe would fall apart without him to fend off those big, bad train robbers."

The conversation wasn't going quite the way McCluskie had expected. In fact, it seemed to be all uphill, with him pulling the load. He decided to try another tack.

"I just got in this afternoon. Thought I'd come down

and invite you out for a bite to eat after you close up
tonight."

"Then we could go up to your room for a drink and
talk about old times."

McCluskie grinned. "Well, something like that had
crossed my mind."

Fire flashed in Belle's eyes, and it was no longer a tiny
flame. "Listen you thick-headed Mick, forget the sweet
talk and trot yourself out of here. You left me high and
dry in Abilene, and once burned is twice beware. So just
scoot!"

"Aw, hell, Belle. It wasn't like—"

"Don't 'aw, Belle' me, you big baboon! Waltz on down
the street and find yourself another sucker. They're a
dime a dozen and standing in line."

Singed around the ears and smoking hot, he headed
for the vestibule. "Well, don't say I never asked you. If
you change your mind I'm stayin' at the National."

"Don't hold your breath," she fired back. "And don't
let the door hit you in the keester on the way out!"

McCluskie didn't. But he came near jarring it off the
hinges when it slammed shut behind him.

CHAPTER 2

MCCLUSKIE STALKED back up Main Street like a mad bull hooking at cobwebs. With each step his temper flared higher and his mood turned darker. There was just no rhyme nor reason to Belle's attitude. There'd never been any understanding between them, and she sure as hell hadn't had any claim on him. She'd known that from the outset when they started keeping company back in Abilene. It was simply an arrangement. Pleasant enough, and something they had both seemed to need at the time. But nothing more. Just two people having a few laughs and enjoying one another whenever the mood struck them.

That was the trouble with women. They could never accept a little monkey business for what it was. Somehow it always came out larded with mush and lickety-split got itself embroidered into a four letter word. L-O-V-E. Even crib girls weren't immune to the disease. Countless times he'd seen blowsy tarts go sweet on a certain man and just eat their hearts out when they couldn't have him all to themselves. While all the time they were plying their trade regular as clockwork.

It surpassed all understanding. Goddamn if it didn't!

Yet, when it got down to brass tacks, that wasn't what had him boiling. Lots of females had got that goofy look after he'd flushed the birds out of their nest. That was something a fellow learned to live with, for it seemed to be the universal affliction of anything that wore skirts. What had his goat—and the mere thought of it set him off in a rage—was that he'd never before been dusted off by a woman.

And a madam to boot!

The gall of the woman, and her not even Irish. If her name was Adair or Murphy or O'Toole, just maybe he could have swallowed it. Understood, anyway. But for the likes of Belle Siddons to think that she had something special! Something he wanted badly enough to let her put a ring through his nose.

Great crucified Christ! It defied belief.

The hell of it was, he'd never given her any reason to think that way. Not the slightest inkling. He'd always been aboveboard, a square shooter from start to finish. Maybe he hadn't discouraged her. Or put the quietus on her syrupy talk. But that was no reason for her to give him frostbite now. Merely because he'd pulled up stakes in Abilene without inviting her along. There just wasn't room for a woman in his line of work. Not a regular woman anyway. Belle had been around long enough to know that. Leastways if she hadn't then she must have had her head stuck in the sand.

Yet she had still kicked his butt out the door!

McCluskie was barreling along under a full head of steam when the doors of the Red Front Saloon suddenly burst open and he collided head on with a half dozen Texans. One look told him that they were pretty well ossified, and mad as he was, he started to let it pass. Just at the moment he figured he had all the troubles he could say grace over. Besides which, there was nothing to be gained in swapping insults with a bunch of trailhands. Shouldering them aside, he plowed through and headed up the street.

"Jes a goddamn minute, friend! Who'ya think yer shovin' around?"

The big talker knew he had made a mistake when the pilgrim in the bowler hat wheeled about and started back. McCluskie was obviously no friend. The Texan wasn't so drunk that he couldn't recognize a grizzly bear when he saw one, and he had the sinking sensation that he was on the verge of becoming somebody's supper. Out of sheer reflex he made a grab for his gun, but he never had a chance.

McCluskie's fist caught him flush on the jaw and he went down like a sack of mud. The suddenness of it was a little too much for the other cowhands. They just stood there slack-jawed and bewildered, gawking at their pole-axed comrade as if he had been struck by lightning.

The Irishman rubbed his knuckles and glowered down on them. "Anybody care to be next?"

Apparently it wasn't a thought that merited deep consideration. Even at five to one the Texans weren't wild about the odds. Not after the way their partner had nearly got his head torn off. They just shook their heads, exchanging sheepish glances, and let it slide.

McCluskie spun on his heel and walked off, just the least bit irked with himself. He shouldn't have let a loudmouth drunk set him off that way. Anger was something to be conserved, held back, so that a man could choose his own time and place to let fly. Otherwise he'd get snookered into fighting on somebody else's terms, which was a damn fine way to wind up with a busted skull.

Still, he wasn't fooling himself on where the score stood. It was Belle that had set him off. Not the Texans. If anything, the cowhand was just an innocent bystander. And any time a woman got a man to acting like a buzz saw it was time to pull back and check the bets.

Satisfied with his estimate of the whole affair, he struck off in search of the big nabobs uptown. It was high time he quit horsing around and got down to business.

Which didn't include yellow cathouses or dagger-tongued madams.

Some twenty minutes later McCluskie wandered into the Lone Star Saloon just north of the tracks. After a stop at the depot, and a brief conversation with Hansberry, he came away with an interesting piece of information. Bob Spivey, owner of the Lone Star and Newton's guiding light, was chairman of the town board. All things considered, it seemed a good place to start.

The barkeep was an amiable sort by the name of Mulhaney, who had a weakness for fellow Irishmen. Before McCluskie had time to polish off his first drink Bob Spivey had been summoned from the back room. Mulhaney positively glowed that his countryman was decked out like a Philadelphia lawyer, and made the introductions as if he were presenting a long lost cousin from the old sod. After filling their glasses, still beaming from ear to ear, the barkeep drifted off to let them get better acquainted.

Spivey hoisted his glass in salute and downed the shot in one neat gulp. Plainly he liked his own whiskey. "Welcome to Newton, Mr. McCluskie. Pardon me for sayin' it, but I can't help admirin' that suit you're wearin'. Real nice duds. Just between you and me and the gatepost, we haven't had many visitors with any real class as yet. Hope you'll decide to stay with us for a while."

"Might take you up on that." McCluskie smiled and tapped the brim of his bowler. "Don't pay any mind to this, though. It's my travelin' outfit. Once I change into workin' clothes you couldn't pick me out in a crowd."

"Is that a fact?" Spivey refilled their glasses, glancing sideways as he set the bottle on the bar. "If you don't mind my askin', what line of work are you in?"

The question was breach of etiquette in a cowtown,

and both men knew it. But Spivey was playing the role of a well-meaning, if somewhat curious, host. His face bore the look of a plaster saint, all innocence.

McCluskie didn't bat an eye. "I'm with the railroad. The Santa Fe."

"Well now, that is news." Spivey's grin suddenly turned spare, inquiring. "Would I be out of line in askin' what brings you to our fair metropolis?"

"Nope, not at all. Understand you folks are gettin' ready to open a bank."

"That a fact. The Cattlemen's Exchange. You might have noticed it directly across the street. But I don't see the connection, just exactly."

"The money shipment will be comin' in on tomorrow evening's train. I sort of look after things like that for the Santa Fe."

"I see." The saloonkeeper's gaze drifted off a moment, then snapped back. "Say, wait a minute. McCluskie? Aren't you the fellow that used to ride shotgun for the K&P up in Abilene?"

"Yeah, I did a turn or two along the Smoky Hill."

"Then you're the one that killed the Quinton brothers when they tried to hold up that express car."

"Guess you got me pegged, all right. Course, that was about a hundred lifetimes ago."

"Well I'll be dipped. Mike McCluskie." Spivey's mouth widened in a toothsome grin. "Hell, I feel safer about our money already. I'm just guessin', but I'd speculate the Santa Fe sent you out here to see that things come off without a hitch."

"That's close enough, I guess." McCluskie paused, knuckling back his mustache, and decided on the spur of the moment that it was time to test the water. "Newt Hansberry tells me you're the he-wolf on the town board. Thought we might have a little talk about this lawman of yours. I'm sort of curious as to how much help he'll be if push comes to shove."

"You mean if somebody tries to rob the train?" When the Irishman nodded, Spivey gave him a concerned look. "That sounds like you know something we don't."

"Wouldn't say that exactly. But when you're talkin' about that much money it never hurts to hedge your bet."

"Then you know the amount being shipped?" Mc-Cluskie just stared at him, saying nothing. "Listen, if there's anything in the wind, I'd like to hear about it. Just between you and me, I own a piece of that bank, and all this talk of train robbers don't do my nerves much good."

"Mr. Spivey, I knew you were in on the bank deal before I came out here. Otherwise I wouldn't even be talkin' to you. But so far as I've been able to find out, there's nobody plannin' a stick up. Like I said, I just wanted the lowdown on this deputy of yours. In case I had to call on him."

"Well there's not a whole lot I can tell you. He's from Wichita, y'see. The county sent him up here after a bunch of us pitched in and raised a kitty to pay his salary. Way we figured it, the town needed some sort of John Law to keep the Texans in line. So far Hazeltine's done the job. Leastways we haven't had no killin's."

"Has anybody braced him yet?"

"Can't say as they have. He don't believe in post-in' a gun ordinance. Says it can't be enforced without a lot of killin'. So far nobody's tried him on for size, if that's what you mean."

"Something like that."

"Guess I can't help you there. All we know is that he's supposed to be some kind o' tough nut. The sheriff says he's a real stemwinder. Evidently made himself a reputation somewheres down in the Nations. Tell you the truth, though, you sort of lost me. What's Hazeltine got to do with a Santa Fe money shipment? I always heard you boys weren't exactly slouches at lookin' after your own business."

"We generally manage." McCluskie's look revealed nothing. "But it don't hurt to take a peek at your hole card, just in case you have to play it. Might be an ace and it might be a joker. Pays to know what you're holdin'."

Spivey fell silent, sipping at his whiskey. He was a short man, tending to bald with the years, and he perspired a lot. Mainly from the bulge around his beltline, which was the result of indulging himself with good food and plentiful liquor. But what he lacked in size and muscle he made up for with an agile, inquiring mind. In the past he had been able to stay a step ahead of bigger men simply by outwitting them, and it was this ferret-like shrewdness which had given him some degree of influence in the affairs of Newton. Right now that inquisitive nature was focused on the Irishman. Something about McCluskie's sudden appearance and his guileless manner just didn't jell. Granted, the money shipment warranted the presence of someone of McCluskie's caliber, but there was something here that didn't meet the eye. Puzzling over it, he decided to try a shot in the dark.

"Say, I just remembered something I wanted to ask you about. You being a railroad man and all." Spivey's expression was bland but watchful, searching for any telltale sign. "What's the word at Santa Fe about this new outfit down in Wichita? Way I heard it, a couple of sharp operators name of Meade and Grieffenstein are tryin' to promote themselves a railroad."

McCluskie didn't even blink. "Beats me. There's so many small-timers around a man's hard put to keep 'em sorted out. Why, they been up here tryin' to dump some stock?"

"Naw, they're smarter'n that." The saloonkeeper hadn't detected anything suspicious, but he wasn't willing to let it drop so easily. "They're tryin' to float a bond issue by organizin' a referendum vote. Course, they got the courthouse crowd in their hip pockets, but that don't go for all of Sedgwick County. Up here, we mean to fight 'em right down to the wire."

"That so? Any special reason?"

"Reason? Why, hell yes! You mean to say you don't know where they intend to build this railroad?"

"Don't recollect hearin' one way or the other."

"That curious, for a fact, since they mean to run a line between Wichita and here. Offhand I'd think the Santa Fe wouldn't let a piece of news like that slip past 'em. Naturally, you can see that if the bond issue ever went through, Newton'd be dead as a doornail. Leastways where the cattle trade is concerned."

Whatever reaction this sparked in the Irishman, Spivey missed it completely. His little game came to an abrupt end as the door burst open and a man stomped in as if he was looking for a dog to kick. The cast of his eye said that it didn't make much difference which dog. Just any that happened to be handy would do nicely.

McCluskie caught the glint of a badge and his interest perked up. The man striding toward them was tall and slim, and there was something glacial about his face. Almost as if it had been shrunk and frozen and nailed down tight, so that nothing moved but his eyes. Nature hadn't let him off that lightly, though. His teeth were stained and square as cubes, not unlike a row of old dice, and his eyes gave off a peculiar glassy sparkle. Queer as it seemed, he looked like a stuffed eagle that had had a couple of marbles wedged into his eye sockets.

Plainly, this was Tonk Hazeltine. Newton's principal claim to law and order.

The deputy marched up to Spivey and gave him a hard as nails scowl. "You heard about it?"

"About what?" Spivey sounded like a befuddled parrot.

"Don't nobody in this town keep their ears open 'cept me?" Hazeltine's curt tone was underscored by a kind of smothered wrath. "Some jasper just cold-cocked a drover down at the Red Front and the lid like t' blew off. I hadda hell of a time talkin' them boys out o' startin' a war. Got it in their heads they was gonna tree the whole shebang 'til they found this bird and hauled his ashes."

"Well, Tonk, that don't sound like a major calamity to me. I mean, it was just a fight, wasn't it?"

"Fight, hell! The way them boys tell the story, it was closer to murder. This feller stiffed him with one punch and come near cripplin' him for life. Why, the boy only woke up a minute ago. He's still stumblin' around like a blind dog in a slaughterhouse."

"Then why don't you just arrest this rowdy for disturbin' the peace? Seems to me that'd be the simplest way 'round the whole thing."

"Can't find him, that's why. Searched all over town and ain't seen hide nor hair of him. Them boys said he was about seven feet tall, with a big bushy mustache, and sportin' one of them hats like the drummers—"

Something clicked in Hazeltine's head and his eyes glistened like soapy agates. Since storming into the saloon he hadn't paused for wind, and in a sudden rush of awareness, he finally swiveled around for a look at the Irishman.

McCluskie grinned. "Deputy, it appears you've got your man."

"Well I'll be go to hell." Hazeltine's jaw snapped shut in a grim line. "Mister, you're under—"

Spivey broke in hurriedly. "Now hold on a minute,

Tonk. This here's Mike McCluskie. Chief security agent for the Santa Fe. You can't go arrestin' him for clobberin' some damn trailhand."

"Who says I can't? 'Sides, I already told you, it weren't no fistfight. It was a massacre. Why, he's likely addled that boy permanent."

Spivey groaned and shot the Irishman an imploring look. "What about it, McCluskie? You must've had some reason to hit that drover."

"Best reason I know of. He tried pullin' a gun on me."

"The hell you say!" Hazeltine's lip curled back over his yellow teeth. "That whole bunch is ready to swear you jumped that boy before he even had time to get unlimbered."

"What you're sayin' is that one of them let the cat out of the bag about him makin' a grab for his gun."

"Is that right, Tonk?" Spivey demanded.

"What if it is? He just reached. Never even cleared leather."

The saloonkeeper let out a long sigh. "What d'ya say we just forget it? Seems pretty clear that Mr. McCluskie was provoked and I got an idea the judge would see it the same way."

Hazeltine glowered back at him for a moment, then turned his gaze on the Irishman. "Mister, you'd better watch that stuff in my town. Next time it won't go so easy. Railroad or no railroad."

McCluskie regarded him with impassive curiosity. "Heard you made quite a name for yourself down in the Nations."

"What's that to you?"

"Nothin'. Just funny, that's all. Way I heard it, the tribes don't allow a white man to wear a badge down there."

Hazeltine tried staring him down and found that he

couldn't. At last, face mottled with anger, he brushed past and stalked out of the saloon. McCluskie watched him through the door, then grunted, looking back at Spivey.

"Just offhand I'd say that's the queerest lookin' breed I ever saw."

"Breed? Why hell, McCluskie, he's got no more Injun blood in him than you do."

"Think not?" McCluskie idly toyed with his glass, joining a chain of wet little rings on the bar.

"Well, maybe you're right. Course, that being the case, I'd give a bunch to know which side he was ridin' with when he made that name for himself."

"What d'ya mean, which side?"

"Why, there's only two sides, Mr. Spivey. Always has been. And one of 'em don't wear badges."

The saloonkeeper started to say something, but couldn't quite manage to get it out. McCluskie filled their glasses again and lifted his own in salute.

"Here's mud in your eye."

CHAPTER 3

THE SUN was an orange ball of fire, settling slowly earthward, when McCluskie came out of the cafe. He paused for a moment, working at his teeth with a toothpick, and speculated on the evening ahead. The train wasn't due in for a couple of hours, which left him with time on his hands and damn few ways to spend it. Wine, women, or cards. That's about what it boiled down to in a whistlestop like Newton. Texans had little use for much else, and the vultures who preyed on them were old hands at keeping the entertainment raw and uncomplicated.

Mulling it over, he decided that women were out. Leastways for tonight, anyway. He still hadn't simmered down from yesterday's donnybrook with Belle, and it bothered him more than he cared to admit. Oddly enough, her raking him over the coals that way had made him want her all the more. There was something about a woman with spirit that made the game a little spicier, and there was no denying that Belle could be a regular spitfire when the notion struck her. Trouble was, she could get awful damned possessive in the bargain. Which sort of threw cold water on the whole deal.

Still the idea of stopping off at one of the other houses left a sour taste in his mouth. Maybe tomorrow, or the next day, after he'd got Belle off his mind. It wasn't like he had to have a woman, anyhow. There were lots of things a man needed worse, although at the moment nothing occurred to him that just exactly fitted the ticket.

Grunting, he snapped the toothpick in half and flipped it into the street. Hell, it was too damned hot to start messing around anyway. That was one thing a man could always count on. Kansas in July. Hotter'n Hades, and not enough shade to cool a midget.

They ought to give it back to the Indians.

With women crossed off his list, that left only cards and whiskey. McCluskie hauled out the makings and started building a smoke. Dusk wasn't far off, and what with the money shipment set to arrive, he didn't rightly have time to get himself snarled up in a poker game. A man needed to be loose and easy when he gambled, with nothing on his mind but the fickle lady. Otherwise some slick operator would punch his ticket and hand him his head on a platter.

Besides, Santa Fe trains had been known to come in on time. Not often, and certainly with nothing that would tempt a man to set his watch by their regularity. But every now and then an engineer somehow managed to limp into a station at the appointed hour. In a way, it was sort of like bucking the roulette wheel. Pick a number and make your bet. There was a winner every time and no such thing as a sure-fire cinch. Which went double for the Santa Fe. The odds went out the window where their train schedules were concerned.

By process of elimination, McCluskie had pretty well whittled down his alternatives. Women and cards would have to wait, and in Newton that made for slim pickings. Whiskey seemed to be the only thing left, and the way things were shaping up, a pair of wet tonsils sounded better all the time. Little gargle water might just do wonders for his mood.

Flicking a match, he lit his cigarette and headed toward the tracks. He could just as easily have crossed the street and had a drink at the Lone Star. But tonight he didn't feel like matching wits with Spivey. It was a dull pastime anyhow. The saloonkeeper was sharp as a tack in his own way, but he was about as subtle as a sledge-hammer. Thought he was going to outfox the big dumb Mick, and all he did was wind up getting himself sand-bagged. If it wasn't so pitiful, it might have been funny. Besides, Spivey would likely turn up at the depot later anyway, so there was no sense wasting good drinking time playing cat and mouse.

South of the tracks was more McCluskie's style at any rate. Everybody down there was crooked as a dog's hind leg and nobody tried to pretend otherwise. In a queer sort of way, it was perhaps the purest form of honesty.

Crossing the tracks, it occurred to the Irishman that he tended to think of them as birds of prey. Most were just vultures. Hovering around, waiting to pick the bones after the trailhands had been shorn of their illusions and their pocketbooks. In this class could be lumped together the soiled doves and dancehall operators and saloonkeep-ers. Of course, there were the turkey buzzards, too. Like Rowdy Joe Lowe and his wife, Crazy Kate. They were the real carrion eaters, the bottom of the heap. What they wouldn't do for a nickel hadn't yet been invented.

Looking at it the other way round, though, the sport-ing crowd had its own brand of nobility. At the top were the hawks, and a mere handful of crafty old owls. This group, small in number and worlds apart from the grungy bone-pickers, was comprised strictly of highrollers, bunco artists, thimble riggers, and slippery fingered gamblers. Not a tinhorn among them. The elite of what-ever underworld they chose to frequent.

Already McCluskie had heard that the highrollers were flocking to Newton like a gathering of royalty. Dandy John Gallagher. Jim Moon. Pony Reid. Names to be reckoned with wherever men talked of faro, three-card monte, chuck-a-luck, or poker. Beside them the likes of Ben Thompson and Bill Hickok and Phil Coe were small potatoes. Amateurs. Chickenfeed sparrows trying to fly high in the company of hawks.

Passing Hoff's Grocery, he noted that the southside was already humming. Cow ponies lined the hitch rails, standing hipshot and drowsy in the dusky heat. Their owners, either three sheets to the wind or fast on their way, were in evidence everywhere along the street. After nearly two years in Abilene, McCluskie could just about slot Texans into the right pigeonhole simply by observing their actions.

The newcomers, fresh off the trail, made a beeline for some place like the Blue Front Clothing Store, splurging a hefty chunk of their pay on fancy duds. Those who had had a bath and sprinkled themselves with toilet water could be found in one of three places. Getting their ears unwaxed down in Hide Park. Swilling snakehead whiskey at two-bits a throw. Or testing their none-too-nimble wits against the slick-fingered cardsharps. The ones who gave lessons in instant poverty.

Lastly, there was the motley crew who were flat on their rumps. Broke, busted, and hungover. Most times they could be spotted cadging drinks, or loafing around Hamil's Hardware eyeballing Sam Colt's latest equalizer. Some of these were reduced to selling their saddles in order to get home, which in a Texan's scheme of things was only slightly less heinous than herding sheep.

McCluskie had to laugh everytime he thought about it. Whichever way a man looked at it, cowhands were a queer breed. They had the brass of a billygoat, but the Good Lord had somehow put their behinds where their brains were supposed to be. Heaven for them didn't have nothing to do with the Hereafter. It was fast women and a jug of rotgut. In just that order.

Shouldering past a bunch of drunks crowding the boardwalk, he pushed through the doors of the Gold

Room Saloon. The Texans paid him no mind this time. He was garbed in a linsey shirt, mule-ear boots, and a slouch hat. Along with the Colt Navy strapped high on his hip, the outfit made him one of the crowd. Taller than most, beefier through the shoulders perhaps, but to all appearances just another sporting man out to see the elephant. Which was exactly how he liked it. Having worked his way up from a track layer, he always felt more at ease among men who sweated for a living. Even Texans.

Apparently the Gold Room was one of Newton's better watering holes. Unlike most of the dives, it wasn't jammed to the rafters with caterwauling trail hands. Then he saw the reason. Standing at the bar was Dandy John Gallagher. High priest of the gambling fraternity.

Plainly he had stumbled upon the lair of the high rollers. Where sparrows and pigeons alike were separated from their pokes with style and consummate skill.

Walking forward, he stopped at Gallagher's elbow, who was in the midst of lecturing another man on the merits of some strange new game called Red Dog.

"Mister, I'm lookin' fer a tinhorn name o' Gallagher. The one they run out o' Abilene fer dealin' seconds."

The gambler went stiff as a board, shoulders squared, and slowly turned around. The look in his eye would have melted a cannonball. Then, quite suddenly, the tight-lipped scowl exploded into an infectious grin.

"Mike! You sorry devil. Put'er there!"

McCluskie clasped his hand in a hard grip. "Been a long time, Johnny."

"Too long, by God." Gallagher gave a final shake, then jerked a thumb at his companion. "Why, not ten minutes ago I was saying to Trick here—hey, you two haven't met. Mike McCluskie, say hello to Trick Brown."

The two men hardly had time to exchange nods before Gallagher was off again. "Anyways, I was saying to

Trick that there just aren't enough real gambling men around these days. No competition. But, hell's bells, now that you're here, I might just change my tune."

"Johnny, you're out of my league. No contest."

"Don't grease me, boy. I've seen you play. Remember?"

"Hell, I ought to. The lessons cost me enough."

"Judas Priest! You could churn that stuff and make apple butter. C'mon now, Mike, what do you say? Let's get a real headknocker going. Table stakes. Straight stud. Just like the old days."

"Well, I guess I might try you on for size. Just for old time's sake, you understand. But it'll have to be later tonight. I've got an errand to tend to first."

The gambler punched him on the shoulder. "Something young and full of ginger, I'll lay odds. Never change, do you?"

McCluskie laughed easily. "You've got a lot of room to talk. I didn't feel any calluses on your hand. Bet you're still coatin' them with glycerin morning, noon, and night, aren't you?"

"Christ A'mighty, Irish! They're tools of the trade. Wouldn't want me to disgrace the profession, would you?"

McCluskie was distracted by someone waving from a faro layout at the back of the room. He looked closer and saw that it was Pony Reid. "Listen, I'm gonna have a quick drink and say hello to Pony. I'll catch up with you somewhere around midnight. Just don't let anybody peel your roll till I get back."

"Fat chance. Take care you don't get waylaid yourself. Remember, Irish, a poker game is elixir for the soul. You keep that in mind, you hear?"

McCluskie was still laughing as he strode toward Pony Reid. Gallagher and Brown watched after him a moment, then turned back to their drinks. Brown sipped at his liquor for a minute, apparently lost in thought, and finally glanced over at his friend.

"Johnny, did I get the drift right? The way you talked that hayseed is some kind of bearcat with a deck of cards."

"He's more than that, Trick. In a straight game he could hold his own with anyone you want to name."

"Yeah? Well I'll bet I've got a few moves that'll leave him cross-eyed. Maybe I ought to sit in on that game myself. We might just clean his plow faster'n scat."

Gallagher seemed vastly amused by the idea. "Trick, you're new to the circuit, so I'm going to give you some free advice. Don't ever try to slick Mike McCluskie. He'll kill you quicker than anthrax juice. Looks are deceiving, my boy, and if you're going to live long in this trade, you'd better learn to size a man up. What you just saw wasn't a hayseed. It's a Bengal tiger crossed with an Irish wolfhound."

The gambler's pale, milky eyes drifted again toward the back of the room. "Besides, he could probably outdeal you with his thumbs chopped off."

McCluskie left the Gold Room an hour or so later. His humor was restored and his mood was considerably lighter. While he'd meant to have only one drink, he found it difficult to quit the genial company. There was a camaraderie among professional gamblers that had always intrigued him, and strangely enough, he felt drawn to it in a way he had never fully fathomed. Not that he was blinded to their flaws. They had feet of clay just like everyone else, and the brotherhood they shared was dictated more by circumstances than any need of fellowship. Essentially they were loners, preying on the unwary and the gullible with no more scruples than an alleycat.

Within the fraternity there were petty squabbles and jealousies, and an incessant bickering as to who held title to King of the Hill. The same as would be found among any group of men who lived by their wits and felt themselves superior to the great unwashed herd.

Yet there was a solidarity among gamblers that was rare in men of any stripe. They saw themselves as a small band of gallants pitted against the whole world. Though each of them was concerned with feathering his own nest, they could close ranks in an instant when it suited their purpose. Such as combining forces to trim a well-heeled sucker, or standing together when confronted by an indignant mob of righteous townspeople. More than that, they seemed to genuinely enjoy each other's company, much as a breed apart prefers its own kind, and their good-natured banter was seldom extended to outsiders. Except for a select few who were somehow allowed to join the inner circle.

McCluskie was one of those. A fellow lone wolf. The fact that he played shrewd poker, and on occasion had sent even the best of them back to the well, was only incidental. They accepted him mainly because, when it got right down to the nub, he shared their outlook on life. The Irishman didn't give a damn for the entire human race, and within a congregation of cynics that made him a kindred spirit.

The offshoot of this mutual affinity was that McCluskie could meet them head-on across a gaming table without fear of being greased. With a morality peculiar to the breed, they never cheated friends. Unless, of course, it tickled their fancy. For just as they were addicted to gambling, so were they congenital scamps. With them the practical joke was a universal pastime, engineered and executed with such flair that it frequently approached an art form. Like the time Pony Reid had palmed a cold deck into the game and dealt each of the players four aces. The betting sky-rocketed like a roman candle, and when it was over every man at the table had raised clean down to his stickpin and pocket watch. The showdown had been nothing short of spectacular, and the look on the players' faces was a classic study in slack-jawed stupe-faction. Even years afterward, it was generally conceded that Pony Reid had taken the brass ring for sheer gall. To cold deck a gathering of one's own confederates was considered the ultimate in technical virtuosity.

McCluskie had prompted Reid to retell the yarn again tonight, when they were on their fourth drink. Now, walking up Main toward the train station, he was still chuckling to himself. Taken as a whole, gamblers were a cutthroat bunch. Born thieves with no more conscience than a hungry spider. But they were likeable rogues, practicing their own brand of honor, and in a curious way, a notch above those who used the law to whitewash their sleazy schemes. Leastways it had always been his observation that not all of a town's rascals came from the wrong side of the tracks.

Mounting the steps to the depot platform, McCluskie's amiable mood did a bellyflop. Standing there, like a double dose of ice water, was Newt Hansberry and his assistant flunky, Ringbone Smith.

"Evenin', Mike."

"Evenin', Newt."

"Howdy do, Mr. McCluskie."

McCluskie just nodded to Smith. They had met earlier in the day and Smith impressed him as a near miss of some sort. A gangling lout whose name was derived from his habit of wearing a hollowed-out marrow bone on his pinky finger. Seeing them together, the Irishman felt his good cheer begin to curdle. A long-nosed busybody and a dimdot who had been shortchanged when the marbles were passed out.

It was a match made in heaven.

Hansberry hawked and spat a wad of phlegm at the tracks. "Gettin' on time for that train of yours. Oughta be seein' it any minute now."

McCluskie eyed him narrowly. "Had any word from up the line?"

"Nope, nary a peep. Seems like ever'body's got lockjaw where that train of yours is concerned."

"Newt, I'm not interested one way or the other especially, but what makes you think that it's *my* train?"

"Well, it ain't like it's a regular run, now is it! I mean, hell's fire and little fishes. I didn't even know the dangblasted thing was comin' in till you told me this mornin'."

"The Santa Fe moves in mysterious ways, Newt. Not that it performs many wonders."

"Humph!" Hansberry snorted and screwed his face up in a walleyed look of righteous indignation. "Y'know, I am the station master around here. Seems like some people has a way of forgettin' that."

"You're thinkin' the brass should've informed you official-like. Instead of leavin' it to me."

"That'd do for openers. Contrary to what some folks think, I ain't the head mop jockey around here. I run this place with a pretty tight hand, and seems to me I oughta know what's what and whyfor."

"Guess it all depends on how you look at it. Some things are for the doing and not the talking. What you don't know can't hurt you. Specially if you keep your trap shut."

McCluskie saw Spivey and Tonk Hazeltine approaching with a stranger. Leaving Hansberry to fry in his own fat, the Irishman walked off to meet the greeting committee. The safest bet in town was that they would have been on hand to oversee the money shipment.

Ringbone Smith whistled softly through his teeth, spraying his chin with spit. "Lordy mercy, Mr. H. That feller must've been brung up on sour milk to get so downright techy."

Hansberry just grunted, and ground his jaws in quiet fury. Sometimes he wished he were back on the farm slopping hogs. Lately he'd come to think that pigs were downright civil alongside some people he knew.

CHAPTER 4

MCCLUSKIE STOPPED short of the three men and waited.
Leaning back against a freight cart, he started rolling a
smoke. Out of the corner of his eye he saw them mount
the steps, and for some reason he was reminded of an old
homily that Irishmen were fond of quoting.

"The fat and the lean are never what they seem."

Spivey and the stranger were both on the stout side.
The charitable word would have been portly, but Mc-
Cluskie wasn't feeling charitable. They looked like a
couple of blubberguts that had just put a boardinghouse
out of business. One thing was for sure. Matched up
against one another, the pair of them would make a hell
of a race at a pie-eating contest.

Trailing behind them, Hazeltine seemed like a starved
dog herding a couple of hogs. He was what Texans called
a long drink of water, only more so. Standing sideways
in a bright sun, his shadow wouldn't have covered a gatepost. The brace of Remingtons cross-cinched over his
hips seemed likely to drag him under if he ever stepped
in a mud puddle.

McCluskie stuck the cigarette in his mouth and lit it,
purposely letting them come to him. It was an old trick,
but effective. Forcing the other man to make the first
move, especially with talk and shaking hands. Somehow
it put them on the defensive, just the least bit off balance.
Considering the unlikely trio bearing down on him, it
was a dodge well suited to the moment.

Spivey commenced grinning the minute he cleared the

steps. "Mike, where the hell you been all day? Thought sure you'd drop by for a drink."

McCluskie exhaled a small cloud of smoke. "Couldn't squeeze it in. Had some business that needed tendin'."

"No doubt. No doubt." Spivey fairly oozed good cheer. "Well don't make yourself a stranger, you hear?" Suddenly his jowls dimpled in a rubbery smile. "Say, I almost forgot you two don't know each other. This here's Judge Randolph Muse, our local magistrate. Randy, shake hands with Mike McCluskie."

The Irishman waited, letting the older man extend his hand. Only then did he take it, nodding slightly. "Judge. Pleased to meet you."

Randolph Muse was no fledgling. He knew the gambit well, had used it on other men most of his life. Still, he'd let himself get sucked in. His ears burned, and despite a stiff upper lip, he felt like a bumbling ass. Perhaps Spivey was right, after all. This ham-fisted Mick would bear watching.

"The pleasure's all mine, Mr. McCluskie. Bob has been telling me about you. According to him, you're about the toughest thing to come down the pike since Wild Bill himself."

"That's layin' it on pretty thick, Judge. From what I hear, Hickok's got Abilene treed about the same way he did Hays City. Just offhand, I don't think I'd want to try twistin' a knot in his tail."

Tonk Hazeltine snorted through his nose. "Hell! Hickok ain't so much. Just got himself a reputation, that's all. There's lots of men that could dust him off 'fore he ever had time to get started."

Spivey and Muse looked embarrassed. McCluskie blew the ashes off his cigarette and studied the coal without expression. It was obvious to everyone that the lawman's raspy statement was sheer braggadocio. A penny-ante gunslick tooting his own bugle. With all the finesse of a lead mallet.

The saloonkeeper cleared his throat and nimbly changed the subject. "Mike, what time's this train suppose to be in, anyway? Near as I recollect, all you ever said was somewhere after suppertime."

McCluskie smiled and cocked one eye eastward along the tracks. "With the Santa Fe it's sorta a case of you pays your money and you takes your chances. I didn't give you an exact time because my crystal ball is busted."

"You mean to say nobody's got any idea of when it'll be in?"

"Your guess is as good as mine, I reckon. Best I can tell you is that we'll know it's here when we see it."

The judge grumped something that sounded faintly like a belch. "That's a hell of a way to run a railroad, if you don't mind my saying so."

McCluskie eyed him closer in the flickering light from the depot lantern. Clear to see, Newton's judicial wizard was a crusty old vinegaroon. Yet his character didn't exactly fit any of the handy little pigeonholes McCluskie normally used to catalogue people. There was something of a charlatan about him. Not just the precise way he spoke, or the high-falutin clothes he wore, but a secretion of some sort. A smell. The kind the Irishman had winded all too often not to recognize it when he was face to face with the live goods. All the same, he exuded a dash of dignity that lacked even the slightest trace of hokum. It was the real article. Which made for a pretty queer mixture, one that didn't lend itself to any lightning calculations. Plainly, Randolph Muse wasn't a man to be underestimated. Especially if he was tied in with Spivey somehow.

"Your Honor, I couldn't agree with you more. Course,

I'm just hired help, you understand. The Santa Fe don't pay me to solve their riddles, frankly, I've never paid it much mind one way or the other. 'Fraid you'll have to take it up with the brass if you want the real lowdown."

Spivey leaped in before the judge could reply. "Now don't get off on the wrong track, Mike. Randy didn't mean nothin' personal. It's just that we've both got a lot at stake in this deal. He's one of the investors in our little bank, and it's only natural he'd be skittish about this train being late and all. Hell, to tell you the truth, I'm sorta jumpy myself. What with everyone in town knowin' we're supposed to open for business tomorrow, it kind o' puts us behind the eightball."

"I wouldn't worry too much, gents." McCluskie took a drag off his cigarette and flipped the stub into the darkness. "The Santa Fe might be slow as molasses, but they're not in the habit of losin' strongboxes. Besides, till the money gets here, it's the railroad's lookout, not yours."

"That's all very well, Mr. McCluskie," Judge Muse remarked. "But it isn't the Santa Fe who must face the townspeople tomorrow morning if those bank doors don't open."

"Like I said, Judge. There's no need gettin' a case of the sweats. Not yet, anyway."

Spivey frowned like a constipated owl. "That's not offering us much encouragement, Mike. Just to be blunt about it, I never did understand why you're bringin' the money in at night, anyhow. Randy and me talked it over, and the way we see it, that's about the worst time you could've picked."

"It's called security. Which means doing things the way folks don't expect. Specially train robbers. So far I haven't lost any strongboxes playin' my hunches. Don't expect to lose this one either."

"Good God, man!" the judge yelped. "Are you standing

there telling us that you shipped one hundred thousand dollars on a hunch?"

"Get a hunch, bet a bunch." The Irishman grinned, thoroughly amused that he'd given the two lardguts a case of the fidgets. "What you fellows can't seem to get straight is that it's out of my hands. Leastways till the train gets here."

"Judas Priest!" Spivey groaned. "That's what we're talkin' about. Where the hell is the train?"

"Somewhere between here and there, most likely. Tell you what. Why don't you and the judge go get yourselves a drink? Little whiskey never hurt anybody's nerves. When the train gets in, I'll bring your money over with a red ribbon on it."

"Don't you fret yourself none, Mr. Spivey." Tonk Hazeltine came on fast, trying to regain lost ground. "I'll stick right here and make sure ever'thing goes accordin' to snuff." He gave the holstered Remingtons a flat-handed slap. "Long as we got these backin' the play there ain't gonna be no miscues on this end."

The other men stared at him as if he had just sprouted measles. McCluskie's earlier suspicions had now been confirmed in spades. As a peace officer Tonk Hazeltine was long on luck and short on savvy. The man's attitude was that of flint in search of stone. Abrasive and needlessly pugnacious. Anybody who went around with that big chip on his shoulder was running scared. It was the act of a tinhorn trying to convince everybody he was sudden death from Bitter Creek. Inside, his guts probably quivered like jelly on a cold platter.

"Deputy, it strikes me you've pulled up a chair in the wrong game." McCluskie's voice was smooth as butter. "If I need help you'll hear me yell plenty loud. Otherwise I guess I'll just play the cards out my own way."

Hazeltine went red as ox blood, and the scorn he read in the Irishman's gaze pushed him over the edge. "Mister, you might be somethin' on a stick with your fists, but you ain't messin' around with no cowhand. I'll go wherever I goddamn please and do whatever suits me. Now if that notion ain't to your likin', whyn't you try reachin' for that peashooter on your hip."

McCluskie smiled and eased away from the freight cart. "Girls first, Tonk. You start the dance and we'll see who ends up suckin' wind."

The goad was deliberate, calculated. An insult that left a man only two outs. Fish or cut bait.

But whatever the lawman saw in McCluskie's face sent a shiver through his innards. Just for a moment he met and held the flinty gaze, then his eyes shifted away. He had a sudden premonition that the Irishman would kill him where he stood if he so much as twitched his finger.

"Another time, mebbe. When we ain't got all this money to keep watch on." Hazeltine's eyes seemed to look everywhere but at the three men. "Guess I'll mosey down and see if Newt's got any word over the wire. Wouldn't surprise me if he knows more about that train than the whole bunch of us."

The deputy walked off as if he hadn't a care in the world. But his knees somehow seemed out of joint, and when he tugged at the brim of his hat, there was a slight tremor to his hand. Spivey and Muse stared after him in pop-eyed befuddlement. They had seen it, but they couldn't quite believe it. Tonk Hazeltine with his tail between his legs. It shook them right down to the quick.

Randolph Muse was the first to recover his wits. "Mr. McCluskie, if I wasn't standing here, I'd swear on a stack of Bibles that such a thing could never happen."

"Me too," Spivey agreed. "Beats anything I ever heard tell of. Why, I would've bet every nickel I own there wasn't nothin' that could make Hazeltine eat dirt."

McCluskie started building another smoke. "Yeah, it's queer awright. The way a man'll lose his starch when his bluff gets called. Interestin' though." He licked the paper and twisted one end of the cigarette. "Seein' which way it'll fall, I mean."

The older men digested that in silence and remained quiet for what seemed a long while. McCluskie's statement, perhaps more than his actions, left them momentarily nonplused. They had seen their share of hardcases since coming west. Cowtowns acted as a lodestone for the rougher element, and the sight of two men carving one another up with knives or blasting away with guns wasn't any great novelty. But they had never come across anyone exactly like the Irishman. The way he'd goaded Hazeltine was somehow inhuman, cold and calculated with a degree of fatalism that bordered on lunacy. Like a man who teases a rattler just to see if he can leap aside faster than the snake can strike. They had heard about men like that. The kind who had ice water in their veins, and through some quirk of nature, took sport in pitting themselves against danger.

McCluskie was the first one they had ever met, though, and it was a sobering experience.

Presently Judge Muse came out of his funk and remembered his purpose in being there. He tried to keep his voice casual, offhand. "Bob tells me you're chief of security for the Santa Fe."

"One handle's as good as another, I guess." McCluskie glanced at him, alerted somehow that new cards had just been dealt. "The railroad's got a habit of pastin' labels on people."

"Now that's passing strange, for a fact." Muse stared

off into the night, reflective, like a dog worrying over a bone.

The Irishman refused the bait. Leaning back against the freight cart, he puffed on his cigarette and said nothing.

After a moment, failing to get a rise out of McCluskie, the judge shook his head and grunted. The act was a good one. He looked for all the world like a man faced with a bothersome little riddle. One that stubbornly resisted a reasonable solution.

"Puzzles always intrigue me, Mr. McCluskie. Just a personal idiosyncrasy, I suppose. But something Bob said struck me as very curious. He told me that neither you nor the Santa Fe had heard about the Wichita & South-western."

"You mean this two-bit railroad somebody's tryin' to promote?"

"That's the one. To be more precise, the men behind it are a certain James Meade and William Grieffenstein. Reputedly, they have connections back east."

"You sort of lost me on the turn, Judge. What's a shoe-string outfit like that got to do with me or the Santa Fe?"

"Well it does seem strange. That a line as large as the Santa Fe would remain in the dark on an issue this vital. Don't you agree?"

"Beats me. Course, in a way, you're talkin' to the wrong man. The Santa Fe don't tell me all its secrets, y'know. There's lots of things the brass keeps to them-selves. Most likely they don't think it's as vital as you do. Assumin' they even know."

"That seems highly improbable. A line between here and Wichita would provide some pretty stiff competition. Unless, of course, the Santa Fe bought it out."

McCluskie held back hard on a smile. The old repro-bate had finally sunk the gaff. He felt Muse's bright eyes boring into him, waiting for him to squirm. It was down-right pathetic. Especially from a man he'd sized up to be a slick article.

"Judge, much as I hate to admit it, all that high finance is over my head. Just offhand, though, I'd say the Santa Fe has got all the fish it can fry. What with the deadline on pushin' rails west, they're stretched pretty thin. Don't seem likely they'd start worryin' about some fleaflicker operation out of Wichita."

Spivey came to life with a sputtered oath. "By damn, there's nothin' silly about it to us! It's just like I told you, Mike. If they ever get that bond issue through, Newton's gonna dry up and blow away."

The Irishman pursed his lips and looked thoughtful. "Well, it's sort of out of my bailiwick, but if I can lend a hand some way, you give a yell. I don't guess the Santa Fe would object to me helpin' you folks out. Not with this being division point and all."

Judge Muse batted his eyes a couple of times on that and started to say something. But as his mouth opened the lonesome wail of a train whistle floated in out of the darkness. The three men looked eastward, and through the night they spotted the distant glow of an engine's headlamp. The light grew brighter as they watched, and the distinct clack of steel wheels meshing with spiked track drifted in on a light breeze. Then the train loomed up out of the darkness, passing between Hoff's Grocery and Horner's Store. A groaning squeal racketed back off the buildings as the engineer throttled down and set the brakes. Like some soot-encrusted dragon, the engine rolled past the station house and ground to a halt, belching steam and smoke and fiery sparks in a final burst of power.

Spivey and the judge stood transfixed, staring at the

slat-ribbed cars in aggrieved bewilderment. It was a cattle train.

McCluskie left them open-mouthed and gawking, and walked off toward the caboose. Tonk Hazeltine, trailed by the station master and Ringbone Smith, followed along. Judge Muse and Spivey exchanged baffled frowns and joined the parade. None of them had even the vaguest notion of what was afoot, but they were determined to see the Irishman play out his string.

Climbing aboard at the forward steps, McCluskie rapped on the caboose door. There was a muffled inquiry from within and he barked a single word in response.

"McCluskie!"

The door edged open and the barrels of a sawed-off shotgun centered on his chest. Somewhere behind the cannon a disembodied voice rumbled to life.

"Everything all right out there, Mike?"

"Right as rain, Spike. Open up."

The door swung back and Spike Nugent ducked through the opening. The shotgun looked like a broomstick in his meaty paws, and the onlookers fully expected him to bound down off the train and start walking on his knuckles. He was what every young gorilla aspired to and seldom attained. Even McCluskie seemed dwarfed by the sheer bulk of the man.

"Any trouble?" McCluskie asked.

"Quiet as a church," the burly guard observed. "Me and Jack played pinochle the whole way."

"Good. You boys get the strongbox out and we'll waltz it over to the bank. Sooner we get their receipt for it, the sooner I can get back to my poker game."

Nugent's laugh sounded like dynamite in a mountain tunnel. He turned back into the caboose and McCluskie scrambled down the steps to the station platform.

Spivey was fairly dancing with excitement. "By God, Mike, I got to hand it to you. That was slicker'n bear grease. Nobody in his right mind would've thought of lookin' in a caboose for a hundred thousand simoleons."

"That was sort of the idea," McCluskie commented.

Tonk Hazeltine stepped out from the little crowd and hitched up his crossed gunbelts. "Now that you got it here, I'll just ride herd 'tween here and the bank to make sure nobody gets any funny ideas."

McCluskie gave him a corrosive look, then shrugged. "Tag along if you want, but remember what I said. This is railroad business. You get in the way and you'll get beefed. Same as anyone else."

The lawman's reply was cut short when Spike Nugent and another man stepped through the door of the caboose. They each had a shotgun in one hand and grasped the handles of an oversized strongbox in the other. McCluskie started toward them but out of the corner of his eye he caught movement. Wheeling, he saw a shadowy figure drop from one of the forward cattle cars and take off running.

Hazeltine's arm came up with a cocked Remington, centered on the fleeing man. The impact of McCluskie's fist against his jaw gave off a mushy splat, and the deputy collapsed like a punctured accordion.

"Spike! Get that box back in the car!"

The Irishman took off in a dead sprint as the two guards lumbered back aboard the caboose. Ahead, the dim shape of a man was still visible in the flickering light from the depot lanterns. But there was something peculiar about him even in the shadowed darkness. Instead of running, he seemed to be bounding headlong in a queer, staggering lurch. Almost as if momentum alone kept him from falling. McCluskie dug harder and put on a final burst of speed.

He overtook the man just back of the engine. When he grabbed, a piece of shirt came away in his hand, and the man stumbled to a halt. McCluskie saw him turn, sensed the cocked fist, and the looping roundhouse blow. Slipping beneath the punch, the Irishman belted him in the gut and then nailed him with a left hook square on the chin. The man hit the cinders with a dusty thud and lay still.

McCluskie stooped over, gathered a handful of shirt, and began dragging the limp form toward the front of the engine. Oddly, the man didn't seem to weigh any more than a bag of wet feathers. Clearing the cowcatcher, McCluskie heaved and dumped the body in the glare of the headlamp. Then his jaws clicked shut in a wordless curse.

It was nothing but a kid. A scarecrow kid.

CHAPTER 5

MCCLUSKIE SAT in a chair across the room, elbows on his knees, staring vacantly at a glass of whiskey in his hands. Every now and then he would glance up, watching the doctor for a moment, and afterward go back to studying his glass. The whiskey seemed forgotten, just something to keep his hands occupied. Whatever it was that might have distracted his mind didn't come in a bottle. Not this night, anyway.

Gass Boyd, Newton's resident sawbones, hovered around the bed like a rumpled butterfly. Though unkempt in appearance, he had a kindly bedside manner; the townspeople had found him to be a competent healer, if not a miracle worker. Since arriving in Newton, something less than a month past, most of his patients had been the victims of gunshot wounds or knifings. The youngster he worked over now had a far greater problem.

Boyd painstakingly bound the boy's ribcage in a tight harness, easing a roll of bandage under his back and around again. The youth's face was ashen, almost chalky, and a bruise the color of rotten plums covered his chin. But that wasn't what concerned the doctor. Even as he worked, he listened, and what he heard was far from encouraging. The boy's breathing was labored, more a hoarse wheezing, and a telltale pinkish froth bubbled at the corners of his mouth. Boyd had seen the symptoms plenty of times after the war, back in Alabama. It was the great ravager. Slow and insidious, without the swift mercy of a rifled slug or a steely knife.

Finished with the bandaging, Gass Boyd once again

took out his stethoscope and placed it on the youngster's chest. He listened intently, moving the instrument from spot to spot, wanting desperately to be wrong. But he heard nothing that changed his diagnosis.

Then he grunted sourly to himself. At this stage it ceased being diagnosis. It became, instead, prognosis.

Folding the stethoscope, he placed it in his bag, snapped the catch shut, and stood. Just for a moment he studied the boy, seeing him for the first time as more than a body with sundry ailments and bruises. Hardly more than eighteen. If that. Haggard, hollow-cheeked, gaunt. A face of starved innocence. One of God's miscalculations. Or perhaps the immortal bard had been right after all. Maybe the gods did make wanton sport of men.

Boyd heard rustling behind him and turned to find the Irishman out of his chair on his feet. Their eyes locked and the doctor had a fleeting moment of wonder about this strange man. Beat a boy half to death and then turn a town upside down to save his life. It was a paradox. Classic in its overtones. From a clinical standpoint, perhaps one of the more interesting phenomena in man's erratic tomfoolery.

The doctor set aside such thoughts and came back to the business at hand. "Mr. McCluskie, the boy has a couple of broken ribs and a badly bruised chin. Fortunately your blow didn't catch him in the nose or he might've looked like a bull-dog the rest of his life."

"Then he'll be all right?"

"I didn't say that."

McCluskie's mouth tightened. "What're you gettin' at, Doc?"

"The boy has consumption of the lungs. Rather advanced case, I'd say."

"Consumption?" McCluskie's glance flicked to the bed and back again. "You sure?"

Gass Boyd sighed wearily. "Take my word for it, Mr. McCluskie. The boy has consumption. He's not long for this world."

The Irishman stared at him for what seemed a long while. When he finally spoke his voice had changed somehow. Gentler, perhaps. Not so hard.

"How long?"

Dr. Boyd shrugged. "It's difficult to say. Six months. A year, perhaps. I wouldn't even hazard a guess beyond that."

"Guess? Hell, Doc, I'm not askin' for guesses. He's just a kid. Don't it strike you that somebody punched his ticket a little bit early?"

"Mr. McCluskie, it's an unfortunate fact of life that God plays dirty pool. All too often the good die young. I've never found any satisfactory answer to that, and I doubt that anyone ever will."

"What you're sayin' is that you've given up on him. Written him off."

Far from being offended, the physician found himself fascinated. McCluskie was a strange and complex man, and the irony of the situation was inescapable. Within a matter of minutes he had run the gauntlet of emotions. From hangdog guilt to concern to outraged indignation. Right now he was gripped by a sense of frustrated helplessness, and the only response he knew was to lash out in anger. It was as if this big hulk of a man had unwittingly revealed a part of himself. The part that was raw and vulnerable and rarely saw the light of day.

"I've hardly written him off, Mr. McCluskie. Matter of fact, I'll look in at least twice a day until we have him back on his feet. He's underfed and weak as a kitten, and we have to get his strength built up. Unless things take a drastic turn for the better, I'd judge he won't set foot out of that bed for at least two weeks."

Boyd tactfully avoided any mention of the beating the youngster had taken. There was no need. The punishment absorbed by the frail body was apparent and spoke for itself. McCluskie could scarcely bear to look at the bed, and the loathing he felt for himself showed in his eyes. Watching him, it occurred to the doctor that victims weren't always the ones swathed in bandages. The Irishman's shame at having thrashed a sickly boy would endure far longer than a broken rib or a bruised chin.

McCluskie still hadn't said anything, as if his anger had been blunted by the doctor's unruffled manner. After a moment Boyd gathered his bag and nodded toward the boy. "I've given him a dose of laudanum, so he should rest easy through the night. I'll come by first thing in the morning and see how he's doing."

"Thanks, Doc. I'm—" The Irishman faltered, having difficulty with the words. "Sorry I talked out of turn."

"Completely understandable. No apologies necessary." Boyd smiled, clamped his hat on his head, and crossed the room. But at the door he turned and looked back. "There is one thing, though. If you don't mind my asking. What prompted you to bring the boy here to your room? Instead of over to my office."

McCluskie blinked, taken off guard by a question he hadn't as yet asked himself. "Why, I can't rightly say." He took a swipe at his mustache and shrugged, fumbling with a thought which resisted words. "Just seemed like the thing to do, I guess."

The doctor studied him a moment with a quizzical look. Then he smiled. "Yes. I can see that it would."

Nodding, he opened the door and stepped into the hall.

The Irishman stared at the door for a long while, overcome with a queer sense of unease. The question hung there, still unanswered, and tried to sort it out in his head.

Why had he brought the kid to his room?

Everything else was clear as a bell. The commotion at the depot. Everybody running and shouting and yelling bloody murder at the top of their lungs. Hansberry bleating some asinine nonsense about train robbers, and the little crowd scattering like a bunch of quail. Then later, Spivey and the judge raking him over the coals for coldcocking Tonk Hazeltine. And later still, somebody carting the deputy off like a side of beef. Somewhere in all the fussing and moaning he'd even managed to get the strongbox over to the bank. That part he remembered clearly. But there was just a big blank spot where the kid was concerned. For the life of him, he couldn't recall when or how he'd gotten the kid to his room.

Or why.

Returning to his chair, he sat down and tried to muddle it through. But it was hard sledding, and all uphill. Distantly, as through a cloudy glass, he got an impression of sending Jack off to fetch the doctor. Then something else. Something to do with Spike.

That must have been when he was carrying the kid across Main toward the hotel.

But it still didn't answer the question. The one Doc Boyd had started rattling around in his head. The one that even now didn't make any sense.

Why the hotel? Why *his* room?

McCluskie reached for the whiskey glass and his eyes automatically went to the bed. Jesus! The kid was nothing but a bag of bones. Didn't hardly put a dent in the mattress. Just laid there wheezing and spewing those little bubbles. Like he was—

The rap at the door startled McCluskie clean out of his chair. He crossed the room in two strides and threw open the door. Just for a moment nothing registered. Then those green eyes nailed him and everything came into focus all of a sudden.

It was Belle.

"Well don't just stand there, you big lummox. Let me in."

Wordlessly he stepped aside, his head reeling. He couldn't have been more surprised if she had materialized out of a puff of smoke.

Belle sailed into the room and whirled on him. "I almost didn't come, you know. Not until Spike told me—"

"Spike?"

"—about the kid."

She stopped and gave him a funny look. "Are you drunk, or what? You did send Spike to get me, didn't you?"

"Yeah, I guess so."

"You guess so?" One eyebrow lifted and she inspected him with closer scrutiny. "Mike, are you all right? You look sort of green around the gills."

Suddenly it all came back to him in a rush. As if somebody had wiped the window clean and he could see it again. The way it had been in those last moments when he walked away from the depot with the kid in his arms.

"Sure I sent Spike. The kid was bad hurt and I didn't know what kind of sawbones they had in this jerkwater burg. You've patched up more men than most of these quacks anyway, so I didn't figure it would hurt nothin' for you to have a looksee."

She gave him that queer look again, still a little leery. "Well, as long as I'm here I might as well inspect the damages." She turned toward the bed. "Where's Doc Boyd? Didn't he show?"

"Yeah, he just left a little while ago."

"What was the verdict? Castor oil and mustard plaster?"

McCluskie had no chance to answer. Belle stopped short of the bed and uttered a sharp gasp. In the pale

cider glow of the lamp the boy looked like he had been
embalmed. Her eyes riveted on the bandages and the
bruised chin and the froth at the corners of his mouth.
Her back went stiff as a poker and she mumbled something very unladylike under her breath. Suddenly galvanized, she wheeled around, and green-fire shot out of her
eyes in a smoky sizzle.

"You miserable excuse for a man! Is that how you earn
your keep? Beating up kids for the Santa Fe?"

"Belle, it's not like it looks. The kid swung on me—"

"Swung on you! My God, Mike, that boy doesn't have
enough strength to kill a fly."

"I know that now." He flushed and went on lamely.
"But it was dark out there and I couldn't tell. I just knew
he was swingin' on me."

"So you let him have the old McCluskie thunderbolt."
Her stare was riddled through with scorn. "You must feel
real proud of yourself. Why aren't you down at the saloon telling the boys all about your big fight?"

McCluskie's shoulders sagged imperceptibly, and he
had trouble meeting her gaze. They stood like that for a
moment, frozen in silence. Then, quite without warning,
Belle felt her anger start to ebb. Something had just
become apparent to her. The big Irishman was ashamed.
Really ashamed! This was none of his slick dodges.
Those cute little tricks he'd always used to get around her
temper. He was genuinely shamed by what he had done.
Which rocked her back on her heels.

So far as she knew, Mike McCluskie had never apol-
ogized to anybody for anything in his entire life. Much
less hung his head and looked mortified to boot.

Curiously, the question she'd been saving for later no
longer needed to be asked. She knew why the kid was
here. In this room. Laid out in Mike's bed.

But the knowing left her in something of a quandary.

One question had been answered yet others were popping through her head like a string of firecrackers. Questions she had never before even considered about the Irishman.

Suddenly it came to her that perhaps she wasn't as good a judge of men as she had thought. Maybe she'd been running a sporting house too long. Saw things not as they were but distorted and flawed, like a cracked mirror.

She took a closer look at Mike McCluskie.

What she saw was different from what she had seen before. Or perhaps different wasn't the right word. Maybe it was just all there, finally complete. Like a jigsaw puzzle that had at last had the missing parts fitted into place.

She decided to withhold judgment for the moment. "What did Doc have to say about the kid?"

"Couple of busted ribs and a sore jaw."

Belle darted a skeptical glance back toward the bed. "That's all?"

"No, not just exactly." McCluskie swallowed hard. "Doc says he's got lung fever. Consumption."

She just stared at him, unblinking. After a while she managed to talk around the lump in her throat. "He's sure?"

"Sure enough. Said the kid had a year at the outside. Leastways if you're partial to bettin' longshots."

She turned and stepped nearer the bed. Her eyes went over the frail, emaciated boy, missing nothing. Hair the color of cornsilk, dirty and ragged, but bleached out by the sun. A sensitive face, with wide-set eyes and a straight nose, and the jawbone squared off in a resolute line. Large bony hands with fingers that were curiously slim and tapering. Like those of a piano player. Or a cardsharp. Or a surgeon.

Or any one of a hundred things this kid would never live to become.

Belle jumped, scared out of her wits, as the pale blue eyes popped open. They reminded her of carpenter's chalk, only with a glaze of fresh ice over the top. But the boy didn't see her. His face mottled in dark reddish splotches, and he started sucking for wind in a hoarse, dry rattle. Belle didn't think, she simply reacted.

"He's choking, Mike! Sit him up."

McCluskie reached the bed in one stride, slipping his arms beneath the youngster, and lifted him to a sitting position. Belle wrenched the boy's mouth open, prying his tongue out, and began gently massaging his Adam's apple. Suddenly the boy heaved, his guts pumping, and went into a coughing spasm that shook the entire bed. Globs of sputum and scarlet-tinged mucus shot out of his mouth and nose, and for a moment they thought he was vomiting his life away right in their arms. Then the coughing slacked off, gradually subsiding, and a spark of color came back to his face. The film slowly faded from his eyes and he slumped back, exhausted. The attack had run its course, but he was still laboring for each breath.

Belle plumped up both pillows and wedged them in behind him. McCluskie eased him back, so that he rested against the pillows in a half-sitting position. Feeling somewhat drained themselves, they just stood there watching him, uncertain what to do next.

Suddenly the boy's lids fluttered and they found themselves staring into the blue eyes again. Only this time they were clear, if not fully alert. The youngster's lips moved in a weak whisper. "Am I back in the hospital?"

McCluskie exchanged puzzled glances with Belle, then shook his head. "You're in a hotel room, kid. We brought you here from the train depot."

The boy closed his eyes and for a minute they thought

he was asleep. Then he was looking at them again. Focusing at last on the Irishman. "You the one that clobbered me?"

McCluskie nodded sheepishly. "Thought you was somebody else."

The kid's mouth parted in a sallow grin. "You got a good punch."

McCluskie smiled. The button had plenty of sand, even flat on his back. "What's your name, bucko? Got any family we could get word to?"

"Just me. Nobody else."

"Yeah, but what's your name?"

"Kinch." The boy's eyelids went heavy, drooping, and slowly closed. "Kinch Riley."

The words came in a soft whisper as the laudanum again took hold. Breathing somewhat easier, he drifted off into a deep sleep.

They watched him for a long while, saying nothing. Oddly enough, though they hadn't touched since Belle entered the room, they felt a closeness unlike anything in the past. Almost as if the boy, in some curious way, had bridged a gap in time and space.

At last McCluskie grunted, and his voice was a shade huskier than usual. "Belle, something damned queer happened to me tonight. I've been in brawls, knife fights, shootouts—and afterward I always remembered every minute of it. Every little detail. But tonight—after I slugged the kid—it's all fuzzy. Just comes back to me in bits and snatches. That's one for the books, isn't it?"

She put her arm around his waist and laid her head on his shoulder. "Mister, would you buy a girl a drink?"

The Irishman pulled her close, warmed by her nearness and the scent from her hair. But his eyes were still on the kid.

Then it struck him. The name.

Riley.

Sweet Jesus on the Cross! No wonder he was a gutsy little scrapper.

The kid was Irish.

CHAPTER 6

MCCLUSKIE RODE past the stockyards, letting the sorrel mare set her own pace. Now that they were headed back to the livery stable she was full of ginger, apparently cured of her tendency to balk and fight the reins. Several times throughout the day he'd seriously considered the possibility that he had rented a mule disguised as a horse. Along toward midday he started wishing for a pair of the roweled spurs favored by Texans, and would have gladly sunk them to the haft in the mare's flanks. Even coming back from Wichita the hammerhead had acted just like a woman. Wanted her own way and pitched a regular fit when she didn't get it.

The Irishman had ridden out of Newton early that morning on the pretext of inspecting the track crew west of town. While he could have hitched a ride on a switch-engine, he let it drop at the hotel and again at the stables that he felt like a hard day in the saddle. Just to work out the kinks and melt off a bit of the lard from city living. The truth was, he had an absolute loathing for horses. Having served under Sherman during the late war, his rump had stayed galled the better part of three years. Upon being mustered out he had sworn off horses as a mode of transportation for the remainder of his life.

Still, renting a horse was the only practical dodge he could think of for a flying trip to Wichita. It had to be done in one day so as not to arouse the suspicions of Spivey and his cronies. Heading west, he had crossed Sand Creek, passed the stockyard, and kept on a couple of miles farther before turning back southeast. Except for

the iron-jawed mare, the twenty miles to Wichita had
proved uneventful. There he had quickly hunted down
Meade and Grieffenstein, and managed to gain entrance
to their offices under an assumed name.

The promoters had been elated when he revealed his
identity and the purpose of his call. Although deeply en-
meshed in a financial conspiracy with the Santa Fe, they
had been kept virtually in the dark by the brass. They
knew only that someone would be sent to Newton, and
that when the time seemed ripe, they would be contacted.

Some six months past the Santa Fe had entered into
an agreement with the partnership of Meade and Grieffenstein. They were to organize a railroad between Wichita and Newton, and float a county bond issue for its
construction. Once it was operating, the Santa Fe would
buy them out at a tidy profit. The pact was struck and now
the vote on the bond issue was less than a month away.
The partners had the political muscle to control the southern townships, Wichita in particular, but the upper part
of Sedgwick County still had them worried. Unless the
referendum carried, the Wichita & Southwestern railroad
would simply evaporate in a puff of dust, and McCluskie's
message brought with it a measure of reassurance.

His orders were to establish himself in Newton working undercover as long as practical, and to influence the
vote of the northern townships to whatever degree possible. Wherever divisive tactics would work, he was to
drive a wedge between the town leaders, splitting them
on the bond issue. The sporting crowd, with whom he
enjoyed a certain reputation, was to be cultivated on the
sly. Hopefully, their ballots could be controlled in a block
and provide the swing vote in Newton itself. Further than
that, he was instructed to give the promoters any help
they might request. But within certain limits. Money and
muscle were not included in the bargain.

Retracing his steps across the buff Kansas prairie, McCluskie had hit the tracks a few miles west of the stockyards and turned the mare toward Newton. So far as anyone would know, he had spent the day in the Santa Fe camp, performing some errand for the head office brass. Which was stretching the truth only in terms of time and place. The errand had been real enough, if not precisely as reported.

Now, entering the outskirts of town, he was reminded again of the Wichita promoters. They were a shifty pair, well versed in the rules of the game, and the Irishman had come away with the impression that they still had a few dazzlers left to be played. After years of rubbing elbows with grifters and bunco artists, he had an instinct for such things. Meade and Grieffenstein were about to sound the death knell on lively little Newton.

Thinking about it as he passed the depot, McCluskie grunted with disgust. All of the skulduggery and underhanded shenanigans left him with a sour taste in his mouth. While he could play the game well enough, it went against the grain. Yet, when it got down to brass tacks, his assignment in Newton was hardly a new role. In a moment of sardonic reflection, it occurred to him that his life had been little more than a lie since the day he headed west.

After the war he had returned to New York, colder and leaner, a man brutalized by the bloodbath that had ended at Appomattox. But he quickly discovered that not all of the casualties had taken place on the battlefield. Only months before, while he rode in the vanguard of Sherman's march to the sea, his wife and small son had been killed in a street riot. Somehow, in those last frenetic days of the war, the army had failed to notify him of their deaths. The homecoming he had dreamed of and longed for during the fighting became instead a

ghoulish nightmare. In a single instant, standing dumbstruck before his landlady in Hell's Kitchen, he became
both a widower and a bereaved father. Kathleen and
Brian, the boy he had never seen, simply ceased to exist.

The blow shook him to the very core of his being. On
a hundred killing grounds, from Bull Run to Savannah,
he had seen men slaughtered. Grown cold and callous to
the sight of death. Accounted for a faceless legion of
Johnny Rebs himself. Killing them grimly and efficiently,
unmoved toward the end by the bloody handiwork of his
saber. Thoroughly accustomed to watching men fall before his gun, screaming and splattered with gore like
squealing pigs in a charnel house. But the death of his
wife and son left him something less than a man. Cold
as a stone, and with scarcely more feeling.

Informed that the riot had occurred at a political rally,
he investigated further and unearthed a chilling fact.
Kathleen and the boy had been innocent bystanders, in
the wrong place at the wrong time. Caught up in a brawl
deliberately staged by the ward boss of an opposing fac-
tion. It was simply another Irish donnybrook, political
rivals battling for control of the ward, except that this
time it had claimed the lives of three men. And a woman
who happened by with her small son.

That very night McCluskie sought out the ward boss
and beat him to death with his fists. Afterward, certain
to be charged with murder, he vanished from Hell's
Kitchen and boarded the first train headed west.

The years since had been rewarding after a fashion,
for he was not a man to brood over things dead and gone.
But the ache, though diminished with time, was still
there. For Kathleen, and for the son he had never seen. It
was a part of himself that he kept hidden, and seldom saw
the light of day. Yet as he passed the depot and reined

the mare across the tracks, he was struck by a curious thought.

He wondered if his boy would have been anything like Kinch.

Somehow he hoped so, and just exactly why didn't seem to matter. It was enough that he might have had a son like the kid. A scrapper who never quit. Never backed off. A boy to make a man proud.

Dismounting in front of the livery stable, McCluskie led the mare inside as the sun settled to earth in a fiery splash of gold. Seth Mabry, the proprietor, looked up from shoeing a horse in the dingy smithy set back against the far wall. When he saw that it was the Irishman, he dropped his rasp and hurried forward, wiping his hands on the heavy leather apron covering his chest and belly.

"Well, Mr. McCluskie. You made a day of it. I was just startin' to wonder if you was gonna get back in time for supper."

"Make it a practice never to miss a meal," McCluskie replied handing over the reins. "Little habit I picked up right after I got weaned."

Mabry's stomach jounced with a fat man's hearty mirth. "Good way to be, Mr. McCluskie. Never was one to pass up a feed myself. Course, there's them that stays partial to milk even when they're full growed. If y'know what I mean."

"Been there myself, Mr. Mabry. Nothin' suits better than going back to the well when your throat gets dry."

"Now ain't that a fact!" The blacksmith squashed a horsefly buzzing about the hairy bristles of his arm. "Say, I didn't even think to ask. Hope Sally gave you that work-out you was lookin' for. She's got a lot of sass when she gets to feelin' her oats."

McCluskie snorted and shot the mare a dark look. "Sass don't hardly fit the ticket. She's got a jaw like a cast-iron stove. 'Stead of a quirt you ought to give people a bung starter when you rent her out."

"Just like a woman, ain't it, Mr. McCluskie? Never seen one yet that wasn't bound and determined to make a monkey of a man. Part of bein' female, I guess. Now, you take my wife—"

"Thanks all the same, but I'll pass. Hell, I had enough trouble just handlin' your horse."

The blacksmith was still laughing when McCluskie went through the door and turned down Main Street. Striding along the boardwalk, he almost collided with Randolph Muse in front of the Cattlemen's Exchange. The judge came tearing out of the bank as if his pants were on fire, and McCluskie had to haul up short to keep from bowling him over. It occurred to the Irishman that Muse never seemed to walk. His normal gait was sort of a hitching lope, like a centipede racing back to its hideout.

"Afternoon, Mr. McCluskie." The judge squinted against the sun, grinning, and his store-bought teeth gave off a waxy sheen. "Looks like you had a hard day's ride somewhere."

McCluskie swatted his shirt, raising a small cloud of dust. "Yeah, rode out to have a looksee at the track gang west of town."

"Everything proceeding smoothly, I trust."

"Right on schedule, Judge. Laying 'em down regular as clockwork."

"Good! Good!" They walked on a few paces together and Muse rolled his eyes around in a sidewise glance. "Don't suppose you heard any word about our competition? That Wichita bunch, I mean."

"Can't say as I did, your honor. Most likely they're keepin' their secrets to themselves."

"Well keep your ear to the ground, my boy. Ear to the

ground! We need all the information we can get on those rascals."

"I'll do that very thing, Judge. Fellow never knows where he'll turn up an interestin' little tidbit."

"Precisely. Couldn't have said it better myself." Muse took to the street and angled off toward the Lone Star. "I'd ask you to join me in a drink, but I've got a matter of business to discuss with Bob. Say, how is that lad of yours doing? Up and around, is he?"

"Gettin' friskier every day. I figure he'll be ready to try his legs just any time now."

"Excellent. Bring him around to see me. Sounds like a boy with real grit."

Muse turned away with a wave of his hand, kicking up little spurts of dust as he churned along. The Irishman chuckled softly to himself, struck again by the wonder of wee men obsessed with themselves and their wee plans. Passing Horner's Store, he stepped off the boardwalk and headed toward the tracks.

Newt Hansberry waved from the depot platform, but McCluskie merely returned the wave and kept going. This was one time he simply couldn't be bothered with the gossipy station master, or the Santa Fe for that matter. He'd earned his pay for the day and had a sore butt to prove it. The whole lot of them could swing by their thumbs for one night. It was high time he cut the wolf loose and had himself a little fling. Maybe even resurrect that card game with Dandy John and the boys.

The thought came and went with no real conviction. Tonight he'd be doing the same thing he had done every night for the last week. Sitting up with the kid. Just jawboning and swapping yarns till it was bedtime and he could sneak off for a quick one over at the Gold Room.

Not that he begrudged the kid those evenings. Truth was, he sort of enjoyed it. The button had more spunk than a three-legged bulldog, and oddly enough, he'd never felt so proud of anybody in his life. Judge Muse had called it grit, but that didn't hardly fit the ticket. The kid had enough sand in his craw to put them all in the shade. With a little to spare.

Doc Boyd had declared it nothing short of remarkable. The way the kid had perked up and started regaining his strength. Almost as if he had pulled himself up by his own bootstraps. Somehow refused to knuckle under. The sawbones had put a fancy handle on it—the instinct to survive—but McCluskie knew better. It was just plain old Irish moxie, with a streak of stubbornness thrown in on the side. The Gaelic in a man didn't let go without a fight, and Kinch Riley had been standing at the head of the line when they passed out spunk.

Already the color had returned to his face, and he'd lost that skin and bones look. Mostly due to Belle stuffing him full of soup and broth and great pitchers of fresh milk. Every day his spirits improved a notch or two, and he had even started talking about getting out of bed. Doc Boyd had put the quietus on that fast enough, leastways for the time being. But one thing was plain as hell. That kid wouldn't let himself be bound to a bed much longer. Not unless they strapped him down and hid his boots.

Thinking about it, McCluskie had to give most of the credit to Belle. She spent the better part of each day with the kid, returning to her house only when it was time for the evening rush to start. Along with hot food and fresh milk she also dispensed a peck of good cheer. Her sense of humor was sort of on the raw side, but she had a way of joshing the kid that made him light up like a polished apple. Maybe it was just Belle's maternal instinct showing through, but whatever it was, it worked. The kid lapped it up as fast as she could dish it out, and it was her gentle nudging that had finally started him talking.

At first, he had been reluctant to say much about himself. Just his name and the fact that he had no kin. But day by day Belle had wormed her way into his confidence, and when he finally let go it turned out to be a real tearjerker. Even Belle had got that misty look around the eyes, and a couple of times had to interrupt so she could blow her nose.

The kid made it short and sweet, just the bare bones. His folks were from Chicago and had been killed in a fire shortly after he turned seventeen. Afterward, working in the stockyards, he had heard about the Kansas cowtowns and decided to come west. His coughing spells got worse, though, riding the rods. He didn't think much about it at first, because he'd had similar attacks off and on over the past couple of years. But train smoke evidently didn't set well with his lungs and in Kansas City he ended up in a charity ward. The doctors there were a friendly bunch, but they hadn't pulled any punches. They told him what he was up against, and just about what he could expect. Once he was back on his feet, he'd skipped out before anybody got ideas about putting him in a home somewhere. He figured he might as well see the elephant while he had time and he started west again. Things got a little hazy after that, except for being chased and the one haymaker he'd thrown in the Newton rail yard. The next thing he knew, he woke up in Mike's bed.

Later, the Irishman talked it over with Belle and they decided that it was a little more than the luck of the draw. The kid's cards were being dealt from a cold deck, and it was going to be a rough hand to play out alone. McCluskie had surprised himself by volunteering to look after the kid. Just till he got his pins back under him.

Belle wasn't the least bit surprised, though. Not any more. She had laughed and said that it merely confirmed her suspicions. Beneath his stony composure he was all whipped cream and vanilla frosting. In other words, Irish to the core, and a born sucker when it came to siding with an underdog. Then she'd taken him up to her room and come very near to ruining him. When he finally crawled out of her place next morning, he'd felt limp as a dish-rag. But good. Restored somehow. Better than he had felt in more than a year.

Now, crossing the hotel lobby, McCluskie had to chuckle to himself as he thought back on it. That was one thing about Belle. Any tricks her girls knew, she knew better, and she could just about cripple a man when her spring came unwound.

Whistling tunelessly, he walked down the short hall-way and entered his room. Or what had once been his room. It was the kid's now. He merely kept his clothes there and paid the rent. For the past week he'd been stay-ing at Belle's, and getting himself worn to a frazzle in the process.

The kid was propped up in bed riffling a deck of cards on his lap. When McCluskie came through the door, he looked around and broke out in a wide smile.

"Mike! We was just about to send the cavalry out lookin' for you."

"Evenin', sport." The Irishman sailed his hat in the general direction of a coat rack and walked to the wash-stand. "Who's we?"

"Why, Belle and me. She just left a minute ago." Kinch laughed and shook his head. "She's a pistol, ain't she? Said she couldn't wait no longer or them cowhands'd be bustin' down the doors."

McCluskie glanced up at him in the mirror. "Belle said that?"

"Yeah, sure. Why?"

"Nothin'." He peeled his shirt and tossed it on a chair. "Guess she figures you're a shade older'n you look."

The boy reared back and scowled indignantly. "Well hell, Mike, I'm pushin' eighteen, y'know. Betcha when you was my age you'd been around plenty."

"Kid, when I was your age I was a hundred years old." McCluskie poured water in a washbowl and began his nightly birdbath. "But that don't cut no ice one way or the other. Now, c'mon, own up to it. You've never had a woman in your life, have you?"

Kinch went red as beet juice and fumbled around for a snappy comeback. "Well I come close a couple of times, don't you worry yourself about that. I'm not as green as I look."

"Hey, cool down. I wasn't rubbin' your nose in it. Just meant there's a few gaps in your education, that's all. Soon's you get the lead back in your pencil we'll have to arrange some lessons down at Belle's."

It took a moment for the meaning to register, and then the youngster burst out in a whooping belly laugh. Suddenly his face drained of color and the laugh turned to a racking cough. The attack was fairly short, and his sputum was no longer flecked with blood, but the pain was clearly evident in his face. Still, he tended to accept it with a stoicism beyond his years. Though hardly an old friend, pain was a familiar companion these days, and lying around on his backsides had given him plenty of time to think it out. There wasn't much to be gained in feeling sorry for himself—and moaning about it wouldn't change anything—so he might as well make the best of what time he had. Besides, what with one thing and another, he'd come out smelling like a rose anyway. It wasn't just everybody that got themselves hooked up with a slick article like the Irishman. Not by a damnsight, it wasn't.

As his cough slacked off, the boy glanced up and saw McCluskie watching him intently. He forced a smile and went back to shuffling the cards. "Y'know, Belle says that

with my hands I wouldn't have no trouble at all learnin'
how to make these pasteboards sit up and talk."

McCluskie finished splashing and started toweling
himself dry. "Seems like Belle's just chock full of ideas
for you."

"She's some talker, awright. Smart, too." Kinch cut the
deck and began dealing dummy hands of stud on the bed.
"But she's right about one thing. I ain't gonna be tied to
this bed forever, and I gotta get myself lined up with
some kind of work. It's real white of you, footin' all the
bills like this, but I'm used to payin' my own freight."

McCluskie stifled the temptation to smile. Sometimes
the kid was so damned serious it was all he could do to
keep a straight face. Sat there chewing his lip and frowning, like a little old man puzzling over some problem
that had confounded the world's scholars. For a button,
he was a prize package. In spades.

"Well now, I'll tell you, sport—I've been giving that
some thought myself. The Santa Fe has got me wore
down to a stump pullin' their chestnuts out of the fire.
Just never seems to be no end to it. Truth is, I've been
thinkin' of hirin' myself an assistant, and I got an idea
you might just fit the ticket. Course, the wages wouldn't
be much to start, but it'd get you by."

"Cripes, I ain't worried about that, Mike. Long as I
got three squares and a bed, I figure I'm livin' high on
the hog."

"You mull it over some. No hurry. When you get back
on your feet if you still like the idea, we'll give it a whirl."

McCluskie pulled a fresh shirt out of the bureau and
started putting it on. The boy was watching his every
move with renewed interest, and a quizzical look came
over his face all of a sudden.

"Say, Mike, I ain't never got around to it, but there's

something I been meanin' to ask you. How'd you get that scar on your belly?"

The Irishman glanced down at the jagged weal running from his ribs to his beltline, then went on buttoning the shirt. "Some hardcase came at me with a knife one night in Abilene."

"God A'mighty! What happened to him?"

"Nothin' special. Just a regular ten-dollar funeral."

Kinch's eyes went round as saucers and he sat there staring, the deck of cards forgotten.

With his shirt tucked in, McCluskie deliberated a moment and then gave the boy a questioning look. "Listen, bud, if you and me start workin' together, I want you to quit using that word *ain't* so much. It's not the word that bothers me, you understand, but it reminds me of somebody that rubs my fur the wrong way. Likely you'll meet him first time we're over at the depot."

The youngster ducked his head. "Sure, Mike. Anything you say. Won't be no trouble at all."

McCluskie grinned. "Tell you what. I'll go get us a supper tray, and after we eat, maybe I'll show you how to make them cards sit up and say *bow wow*."

Kinch's face lit up and he got busy shuffling the cards. But as the Irishman went through the door he sobered with a sudden thought and gave a loud yell.

"Tell 'em to hold the milk! Belle's got me swimmin' in the stuff."

CHAPTER 7

THE DAY was bright as brass, a regular Kansas scorcher. Lazy clouds hung suspended against the blue muslin of the sky, and the sun hammered down with the fury of an open forge. The air was still, without a hint of breeze, and across the prairie shimmering heat waves drifted soft as woodsmoke. Already the morning was a small slice of hell, and by noon the blazing fireball overhead would wilt anything that moved.

But it was the kind of day McCluskie liked. Clear and windless, and hot enough to keep a man's joints oiled with sweat. Perfect for burning powder, and testing himself against his keenest rival.

The one that dwelled within himself.

The Irishman came each morning to the rolling plains north of town. There, in a dry wash fissured through the earth's bowels, he played a game. The object was to beat his shadow on the gully wall. To draw and fire the Colt Navy a split second faster than his darkened image. Yet that was only part of the game. For while his shadow was allowed to miss, he granted himself no such edge.

Each slug must strike the target—a kill shot—or the game was lost.

McCluskie had been playing this game for three years, since the spring of '68 when he came west with the K&P. Not unlike most things he did, it was calculated and performed with solemn deliberation. Broiling his guts out with a track gang, laying rails across the parched Kansas plains, he had decided to make something better of himself than a common laborer. Watching and waiting, he studied the matter for a time, and concluded that the job of railway guard would be the first step. That required a certain aptitude with a gun, and with no one to school him, he taught himself. He invented the game and began practicing in his off time. Through trial and error he perfected the rudiments of what would later become rigid discipline, and shortly thereafter, his newly acquired skill came to the attention of company officials.

Later, after he had killed three men, people stopped joshing him about the game. They had seen the results, and the greatest skeptic among them became a devout believer.

McCluskie, along with Hickok and Hardin and a handful more, was a man to be cultivated. Befriended or won over somehow. Failing that, it was best to simply stay clear of him.

Even now, the Irishman still practiced the game religiously. Since killing the Quinton brothers, when they attempted to rob a K&P express car the summer of '69, there had been no occasion to draw the Colt in anger. His name was known, and anyone deadly enough to match his skill had better sense than to try. But this in no way diverted him from the game. The world was full of men too dumb, or too hotheaded, to back down, and in his trade, the risk of coming up against these hardcases was always there. With spartan discipline, he practiced faithfully, seven days a week. It was a demanding craft, one that allowed no margin for error. A man's first mistake might well be his last, and the prize for second place wasn't a gold watch.

McCluskie had never begrudged the time demanded by the game. Curiously, he'd always thought of it as an investment. Money in the bank. Better to have it and not need it than to need it and not have it. Which in his line of work made a pretty fair maxim all the way round.

So he practiced and improved and waited.

The past week had been a little different, though. Generally he played the game solitaire, but lately he'd started bringing Kinch along. The boy was recuperated, at least as much as he ever would be, and Doc Boyd had agreed that fresh air and sunshine were curatives in their own right. McCluskie enjoyed the company, and the kid seemed fascinated by the game, so the mornings had become a special time for them both.

There was only one thing that bothered the Irishman. Puzzled him in a way he couldn't quite fathom. The kid had been watching him for days now and never once had he asked to fire the pistol. Hadn't even asked to touch it, or evidenced the slightest curiosity in how it worked. Apparently his only interest was in the game itself, trying to judge who was the fastest. Man or shadow.

All of which seemed a bit queer to McCluskie. Most boys would have given their eyeteeth to sit in on these sessions. More to the point, though, they would have broken out in a case of the blue swivets waiting to get their hands on the gun. To see how good they could do. To learn. To feel the Colt buck and jump and spit lead. That's what he would have expected from any kid old enough to wear long pants.

But Kinch just hung back, watchful as a hawk, plainly satisfied to remain nothing more than a spectator.

McCluskie couldn't figure it, but as yet he hadn't pushed it either. There were lots of reasons that could make the kid shy off. None of them worthwhile from a man's standpoint, and some of them too repulsive even to consider. But he left it alone, saying nothing. The kid would come around in his own time, and if he didn't, there would be plenty of chances to find out why.

This was the fifth morning Kinch had tagged along, and by now the boy was accustomed to the ritual. Squatting down against one side of the gully, he observed silently as McCluskie set about the game. The first step was a target, and for this they had brought along a gunnysack stuffed with empty tin cans. The tins were of assorted sizes, mostly pints and quarts. McCluskie had wedged a plank between the walls of the gully about chest high, and on this he arranged five tins at spaced intervals. Then he stepped off ten paces and turned, facing the target. From his pocket he withdrew a double eagle and placed it in his left hand. Ready now, he stood loose and easy, arms hanging naturally at his sides. The only tenseness was in his eyes, and to the watching boy, it seemed that every fiber of his being was concentrated on the five cans.

Like most Westerners, McCluskie carried the Colt high on his hip, with the butt of the gun resting just below waistline. There were those who used tied-down triggers, low-slung holsters, even swivel affairs that allowed a man to twist the gun upward and fire while it was still in the holster. But experience, and three years of watching self-styled badmen commit suicide, had convinced him that such devices were strictly the work of amateurs. Flash-in-the-pan braggarts who thought an edge in speed could overcome a shortness in guts. The place for a gun was where it rode comfortable, easy to reach sitting or standing, and where it came natural to the hand when a man made his move.

The Irishman's left hand opened and the double eagle tumbled out. There was a space of only a split second before it hit the rocky floor of the wash. The metallic ring was the signal, and with it McCluskie's right arm moved. To the naked eye it was merely a blurred motion, but the Colt suddenly appeared in his hand and exploded flame.

The center can leaped off the plank and spun away.

Alternating his shots left to right, McCluskie sent the remaining tins bouncing down the gully. From first shot to last, the whole thing had consumed no more than a half-dozen heartbeats. Working with deliberate speed, McCluskie pulled out powder and ball, and began reloading.

Kinch was no less fascinated than the first time he had seen it happen. There was something magic about it, like a man pulling a rabbit out of a hat. One minute McCluskie was just standing there, and in the blink of an eye the gun was in his hand and whanging tin cans all over the place. It was hard to believe, except that he'd seen it repeated five mornings in a row.

Grinning, he picked up a rock and chunked it at one of the tins. "Better watch it, Mike. The shadow almost caught you that time."

McCluskie grunted, smiling. "Un-huh. Toad's got six toes, too. You keep a sharp lookout, though, sport. Can't let the bogeyman get too close or I'll have to take up cards for a livin'."

The Irishman directed his attention to the cans once more, and for the next half-hour blasted his way through what had become by now a ritualized drill. First, he increased the distance to twenty paces and began walking toward a fresh row of cans. Suddenly he halted in midstride, dropped into a crouch and started firing. Five tins again winged skyward.

Next, he stood with his back to the plank and held his arms in unusually awkward positions. Overhead, out to the side, scratching his nose. The way it might happen if he were taken by surprise. On signal from the coin, he would wheel around and open fire. Again and again he practiced these movements, spinning to the right on one exchange and to the left on another, each time changing the order in which he potted the cans.

Finally, he walked off down the gully a good fifty yards and halted. Turning sideways, he assumed the classic duelist's stance. Thumbing off each shot with precise care, using the sights for the first time, he started on the left and ticked off the cans in sequence. He missed on the last shot.

Kinch felt like the inside of his skull was being donged by the clapper in a church bell. The morning's barrage had left him all but deaf, and reverberations from the staccato bark of the pistol still rang in his ears. But the noise had little to do with the reason for shaking his head. By exact count, the Irishman had fired fifty shots.

He had missed only once. The last can.

While the boy was visibly impressed, McCluskie himself was muttering curses as he walked forward. Granted, it was the best score he'd racked up this week. But it wasn't good enough. Not in this game. The missed shot might have been the very one to put him in a box with a bunch of daisies in his hand. Concentration! That's where he had slipped up. Plain and simple.

Lack of concentration.

The Irishman squatted down beside the boy and began disassembling his pistol. This was something else that fascinated the youngster, the almost reverent care McCluskie lavished on the weapon. Kinch knew that later he would scrub out the black powder residue with soap and hot water. But for now he made do with swabbing a lightly oiled cloth through the barrel and the cylinder chambers.

McCluskie glanced up and smiled at the kid's solemn expression. "Well, bud, we didn't win the war but we scared the hell out of 'em. Still can't figure how I missed that last shot."

"It's important to you, ain't"—he grinned and made a face—"I mean, isn't it?"

McCluskie acted as though he hadn't noted the slip. "Damn right it's important. Not just because it's part of my job, either. Y'know, you're not back in Chicago any more. Out here a man has got to look out for himself."

"Yeah, but they got law in Newton. I mean, it's not like you was off in the mountains somewheres with a bunch of wild animals."

McCluskie snorted and peered down the barrel of the Colt. "Lemme tell you something, sport. The tough things in this life are sort of like takin' a leak. You've got to stand on your own two feet and nobody else can do it for you. That goes double in a place where everybody and his dog carries a gun. The law might arrest your murderer—maybe even hang him—but that's not likely to do you a whole lot of good. Dead's dead, and that's all she wrote."

Kinch picked up a pebble, studying it a moment, then shot it across the gully like a marble. "Belle says you've killed three men."

"Judas Priest, there's nothin' that woman won't talk about, is there?"

The boy gave him a sideways glance, then looked away again. Something was eating at him and it was a while before he could find the right words. "Is it hard to kill a man, Mike?"

"Well, I don't know." The Irishman paused and pulled reflectively at his ear. "Most times you don't think about it when it's happenin'. It's like fightin' off bees. You just do what needs doing to keep from gettin' stung."

"Yeah, but afterward don't you think about it? Maybe wish you hadn't done it?"

"Like feelin' sorry, you mean?"

Kinch nodded, watching him intently.

"What you're talkin' about is all that stuff in the Good Book. Thou shalt not this and that. The way I look at it, guilt is for them that needs it."

"I don't get you."

"Well, it's like this. Some folks are just miserable inside unless they've got something to feel guilty about. Sort of like it'd been bred into 'em, the same as horns on a cow. They're not really happy unless they're sad. All choked up with guilt. Y'see what I mean?"

The boy mulled it over a minute, frowning thoughtfully. "You're sayin' that if they kill a man to keep from gettin' killed, they still feel guilty. Like it was wrong doing it even to save themselves."

"That's about the size of it, I guess."

"But shouldn't you feel sorry, even a little bit? Somehow it don't seem the same as slaughterin' a pig or knockin' a steer in the head."

"Sport, it's not ghosts that haunt our lives. It's people. The live ones are who you've got to worry about. Don't waste your time on the dead. Where they are, it won't make a particle of difference."

Kinch again looked away, troubled by something he couldn't quite come to grips with. The game McCluskie played was fun to watch, the same way there was something grimly fascinating about watching a snake rear back and shake its rattles. But all week something had bothered him about the gun. Not anything he could exactly put his finger on, just a worrisome thought that wouldn't go away. Now he knew what it was.

The game had only one purpose. And it wasn't to perforate tin cans.

Since his little siege in the charity ward back in Kansas City, Kinch had had plenty of time to think. Mostly about death, and especially his own. In some queer sort of way it was as if he and Death had become close acquaintances, without a secret between them. Yet in the closeness came a curious turnabout. It wasn't that death frightened him so much as that life had suddenly become very precious. Each day was somehow special, a thing

to be treasured, and every breath his lungs took seemed
sweeter than the one before. Death in itself was sort of
shrouded, a misty bunch of nothing that even the preachers couldn't explain too well. But the loss of life was
very real, something he could understand all on his own.
When the candle was snuffed out, everything he was or
might have been just stopped. Double ought zero.

The thought of killing someone wasn't just repugnant.
It was scary in a way that resisted words. Like killing
another man would somehow kill a part of himself. Almost as if the time he had left would be whittled down
in the act of stealing from another what he himself prized
the most.

Then again, maybe it was like the Irishman said. Life
couldn't be all that precious if a man wouldn't fight to
save it. Only something of little value was tossed aside
lightly, and that didn't include the privilege to go on
breathing.

Kinch glanced at the big man out of the corner of his
eye. Since the loss of his family a year past he had been
drifting aimlessly, with no real goal in mind except to
taste life before his time ran out. McCluskie was the first
person to show any interest in him, to take the time and
trouble to talk with him. Strangely enough, these talks
somehow put him in mind of quiet evenings back in Chicago. When he and his father would sit on the tenement
stoop and discuss all manner of things. But that was before the fire. And the screaming and smoke and charred
stench of death.

He shuddered inside, remembering again how it had
been. Then he took hold of himself and wiped the thought
from his mind. There was nothing to be gained in living
in the past. Just bitter memories and grief and a void that
ached to be filled. Here and now, with the Irishman, he
had the start of something new. A friendship certainly,

otherwise McCluskie would never have taken him in and cared for him and given him a job. But over and above that there was something more. A closeness shared, unlike anything he'd ever known for another man. Except maybe for his father, and even that was somehow different.

Despite McCluskie's brusque manner and gamy joshing he felt drawn to the man. Not that McCluskie treated him as full grown. Nor was it just exactly a father to son kind of thing. Instead, it was something in between, a partnership of sorts, and perhaps that was what made it different. One of a kind. A rare thing, and exciting.

Puzzling over it, Kinch decided on the spur of the moment that he could have picked worse spots than Newton to pile off the train. Lots worse. Truth to tell, getting clobbered by the Irishman might well have been an unusual stroke of luck. They made a pretty good team, and it came to him all of a sudden that he had found something he didn't want to lose. Something damned special. And he wasn't about to rock the boat.

Whichever way the Irishman led, he meant to follow.

McCluskie finished assembling the Colt and started loading it. Seating a ball, he rammed it down and looked over at the kid. "Y'know, there's nothin' stoppin' you from tryin' your hand with this thing. Wouldn't be no trouble at all to show you how it's done. Matter of fact, what with you being my assistant, it might be a good idea. Never yet hurt a man to know one end of a gun from the other."

Kinch uncoiled slowly and got to his feet. "I'll give 'er a try. So long as we stick to shootin' at cans."

"Meanin' you're not ready to try your luck with something that shoots back."

The boy grinned. "I'd just as soon not."

"Bud, I hope it never comes to that. What I said a

while ago about guilt and all—I meant that. But it's not much fun killin' a man. Just between us, I could do without it myself."

McCluskie devoted the next hour to demonstrating the rudiments of what he had learned through nearly three years of trial and error. Instructing someone in the use of a gun seemed awkward at first, but he found Kinch an eager pupil. Things he had never before put into words made even more sense when he heard himself explaining it, and the boy's sudden interest gratified him in a way he would never have suspected. Nor did he fully understand it. He was just damned pleased.

Concentration and balance and deliberation. According to the Irishman, these were the sum and substance of firing a pistol accurately. Distractions of whatever variety—movement, sound, even gunfire—must be blocked out of a man's mind. Every nerve in his body must be focused with an iron grip on the target. Almost as if he were blinded to anything except the spot he wanted to hit. Without this intensity of concentration, he would more likely than not throw the shot off. Since the first shot was the one that counted, to waste it was a hazardous proposition at best.

Balance had to do with a man's stance and his aiming of the gun. McCluskie demonstrated by dropping into a crouch, feet slightly apart, and leveling the gun to a point that his arm was about equidistant between waist and shoulder. Each man soon determined the position most natural to himself, but the crouch was essential. It not only made him a smaller target, but more importantly, it centered the gun on his opponent's vitals. The chest and belly. At that point a man forgot the sights and aimed by instinct. Much the same as pointing his finger. With his body squarely directed into the target, and the gun jabbed out as an extension of his finger, he had only to bring his arm level and the slug would strike pretty much dead center every time.

McCluskie paused, mulling over the next part, and tried to frame his words to capture the precise meaning of a single thought.

"Forget about speed. That'll get a man planted quicker'n anything. It's not how fast you shoot or how many shots you get off. What counts is that you hit what you're shootin' at. With the first shot. If you can't learn to do that, then you've got no business carryin' a gun."

Kinch gave him a skeptical look. "You sound like one of them preachers that says 'do as I say, not as I do.' Cripes, I've been sittin' here for a whole week watchin' you whip that thing out like it had grease on it."

"That's because you've been watchin'," McCluskie growled, "instead of payin' attention. You've got fast mixed up with sudden. There's difference, and not understandin' that is what gets a man a one way ticket to the Pearly Gates."

The Irishman leveled his pistol at arm's length. "Right there's where you hesitate before you pull the trigger. But it's only a little hesitation, a fragment of a second. Nothin' a man could count even when he's doing it. Just a split-hair delay to catch the barrel out of the corner of your eye and make sure it's lined up on the target. Then you pull the trigger."

The Colt roared and a can spun off the plank.

"Learn that before you learn anything else. It's the difference between the quick and the dead. Deliberation. Sudden instead of fast. Whatever you want to call it. Just slow down enough so that your first shot counts. Otherwise you might not get a second."

McCluskie positioned the boy only five paces from the plank to start. They worked for a while on stance and gaining a feel for pointing the gun. Then he had the kid hold the Colt down at his side and concentrate on a single can. The label on it showed a bright golden peach.

"Whenever you're ready."

Kinch whipped the gun up and blasted off four shots in a chain-lightning barrage.

The can hadn't moved.

"No goddamnit, you're not listenin'. I said hesitate. Take your time. Hell, any dimdot can stand there and just pull the trigger. Now load up and try it again. Only slow down, for Chrissakes."

The next half-hour was excruciating for both teacher and pupil. The boy fired and loaded four cylinders—twenty shots—before he hit the juicy-looking peach. All the while McCluskie was storming and yelling advice and growing more exasperated with each pull of the trigger. Oddly enough, he seemed madder than if he himself had run out the string of misses.

But something had clicked on that last shot, the hit. Understanding came so sudden that Kinch felt as if his ears had come unplugged. The delay had been there. Right under his fingertips, like a sliver of smoke. He had felt it, sensed that it was waiting on him. Known even before he feathered the trigger that the can would jump.

He reloaded, blocking out McCluskie and the heat and the ringing in his ears. Then he crouched, leveling his arm, and the gun began to buck. Spaced shots, neither slow nor fast, with a mere trickle of time between each report.

Three cans out of five leaped from the plank.

The Irishman just stood there a moment, staring at the punctured tins. Then his mouth creased in a slow smile.

"Well I'll be a sonovabitch. You rung the gong."

CHAPTER 8

MCCLUSKIE HAD given the matter of Kinch's birthday considerable thought. The kid was turning eighteen, which was sort of a milestone in a youngster's life. The day he ceased being a boy and set about the business of becoming a man.

Not that a youngster couldn't have fought Indians or rustled cattle or killed himself a couple of men by that time. There were many who had, and lots more who fell shy by only the slimmest of margins. Wes Hardin, who had treed Abilene just last month, was scarcely eighteen himself. Yet, according to newspaper claims, he had even run a sandy on Wild Bill Hickok.

Life west of Kansas City forced a boy to grow up in a hurry. All too often, though, it killed him off before he ever really got started.

Personally, the Irishman had never set much store with this thing of birthdays. The idea of a boy becoming a man just because he'd chalked up a certain number of years seemed a little absurd. That pretty much assumed a kid couldn't cut the mustard, and McCluskie knew different. He had joined the Union army at the advanced age of nineteen, and nobody had ever been called upon to hold his hand. From the opening gun he had pulled his own weight, and when the Rebs finally called it quits, he'd felt like the old man of his outfit.

The killing ground did that. Seared the childish notions out of a boy's head and made him look at things in a different light. Like a man.

McCluskie had learned that lesson the hard way. First

hand. When he came west after the war, he was a man stripped of illusions. Life fought dirty in the clinches, so he had discovered, and it didn't pay to give the other fellow an even break. Just as he felt no remorse over the men he had killed in the war, so it was that he felt nothing for the ward boss in Hell's Kitchen, or the three hardcases he had planted in Abilene. There were some people just bound and determined to get themselves killed. The fact that he was the instrument of their abrupt and somewhat unceremonious demise was their lookout, not his. Not by a damnsight. Yet, in some queer way that he'd never really fathomed, he took neither pleasure nor pride in killing. It was like he had told the kid.

It's not much fun killin' a man.

Still, it was one thing to feel a twinge of regret and something else entirely to turn the other cheek. A man tended to his own business and tried not to step on the other fellow's toes. But he also fought his own fights, and anyone who came looking for trouble deserved whatever he got. Whether it was a busted nose or a rough pine box. That's the way the game was played, and while he hadn't made the rules, he wasn't about to break them either. Only dimdots and faint-hearts came west expecting to get a fair shake from the next man, and more often than not, they were the ones who ended up on an undertaker's slab.

Understandably then, McCluskie didn't believe in mollycoddling. The sooner kids learned to wipe their own noses, the better off for all concerned. Curiously enough, though, he had been at some pains to make an event of Kinch's birthday.

The excuses he gave himself were pretty lame. Generally he didn't allow feeling to stand in the way of common sense. He saw himself as a realist in a hard and uncompromising world. A man who met life on its own terms and handed out more licks than he took. Underneath his flinty composure, it grated the wrong way to admit there was still a soft spot he hadn't whipped into line. But he'd never been a man to fool himself, either. It all boiled down to one inescapable fact.

There wouldn't be any more birthdays for the kid. Eighteen was where the string ran out.

Oddly enough, the Irishman was having a hard time dealing with that. It confused him, this feeling he had for the kid. Part of it had to do with a small boy killed in a street brawl, the one he'd never seen. And he understood that. Accepted it as natural that a man would dredge up old feelings, musty and long buried, and allow a skinny, underfed kid to touch his soft spot. Even a man who made his living with a gun wasn't without a spark of emotion. No matter how many times he'd killed. Or told himself there was nothing on earth that could get under his skin and make him breathe life into thoughts dead and gone. That part held no riddle for him, and he had come to grips with it in his own way.

What bothered him, and left him more than a little bemused, was the extent of his feeling. Somehow the kid had penetrated his soft spot far deeper than he'd suspected at the outset. Little by little, over the course of their weeks together, the youngster had burrowed clean into the core. Like a worm that slowly bores a passage in hard-packed earth. Now the Irishman found himself face to face with something he couldn't quite handle. It was Hell's Kitchen all over again. Only this time he was there. Forced to stand helplessly by, as if his hands were tied, and watch it happen. Almost as though life had felt cheated the first time, and out of spite had summoned him back to observe, at last, the death of a boy.

In some diabolic fashion, the death of his own son.

That evening, when he got to the hotel, Kinch had himself all decked out in a new set of duds. The Irishman had forewarned him that this was the night. After nearly three weeks of taking it easy and soaking up sunshine, it was high time he got his feet wet.

Tonight they were out to see the elephant.

Kinch had splurged like a cowhand fresh off the trail. The wages McCluskie paid weren't princely by any yardstick, but the best at the Blue Front Clothing Store had been none too good. Candy-striped shirt, slouch hat, boots freshly blacked, and a peacock blue kerchief knotted around his neck. He was clean scrubbed and reeked of rose water, and his hair looked like it had been plastered down with a trowel.

McCluskie whistled and gave him the full once over. "Well now, just looky here. Got yourself all tricked out like it was Sunday-go-to-meetin'."

The boy preened and darted a quick look at himself in the mirror. "Just followin' orders. You said bright-eyed and bushy-tailed."

Damned if I didn't. Sort of took me at my word, too, didn't you?"

"Guess I did, at that. Put a dent about the size of a freight engine in my pocketbook."

The Irishman suddenly remembered the package he'd brought along and thrust it out. "Here. What with it being your birthday and all, I figured you was due a bonus."

"Aw, hell, Mike. You didn't have to buy me nothin'."

The sparkle in the kid's eyes belied his words, and it was all he could do to keep from ripping the package open. Setting it on the dresser, he forced himself to slowly untie the cord and peel back the wrapping paper. Then he removed the box top and his jaw popped open in astonishment.

"Hooooly Moses!"

Inside was a Colt Navy with a gunbelt and holster.

Kinch just stood there, mesmerized by the walnut grips and blued steel and the smell of new leather. After a while McCluskie chuckled and gave him a nudge. "Go ahead, try it on. It's not new, you understand, but she shoots as good as mine. I tried'er out this afternoon."

The boy pulled the rig out of the box as if it were dipped in gold and buckled it around his hips. It fitted perfectly, and he knew without asking that McCluskie had had it special made. There wasn't a store-bought gunbelt the near side of Kingdom Come that wouldn't have swallowed his skinny rump.

The Irishman took his shoulders and positioned him in front of the mirror. "Take a gander at yourself, bud. Don't hardly look like the same fellow, does it?"

Kinch just stared at the reflection in the mirror, dumfounded somehow by the stranger who stared back.

McCluskie grinned. "Much more and you'll bore a hole clean through that lookin' glass. C'mon, say something."

The kid's arm moved and they were both staring down the large black hole of the Colt's snout. The youthful face in the mirror laughed, eyes shining brightly. "D'ya see it?"

"See it?" McCluskie's grin broadened. "That's a damnfool question. What was it I taught you, anyway?"

That the hand's faster than the eye."

"Well you've got your proof right there in that mirror. The fellow you're lookin' at didn't even see it. He's still blinkin'."

While it was a slight exaggeration, McCluskie's comment wasn't far wide of the mark. The truth was, he hadn't seen the kid draw. Nor did it surprise him.

Not after the last couple of days in the gully north of town.

The swiftness with which the kid learned was nothing short of incredible. In two weeks he had mastered what some men never absorbed in a lifetime. Part of it was the will to learn, and some of it was McCluskie's dogged insistence on practice. But most of it was simply the boy's hands. Slim and tapered, hardened from work, but with a strength and quickness that was all but unimaginable. What those hands knew couldn't be taught. It was there all along, waiting merely to be trained. Reaction and speed was a gift. Something a man was born with. The rest was purely a matter of practice.

Kinch wasn't as good as he would be. Or as yet anywhere close to McCluskie. But he was fast. Even too fast, perhaps. The best score he'd racked up so far was three out of five cans. While he was fairly consistent, and improving every day, he still hadn't overcome a tendency to rush. Quite plainly, despite the Irishman's constant scolding, he had been bitten by the speed bug.

Still, this obsession with speed wasn't what troubled McCluskie the most. That would pass soon enough. As the kid got better, and gained confidence in himself, he would see that sudden beat fast everytime. The worrisome thing was Kinch's attitude. He still looked on the whole deal as one big game. Just a lark. A sporting event of some sort where the only casualties were a bunch of tin cans.

McCluskie wasn't completely unaware of what lay behind the kid's lighthearted manner. Perhaps any man, faced with the prospect of his own death, would have reacted the same way. Yet it was hard to accept, for it overlooked a salient detail. Places like Newton often pitted a man against something besides tin cans. Something that could shoot back.

Thinking about it now, as Kinch preened in front of the mirror, he wondered if he had done the right thing. Maybe giving the kid a gun wouldn't change anything. That remained to be seen. But one thing was for damn sure. It had put a spark in his eye that wasn't there before, and for the moment, that in itself was enough.

When they left the hotel dusk had already fallen, and the southside was a regular beehive of activity. Trailhands thronged the boardwalk, drifting from dive to dive with the rowdy exuberance of schoolboys playing hooky. Along the street rinky-dink pianos tinkled in witless harmony, and over the laughing and shouting and drunken Rebel yells, it all came together in a calliope of strident gibberish. Every night was Saturday night in Newton, and so long as the Texans' money held out, they flung themselves headlong into a frenetic swirl of cheap whiskey and fast women.

McCluskie angled across the street toward the Gold Room. That seemed like as good a place to start as any, but by no means would it be their last stop. Before introducing the kid to Belle's girls he figured to hit at least three or four dives. Somehow he just couldn't picture the youngster waltzing into a whore-house stone-cold sober. Better to float his kidneys first, and then let the ladies instruct him in the ancient and noble sport of dip the wick.

They came through the door with Kinch hard on his heels and headed for the bar. Every couple of steps the youngster took a hitch at his gunbelt, as if checking to make sure it was still there. The pistol felt strange and somehow reassuring on his hip, and the temptation to touch it was too much to resist. Had it been a wart between his eyes he wouldn't have been any less conscious of its existence.

Pony Reid greeted them at the bar. "Evenin', Mike. Kinch. You boys are gettin' an early start, aren't you?"

"Pony, we're out to see the elephant." McCluskie clapped the kid across the shoulders. "Not that you'd remember back that far, but Kinch just turned the corner on eighteen. He's ready to cut the wolf loose and let him howl."

By now everyone in town knew the story on the Irishman's young assistant. They had become all but inseparable, and it required only a moment's observation to see that the kid idolized McCluskie. In the manner of rough-natured men, the sporting crowd had adopted Kinch as one of their own.

"Hell's bells, that calls for a drink!" Reid signaled the barkeep. "Set 'em up for my friends here. Celebration like this has to get started off proper."

The bartender poured out three shots and Reid hoisted his glass. "Kinch, here's mud in your eye. Happy days."

The gambler and McCluskie downed their whiskey neat. Kinch hesitated only a moment and followed suit. When the liquor hit bottom it bounced dangerously, exploding in a series of molten eruptions. His eyes watered furiously and he felt sure smoke would belch out of his ears at any moment. But somehow he managed to hold it down, and after a couple of quick breaths, he gave the older men a weak smile.

"Mighty good drinkin' whiskey. Next one's on me."

"The hell you say!" The Irishman slapped a double eagle on the bar and winked sideways at Pony Reid. "Treat's on me. The rest of the night. Barkeep! Set 'em up again."

Kinch had the sinking sensation that another round might just paralyze him, but he merely grinned and bellied up closer to the bar. This was the first time the Irishman had allowed him anything stronger than a warm beer, and he wasn't about to back off now.

Then, as he lifted the glass again, his nose twitched.

Cripes! No wonder they called it coffin varnish. That's what it smelled like. Only worse.

They came through the door of Belle's house arm in arm. Kinch was listing slightly, but still navigating under his own power. This, along with his clear eye and steady speech, had the Irishman a little puzzled. After a whirlwind tour of three saloons in the past two hours he'd fully expected to have the youngster ossified and walking on air. But it hadn't worked out that way.

Apparently the kid had a greater tolerance for whiskey than he'd suspected. That or a hollow leg.

Halting in the entranceway to the parlor, they surveyed the room with a look of amused dignity. McCluskie swept off his hat and made a game try at what passed for a bow.

"Ladies, we bring you greetings." Straightening, he gestured toward the boy, who was propped up against the doorjamb. "This here is Mr. Kinch Riley, sportin' man supreme."

Everything in the room came to a stop. Belle, along with three cowhands and five girls, stared back at them as if man and boy had suddenly sprung whole from a crack in the floor. Kinch pulled his hat off and grinned like a cat with a mouthful of feathers. But he had a little trouble duplicating McCluskie's bow. All at once his joints seemed limber as goose grease and he couldn't quite manage to peel himself off the doorjamb.

Belle crossed the room and planted herself directly in their path. She looked them both up and down, shaking her head ruefully. Then she sniffed, as if one of them had broken wind, and her gaze settled on the Irishman.

"Just proud as punch, aren't you? Finally managed to get him drunk."

"Drunk?" McCluskie tucked his chin down and gave her an owlish frown. "Who?"

"Him!" Belle's finger stabbed out and Kinch jerked back, banging his head against the door frame.

McCluskie's frown changed to a sly smirk, as if he had just heard a lie so preposterous it defied belief. "God-damn, Belle, he's sober as a judge. You better get your-self some specs."

"You really are thick, aren't you?" Her words came clipped and sharp, like spitting grease. "You big baboon, you're so drunk he looks sober. And him sick, too. Just wait till Doc Boyd gets wind of this."

"Cough syrup," Kinch muttered.

They both blinked and gave him a peculiar look. Belle shrugged, not sure she had heard right, and after a moment McCluskie bent closer. "How's that, bud?"

"Cough syrup."

"Yeah, what about it?"

"Tastes just like cough syrup."

"You mean the whiskey?"

"Just like what they gimme at the hospital."

"What them doctors gave you back in Kansas City?"

"Only better. Lots better."

McCluskie sifted it over a minute and all of a sudden the kid made perfect sense. Canting his head back, he gave Belle a crafty look. "Thick, huh? Case you hadn't noticed, he's not coughin'. Matter of fact, he hasn't since we started drinkin'. What d'ya think of that?"

"Oh, pshaw!" she informed him. "That's no excuse to take a boy out and get him drunk."

"Belle, you're startin' to sound like a mother hen. Be-sides which, we didn't need an excuse. This is his birth-day. Or maybe you forgot."

"I didn't forget and you know it very well. But he was supposed to get his birthday present here, not soaking up rotgut in some dingy saloon."

"Well Jesus H. Christ! Whyn't you quit makin' so

much noise, then, and do somethin' about it? Hell, he's been standin' here five minutes and you haven't even introduced him to the girls."

Belle started to say something, but thought better of it. She pried Kinch off the doorjamb and waltzed him out to the middle of the parlor. The girls had watched the entire flurry with mild wonder, and now, as she graced them with a dazzling smile, they sensed that something unusual was brewing.

"Girls, you've all heard me talk about Kinch. Well, tonight is his birthday and he's come to spend it with us. Whatever he wants is on the house, so whoever gets picked, make sure he has a good time."

Nothing about her smile changed, but something in her eyes did. "Understand?"

The girls got the message. They dropped the three cowhands like so many hot rocks and came swarming over the kid. A henna-haired redhead reached him first, and wedged herself up next to his chest like a mustard plaster. Close behind came a blond with soft, jiggly breasts the size of gourds. She latched onto his other arm and started running her hand through his hair. Another blond and a mousey brunette charged into the melee, and before he had time to take a deep breath, Kinch was up to his ears in squealing females.

"Sweetie, do you like Lulu?" purred the redhead.

Kinch cast a trapped look back over his shoulder at the Irishman. But he got no sympathy there. McCluskie and Belle were going at it hammer and tongs. Evidently their little spat had only just started.

The blond stuck her melons under his nose and whispered a blast of hot air into his ear. "Ditch these others, honeybunch. Let Francie give you a trip around the world."

The boy felt as though he were drowning in a sea of

arms and bosoms and clawing hands. Every time he struggled to the surface they dragged him under to the floor. Suddenly he pitched forward, spun completely around, and broke clear. Dazed and still somewhat numb from the whiskey he'd absorbed, he lurched away and almost plowed over the fifth girl. Drawing back, he swayed dangerously and tried to bring her into focus.

She was smaller than the others, just a little sprite of a girl. Her hair was black as tarpitch, and she had large almond eyes that stared out wistfully from a kewpie-doll face. Just at that moment he thought she was the most beautiful creature he'd ever seen. More importantly, if it came down to it, he thought he could whip her in a fair fight. The others he wasn't too sure about.

"Hi." Her mouth dimpled in a smile. "I'm Sugartit."

That threw him off stride and for an instant he couldn't get his jaws working. Then he felt the pack closing in behind him and he grabbed her hand.

"Let's go!"

Kinch didn't know where they were going, but right about then his choices seemed pretty limited. He reeled forward, head spinning crazily, aware of nothing but the girl before him.

Sugartit clutched his hand and took off toward the rear of the parlor. The thing he always remembered most afterward was her laugh as they went through the door.

It was like the patter of rain on a warm spring night.

CHAPTER 9

KINCH WAS having a hard time looking at the girl. Buttoning his shirt, he kept sneaking peeks at her out of the corner of his eye. If she noticed, she didn't say anything, but he found nothing unusual in that. Anybody with a name like hers was probably used to being stared at. Maybe even liked it.

Watching her dress gave him a strange sensation down around his bellybutton. It was almost as if he could see straight through her clothes. The way she'd been in bed, soft and naked and cuddly warm. All of which was in his mind's eye, of course. He kept telling himself that as his hands fumbled with the shirt buttons. But it made the image in his head no less real.

What he saw wasn't so much the girl as the sum of her parts. Brief flashes that came and went, like lightning bugs in a dark room. Her impish smile and those big, waifish eyes. The delicate buttercup of her breasts. The gentle swell of her hips. And most of all, somehow flickering brighter than the rest, the soft black muff between her legs. That came strong and clear, sharply in focus.

It was something he would never forget. The warmth and pulsating throb and pleasure so sweet it became almost pain.

What he felt just then was so distinct and real that his mind turned inward, living it over again. Suddenly something touched him and a shiver rippled along his spine. He blinked, awareness returning in fits and starts, much as a dream fades into wakefulness. Then, all in a rush, he saw Sugartit standing before him. She was buttoning his shirt, her mouth dimpled with that small enigmatic smile.

His hands were motionless, frozen somehow to his shirtfront, just where they were before his mind wandered off. All at once he felt green as grass, clumsy and very foolish, and he quickly lowered his hands.

Sugartit finished the buttoning and began tucking his shirt into the waistband of his trousers. He just stood there watching her, gripped by a sensation so acute he couldn't put a name to it. Goosebumps popped out on his skin and a static charge brought tingly little prickles to every nerve in his body. Curiously, he was overcome by a feeling of utter helplessness. As if this mere slip of a girl, through some witchery he failed to comprehend, had cast a spell and turned him into a bumbling jackass incapable of the simplest thought.

The girl ran her arms around his waist and pressed herself close to his chest. He could feel the taut little nipples of her breasts through his shirt, and his mouth suddenly went thick and pasty. Mechanically, like some wooden Indian come to life, he put his arms around her. He felt light in the head, queer somehow, as if he were standing off in a corner watching it happen to someone else.

"There's sure not much of you." Sugartit ran her fingers over his ribs like a piano player testing chords. "You're just all bone and gristle, aren't you?"

Kinch swallowed a wad of paste. "I guess."

"Well, don't worry about it, lover." Her head arched back and the almond eyes seemed to soak him up in great gulps. "Maybe you got shortchanged on muscle, but you're all bearcat where it counts."

Suddenly he felt about eight feet tall. "You ain't exactly tame yourself."

She laughed softly and snuggled closer. "Did you like it?"

"Better'n a duck likes water." Curiously, his tongue had come unglued and he felt slick as a street-corner pitchman. "What about you?"

"Silly, of course I did. Couldn't you tell?" She gave him a tight little squeeze. "I've had it lots of ways, but never like that. Not even once."

The scent of her hair was like perfume and for an instant he couldn't get his breath. "You're joshin' me."

Sugartit put her arms around his neck and pulled his head down. Her lips came over his mouth, soft and warm, and her pink little tongue started doing tricks. Then her hips moved, undulating and hungry, and a jolt of lightning hit him just below the belt buckle. She pulled back and searched his face with a devilish smile.

"Still think I'm joshing?"

Kinch bent and lifted her in his arms. She was surprisingly light, and it pleased him that he could heft her so easily. As he carried her toward the bed, Sugartit laughed that soft laugh again and began nibbling on his ear.

When they entered the parlor some time later everything was back to normal. Belle and the Irishman were wedged into a settee like a couple of lovebirds, and from the looks they were giving one another, it was clear that a truce of some sort had been negotiated. The girls had themselves a fresh batch of Texans, and they were paired off around the room making sweet talk. Everybody knew that this was what made Belle's prices so stiff, all the sugar and spice that came beforehand. But the cowhands didn't seem to mind in the least. They were lapping it up as fast as the girls could dish it out.

So far as the kid could see, it was business as usual.

McCluskie spotted him first and gave Belle the high sign with a jerk of his head. She looked around and then they both stood up, waiting for Sugartit and Kinch to cross the room. Belle whispered something and the Irishman smiled, but oddly enough, they had the look of expectant parents. Almost as if they were awaiting news of a blessed event.

"Bud, I'd just about given you up for lost," McCluskie grinned and tried to make it sound offhand. "Enjoy yourself, did you?"

Kinch flushed despite himself. "Yeah, sure. Best birthday I ever had."

The girl giggled and Belle eyed her speculatively. "Sugartit, I hope you showed our young friend a good time."

"Why, Belle, I just put the frosting on his cake. I taught him the French twist, and the half-and-half, and—"

"Whoa, Nellie!" McCluskie threw up his hand. "All that racy talk is liable to give an old man like me dangerous notions. C'mon, sport. Let's go get ourselves a drink. After a workout like that I've got an idea you need fortifyin'." He dropped an arm over the kid's shoulders and headed for the door. "Belle, I'll see you later. And if I don't, you'll know ol' hollow-leg here had put me under the table."

"Mike McCluskie, you remember what I said! Don't you dare get that boy drunk again. I'll hear about it if you do."

McCluskie laughed and kept on walking. The boy darted a look over his shoulder as he was being hustled into the hallway, and Sugartit gave him a bright smile.

"Come back soon, lover. Don't forget, you hear?"

Kinch's disembodied voice floated back through the parlor entrance. "I will. First thing tomorrow."

Then the door slammed and Belle shot the girl a funny look. Sugartit sighed and dimpled her cheeks in a pensive little frown, wondering if he really meant it.

Outside, McCluskie headed the boy uptown and they walked along at a steady clip for a few paces. After a while the Irishman grunted and shook his head.

"Let that be a lesson to you, bud. Don't ever let women get started runnin' their gums. Once they build up a head of steam, there's no stoppin' them. I got us out of there just in time."

Kinch gave him a quizzical glance. "I don't get you. What's wrong with talkin'?"

"Talkin'? Hell, there wouldn't be no talkin' to it. Just listenin'. They'd sit there and rehash the whole night, and feed it back to you blow by blow. Time they got through you'd come away thinkin' you'd lived it twice."

"Yeah, I guess I see what you mean."

They walked along in silence for a few steps, but McCluskie's curiosity finally got the better of him. Not unlike the temptation to peep through a knothole, there was a question he just couldn't resist.

"What'd you think of Sugartit?"

"She's nifty, Mike. Cuter'n a button, too."

Something in the kid's voice sounded peculiar. Just a little off key. "Well, I didn't mean her, exactly. I was talkin' about what she did for you. How'd you like that?"

Kinch didn't say anything for a moment, but an odd look came over his eyes. "It was like a big juicy toothache that don't hurt no more. All of a sudden *whammo!* And then it's fixed."

"Yeah?" McCluskie detected something more than mere excitement. "Tell me about it."

"Well, I don't know. It was like colored lights whirlin' around inside your head. Y'know, the way a skyrocket does. There's a big explosion and then for a while you can't see nothin' but streaks and colors and bright flashes. Cripes, she was somethin', Mike."

"I'm startin' to get a hunch you were drunker'n I thought."

"No I wasn't, neither. After the first time I was sober as all get out."

"First time!"

The boy grinned sheepishly. "Yeah. Y'see, we was getting' dressed and then she started rubbin' around on me and—"

"I get the picture. What you're sayin' is that you liked it more'n you thought."

"I liked her. There's somethin' about her, Mike. She's not like the others. Not even a little bit."

The Irishman slammed to a halt and faced him. "Say, you're not gettin' sweet on that girl, are you?"

"I might be." Kinch stuck out his chin and stared right back. "What's wrong with that?"

McCluskie had seen lots of men go dippy over whores. In a cowtown there was always a scarcity of women, and sometimes a man settled for what he could get. But the kid deserved better than that. The only thing special about Sugartit was that she had probably laid half the cowhands in Texas. And her hardly older than the kid, for Chrissakes!

"What's wrong is that she's a whore. Has been since Belle stole her away from a dancehall back in Abilene. That was close to three years ago. You got any idea how many men she's screwed in—"

"Mike, I ain't gonna listen to that. Don't you go bad-mouthin' her, y'hear me!"

The boy was bristled up like a banty rooster and Mc-Cluskie had to clamp down hard to keep from laughing. "Don't get your dander up, bud. I was just tryin' to show you what's what."

"Well, lay off of her. I told you, she's not like the others."

"Awright, just for the sake of argument, let's say she's not. But what do you think she's doin' back there right now?"

"What kind of crack is that?"

"You think about it for a minute. She's not workin' in a sporting house for her health, y'know. There's cowhands walkin' in there regular as clockwork, and before the night's over she'll have humped her share."

Kinch glared at him for a long time, then he shrugged and looked away. "Nobody's perfect. She was probably starvin' and plenty hard up when Belle took her in."

"That's right, she was."

"Same as me, the night you caught me down at the depot."

"Not just exactly. That's what I'm tryin' to get through your head. Call her whatever you want: Soiled Dove. Fallen Sparrow. The handle you put on her won't change nothin'. The plain fact of the matter is, she's a whore."

"Well, holy jumpin' Jesus, that ain't no crime, is it? Cripes, if I was a girl and got stuck in a cowtown, I might've wound up a whore myself."

"All I'm sayin' is that you shouldn't get calf eyes over your first piece of tail. There's lots of women around. Some of 'em better'n Sugartit, maybe. You ought to shop around a little before you let yourself get all bogged down."

"I don't see you makin' the rounds. Seems to me you stick pretty close to Belle."

The kid halfway had a point. McCluskie grunted and turned back uptown. They clomped along without saying much, each lost in his own thoughts. At last, somewhat baffled by the youngster's doggedness, the Irishman decided to try another tack.

"Y'know, it's funny how things work out between a man and a woman. Now you take Belle and me, for instance. Once I get her in bed she's tame as any tabby-cat you ever saw. But the rest of the time she's got a temper that'd melt lead. Hell, I don't need to tell you. Not after some of the tantrums you've seen her pitch."

Kinch gave him a suspicious look. "What's that got to do with me and Sugartit?"

"That's what I was workin' around to. You see, it's like this: When a man's puttin' the goods to a woman, she's putty in his hands. There's not a promise on earth she wouldn't make while he's got his shaft ticklin' her fun-nybone. But out of bed it's a different story. Then she knows he's got his mind on the next time, and that gives her the whiphand. She'll make him sweat and do all kinds of damnfool things before she lets him climb in the saddle again."

"I still don't see what that's got to do with anything."

"You're not listenin', bud. What I'm sayin' is that women calculate things. Plan it all out. A man's brains are between his legs, and that's where he does most of his thinkin'. A woman thinks with her head, leastways when you haven't got her on her back, and she generally winds up getting' what she wants."

"What you're sayin' is that women know how to wind a man around their little finger."

"That's exactly what I'm sayin'. Just remember, a man rules in bed, but the rest of the time it's the woman that calls the tune. They'll make you dance whatever jig they want just for the honor of pumpin' on 'em every now and then."

"And you think that's what Sugartit has got planned for me?"

"She's female, and I'm just tellin' you that's the way they work."

Kinch screwed up his face in a stubborn frown. "Mike, that's the biggest crock I ever heard. Maybe I'm wet behind the ears, but I'm not stupid. Sugartit is different, and nothin' you say is gonna budge me one iota."

It suddenly dawned on McCluskie that he was up against a stone wall. Not only that, but he was trying to play God in the bargain. Here was a kid who'd be lucky if he lived out the winter, and the last thing he needed was a bunch of second-hand advice—especially from somebody who hadn't made any great shakes of his own life. If the kid wanted a playmate till his string ran out, then by damn that's what he would have. Sugartit was handy and seemed willing, so it was just a matter of working it out with Belle. The button wouldn't even have to know.

McCluskie threw his arm over the boy's shoulders. "Sport, I learned a long time ago not to argue with a man when he's got his mind set. Besides, maybe you know something I don't. Hell, give it a whirl. You and Sugartit might hit it off in style. Just remember what I said, though. Keep your dauber up and she'll treat you like Jesus H. himself."

The kid grinned and started to reply, but all at once his throat constricted and he began coughing. It wasn't a particularly severe spasm but it was the worst of the night. Watching him gasp for air, the Irishman was again reminded of his promise to himself. This kid was going to have whatever he wanted. Served up any way he liked.

"Goddamn, I knew it!" McCluskie growled. "You sobered up and now you're back to coughin'. C'mon, bud, what you need is a drink. Let's find ourselves a waterin' hole."

They crossed the street and entered Gregory's Saloon. This was a Texan hangout and a place McCluskie normally wouldn't have frequented, but just then he wasn't feeling choosy. Whiskey was whiskey, and the kid needed a dose in the worst way.

The dive was packed shoulder to shoulder with trail-hands, and reeked of sweat, cow manure, and stale smoke. McCluskie bulled his way through the crowd and wedged out a place for them at the bar. Some of the men he shoved aside muttered angrily, and a curious buzz swept back over the room as others turned to look at the choking, red-faced kid.

The bartender sauntered over, absently munching a toothpick. "What'll you have?"

"The good stuff," McCluskie informed him. "With the live snake in it."

That didn't draw any laughs but it produced a bottle. The Irishman poured and got a shot down Kinch without any lost motion. Apparently even snakehead whiskey was not without medicinal qualities. It had no sooner hit bottom than the kid stopped coughing and commenced to look like himself again. McCluskie poured a second round just for good measure.

"Say, Irish, when'd ya start collectin' strays?"

Several of the men close by chuckled, and McCluskie turned to find Bill Bailey standing a few feet behind him. They had crossed paths back in Abilene and shared a mutual dislike for one another. Bailey was a big man, heavier than McCluskie, with a seamed, windburned face the color of plug tobacco. His legs bowed out like a couple of barrel staves, and it was no secret that he had once been a top hand for Shanghai Pierce. According to rumor, he had a checkered past and couldn't return to Texas—something about a shootout over a card game that had left a reward dodger hanging over his head. But he was a great favorite with the trailhands, and through one device or another, managed to leave them laughing as he separated them from their pay.

McCluskie gave him a brittle stare. "Bailey, I only allow my friends to call me Irish. That lets you out."

"Hell, don't get your nose out of joint." Bailey jerked a thumb at Kinch. "I was just curious about your pardner. Looks a mite sickly to be runnin' with you."

"Don't let his looks fool you." McCluskie turned his head slightly and winked at the kid. "For a skinny fellow he's sorta sudden."

Bailey cocked one eyebrow and inspected the boy closer. "Yeh, that popgun he's wearin' looks real, sure enough. Course, I've seen more'n one pilgrim shoot his toes off tryin' to play badman. What about it, squirt, you lost any toes lately?"

McCluskie leaned back against the bar and studied the ceiling. The kid glanced at him and got no reaction whatever. Then it came to him, what was happening here, and a smile ticked at the corner of his mouth.

The Irishman had slyly brought the game full circle.

Kinch turned his attention back to the Texan. "Mister, that's a bad habit you've got, callin' people names. Some folks might not take kindly to it."

Bailey's eyes narrowed and he darted a puzzled look at the Irishman. "Listen, sonny, my beef's with your friend here. Just button your lip and I'll act like I didn't hear you."

All at once the kid knew what McCluskie had been talking about every day out in the gully: the difference between a tin can and a man. It brought a warm little glow down in the pit of his belly.

"What's the matter, lardgut? Lost your nerve?"

"Boy, I'm warnin' you, don't rile me. You're out of your class."

It was just like McCluskie had said! A four-flusher always toots his horn the loudest. He smiled and edged clear of the bar.

"Try me."

Bailey's hand twitched and streaked toward the butt

of his gun. Then he froze dead still. The kid was standing there with a Colt Navy pointed straight at his gut. What the Texan took to be his last thought was one of sheer wonder. He hadn't even seen the kid move.

McCluskie waited a couple of seconds, then looked over at the boy. "You figure on shootin' him?"

Kinch shook his head. "Nope, He's not worth it."

McCluskie shrugged and headed toward the door. The boy backed away, keeping Bailey covered, and only after he was outside did he holster the Colt. The Irishman was already striding up the street, and as Kinch came alongside he grunted sourly.

"That was a damnfool play. A gun's like what you've got between your legs. If you're not going to use it, then keep it in your pants. Saves a whole lot of trouble later on."

CHAPTER 10

THE FIVE men were seated around a table in the Lone Star. They were alone, for sunrise was scarcely an hour past, and none of the saloon help had yet arrived. Spivey and Judge Muse, flanked by Tonk Hazeltine, occupied one side of the table. Seated across from them were McCluskie and Bill Bailey.

Not unlike dogs warily eying one another, the Texan and McCluskie had their chairs hitched around sideways to the table. They had exchanged curt nods when the meeting began, and afterward seated themselves so they could keep each other in sight. This guarded maneuvering was hardly lost on the others, yet none of them displayed any real surprise. The story of Bailey's humiliation at the hands of the kid was by now common knowledge. It had created a sensation on both sides of the tracks, and except for the upcoming bond issue, the townspeople had talked of little else for the last week.

Word had spread that Bailey meant to even the score, and hardly anyone doubted he would try. Unless McCluskie got to him first, which seemed highly likely. Still, betting was about evenly split, and speculation was widespread as to the outcome if it ever came to a showdown.

When the men first sat down, Spivey had attempted to ease the tension with some idle chitchat. But it quickly became apparent that his efforts were largely wasted. While Muse joined in, the others simply stared back at him like a flock of molting owls. Hazeltine and Bailey shared a bitter dislike for the Irishman, who in turn, looked through them as if they didn't exist. Spivey finally gave it up as hopeless and at last got down to business.

"Gents, I called this meetin' so we could get everything squared away neat and proper. Once the votin' commences I don't figure we're gonna have much chance to get our heads together. Whatever's got to be ironed out, we'd best get to it now. Later we likely won't have time."

There was a moment of silence while everybody digested that. After a while Hazeltine cleared his throat. "I don't follow you. What's left to be done?"

"Well, Tonk, when we agreed to deputize these boys"—Spivey waved his hand in the general direction of McCluskie and Bailey—"we sort of thought you'd make good use of 'em. I kept waitin' but as of last night you hadn't said yea or nay. Seemed to me we oughta talk about it."

"What's to talk about?" The lawman gave him an indignant frown. "I'm the law here and I'll see that everything comes off the way it's s'posed to."

Spivey and Muse exchanged glances. Then the judge made a steeple of his fingers and peered through them at Hazeltine. "Deputy, we're not casting aspersions on you personally. Nothing of the sort. We're merely asking what your plans are."

"Hell, we don't need no plans. You talk like we was electin' a new President or somethin'. It's nothin' but a measly goddamn bond vote."

Spivey swelled up like a bloated toad. "Measly, my dusty rump! Just in case it slipped your mind, what happens today could put the quietus on this whole town. What's at stake here is Newton itself."

"Bob's right," the judge agreed hurriedly. "We're fighting for our lives. Now let me tell you something. Six months ago this town was nothing but a cow pasture.

Today we have a bank, hotels, businesses. A thriving economy. And something more, too. The potential—"

McCluskie turned a deaf ear to the judge's harangue. The past month had left him with a sour taste in his mouth for the grubby little game being played out here. Wichita was trying to shaft Newton. The Santa Fe was shafting everybody. And he was caught squarely in the middle.

All because the head office brass wanted to squeeze a lousy two hundred thousand dollars out of Sedgwick County.

But then, that's how the rich got fat and the poor got lean. The big dog kept nibbling away, bit by bit, at the little dog's bone. Which didn't concern him one way or the other. Except that the brass acted like they had a case of the trots and couldn't find the plug.

They had ordered him to split Newton down the middle and that's what he'd done. Pony Reid and John Gallagher started talking it up and before long the sporting crowd had swung over to Wichita's side of the fence. All of which made good sense from their standpoint. Wichita was farther south than any of the cowtowns and was sure to attract a greater number of the Texas herds.

Then, out of a clear blue, the brass told him to lay off. They had decided, according to their last letter, to let Sedgwick County resolve its own internal affairs. Stripped of all subterfuge, it simply meant they intended to play both ends against the middle. Whoever won— Newton or Wichita—the Santa Fe would still wind up with all the marbles.

If it wasn't so infuriating he might have laughed. The fact that they paid him to waste his time and effort only made it more absurd. Like a dog chasing its tail, he had accomplished nothing.

Judge Muse brought him back to the present with a sharp rap on the table. "We're fighting for nothing less than our very lives! Everything we possess has been poured into this town. Speaking quite frankly, Deputy, I think that demands some added effort on your part also."

Tonk Hazeltine gave him a glum scowl. "I already said my piece. Trouble with you fellers is you're makin' a mountain out of a molehill."

"Like hell we are!" Spivey replied hotly. "This town'll be swamped with Texans today, and if I know them they won't miss a chance to hooraw things good and proper. It's our election, but odds are they'll use it as an excuse to pull Newton up by the roots."

"Which could disrupt the voting," Muse added, "and easily jeopardize whatever chance we have of defeating the bond issue."

Hazeltine said nothing, merely staring back at them. Spivey and the judge looked nonplused, but it was all the Irishman could do to keep from grinning. What he had suspected from the outset was now quite apparent. The lawman was all bluff, and he plainly wasn't overjoyed by the prospect of cracking down on the cowhands. Muse and Spivey had blinded themselves to the truth, staking their hopes on his much publicized reputation. Right now he was the only law the town had, and they couldn't see past the glitter of his tin star.

The silence thickened and after a moment Spivey glanced over at the Irishman. "What d'ya think, Mike? Isn't there some way we could keep the lid on till after the votin' is done with?"

"Why the hell you askin' him?" Bailey snarled. "The only thing he ever give Texans was a hard time, and you'd better believe they ain't forgot it neither."

Judge Muse raised his hand in a curbing gesture. "Mr. Bailey, may I remind you that you and Mr. Mc-

Cluskie were deputized in an effort to even things out. You're a Texan, and you should be able to reason with them if things get out of hand. Mr. McCluskie, on the other hand, is versed in—shall we say, keeping the peace—and that, too, has its place. All things considered, it seems like a good combination."

"Like hell!" Bailey rasped, edging forward in his chair. "You turn him loose with a badge and I guaran-damn-tee you there's gonna be trouble. He's got it in for Texans and everybody knows it."

McCluskie pulled out the makings and started building a smoke. "There's only one Texan I'm on the lookout for, and you're sittin' in his chair."

"You're gonna get it sooner'n you think." Bailey half rose to his feet, then thought better of it and hastily sat down. "That goes for your snot-nosed side-kick, too."

The Irishman fired up his cigarette and took a deep drag. Then he tossed the match aside and smiled, exhaling smoke. "Bailey, you monkey with me and I'll put a leak in your ticker. Any time you think different, you just try me."

Spivey broke in before the Texan could frame an answer. "Now everybody just simmer down. Whatever personal grudge you've got is between you two. But for God's sake, let's keep the peace today. C'mon now, what d'ya say? Do I have your word on that—both of you?"

When neither man responded, the saloonkeeper hurried on as though it were all settled. "Good. Now, Mike, you never did answer my question. What do we do to keep the lid on?"

McCluskie puffed thoughtfully on his cigarette. "Where's the votin' booth? Horner's Store, isn't it?"

"That's right. What with it bein' just north of the tracks, we figured it was handy to everybody concerned."

"Yeah, that sounds reasonable." The Irishman took a

swipe at his mustache, mulling some thought a moment longer. "Way I see it, the thing to do is to keep the cowhands from crossin' the tracks in any big bunches. Hazeltine could watch over Horner's, and me and Bailey could patrol opposite sides of the street down on the southside. That way if any trouble starts we could close in on it from three sides. Oughtn't to be that much of a problem if we handle it right."

Hazeltine stiffened in his chair and glared around at Spivey. "Who's callin' the shots here, me or him?"

McCluskie chuckled and flipped his cigarette in the direction of a spittoon. "Tonk, the man just asked for some advice. I wouldn't have the job on a bet."

Spivey nodded vigorously, looking from one to the other. "Course, you're callin' the shots, Tonk. Wouldn't have it any other way. But you'll have to admit, he's got a pretty good idea."

The deputy pursed his lips and shrugged with a great show of reluctance. "Yeah, I guess so. Probably wouldn't hurt none for me to stick close to that votin' booth."

McCluskie wiped his mouth to hide a grin. *Wouldn't hurt none.* What a joke! The sorry devil had been oozing sweat at the thought of patrolling the southside. Holed up in Horner's was just his speed. Likely what he had intended doing all along.

Judge Muse climbed to his feet, smiling affably. "Then it's all settled. Gentlemen, I'm happy to see we've reached an accord. I, for one, have a feeling this is going to be a red-letter day in the history of Newton."

The men pushed out of their chairs, standing, and Bailey's gut gave off a thunderous rumble. Someone suggested breakfast and the others quickly agreed. Despite Randolph Muse's optimistic forecast, they shared a hunch that it wasn't a day to be faced on an empty stomach.

Walking back to the hotel, McCluskie couldn't shake

an edgy feeling about Bailey. The man was a loudmouth and a bully, but he was no coward. Not that he wouldn't backshoot somebody if that seemed the best way. He would and probably had. Yet even that took a certain amount of sand, and Bailey had his share.

The Irishman wasn't worried about himself. Characters like Bailey were strictly penny-ante, and there was a certain savor in beating them at their own game. But the threat against the kid was another matter altogether. It was very real, and Bailey had ample reason to want the youngster dead. Making a fool of a hardcase, who had set himself up as bull-of-the-woods, was a risky sport. It could get a man—or a boy—gunned down in a dark alley. Or in bed. Or just about any place where he least expected it.

Thinking of the kid made him chuckle, but it was amusement heavily larded with concern. These days the button was cocky as a young rooster. That he had shaded Bailey on the draw was only part of it. Mostly it had to do with a girl named Sugar, and the fact that she had become his regular girl. Not that she was his alone, but she came as close as she could. Sugar was one of Belle's girls, and Belle was a businesswoman first and last, and even for the kid her generosity had certain limits. After listening to McCluskie's arguments she had agreed to a compromise of sorts. Sugar could see the kid all she wanted on her off time, and so long as he made a definite appointment at night, Belle wouldn't use the girl for the parlor trade. Otherwise Sugar would work the same as usual, which meant that she was the boy's private stock, but only about halfway.

The kid wasn't exactly overjoyed by the arrangement, yet he couldn't help but strut his stuff the least little bit. Sugar had a knack about her, there was no denying that. She had convinced him that he was the only real man in

her life, and every time they were together, he came away
fairly prancing. What they had wasn't just the way he
wanted it, but it was far more than he'd ever had before.
Life had dealt him enough low blows so that having
Sugar, even on a part-time basis, seemed like a stroke of
luck all done up in a fancy ribbon. The way he talked it
was as if the bitter and the sweet had finally equaled out.
He was happy as a pig in mud, only he couldn't stop
wishing the wallow was his alone.

When McCluskie entered the room, he found the kid
standing before the mirror, practicing his draw. Every
day the boy got a shade faster, but smooth along with it,
as though somebody had slapped a liberal dose of grease
on a streak of chain-lightning. The Irishman felt a little
like God, profoundly awed at what he had wrought.

Kinch saw him in the mirror and turned, holstering
the Colt in one slick motion. "Just practicin' a little. I
been waitin' breakfast for you."

"Already had mine." McCluskie cocked his thumb and
forefinger and gestured at the pistol. "You've got yourself honed down to a pretty fine edge. What's the sense
if you won't shoot nothin' but tin cans?"

"Same song, second verse. You're talkin' about Bailey again, aren't you?"

"That'll do for openers."

"Mike, I done told you fifty zillion times. I had him
cold. There wasn't no need to shoot him. He was froze
tighter'n an icicle."

"There's some men that would've dusted you on both
sides while you was standin' there admirin' how fast you
were. You try pullin' a fool stunt like that again and the
jasper you're facin' might just be the one that proves it to
you."

"Okay, professor." The kid smiled and threw up his

hands to ward off the lecture. "You don't have to keep beatin' me over the head with it. I got the idea."

"Yeah, but have you got the stomach for it? I've been tellin' you not to wear that gun unless you mean to use it next time. So far you've given me a lot of talk but you haven't said anything."

"Awright, I'm sayin' it. Next time I won't hold off."

McCluskie eyed him skeptically. "Sometimes I think it was a mistake to give you that gun. Might have saved us all a pile of grief."

"You lost me. Where's the grief in me packin' a gun?"

"I just came from a meetin' with the big nabobs." The Irishman hesitated, turning it over in his head, and decided there was nothing to be gained in holding back. "Bailey was there and he started makin' noises about nailin' you. Course, he's been makin' the same brag all over town, so it's not exactly news. But it's past the talkin' stage now. He'll have to make his play soon."

"Aren't you and him gonna be workin' together today?"

"Now what's that got to do with the price of tea?"

"Nothin'. I was just thinkin' I might tag along with you."

McCluskie grunted, shaking his head. "Bud, you're barking up the wrong tree. Bailey knows better than to mess with me. It's you he's after."

"Still wouldn't do no harm."

"Maybe. But we'll never find out. I want you to stick close to the room today. I'll have the cafe send up your meals."

"Aw, cripes a'mighty, Mike. I'm not a kid no more. If he's spoilin' for a fight it might as well be sooner as later."

The Irishman studied him a moment, weighing the alternatives. "No soap. I'll sic you on him when I'm convinced you won't hold off pullin' the trigger. Meantime, you keep your butt in this room. Savvy?"

Kinch spun away and kicked a chair halfway across the room. "Horseapples!"

McCluskie walked to the door, then turned and glanced back. "How's your cough today?"

The kid wouldn't look at him. "Why, you writin' a book or somethin'?"

"Keep your dauber up, sport. There's better days ahead."

The door closed softly behind him and an oppressive silence fell over the room. Kinch flung himself down on the bed and just lay there, staring at the ceiling. Then he felt the first tingle deep down in his throat.

He waited, knotting his fists, wondering what his lungs would spew up this morning.

Shortly after the noon hour Hugh Anderson and his crew rode into town. McCluskie saw them pull up and dismount before the Red Front Saloon, and his scalp went prickly all of a sudden. That explained it. Why things had been so quiet all morning. The Texans crowding the saloons up and down the street had been biding their time. Waiting for the big dog himself to start the show.

Anderson and his hands were the bane of every cowtown in Kansas. They were wild and loud, rambunctious in the way of overgrown boys testing their manhood. Only their pranks sometimes got out of hand, and they had a tendency to see how far a town could be pushed before it stood up and fought back. Their leader was an arrogant young smart aleck, the son of a Texas cattle baron, and he had developed quite a reputation for devising new ways to hooraw Kansas railheads. Worse yet, he fancied himself as something of a gunslinger, and had an absolute gift for provoking senseless shootouts.

McCluskie knew what was coming and headed toward the tracks at a fast clip. Crossing Fourth, he scanned the street for Bailey, meaning to give him the high sign, but the Texan was nowhere in sight. Before he could reach the next corner, men began boiling out of saloons and Anderson's crew was quickly joined by another forty or fifty cowhands. There was considerable shouting and arm waving, and suddenly the crowd split and everybody raced for their horses. The Irishman jerked his pistol and took off at a dead run.

But he was no match for them afoot, and they thundered across the tracks even as he passed the hotel. Townspeople were lined up outside Horner's Store waiting to vote and the Texans barreled down on them like a band of howling Indians. Anderson opened fire first, splintering the sign over the bank, and within moments it sounded as if a full scale war had broken out. Glass shattered, lead whanged through the high false-front structures overhead, and above it all came the shrill Rebel yells of Texans on the rampage.

Most of the town had gathered to watch the balloting, and now they stampeded before the cowhands like scalded dogs. Women clutched their children and ran screaming along the street, while men scattered and leaped into nearby doorways seeking shelter. The Texans made a clean sweep up North Main, laughing and whooping and drilling holes through anything that even faintly resembled a target. Then they whirled their ponies and came charging back toward the tracks.

Tonk Hazeltine made the mistake of stepping out of Horner's Store just at that moment. Had he remained inside the cowhands would probably have kept on going, satisfied that they had taught the Yankee bloodsuckers a lesson. But the sight of a tin star was a temptation too great to resist.

Hugh Anderson skidded his horse to a halt, and the Texans reined in behind him, cloaked in a billowing cloud of dust. Hazeltine stood his ground on the boardwalk, watching and saying nothing as they walked their horses toward him. When they stopped, Anderson hooked one leg over his saddlehorn and grinned, gesturing toward the deputy.

"Well now, looka here what we caught ourselves, boys. A real live peace officer. Shiny badge and all."

The Texans thought it a rare joke and burst out in fits of laughter. Circling around behind them, McCluskie saw the lawman's face redden but couldn't tell if he said anything or not. It occurred to him that Hazeltine was probably too scared to draw his gun. Still, if he could just get the drop on them from behind it might shake the deputy out of his funk. Once they had the cowhands covered front and rear that would most likely put an end to it.

McCluskie raised his pistol but all at once cold steel jabbed him in the back of the neck. With it came the metallic whirr of a hammer being thumbed back and a grated command.

"Unload it, Irish! Otherwise I'll scatter your brains all over Kingdom Come."

One of McCluskie's cardinal rules was that a man never argued with a gun at his head. Slowly, keeping his hand well in sight, he lowered the Colt and dropped it in the street. Then he stood very still.

There was no need to look around. Bill Bailey's voice was one in a hundred. Maybe even a thousand.

With or without a cocked pistol.

CHAPTER 11

BAILEY MARCHED the Irishman forward, nudging him in the backbone every couple of steps with the pistol. The cowhands' attention was distracted from Hazeltine for a moment, and they turned in their saddles to watch this curious little procession. McCluskie looked straight ahead, ignoring their stares, and took his lead from the jabs in his spine. They circled around the skittish ponies and came to a halt before Hugh Anderson.

"What've you got there, Billy?" Anderson was casually rolling himself a smoke. "Another lawdog?"

"He's the one I told you about. Pride and joy of the Santee Fe. Ain't you, Irish?"

McCluskie kept his mouth shut, coolly inspecting Anderson. The Texan was older than he expected. Pushing thirty, with a bulge around his beltline that spoke well of beans and sowbelly and rotgut whiskey. A hard drinker, clearly a man with a taste for the fast life. But for all the lard he was packing, there was nothing soft about him. His face looked like it had been carved out of seasoned hickory, and back deep in his eyes there was a peculiar glint, feverish and piercing.

All of a sudden McCluskie decided to play it very loose. He had seen that look before. Cold and inscrutable, but alert. The look of a man who enjoyed dousing cats with coal oil just to watch them burn.

"McCluskie." The word came out flat and toneless. Anderson flicked a sulphurhead across his saddlehorn and lit the cigarette.

"You're the one that had everybody walkin' on eggshells back in Abilene."

"Yeah, that's him," Bailey crowed. "The big tough Mick. Leastways he thinks he is."

"Bailey, whatever I am," McCluskie observed softly, "I don't switch sides in the middle of a fight."

"He's got you there, Billy." Anderson smiled but there was no humor in his eyes. "Folks hereabouts are gonna start callin' you a turncoat, sure as hell."

"No such thing," Bailey declared hotly. "I just played along, that's all. So's you boys would get the lowdown."

He rammed McCluskie in the spine with the gun barrel. "You smart-mouth sonovabitch, I oughta fix your wagon right now."

Anderson laughed, thoroughly enjoying himself. "Hold off there, Billy. We can't have people sayin' we go around murderin' folks. Besides, I got a better idea." His gaze settled on McCluskie and the odd light flickered a little brighter. "You. Trot it on over there beside jellyguts."

The Irishman's expression betrayed nothing. He walked forward, mounted the boardwalk, and took a position alongside Hazeltine. The deputy shot him a nervous glance, but just then he couldn't be bothered. His attention was focused on Anderson.

The Texans were also watching their leader, not quite sure what he had in mind. But knowing him, there was unspoken agreement that it was certain to be a real gutbuster. Whatever it was.

Anderson just sat there, leg hooked over the saddlehorn, puffing clouds of smoke as he contemplated the lawmen. People appeared from buildings along the street and started edging closer, drawn in some perverse way to the silent struggle taking place in front of Horner's Store. At last Anderson smiled, nodding to himself, and flipped his cigarette at Hazeltine's feet.

"Let's see how fast you two can shuck out of them duds." Idly he jerked his thumb toward the southside. "We're gonna have ourselves a little race. Last one to hit the town limits gets his head shaved."

The cowhands cackled uproariously, slapping one another on the back as they marveled at the sheer artistry of it. Goddamn if Hughie hadn't done it again, they shouted back and forth. Come up with a real lalapalooza! On the whole they looked proud as punch, as if the sentence rendered by Anderson somehow reflected their own good judgment. The jeers and catcalls they directed at the lawmen made it clear that they wanted no time lost in getting the show on the road.

Hazeltine began shaking like a dog passing peach pits, and it was plain to everyone watching that he was scared out of his wits. Without his badge to hide behind, divested of even his clothes, there was no telling what these crazy Texans would do to him. He had thought to talk them back over to the southside once they'd had their fun, but it was obvious now that he would be lucky to escape with his life. The fear showed in his face, and not unlike a small child being marched to the woodshed, he started peeling off his shirt.

McCluskie just stood there.

Anderson eyed him a moment, then grinned. "Hoss, you better get to strippin'. Jellyguts there'll outrun you six ways to Sunday if you try racin' in them boots."

The Irishman met and held his gaze. "I guess I'll stand pat."

"Cousin, you don't seem to get the picture. I ain't offered you a choice. I only told you how it was gonna be. *Sabe?*"

McCluskie did something funny with his wrist and a .41 Derringer appeared in his hand, cocked and centered squarely on the Texan's chest. "Your boys might get me, but I'll pull this trigger before I go down. What d'ya say, check or bet?"

"Well now, don't that beat all? Got himself a hideout gun." Anderson was laughing but he didn't make any sudden moves. At that range the Derringer would bore a hole the size of a silver dollar. "I got to hand it to you, cousin. You're bold as brass, damned if you ain't."

"Yeah, but I get nervous when I'm spooked. You talk much more and this popgun's liable to go off in your face."

Anderson studied him a couple of seconds, then shrugged. "What the hell? It wouldn't have been much of a race anyhow."

"Judas Priest, Hugh!" Bailey scuttled forward, waving his pistol like a divining rod. "Don't let him back you down. He's runnin' a sandy. Can't you see that?"

"Bailey, my second shot's for you." McCluskie's voice was so low the Texans had to strain to catch his words. "Keep talkin' and you'll get an extra hole right between your eyes."

"Back off, Billy!" Anderson's command stopped Bailey dead in his tracks. "Trouble with you is you never could tell a bluff from the real article. He's holdin' the goods."

Bailey kicked at a clod of dirt and walked off. After a moment Anderson's mouth cracked in a tight smile. "McCluskie, we'll just write this off to unfinished business. There's always another day. Now, why don't you make tracks before some of my boys get itchy?"

"What about Hazeltine?" the Irishman asked.

"What about him?"

"I thought maybe I'd just take him along with me."

"Don't push your luck, cousin." Anderson scowled and the feverish glow again lighted his eyes. "Our deal don't include him."

When McCluskie hesitated, he laughed. "Mebbe you're thicker'n I thought. You got some notion of gettin' yourself killed over a two-bit marshal?"

McCluskie glanced at the lawman out of the corner of his eye, then shook his head. "Nope. Just figured it was worth a try."

"So you tried," Anderson remarked, dismissing him with a jerk of his head. "See you in church."

The Irishman stepped off the boardwalk and backed away, keeping Anderson covered as he circled around the milling horses. Once clear, he saw Spivey and Judge Muse standing in the doorway of the Lone Star and made a beeline to join them. Both men looked grim as death warmed over, and at the sight of the Derringer in his hand they paled visibly. While they had caught only snatches of the conversation between Anderson and the Irishman, there was no need to ask questions. It was all too obvious that a killing had been averted by only the slimmest of margins. McCluskie retrieved his pistol from the street and came to stand beside them in the doorway.

Tonk Hazeltine was left the star attraction of the Texans' impromptu theatrical. Accompanied by a chorus of gibes and hooting laughter, he skinned out of his clothing a piece at a time. Shirt, gunbelt, pants, and boots hit the street in rapid succession, and at last he stood before them in nothing but his longjohns and hat. Bare to the waist, he made a ludicrous figure, like some comic scarecrow being ridiculed by a flock of birds. Half-naked, humiliated in the eyes of the townspeople, he had been stripped of much more than his clothes. The reputation he had brought to Newton was gone, vanished in an instant of shame, and with it the last vestiges of his backbone.

He stood alone and cowering, a broken man.

The Texans gave him a head start and choused him

south across the tracks at a shambling lope. His hat flew off as he passed the depot and every few steps they dusted his heels with a flurry of gunshots. All along the street the sporting crowd jammed the boardwalks watching in stunned silence as his ordeal was played out to its conclusion. Never once did Hazeltine utter a sound, but his eyes were wild and terror-stricken, and tears sluiced down over his cheeks even as he ran. The last they saw of him, he was limping aimlessly across the prairie, a solitary wanderer on the road to his own private hell.

Anderson and Bailey hadn't joined in the chase. They watched from in front of Horner's Store, seemingly content to let the cowhands share whatever glory remained in the final act. Now, grinning and thoroughly delighted with themselves, they became aware of the three men standing outside the Lone Star. Anderson reined his horse about, with Bailey walking alongside, and they crossed the street. Halting a few paces off, the cattleman gave McCluskie a gloating smile, then turned his attention to Spivey and Muse.

"Gents, it would appear your little metropolis needs itself a new marshal."

Judge Muse bristled and shook his finger at the Texan. "Anderson, you've brought yourself a peck of trouble. That was a deputy sheriff you ran off, which makes this a county matter. Tomorrow at the latest the sheriff himself will be up here with a warrant for your arrest."

"Is that a fact?" Anderson studied him with mock seriousness for a moment, as if amused by the jabber of a backward child. "What would you like to bet that the sheriff don't get within ten miles of Newton?"

Bailey laughed, plainly taken with the idea. "Yeah, he ain't comin' up here to pull your fat out of the fire. Hell, we'd send him hightailin' in his drawers the same as Hazeltine."

"Which come election time," Anderson added, "might look real bad to the voters. Or don't you gents agree?"

The logic of Anderson's argument was all too persuasive. Spivey and the judge exchanged bemused glances, and in the look was admission of defeat. Whatever help there was for Newton wouldn't come from a sheriff whose bread was buttered by Wichita voters. The town was on its own, and like storm clouds gathering in a darkened sky, it was plain for all to see.

"By damn, it don't end there," Spivey declared. "We'll just hire ourselves a marshal of our own. That's what we should've done in the first place."

Anderson leaned forward, crossing his arms over the saddlehorn. "Now I'm glad you brought that up. Fact is, I was thinkin' along the same lines myself."

Muse eyed him suspiciously. "I fail to see where it concerns you."

"That's where you're wrong, judge. Case you don't know it, me and my boys have got this town treed. Just offhand, I'd say that gives us quite a voice in who gets picked as lawdog."

"By any chance," Muse sniffed, "were you thinking of nominating yourself for the job?"

"You got a sense of humor, old man. I like that." Anderson grinned and dropped his hand on Bailey's shoulder. "No, the feller I had in mind was Billy here. With him totin' that badge you'd have a townful of the friendliest bunch of Texans you ever seen."

Spivey's face purpled with rage. "I'll kiss a pig's tail before that happens. Newton's not gonna have any backstabbin' jackleg for a marshal."

Bailey jerked as if stung by a wasp and started forward. "Swizzleguts, I'm gonna clean your plow."

McCluskie had been standing back observing, but

now he shifted away from the door. "Bailey, you're liable to start something you can't finish."

The Texan stopped short and his beady eyes narrowed in a scowl. "Big tough Mick, aren't you? Think you're fast enough to take both of us?"

McCluskie smiled, waiting. "There's one way to find out."

Anderson had seen other men smile that way. Cold and taunting, eager somehow, like a hungry cat. The odds didn't suit him and he very carefully left his arms folded over the saddlehorn. Bailey glanced around, suddenly aware that he was playing a lone hand. After a moment he grunted, ripping the deputy badge from his shirt, and flung it to the ground.

"Jam it! I got better things to do anyway."

Everybody stood there and looked at each other for a while and it was finally Anderson who broke the stalemate. "Judge, you and Spivey oughta think it over. Not go off half-cocked, if y'see what I mean. You put that tin star on anybody besides Billy and I got an idea Newton's in for hard times."

Then his gaze fell on the Irishman. "You've braced me twice today. Third time out and your number's up."

McCluskie gave him the same frozen smile. "Don't bet your life on it."

Anderson reined his horse back and rode off toward the southside. Trailing behind, Bailey ambled along like a bear with a sore paw. From the doorway of the Lone Star, the three men watched after them, and at last Spivey let out his breath between clenched teeth.

"Christ!"

Late that afternoon nine men gathered in the small back-room office of the Lone Star. Among them were saloon-keepers, businessmen, one judge, and a blacksmith. They comprised the Town Board, and their chairman, Bob Spivey, had called them into emergency session. None of them questioned why they were there, or that a crisis existed. But as they stood around the smoke-filled room staring at one another, few of the men had any real hope of solving what seemed an insoluble mess.

When the last member arrived, Spivey rapped on his desk for order and stood to face them. "Men, I'm not gonna waste time rehashin' what's happened today. Most of you saw it for yourselves, and them that didn't has heard the particulars more'n once by now. The thing is, we've got ourselves a real stemwinder of a problem, and before we leave here we're gonna have to figure out what to do about it. Otherwise you can kiss the town of Newton good-by. That goes for whatever money you've got invested here, too. Now, instead of me blabberin' on about the fix we've got ourselves in, I'm gonna throw the floor open for discussion. Who's first?"

The men looked around at one another, hesitant to take the lead, and after a moment Randolph Muse cleared his throat. Rising from his chair, he studied each face in turn, as if in the hope of discovering some chink in their stony expressions. Though he had tussled with the problem all afternoon, he had yet to settle on the best approach. They were a disparate group, with conflicting interests and loyalties, and it would be no simple matter to hammer out an accord. Not a man among them could be bullied, and logic was an equation foreign to their character. That narrowed the alternatives considerably. Leaving perhaps only one appeal which might muster some solidarity in what lay before them.

"Gentlemen, what I have to say will be short and straight to the point. Where there is no law all values disappear. Whether on life or on property. Newton was founded on a cornerstone of greed, and I think each of us is honest enough to admit that to ourselves. We came here hoping to make our fortune, and for no other reason. Unless we restore law and order to this town there is every likelihood we will leave here paupers."

He paused, screwing up his most judicious frown. "Without restraints of some sort, the Texans will turn this into one big graveyard long before you can unload your business on some unwary sucker. If you don't believe that, you have only to wait and watch it happen."

Val Gregory lashed out angrily. "That's a lot of hot air. I say give the drovers their way. They're about the only ones that come in my place, and god-damnit, I don't mean to bite the hand that feeds me. You think about it a minute and most of you'll see that you're rowin' the same boat."

Perry Tuttle, the dancehall impresario, readily agreed. But the others evidenced less certainty, muttering and shaking their heads as they tried to unravel what seemed a very tangled web. Seth Mabry, still covered with grime from the smithy, pounded a meaty fist into the palm of his hand.

"No, by God, I don't agree. It's like the judge says. You give in to 'em, and make Bill Bailey marshal, and we'll wind up presidin' over a wake."

"That's right," Sam Horner growled. "Inside of a month they'd tear this town down around our ears."

Charlie Hoff and John Hamil, whose stores were south of the tracks, both chimed in with quick support. That seemed to shift the scales off center, and for a minute everybody just stood around and glared at one another.

Harry Lovett, who operated the Gold Room, finally sounded a note of moderation. "Seems to me we're all after the same thing. It's just a matter of how we get it. Hell, nobody wants to rankle the Texans. Most of my business is with highrollers, but I still turn a nice profit on the cowhands. The long and the tall of it boils down to one thing. We can't operate in a town where every store and saloon and dancehall has to be its own law. That'd be like fightin' a fire with a willow switch. There just wouldn't be no stoppin' it. What we need is somebody the drovers respect. Just between us, I don't think Bailey's the man."

The gambler had presented a convincing argument, and before anyone could object, Bob Spivey came out swinging. "Harry, you hit the nail right on the head. Only I'd take it a step farther. What we need is not so much a man they respect, but a man they're afraid of. We've got the same problem Abilene had, and everybody here knows how they solved it. Bear River Tom Smith and Wild Bill Hickok. Texans are like any other jackass. You can't reason with 'em and being nice to 'em is a waste of time. You've got to teach 'em that every time they step out of line somebody's gonna get a busted skull. That's the only thing they understand."

The men stared back at him, somewhat dumbstruck by his heated tone. Spivey wasn't a violent man, and when he used words that strong it seemed prudent to weigh them carefully. None of them said anything simply because there was no way to refute his statement. It was all true.

After a while Val Gregory grunted and gave him a wry look. "I suppose you just happen to have a man in mind?"

Spivey walked to the door, yanked it open, and gestured to someone in the saloon. There was a brief wait and a slight stir of expectancy, but it came as no great surprise when McCluskie entered the office.

"Boys, I think you all know Mike McCluskie." Spivey slammed the door, and while everybody was still nodding, he gave them another broadside. "Mike, if we was to appoint you city marshal, how would you go about handlin' the Texans?"

McCluskie saw no reason to mince words. "Same as I would a mean dog. Educate 'em as to who's boss. That'd likely mean some skinned heads, and maybe even some shootin'. But it's the only thing that'd get the job done."

"What about the Santa Fe?" Perry Tuttle asked. "Wouldn't think they'd hold still for you gettin' mixed up in a thing like this."

"I cleared it with 'em this afternoon." The Irishman nodded at Spivey. "Soon as Bob put it to me I got on the telegraph."

Sam Horner rubbed his jaw and looked thoughtful. "Where would you start? Educatin' the Texans, I mean."

McCluskie smiled. "Best way to kill a snake is to cut his head off."

The room went still and Spivey glanced around at the solemn faces. "Anybody opposed?"

When none of the men offered objection, he pulled out a badge and pinned it to McCluskie's shirt. Then he sighed wearily and a grave smile touched the corners of his mouth.

"Marshal, I guess you better get to killin' snakes."

CHAPTER 12

McCLUSKIE WASTED little time. What he had in mind depended not so much on nerve or guts or even luck. It required mainly an element of surprise. The Texans had to be taken off guard, hit fast when they least expected it. But if it was to work he had to make his move before the board members scattered and spread the word. Otherwise the chances of taking Anderson and Bailey unawares would be pretty well eliminated.

While Spivey and the board were still hashing it around, he excused himself and made a hasty exit from the Lone Star. None of them expected anything rash on his part—they were the kind that believed in coppering their bets—and it would never occur to them that he might go the limit strictly on his own hook. That gave him an edge of perhaps a quarter hour, certainly no more. He meant to use it to best advantage.

His advantage.

Turning south, he crossed the tracks past the depot and began checking saloons along the street. His plan was already formulated, had been since that afternoon, yet he wasn't fooling himself about the risks. It boiled down to one of two things. Brace Anderson outright or make an object lesson out of Bailey. The latter alternative seemed the slicker move. Dusting Bailey off would serve as warning, and it might just avert a showdown with Anderson and his crew. That was something he wanted to avoid if at all possible, for Anderson had the men and the guns to turn Newton into a battleground. Still, the plan fairly bristled with danger. There were simply too many unknowns. If he had guessed wrong, and Anderson decided to deal himself a hand, the fat was in the fire.

But in the end that's what life was all about. Get a hunch, bet a bunch. Logic might make a man rich, but it was no substitute for raw instinct. Not when the other players carried guns.

A fellow either backed his hunches or he folded his cards and got out. Yet a man who cultivated the habit of running really wasn't worth his salt. To himself or anyone else.

Tony Hazeltine had proved that.

McCluskie found what he was looking for in front of Gregory's Saloon. The hitchrack was crowded with horses bearing the Flying A brand, and among them was Anderson's chestnut gelding. Odds were that Bill Bailey wouldn't be far from his Texan friends on this night.

The Irishman paused outside the batwing doors and surveyed the house. Anderson and Bailey were standing shoulder to shoulder at the bar, and the room was jammed with cowhands. There seemed to be a contest of sorts taking place. Whoever yelled the loudest got the floor and tried to top the others with some whopper about the afternoon's chief sporting event. Though they had been at it for some hours, the stories seemed to get better the longer they drank, and there was no dearth of laughter. Apparently Hazeltine's one-man race was the favorite topic, with the stampeded voters running a close second, and every time someone launched into a fresh version it was greeted by raucous shouts from the crowd.

McCluskie slapped the doors open and walked in as if he had just foreclosed on the mortgage. Hardly anyone noticed him at first, but as he crossed the room a ripple of silence sped along before him. When he came to a halt in front of Anderson and Bailey the saloon went still as a graveyard.

Anderson leaned back against the bar and gave Bailey a broad wink. "Well, looka who's here, Billy. The holy terror hisself." Suddenly he blinked drunkenly and peered a little closer. "Goddamn my soul. Billy, I think that's your badge he's wearin'."

"Let's get something straight," McCluskie warned him. "I didn't come here lookin' for trouble with you or your boys. My beef is with Bailey. You stay out of it and we'll just chalk this afternoon up to one for your side."

"Sort of a Mexican standoff."

"Something like that."

"Maybe it don't suit me to let it ride. You're a feller that needs his wick trimmed, 'specially after today."

"Then we can settle it later. Right now all I want is Bailey. Course, you can step in if you like. There's nothin' I can do to stop you. But it's gonna start folks to talkin'."

Bailey finally caught the drift and got his tongue untracked. "Hugh, he's bluffin' again. Can't you see that?"

Anderson's gaze never left the Irishman. "What kind o' talk?"

"Why, the sort of stuff they're already sayin'. That one Texan hasn't got the sand to go up against a lawman by himself."

The saloon went deathly still. Anderson's face turned red as ox blood and for a moment he almost lost his steely composure. Then a tiny bead kindled back deep in his eyes and a crafty smirk came over his mouth. Turning sideways, he leaned into the bar and gave Bailey a speculative look.

"What about it, Billy boy? Think you can haul his ashes?"

Bailey swallowed hard. Every man in the room was watching him and he knew it. They had heard his brag for the past week, and Anderson's question now made it a matter of fish or cut bait.

"Hell, yes, I can take him. Won't hardly be no contest at all."

McCluskie moved while he had the advantage. "Bailey, you've got your choice. Get out of town or go to the lockup."

"Lockup? You're talkin' through your hat. I ain't broke no law."

"You were deputized and you broke your oath. That's good for about six months accordin' to Judge Muse."

Bailey's lip curled back and he launched himself off the bar. Whiskey had given him a measure of false courage but it hadn't clouded his judgment. Somewhere deep in his gut he knew that if he touched his gun the Irishman would kill him. But in a rough and tumble scrap it might just go the other way. He was bigger and stronger and he'd never yet lost a barroom brawl. Nor did he intend to lose this one. Hurtling forward, he let go a haymaker that would have demolished a stone church.

Except that it never landed. McCluskie slipped under the punch and buried his fist in the Texan's crotch. Back in Hell's Kitchen, one of New York's grimier slums, Irish youngsters were educated at an early age in the finer points of survival. What he didn't know about dirty fighting hadn't yet been written. Though he would have preferred to kill Bailey, he felt a certain grim satisfaction that it was to be settled with fists.

The Texan jackknifed at the middle, and as his head came down McCluskie's knee met it in a mushy crunch. Bailey reeled backward, his mouth and nose spurting blood, but he didn't go down. He was hurt bad, blinded by a chain of explosions that felt like a string of firecrackers inside his skull. Yet, in the way of a wounded beast, the pain only compounded his rage. Spitting teeth and bright wads of gore, he waded in again, flailing the air with a windmill of punches.

McCluskie gave ground, ducking some of the blows, warding off others. But he was hemmed in on all sides by shouting cowhands and there was no way of avoiding the burly Texan altogether. The air suddenly seemed filled with knuckles and for every punch he slipped past another sledgehammered off his head. With no room to maneuver, he had little choice but to absorb punishment and wait for an opening. His eyebrow split under the impact of a meaty fist and blood squirted down over his face. All at once it dawned on him that he was in grave danger. If he ever went down Bailey would stomp him to death, and the longer the fight lasted the more likely it was to happen. He had to end it fast or there was every chance he wouldn't end it at all. Operating now on sheer reflex, he stopped thinking and let his body simply react.

Shifting and dodging, he feinted with a left hook and suckered the Texan into a looping roundhouse right. The blow grazed past his ear and he slipped under Bailey's guard. Setting himself, he put his weight behind a whistling right that caught the other man squarely in the Adam's apple. Bailey's mouth flew open in a strangled gasp and his lungs started pumping for air. Both hands went to his throat and he doubled over, wretching in a hoarse, grating sound as he sucked for wind. McCluskie stepped back, planted himself, and kicked with every ounce of strength he possessed. The heel of his boot collided with Bailey's chin and the big man hurtled backward as if shot from a cannon. Cowhands scattered in every direction as the Texan went head over heels through the batwing doors and collapsed in a bloody mound on the boardwalk. Like a great whale snatched from the ocean's depths, he gave a blubbery sigh and lay still.

He was out cold.

McCluskie retrieved his hat, jammed it on his head,

and somehow made it to the door without falling. He slammed one wing of the door open and leaned against it for support, inspecting the battered hulk with the cold, practiced eye of a mortician. Then he turned, glowering back at the crowd until his gaze came to rest on Anderson.

"When he comes to, give him the word. If he's not out of town in two hours he goes in the lockup."

The door swung shut behind him and he lurched off in the direction of the hotel. Except that he was walking, he would have sworn that somebody had just beaten the living bejesus out of him. Even his hair felt sore.

Kinch was stretched out on the bed with his hands locked behind his head. When McCluskie entered the room he gave him a sullen glance and looked away. Then it hit him, and he sat bolt upright, staring slack-jawed at the Irishman's eyebrow. The cut itself was crusted over with dried blood and didn't look so bad. But a knot the size of a hen egg had swollen his brow into an ugly, discolored lump.

McCluskie gave him a tight grin and headed for the washstand. "You're gonna catch lots of flies if you leave your mouth hangin' open."

The kid's clicked shut and he bounded out of bed. "Holy jumpin' catfish! What'd you do, butt heads with a steam engine?"

"Just about. Closest thing on two legs anyhow."

McCluskie sloshed water into a washbowl and then dampened one end of a towel. Inspecting himself in the mirror, he understood why the kid looked so startled. The lump over his left eye was the color of rotten squash and a jagged split laid bare the ridgebone along his brow. It was a souvenir he wouldn't soon forget. The same as his busted nose and scars from other fights. From the looks of this one, though, it would turn out to be a real humdinger.

After squeezing the towel out he began scrubbing caked blood off his face and mustache. The wound itself he left untouched. It had stopped bleeding and the flesh seemed pretty well stuck in place. Washing it now would only start the whole mess bubbling again. Ugly as it was, it would have to do for the moment.

Kinch came around and took a closer look at the cut. For a while he just stared, saying nothing, then he whistled softly under his breath. "Mike, that's clean down to the bone. Doc Boyd's the one that oughta be workin' on it, not you."

McCluskie grunted, swabbing dried blood out of his ear. "I'll let him patch me up later."

"Yah, but cripes, that thing needs stitchin'. You're hurt worse'n you think."

"Bud, I can't spare the time now. It'll have to wait."

The boy glanced at him in the mirror, struck by a sudden thought. "It was Bailey, wasn't it?"

"All five hundred pounds of him."

"What happened?"

"He beat the crap out of me, that's what happened. I finally got in a lucky punch and put him to sleep."

"C'mon, I'll bet there weren't no luck to it at all. You could take him with one hand strapped down."

The Irishman met his gaze in the mirror. "Much as I hate to admit it, that's one bet you'd lose."

Kinch blinked a couple of times, clearly amazed. "Tougher'n you thought he was?"

"Well, let's just say he wasn't exactly what you'd call a creampuff. Fact is, if I had it to do over, I'd sooner fight a real live gorilla. Probably stand a better chance all the way round."

"Quit funnin' me. You whipped him, didn't you?"

"Just barely, sport. Just barely."

McCluskie stripped off his shirt and tossed it in a corner. Crossing the room, he opened a dresser drawer and selected a fresh shirt. His arms and chest were covered with splotchy bruises from the pounding he'd taken, and every movement was a small agony in itself. Slipping into the shirt even made him wince, but as he turned back to the kid he forced himself to smile.

"Never seen it fail. Clean shirt and a little birdbath and it'll make a new man out of you every time."

"Malarkey!" Kinch obviously wasn't convinced. "The way that eye's puffed out, I'd say you need a sawbones more'n anything else."

"All in good time, bud. There's a few things that still need tendin' before I call it a night."

"You mean Bailey? I thought you said you whipped him."

"Some folks might give you an argument on that." McCluskie finished buttoning his shirt and began tucking it in his pants. "Thing is, I posted him out of town. Now I've got to make it stick."

The boy gave him a look of baffled aggrievement. "You knew it was gonna happen, didn't you? Even before you went down and talked with Spivey and his bunch, you knew you was gonna take that badge and go after Bailey and then start cleanin' house on the Texans. That's the way you had it figured all along, wasn't it?"

"Yeah, I guess it was. So what, though? You're talkin' like it was some skin off your nose."

"Damn right it is! You got me locked up in this room instead of lettin' me pitch in and help. That ain't my idea of what friends are for."

"Don't say ain't."

"Aw, horseapples. I'm serious and you're standin' there grinnin' like it was some kinda joke."

"Nope, it's a long ways from being a joke. Fact is, things are gettin' sorrier and sorrier. Regular as clockwork, too."

"You're gonna go lookin' for Bailey tonight, aren't you?"

McCluskie smiled and shook his head. "Most likely he's already left town. I'll just sashay around a while and see what's what."

"I'm goin' with you," Kinch announced.

"Some other time, bud. Tonight's liable to get a little dicey."

"Goddamnit, Mike, you got no call to treat me that way. I don't need nobody to wipe my nose. That's what you said, wasn't it? Out here a man's got to look after himself. Well I'm as fast as you are and I'm near about as good a shot, too."

"There's more to it than that. I've told you before, tin cans don't shoot back."

"Yeah? Well what if you go lookin' for Bailey and them drovers back his play? Where'll you be then?"

"That's the luck of the draw. A man has got to play whatever hand he's dealt. But that don't change nothin'. Like it or lump it, you're still not invited."

Kinch's eyes went watery all of a sudden, like a scolded child, and it was all McCluskie could do not to reach out and touch him. The kid was right. He didn't need anyone to wipe his nose. But for all the wrong reasons.

The last couple of days had been the hardest of the Irishman's life. After considerable self-examination he'd decided he didn't like what he saw in himself. Or what he'd done to the kid. Before he got to Newton, Kinch had been a decent, God-fearing youngster. Raised up proper, taught right from wrong. Innocent as a lamb if a man got down to brass tacks. Now he had himself a gun and

somebody had showed him how to use it. Worse than
that, though, he no longer had any qualms about using
it. That *somebody* had drilled him so good he was all
primed and ready to pop. Like a puppy that had been fed
raw meat and gunpowder till he just couldn't wait to bust
out and kill the first thing that moved.

Not that he wanted to kill anybody. Or even liked the
idea. But just so he could prove to his teacher that he was
everything a man ought to be. Cold and unfeeling and
pitiless. The badge of manhood that had been drilled into
him by someone who saw life at its very elemental worst.

The quick and the dead.

McCluskie wasn't proud of himself. Not any longer.
He hadn't done the kid any favors, and that was an itch
he'd have to learn to live with. But it was no longer just
a matter of the kid killing someone. It had worked down
to someone wanting to kill the kid. That was the one
thing he wouldn't allow to happen.

However much he had to hurt the boy's feelings.

Watching him now, McCluskie made it even stronger.
"Let's get it straight. You don't budge out of this room
tonight. Got me?"

"Aw, c'mon, Mike." Kinch's look changed from one
of hurt to disappointment. "I got a date with Sugar."

"What time?"

"Eight. I set it up with Belle yesterday."

The Irishman flipped out his pocket watch and gave
it a quick check. "Okay. Just to Belle's and nowhere else.
I'll walk you down there, but I want you to leave that gun
here."

"Cripes a'mighty, don't you never give up? How am I
gonna look out for myself if you make me walk around
naked?"

McCluskie was forced to agree. It was just possible
that Bailey hadn't left town. That he might be laying for

the kid somewhere, hopeful of settling at least one score before he made tracks. Even with a gun the kid would be in a bad fix. Without it he wouldn't have the chance of a snowball in hell.

"You got a deal. But remember, just Belle's. Nowhere else. Okay?"

Kinch grinned and gave him a shrug more elaborate than words.

After dropping the kid off at Belle's the Irishman headed for Hide Park. He hadn't spotted any of Anderson's horses along the street, which meant the Texan and his crew had probably adjourned to the sporting houses. Wherever they were that's where Bailey would be. If he was still in town. Oddly enough, he halfway wished Bailey had lit out for parts unknown. It would set his mind at rest about the kid.

But it wasn't a hope he meant to stake his life on. Wherever possible he stuck to the shadows, passing lighted windows quickly, without bothering to peek inside. Hitchracks were what interested him, and at the corner of Second and Main, he found what he was looking for. The same bunch of Flying A cow ponies, Anderson's chestnut included, standing hipshot in front of Tuttle's Dancehall.

Nearing the entrance, he slowed and moved up cautiously. If Bailey was inside he wanted to know precisely where, and more importantly, the best way to approach him. Otherwise, it was walk in blind and take a chance on getting his head shot off. Edging closer to the door, he stuck his head around the corner and slowly scanned the dancehall. Anderson's men were plainly visible, stomping and howling as they swung the dollar-a-dance girls around the floor. But Bailey himself was nowhere in sight.

Then, as his gaze swept the room once more, the door
frame above his head splintered and an instant later he
heard the snarl of a slug. Dropping and rolling, he came
up on one knee as another shot chunked into the wall
behind him. He saw Bailey across the street, scuttling
along the boardwalk, firing as he ran. McCluskie drew a
bead, waiting, enjoying it. The bastard had set him up
like a duck in a shooting gallery. And it would have
worked, slick as a whistle, except that the numbskull
couldn't shoot worth a lick.

When Bailey silhouetted himself against the window
of Krum's Dancehall, the Irishman opened fire. The first
slug nailed him in his tracks, and the next two sent him
crashing through the window in an explosion of sharded
glass. When he collapsed on the floor inside only the
soles of his boots were visible over the windowsill.

McCluskie uncoiled and came to his feet. There was
considerable commotion inside Krum's and the thought
of it made him chuckle. It wasn't every day that a dead
man came sailing through the window. Not even in Hide
Park. He was halfway across the street when the kid's
voice rang out in a hard, businesslike growl.

"Hold it! First man that moves gets drilled."

The Irishman wheeled around, dropping low in a
crouch as he brought the Colt to bear. Hugh Anderson
and most of his crew were framed in the spill of light
from the doorway of Tuttle's. Bunched together, they
stood still as church mice, looking pretty sheepish in the
bargain. Kinch had them covered from the side, over near
the corner of the building.

McCluskie didn't know whether to laugh or curse.
Somehow neither one seemed appropriate, so instead
he just shook his head in mild wonderment. Plain to see,
the kid had snuck out of Belle's and covered his back the
whole time he was pussyfooting down the street. Like as

not, the little wiseacre had it planned all along. But it proved one thing nobody was likely to question any more.

The kid had grit, clean through.

Chuckling to himself, McCluskie turned and started back across the street.

"Keep 'em covered, bud. I'll have a looksee and make sure our friend is out of his misery."

Kinch just grinned and kept his pistol trained on the Texans. There wasn't any need to answer.

It had all been said.

CHAPTER 13

McCLUSKIE GOT the word over his second cup of coffee. Seated in the kitchen, watching Belle slap together some bacon and eggs, he was congratulating himself on last night's little fracas. It had been a nice piece of work. Bailey laid out on a slab and the Texans sent packing. That was one Anderson and his boys could paste in their hats and think about while they were out herding cows. Letting a slick-eared kid get the drop on them. They'd be a long time living that down.

Sweet Jesus! It was a sight to warm a man's heart. The way the kid had stood there, grinning, holding that Colt steady as a rock. Just like if someone had run up and primed his pump, he'd have hauled off and spouted a pail of ice water. Nervy didn't hardly describe it. The kid was ironclad and brass-bound. More guts than a bulldog with a new bone.

The thought brought his mind back to Belle. Last night had been something extraordinarily special. Maybe she was so glad he'd come out alive she just naturally put her heart into it. But whatever the reason, he felt like he'd been put through the wringer and hung out to dry. The lady knew what pleasured a man, and she flat turned into a wildcat once she came unwound.

Like this breakfast. Belle Siddons hadn't cooked a meal in all the time he'd known her. Hell, maybe never. But here she was, bustling around the kitchen, cursing every time the bacon grease spit the wrong way, determined to make this a very special day for him. All because he'd come through last night with his hide still intact.

He smiled and suddenly winced, reminded that his hide wasn't exactly intact after all. The swelling over his eye had gone down a bit, but he could scarcely stand to blow his nose. If he ever sneezed, he was a goner for sure.

That was more of Belle's doing. Pitching a fit till he'd agreed to let Doc Boyd stitch him back together. That old quack had the touch of a butcher, and with a needle he was nothing short of a menace. Still, the eyebrow was back in one piece, and seemed to be healing, so he had little room for complaint. Actually, he couldn't blame anybody but himself.

He should've learned to duck better.

Reflecting on that bit of wisdom, he had just started on a second cup of coffee when the kid burst through the door. He was breathing hard, as if he'd been running, and as he slammed to a halt before the table it suddenly caught up with him. He began to choke and a moment later his lungs gave way. McCluskie grabbed a bottle of whiskey and in between coughs forced a jigger down his throat. The liquor took hold slowly, trickling down through his system, and after a few more heaves and shudders, the spasm petered out. Gulping wind, blinking furiously to clear his eyes, the kid began sputtering in a hoarse, wheezing rattle.

"Slow down, goddamnit!" McCluskie barked. "The world's not comin' to an end. Just take your time, for chrissakes."

His gruff tone brought a withering look from Belle, but she didn't say anything. Bacon and eggs now forgotten, she moved around the table and eased Kinch into a chair. The boy nodded, still sucking air, and made a game attempt at smiling. Presently his color returned, and he seemed to have caught his breath, but his voice was still shaky.

"Mike, they're after you. It's all over town." He gasped and took another long draught of wind. "Soon as I walked into the cafe ever'body and his brother started givin' me the lowdown."

"Bud, you're not makin' sense. Who's after me?"

"The Texans. That's what I'm tryin' to tell you. They sent word in this mornin'."

"What d'ya mean, sent word? Who to?"

"I don't know. But it's all up and down the street. They aim to run you out of town or kill you. Cause of what you did to Bailey."

"Now is that a fact?" McCluskie tilted back in his chair and pulled out the makings. "Y'know, I always heard that pound for pound a Texan would assay out to about nine parts cowdung. Maybe we'll just find out before the day's over."

"You thickheaded Mick!" Belle squawled. "That's just what you'd do, isn't it? Sit there and wait for them to come kill you."

"Cripes, Belle, what d'ya want him to do?" Kinch gave her the look men reserve for hysterical women. "He can't back down or his name'd be mud."

"Sport, you hit it right on the head!" The Irishman slammed his fist on the table so hard his coffee mug bounced in the air. "Once a man runs he's got to keep on runnin'. You mark what I tell you. Them Texans are all hot air and taffy. Anybody that gets hisself in a swivel over that needs his head examined."

"Men!" Belle stamped her foot and glared down on them. "There's no end to it, is there? Just have to go on proving how tough you are."

McCluskie put a match to his cigarette and gave her a

wry grin. "Belle, I don't like to bring it up, but you're burnin' my breakfast to a cinder."

Belle screeched and turned back to the stove. Kinch and the Irishman exchanged smiles as she commenced slinging smoking skillets in every direction. Just then the door banged open and Dora, the colored maid, came rushing in. The whites of her eyes were flared wide and she was waving a scrap of paper in her hand.

"Miz Belle! Miz Belle! Some man near broke the door in an' tol' me to give this to Mistah Mike. Said it was a mattah o' life and death."

Sugar raced into the kitchen before the others had time to collect their wits. "What's all the commotion about? Honest to Christ, Dora, you could wake the dead." All of a sudden she stopped and glanced around uneasily. "Well land o' Goshen, why is everybody staring at me like that?"

McCluskie took the piece of paper from Dora's hand and unfolded it. Inside was a scrawled message, and as he started reading the others scarcely dared to breathe. Finished, he flipped it on the table and let go with a sour grunt.

"Seems like Mr. Spivey has called a meetin' of the Town Board. Says for me to get up there pronto."

The room went still as a tomb and everyone just stared at him for a moment. Sugar gave a rabbity little sniff and wandered over behind Kinch. She leaned down and put her arms around his neck.

"Sweetie, what's going on? Everybody looks like they've just come from a wake."

Kinch took her hands and drew her down closer, but he kept his eyes on the Irishman. After a while McCluskie climbed to his feet and gave Sugar a grim smile. "Little lady, you're pretty close to right. Only thing is, the wake's just gettin' started."

"Sure'n begorra, the great Mick has spoken." Belle shot him a scathing look. "Now why don't you take a peek in your crystal ball and tell us who the corpse will be."

"Why, Belle, that's simple." McCluskie grinned. "He'll be wearin' big jingly spurs and a ten-gallon hat, and after they kick all the dung out of him, they're gonna bury him in a matchbox."

"Very funny," Belle snapped. "I suppose you do song and dance, too."

"Just on request. Weddings and funerals and such. But in your case, I'll make an exception. Like tonight, maybe."

He chucked her under the chin, still smiling, and headed for the door. Then, struck by a sudden thought, he turned and looked back. "Say, you still keep a greener around the house?"

Belle stiffened and her eyes went wide with alarm. "What—what do you want with a shotgun?"

"Why, hell's bells, I didn't get no breakfast, that's what. Thought I might scare up a covey of birds on my way uptown."

"With buckshot?"

"There's all kinds of birds, honey. Some are just bigger'n others, that's all."

Belle moved past him without a word and stepped into the hall. She opened the door of a linen closet, reached inside, and pulled out a sawed-off shotgun. When she returned, McCluskie took it from her, broke it open, and checked the loads. Satisfied, he snapped it shut and thumbed the hammers back to half-cock. Looking up, he smiled, trying to lighten the moment.

"Jesus, I hope you never have to shoot this thing. With what you weigh a ten-gauge would knock you on your keester."

Her eyes went glassy with tears and she turned away. The others watched on in frozen silence, struck dumb by the Irishman's jovial manner. Sugar and Dora couldn't make heads or tails of the whole affair, but the look on Belle's face sent cold shivers racing through them. The girl clutched tighter at Kinch, as if some unseen specter might suddenly snatch him away.

The kid pushed her hands off and started to rise. Then he caught McCluskie's eye and slumped back in his chair. "I guess I don't have to ask. You want me to stay here and suck my thumb."

"Sport, you're gettin' to be a regular mind reader." The Irishman smiled, but there was something hard about his eyes. "If that's not plain enough, lemme give it to you straight. You pull another stunt like last night and I'll swap ends on this scattergun and paddle your rump. Savvy?"

Without so much as a backward glance, he wheeled about and marched off down the hall. The sound of his footsteps slowly faded and moments later they heard the front door slam shut.

Kinch just sat there, grinding his teeth in quiet fury, while Sugar stroked his hair with the soft, fluttering touch of a small bird.

The shotgun didn't draw a crowd, but all along the street people rubbernecked and gawked as if the circus had come to town. McCluskie's appearance brought them out of stores and saloons like flies to honey, and as he strode past they gathered in buzzing knots to discuss this latest wrinkle. Word of the Texans' threat had spread through town only within the last hour, but already the gamblers were giving six-to-five that the Irishman wouldn't run. His tight-lipped scowl, and the double-barreled greener, seemed to reinforce those odds substantially.

Far from running, it appeared McCluskie had declared war.

The sensation created by his passage left the Irishman grimly amused. There was nothing quite like a killing, or better yet the chance of a massacre, to bring the fainthearts out of their holes. Not that they wanted to risk their own necks, or in any way get involved. They just wanted to watch. It spoke eloquently of man's grubby character.

But while he ignored the townspeople, McCluskie's eyes were busy scanning the street. Oddly enough, the hitchracks stood empty and there wasn't a cowhand in sight. That in itself was a sign. More ominous, perhaps, than the warning delivered to Spivey.

Passing Hamil's Hardware, he noted that the doors were locked, and at the next corner Hoff's Grocery was also closed. Plain to see, the buzzards had come to roost at their favorite watering hole. Probably squawking and bickering among themselves while they waited for him to rout the bogeyman and lay all ghosts to rest.

Cursing fools and fainthearts alike, he crossed the tracks and headed for the Lone Star.

When he came through the door of Spivey's office the talk ground abruptly to a halt. The room was filled with smoke, and a sense of something queer, not as it should be, suddenly came over him. The men gathered there stared at him with eyes that were flat and guarded, and as his gaze touched their faces, he saw part of it. Apprehension and alarm and maybe even a little panic. Yet there was something more. Something he couldn't quite put his finger on. Mistrust, perhaps, or just a tinge of hatred. Whatever it was, it eluded him, and for the moment he set it aside. He shut the door but advanced no farther into the room. Someone coughed, and as if the spell had been broken, he nodded to Spivey, who was seated behind the desk.

"I got word you wanted to see me."

"Well, not just me, Mike." Spivey smiled and waved his hand at the others. "The boys here thought you ought to sit in on this. Sort of kick it around and see where we stand."

The rest of the men looked glum as undertakers, and Spivey's smile was far short of convincing. McCluskie felt the hair come up on the back of his neck. "Kick what around?"

"This goddamn mess you've got us in!" Perry Tuttle snarled. "What the hell'd you think we'd be meetin' for?"

The Irishman looked him over with a frosty scowl. "Mister, lemme give you some advice. Talk to me civil or don't talk to me at all. Otherwise you'll wind up with a sore head."

"Judas Priest, what'd I just get through tellin' you not ten minutes ago?" Val Gregory threw his cigar to the floor and glared around at the other men. "You can't say *boo* to him without getting' your skull caved in. Or shot dead. Hell, it's no wonder the Texans are on the warpath."

"Gentlemen, please!" Judge Muse stepped to the center of the room, motioning for silence. "We have enough trouble on our hands without fighting among ourselves."

"You can say that again," Sam Horner muttered. "What beats me is why you go on jabbering about Texans. Newton's dead as a doornail anyway." His glance flicked around to the Irishman. "Case you haven't heard, we lost the referendum. Wichita will get its railroad."

Everyone fell silent, watching for his reaction. He let them stew for a minute, then pursed his lips. "Sorry to hear it."

"Yeah, sure," Perry Tuttle rasped, "we can see you're all broken up."

"Tuttle, I warned you once. Don't make me do it again."

"For Chrissakes, can't you fellas stick to one problem at a time?" Harry Lovett sounded as exasperated as he looked. "That railroad's a year down the line. Today's right now, and I'm a sonovabitch, it seems to me we ought to be thinkin' about the Texans."

"You're right, Harry. Dead right." Spivey looked over at the Irishman, but he was no longer smiling. "Mike, we got ourselves some powerful trouble this time. Anderson sent one of his boys in with a message. Short and sweet and to the point. Either you're on the noon train or they'll kill you and burn Newton down to the ground. I don't think they're foolin' either."

McCluskie shrugged, his expression wooden, almost detached. "Maybe. Leastways they might try. But they won't get very far."

"What makes you so sure?"

"This." McCluskie raised the shotgun, and in the closely packed room it was like looking down a cannon. "Double-ought at close range has a way of discouragin' a man."

"Who're you kiddin'?" Gregory inquired acidly. "Puttin' a couple of loads of buckshot into that crowd'd be like spittin' on a brush fire. Hell, there'll be a hundred of 'em. Maybe more."

"So you can hire yourself a new marshal. Thing is, they won't do nothin' to the town. That'd bring the army down on 'em, and not even Anderson's that dumb."

Judge Muse hawked and cleared his throat. "Mike, I'm afraid that's a risk some of these men feel they can't afford to take."

McCluskie sensed it again, the queer feeling that had come over him when he'd entered the room. "Care to make that a little plainer?"

"Yes, I suppose it's time. Understand, there is nothing personal in this. It's just that we have to consider what is best for the town."

Spivey broke in. "Mike, what he's tryin' to say is that we're between a rock and a hard place. If we keep you on, the Texans are gonna pull this town up by the roots."

McCluskie gave him a corrosive stare. "What you're sayin' is that I'm fired—"

"Now I didn't say that, Mike."

"—and if I don't hightail it you'll throw me to the wolves."

"Damnit, you're puttin' words in my mouth. Fact is, I don't know what we'd do without you. We're damned if we do and damned if we don't."

"If you wanted another Tonk Hazeltine that's what you should've hired." The Irishman tapped the badge on his shirt. "As long as I'm wearin' this it's up to me to pull the fat out of the fire. I'll handle Anderson and his bunch my own way. You boys just get yourselves a good seat and sit back and watch. It'll be worth the price of admission."

He turned to leave but the judge's voice brought him up short. "Mike, before you go, let me ask you one question. You have every right to get yourself killed. That's your privilege. But if you face that mob of Texans other people will get caught in the crossfire. Now, do you really want the blood of innocent bystanders on your hands? Won't you agree that's rather a high price to pay for one man's pride?"

McCluskie just glared at him and after a moment the judge smiled. "I suspect you're too decent a man to take that chance. And it's not like you were running. I mean, after all, once things have calmed down there's nothing to stop you from coming back."

"Judge, that's the trouble with this world. There's too

many runners and not enough stayers. Looks to me like it's time somebody drew the line."

The door opened and closed, and the men were left to ponder that cryptic observation. Nobody said anything, but as the silence deepened they found it difficult to look one another in the eye.

Belle gave a little start and jumped from her chair as he entered the parlor. Kinch and Sugartit also came to their feet, but none of them said a word. The dark rage covering his face was unlike anything they had ever seen, frightening in the way of a man touched by the sun. He stalked across the room and halted in front of Belle, thrusting the greener at her.

"Guess I won't be needing this after all."

"I don't understand." She took the shotgun, staring at him numbly. "What happened?"

"Spivey and the Judge just informed me that they don't want a war. Seems like Anderson sent word for me to be on the noon train and that bunch uptown don't know whether to blink or go blind."

Belle clapped her hands with delight. "Then you're leaving! You're really leaving."

"Hell, no, I'm not leavin'. Wild horses couldn't get me out of here now. I'm just gonna give 'em a little war instead of a big one."

"Oh, God." She seemed to wilt and slumped back into her chair. "There's just no end to it. No end."

She let go of the shotgun and McCluskie grabbed it before it hit the floor. "That's where you're wrong. I mean to end it once and for all. Anderson's about to find out he treed the wrong town."

He hefted the greener, studying it a moment, then laid it across the table. "If I meet 'em without this, I've got an idea I can keep it between him and me. Thought it all out on the way back down here. That way Spivey and his bunch will just get that little war I was talkin' about."

"Mike McCluskie, you're a fool." Belle's lip trembled and she looked on the verge of tears. "Do you know that? A stubborn, thickheaded fool!"

Over her shoulder he saw the kid watching him intently and he smiled. "Well, it takes all kinds. Course, the nice part about being a fool—"

"—is that they walk in where angels fear to tread." Belle gave him a withering look. "Isn't that what you started to say?"

The kid blinked a couple of times, as if he couldn't believe what he was hearing. "Cripes a'mighty, he can't just take off like a scalded cat. Them Texans would be tellin' it all over that they scared him out of town. Then where'd he be?"

"Kinch Riley, you stop that!" Belle snapped. "He'd be alive, that's where he would be. If he doesn't get on that train they'll kill him. Is that what you want?"

"Stay out of it, Belle." McCluskie shot her a harsh look, then glanced back at the kid. "You're right, sport. Sometimes a fella does a thing just because it needs doing. That's what separates the men from the boys. Knowin' when to stop talkin' and get down to business. That's the kind of lingo Anderson will understand."

Belle uttered a small groan and sunk lower in her chair. "Talk never killed anybody. Or running either. If you weren't so pigheaded, you'd see that."

"Better a live coward"—McCluskie grinned—"isn't that how it goes?"

She turned away from him and began dabbing at her eyes with a handkerchief. Sugartit moved up behind the chair and laid a comforting hand on her shoulder. The

Chapter 14

Newt Hansberry waited on the platform as the evening train rolled to a halt. This was the last train of the day, and the station master felt a weary sense of relief that it was only an hour late. All too often it was midnight or later before he closed the depot, and he was grateful for any small favors the Santa Fe passed along. Hansberry waved to the conductor as he stepped off the first passenger coach, then turned and headed toward the express car. Once he had the mailbag locked away he could call it a day and begin thinking about himself for a change. Heading the list was a good night's sleep, something that had been rare as hen's teeth since he took over in Newton.

Out of the corner of his eye Hansberry saw something that suddenly made him forget late trains and mailbags and even his weary bones. He wheeled around and peered intently toward the street. Just for a moment he thought his eyes were playing tricks on him. The flickering light from the station lamps was poor at best, and shadows often fooled a man into seeing things that weren't there. Then he took a closer look and grunted. What he saw wasn't imagination, and it had nothing whatever to do with shadows. It was the real article. A yard wide and big as life.

The station master couldn't seem to collect his wits, and he just stood there as the Irishman crossed the tracks and headed toward the southside. Before he could call out it was too late. McCluskie melted into the darkness at the end of the platform and vanished from sight. Hansberry

blinked and rubbed his eyes, looking again. There was
something spooky about it. Like waking from a dream
bathed in sweat. Yet there was nothing unreal about this,
or the sudden chill that swept along his backbone. It was
just damned hard to accept, and perhaps frightening in a
way he didn't wholly understand.

McCluskie got much the same reaction from people
he passed on the street. Particularly the Texans. They
stopped, hardly able to credit their eyes, and stared after
him with a look of bemused disbelief. That he hadn't quit
and run, boarding the noon train, they could accept.
Some of them, the ones with gumption, liked to believe
they would have done likewise. But that he was out
prowling the streets—fully aware of what he faced—was
beyond reason. The act of a man who had crossed the line
separating fool-hardiness from common ordinary horse
sense.

Angling across Main, McCluskie hesitated before the
hotel and then walked on. With everybody staring at him
like he was some kind of tent show freak, he wasn't about
to give them that satisfaction. They could guess and be
damned, but his reasons for staying were his own. He
meant to keep it that way.

The baffled expression of everyone along the street
gave him a moment of sardonic amusement. Before the
night was out they would have talked themselves dry trying to put a label on it. But they wouldn't even come
close, and in a grim sort of way, it made everything easier knowing he had them stumped. Most of them would
chalk it up to lunacy or pride, and they weren't far wide
of the mark. Perhaps, after all, it did take a certain brand
of madness to stand and fight. To shoulder the burden of
an entire town and accept the responsibility of the cheap
piece of tin pinned on his shirt.

But there was a simpler truth, one not so readily apparent, and only after considerable thought had he seen it for what it was. *Each man in his own way feared certain things worse than he feared death itself.* The lucky ones were never forced to take that close a look at themselves, and what it was they feared most went to the grave with them. The vagaries of fate being what they were, McCluskie hadn't been that fortunate.

He had found his secret fear in the eyes of a kid.

That revelation had come hard, after searching his innermost self with a fine probe. Somehow it was all jumbled together. The town and the kid. Since the war he hadn't given a tinker's damn for anyone or any place. A nomad answerable to no one but himself, with no ties to bind him and no obligations he couldn't sever on the whim of the moment. Now, after grappling with it most of the day, he knew that it was only partly pride, and an even smaller sense of duty, which had prompted him to goad the Town Board. To back them into a corner and force them to let him stay and fight their fight. Underneath it all, perhaps overshadowing his own flinty pride, was the kid. That was the part which had come clear and crystal bright.

Quitters finished last.

Kinch had proved that in the siege with his own special devil. After all that had passed between them, McCluskie could do no less. The look he'd seen in the kid's eyes, exultant at his determination to stay and fight, had made it all worthwhile.

Whatever happened.

Along with a fitful day, holed up in Doc Boyd's office, this newly acquired awareness hadn't given him much rest. Which struck him as neither odd nor unreasonable. Somehow it seemed merely fitting. Luckily, he wasn't forced to dwell on it any longer.

Approaching Third, he saw the yellow parlor house

and his thoughts turned to Belle Siddons. While he had curbed the impulse to stop at the hotel, there was no reason to avoid Belle. She was the closest thing he'd ever had to a sweet tooth, and tonight seemed a little late in the game to start resisting temptation.

When he entered the parlor, Belle uttered a small gasp and the color drained from her face. Several Texans were lolling about making smalltalk among themselves, and the conversation fell off sharply as he stepped through the doorway. Apparently they were passing time, waiting, for there wasn't a girl in sight. Somewhat taken aback, the cowhands stared at him as if he had dropped out of a tree. None of them said anything, but they suddenly got very careful with their hands. Galvanized at last, Belle came out of her chair as if touched by a hot poker.

She grabbed his arm, raking the Texans with a fiery glance, and marched him through the door and down the hall to the kitchen. Only after she had drawn the shade on the back door did she turn on him. Somehow, though it came to him only at that moment, McCluskie had always liked her best when she was angry. She was plainly in one of her spitfire moods right now and the look on her face made him smile.

"Mike, for God's sake, stop grinning at me like a jackass. Don't you know what's happening?"

"Yes, ma'am." He doffed his hat and gave her a half bow. "You see I heard stories about this lady that snorts fire like a dragon, and I've come to pay my respects. Queer thing is, them stories weren't the least bit exaggerated."

"Stop it! Stop it!" A tear rolled down over her cheek and her bottom lip trembled. "They're going to kill you. Do you hear me, Mike? Anderson and his men are in town right now. This very minute. Don't you understand that?"

He crossed the kitchen and took her in his arms, sobered by what he had seen in her face. She met his embrace with a fierce hug and buried her head against his chest. After a moment he raised her chin and kissed her, slowly and with a gentleness he'd never shown before. When their lips parted, she gave a small sniffle and he smiled, wiping a tear off her cheek.

"There's lots of things I understand better than I did this morning."

Belle kissed his hand, then blinked as the words slowly took hold. "Why do you say that?"

"Well, I guess because I had plenty of time to do some thinkin'. I've been holed up in Doc's office all day, waitin' for things to cool down before I braced Anderson. Just sat there starin' at the wall for the most part, figuring things out."

"What things?"

McCluskie let her go and drew back. He pulled out the makings, trickling tobacco onto paper, and started building a smoke. There was something deliberate and unhurried about his movements, as if he was stalling for time, keeping his hands occupied while he collected his thoughts. Belle waited him out, and at last, when he had the cigarette going, he met her gaze.

"I was thinkin' about the kid."

She gave him a quick intent look. "Kinch? Why, there isn't any reason to worry about him. He's just a boy. Texans aren't even low enough to take their spite out on a boy."

"That wasn't what I meant, just exactly." The Irishman took a deep drag and exhaled, studying the coal on the tip of his cigarette. "I was thinkin' about the

way he looked at me this mornin' when he heard I
hadn't quit."

"My god!" Belle paled and her eyes widened with
comprehension. "You stayed so he would go on thinking
you're some kind of holy terror."

"Something like that. I'd already made up my mind
anyway, but it came to me sort of gradual that I stayed
for the kid as much as for myself."

"And you're going to hunt Anderson down just to
prove it?"

"That's about the gist of it, I guess." McCluskie flicked
ashes toward the stove and smiled. "Seems odd, don't it?
Can't say as I've quite gotten used to the idea myself."

"Not odd, Mike. Insane. Do you hear me? Crazy mad!
You'll get yourself killed for nothing." She waited for an
answer but he just stared at her. "He's dying, Mike. Don't
you understand? In a few months he'll be dead and whatever you proved to him won't mean a thing."

"That's the point I've been tryin' to make. It'll mean
a whole lot." His brow wrinkled and he took a swipe at
his mustache. "Funny thing is, it's hard to explain, but
when you get it boiled down, it's real simple. The kid
don't have much besides me. When his string runs out
I'd like to think nothin' between us had changed."

"You're just kidding yourself, don't you know that?
He's in Sugar's room right now. Does that sound like
someone who's all busted up because his idol might wind
up dead?"

"Belle, you've been in the business long enough to
know better'n that. Sugar's like a toy, just something to
keep him from suckin' his thumb. Case you don't know
it, he spent most of the day searchin' all over town for
me. Doc told me so himself."

He took a final puff and ground out the cigarette in
an ashtray. "You say he's in her room now?"

"Yes, has been for the last hour. Why?"

"Nothin'. Just hadn't planned on seein' him, that's all."

"Well that takes the cake! I'll swear to God, it does."

"What's the matter?"

"Matter? Oh, nothing at all. Just that you're willing to get yourself killed, but you can't face Kinch and tell him why. Doesn't that strike you as a little strange?"

"Depends on how you look at it. First off, it's not all because of him. Never was. And there's no sense makin' it out to be something it's not. Next thing is, I don't plan on gettin' killed. Likely there's some that could punch my ticket, but Anderson's not one of 'em."

He paused and gave her a tight grin. "Tell you the truth, there's an even better reason. Hell, you know how the kid is. If I told him what's up, he'd raise a fuss to go along. I want him kept out of it."

"You're crazy, Mike McCluskie, do you know that?" Belle stomped off a couple of paces and turned, glaring at him. "Just once in your life couldn't you stop being so bullheaded? Anderson isn't about to stick to some silly set of rules. He wants you dead, and he'll use every dirty trick in the book to make sure it comes out that way."

The Irishman shrugged and grinned. "I'm not much for playin' by the rules myself. Like the fella said, there's more'n one way to skin a cat."

"Whose cat you gonna skin?"

Startled, they looked around and saw Kinch standing in the hallway door. There was no way of knowing how much he had overheard, yet it was apparently enough. His eyes were fastened on McCluskie, and as he stepped into the kitchen, a wide grin spread over his face.

"You've been sorta scarce today. Everybody said you was hidin' out, but I told 'em they was full of beans. I knew you'd show up."

"Well you had me shaded there, bud. I wasn't real sure myself till the sun went down."

"Yeah, but I knew. I got to thinkin' about it after you left this mornin', and I told myself there wasn't nothin' on earth that'd stop you. I was right, too."

"Guess you were, at that." McCluskie smiled and punched him on the shoulder.

Kinch paused and eyed him steadily for a moment. "You're gonna go lookin' for Anderson, aren't you?"

The Irishman cocked one eyebrow and nodded. "Guess it's time somebody called his hand. Seein' as I'm still wearin' the badge, it might as well be me."

"You'll need some help. Like that night with Bailey, remember? Wouldn't hurt none a'tall for me to back your play."

"Not this time, bud. It's personal. Something Anderson and me have got to settle ourselves."

McCluskie expected the kid to sull up and start pouting. Oddly enough, it fell the other way. Kinch nodded, as if he understood perfectly, and for once showed no inclination to argue the matter. They stared at one another a while and the Irishman finally chuckled.

"Tell you what. You wait here for me and after I'm finished we'll go up and check the yards together. Fair enough?"

"Whatever you say," the boy agreed. "Don't make it too long though. I'd like to get back to Sugar sometime tonight."

McCluskie laughed and turned back to Belle. She was fighting hard, determined not to cry, and from somewhere, she dredged up a tiny smile.

"Take care, Irish."

He grinned and gave her a playful swat on the rump. "Keep the lamp lit. I'll be home early."

"I'll be waiting."

Her words had a hollow ring, and as he entered the hallway she couldn't hold back any longer. Tears sluiced down over her cheeks, and when the front door slammed her heart seemed to stop altogether. Behind her another door closed softly, eased shut with only a slight click of the latch. Somehow she knew even before she looked, and a spark of hope fanned bright as she spun around.

Kinch was gone.

McCluskie had thought it all out at Doc Boyd's while he waited for it to grow dark. The choice was between Gregory's Saloon and Perry Tuttle's Dancehall. Those were Anderson's favorite hangouts, and sooner or later he was bound to show. Tuttle's somehow seemed the more appropriate of the two dives. That was where he had killed Bailey, and it was only fitting that the big dog himself be accorded the same honor.

Striding along toward Hide Park, the Irishman amused himself with a wry thought. Chances were it wouldn't be so much a matter of him finding Anderson as it would of Anderson finding him. While he had been on the street less than an hour, it stood to reason that word had already spread through town. The Texan likely knew every move he was making, and by now any chance of surprise would have worn off. The fact that he chose to flaunt his decision by invading Tuttle's made it a challenge Anderson could hardly overlook. That was something he counted on heavily. Bait of sorts.

Only in this case it was a tossup. He hadn't quite decided whether he was the hunter or the hunted. Not that he would have too long a wait to find out. The question would be resolved soon enough.

Tuttle's was packed to the rafters and going full blast when he came through the doors. He swept the room with a slow look, assuring himself that Anderson wasn't present, but even that seemed more out of habit than any sense of caution. Tonight he didn't feel wary. Quite the opposite, he felt reckless and anxious to have it done with. He had come here to kill a man, and the sooner it could be arranged the better. Perhaps he wouldn't walk away himself, but that had ceased to trouble him. For an assortment of reasons, none of which he had bothered to explore, he was riding a crest of fatalism. It was a thing that needed doing and he had tapped himself for the job. That was explanation enough.

Spotting an empty table against the far wall, he began threading his way through the crowd. That was an edge of sorts—having his back against a wall—and it might just make the difference. At least they couldn't get him from behind. Approaching the table, he noted that the one next to it was occupied by two Santa Fe men. An engineer, Pat Lee, and his fireman, Jim Hickey. When they glanced up, he shook his head, warning them off, and slipped into a chair on the far side of the table.

He ordered a bottle and when it came, poured himself a single shot. Leaning back in his chair, he sipped at the whiskey and kept one eye on the door while he watched the mad whirl on the dancefloor. The trail-hands turned the whole affair into one big struggle, pushing and shoving and shouting, like a gang of wrestlers who just happened to wear spurs and six-guns. Their antics alone were worth the price of admission, and in passing, it occurred to him that dancehall girls earned every nickel of their money. After a night on the floor with the Texans, most of them were probably nothing short of a walking bruise.

McCluskie was still nursing the same drink when the doors flew open and Hugh Anderson strode into the room. Behind him were five hard-looking cowhands, and they all came together in a little knot, quickly scanning the crowd. One of the hands spotted him sitting alone at the table and nudged Anderson. The Texan's gaze jerked around, settling on him at last, and an instant later the men separated. Anderson came straight toward him, but the others fanned out and moved across the floor from different directions. The Irishman grunted to himself, smiling slightly, and climbed to his feet.

Now he had his answer. It was the hunters who had come for him. Which was just as well. He'd never been one to bet short odds, anyway.

Anderson stopped before the table, his lip curled back in a gloating smirk. "Mister, you got enough brass for a whole herd of monkeys."

"Want to borrow some?"

"Come again?"

"Why, it's pretty simple, Anderson." The Irishman jerked his chin at the five hands. They were now spread out in a rough crescent that had him caught in a crossfire from all sides. "If you had the starch to fight your own fights you wouldn't need so much help."

"You stupid sonovabitch. This ain't no church social. That plain enough, or you want me to draw you a picture?"

McCluskie started to answer but movement off to the left caught his eye. The moment his gaze flicked in that direction he knew he'd been suckered. The cowhand farthest down the line had shifted positions, distracting him for a crucial instant, and it had worked perfectly. Even as his eyes swung back he sensed it was too late.

The gun in Anderson's hand was out and cocked, pointed straight at him. It was as if time and motion had been arrested. He saw the hammer fall, glimpsed the first sparks of the muzzle flash, and then went stone blind as the pistol exploded in his face. The slug mushroomed through his throat, slamming him back against the wall, and he felt something warm and sticky splash down over his shirt. Then his knees buckled and he was suddenly gripped with the urgency of killing Anderson.

The trainmen seated at the next table leaped to their feet just as the other Texans opened fire. The shots were meant for the Irishman, but they were hurried and wide of the mark. Lee collapsed, drilled through the bowels, and Hickey screamed as a slug shattered the thigh bone in his right leg. McCluskie heard the gunfire and the terrified shrieks of dancehall girls, sensed the crowd scattering. But it was all somehow distant, even a little unreal. Blinded, falling swiftly into darkness, he willed his hand to move. To finish what he had come here to do.

Another bullet smacked him in the ribs, but like a dead snake, operating on nerves alone, his hand reacted and came up with the Colt. That he couldn't see Anderson bothered him not at all. In his mind's eye he remembered exactly where the Texan was standing, and even as he pressed the trigger, he knew the shot had struck home.

Anderson staggered backward, jolted by a fiery blow in the chest. His legs gave way and he started falling, but with some last reserve of strength he raised his pistol. The floor and his rump collided with a jarring crash, and in a final moment of consciousness, he shot the Irishman in the back.

McCluskie grunted with the impact of the slug and pitched headlong between the tables. His leg twitched and his hand slowly opened, releasing its grip on the Colt. Then his eyes rolled back, the sockets empty and sightless, and he lay still. A wispy tendril of smoke curled out of the gun barrel and disappeared. Afterward there was nothing.

Hurriedly, the five cowhands moved forward and gathered around their boss. The instant they came together the sharp crack of a pistol racketed across the dancehall. One of them clutched at his stomach and slumped forward, and the crowd again dove for cover. But the Texans seemed frozen in their tracks, unable to move, staring at the fallen man in a numbed stupor.

Standing just inside the doorway, Kinch thumbed the hammer back and fired again. There was nothing rushed in either his manner or in his soft feathering of the trigger, yet the shots thundered across the room in a staccato roar. Coolly, just as the Irishman had taught him, he spaced the shots evenly and drilled each one precisely where he meant it to go. Every time the worn Navy bucked, another Texan went down, and within a half-dozen heartbeats it was over. When the gun clicked at last on an empty chamber not a single cowhand was left standing.

The kid slowly lowered his arm and stood there a moment, looking at the tangled jumble of bodies. Something inside tugged at him, demanding that he cross the room and make sure. But he shook it off, touched by the grim certainty that there was no need. He had seen McCluskie go down, felt that last slug as if it had been pumped into his own back. Whatever the Irishman had been in life, he was just a dead man now. Nothing more. That wasn't the way Kinch wanted to remember him.

Backing away, he holstered the Colt and brushed through the doors. There was a sudden chill in the air and he shivered. Then he knew it for what it was and hurried on into the night.

CHAPTER 15

THE KITCHEN was still as a crypt. Kinch sat slumped in a chair, elbows on his knees, staring at nothing. He hadn't moved in the last hour, as if he had retreated within himself, locked in some private hell all his own.

Seated nearby, Sugartit looked on helplessly. She wanted to touch him, take his hand, comfort him in some way. But she knew there was nothing she could say or do that would ease his grief. Years ago she had lost her own family, and she remembered all too well the cold, deadened sensation that clutched at a person's heart. Remorse came quickly, but it released its hold with infinite slowness. Only time would heal the feeling of rage and loss that gripped him now, and difficult as it was to remain quiet, the girl merely watched and waited. When he was ready, in his own fashion, Kinch would find some way to talk about it. However long it took, Sugar meant to be there when he needed her.

The only sound in the room was the soft shuffling of Belle's footsteps. She circled the kitchen like some distracted ghost, wan and ashen-faced. She had long since cried herself out, and now she felt drained of all emotion and feeling. Her hands were icy cold, though the room was sticky with summer warmth, and she kept her arms wrapped around her waist. Somehow she couldn't bring herself to take a seat at the table. She felt some restless compulsion to keep moving, almost as if in her mindless pacing she could outdistance the dreaded truth.

That he was gone, lying dead at that very moment, she still couldn't accept. He had always been so charged with life, full of strength and wit and energy, and it just wasn't possible. Someone with his lust and vitality simply couldn't be extinguished that easily. Like snuffing out a candle. Whatever God watched over Irishmen wasn't that capricious or impersonal. To cut a man down in his prime, kill him needlessly and without purpose, was a waste she couldn't comprehend. A truth so appalling her mind simply wouldn't accept it as fact.

Yet she had known it the minute Kinch walked through the door. The sickly pallor covering his face, and the shock etched deep in his eyes, bespoke the horror of what she had feared most. Stunned, unwilling to believe, she had stared at him a long time, until finally he lowered his head. His words still rang in her ears.

"They got him."

That was all he said. Having spoken those simple words, a death knell sounded in a quavering voice, he slumped into a chair and hadn't moved since. A rush of tears stung her eyes, and something vile and thick clogged her throat. She hadn't questioned him then, and later, after she stopped crying, it didn't seem to matter. Whatever had happened, she chose not to hear it. Somehow, in a way she hadn't yet reconciled, if she didn't hear it then it couldn't be true. But even as she witlessly paced the floor, frantically seeking to elude the truth, she knew deep down that she was only fooling herself.

Mike McCluskie was dead, and all the King's horses and all the King's men couldn't bring him back again.

The nursery rhyme jarred her to a halt.

Humpty Dumpty sat on a wall. Humpty Dumpty had a great fall. *God, she must be going mad.* Reaching back into her childhood, dredging up some silly nonsense to cushion a blow she hadn't yet been able to accept. That's what it was. Some form of lunacy. Letting her mind play tricks on her. Turning a tall, sandy-haired hellraiser into a dumpy little innocent. Watching him tumble from the wall and shatter to pieces. It was a device. A childish game. Something conjured up from God knew where to convince herself that he really couldn't be scraped up and glued back together again.

Life didn't work that way. Only in fairy tales did the good guys win. Out in the harsh reality of the world it was the bastards who walked away with the marbles. They never died. Or perhaps, because there were so many of them, it merely seemed that their numbers never dwindled.

She turned and was amazed to see Sugartit sitting beside the boy. Though her mind seemed lucid and clear, she couldn't recall the girl entering the kitchen. But obviously she had, and plain to see, she was wholly absorbed in the boy's sorrow. Then, in a moment of self-loathing, Belle realized that for the past hour she had dwelt on nothing but her own grief. She had given no thought whatever to Kinch. Wasted and sickly, dying by inches as some ravenous thing consumed his lungs, he sat there stricken with remorse. Not for himself, but instead for what he had lost. The one man who had befriended him, given him a reason to live, made him forget for a small moment in time that he was marked for an early grave.

All at once she felt an outpouring of pity that completely overshadowed her own misery.

She crossed the room and gently laid her hand on the kid's head. "Mike wouldn't like this. Do you know that? If he walked through the door and caught us moping around this way, he'd just raise holy hell."

Kinch kept his eyes fastened on the floor. "He ain't comin' through that door no more."

"No, I suppose not." Belle's stomach churned, queasy and fluttering, as if she had swallowed a jar of butterflies. She took a deep breath to steady herself. "But that's no reason for us to crawl off and call it quits. Mike lived more in thirty years than most men would in a couple of lifetimes. And he enjoyed every minute of it, too. Do you know what he would say if he was here right now? He'd laugh and then he'd say, 'Bud, it's nothin' but the luck of the draw. You pays your money and you takes your chances.'"

Sugartit placed her hand on the boy's arm. "Belle's right, honey. You mustn't blame yourself. These things just happen."

Kinch slammed out of the chair, jerking away from them. "What d'you know about it? You weren't there."

The girl winced as if she had been slapped in the face and stared after him in bewilderment. He stalked across the room and stopped beside the stove, refusing to look at them. The heat of his words left them startled, and for a while no one said anything. Sugartit had plainly hit a nerve, and the boy's wretched look disturbed them in a way they couldn't quite fathom.

Presently Belle got a grip on herself and decided to have another try. Whatever was bothering him had to be brought out into the open. Left to fester and feed upon itself, it would only get worse.

"Are you blaming yourself, Kinch? Is that why you can't look at us?"

He still wouldn't turn around. "I waited too long. I should've gone in there with him. If there'd been two of us they would've backed down."

"Don't you think Mike thought of that?"

"I dunno."

"Yes you do. You know it very well. He told you to stay here because he didn't want you mixed up in this business."

"Yeah, but he was always sayin' that. I shouldn't have listened."

"That's just the point. You didn't listen. You followed him anyway. Nobody could have asked any more of you than that. Why should you expect more of yourself?"

"She's right," Sugartit blurted. "You did what you could, and that's the most anybody can do."

"Cripes, you two don't understand nothin', d'you? I should've talked him into lettin' me back his play. He'd have let me if I just spoke up."

"You're wrong, Kinch." Belle's tone had the hard ring of certainty. "He would have tied you hand and foot before he let that happen."

"Don't be too sure. He knew how good I was with a gun."

"Yes, but there's something you don't understand. He thought the sun rose and set in your hat. Why else do you think he stayed here? You just think about it a minute and you'll see he would never have let you go along."

Belle realized her mistake only after the words were out. She damned herself for speaking out of turn, but by then it was too late. Kinch whirled around, his eyes distended and flecked through with doubt.

"What're you talkin' about? It was his job. He stayed here to get Anderson, didn't he?"

"Of course he did. I just meant he thought too much of you to risk getting you in a jam with the Texans."

"That's not what you meant. You're lyin' to me, Belle." The kid scrunched his eyes up in a tight scowl. "I got a right to know, and you got no right to hold back on me."

She just stared at him a moment, feeling helplessly trapped. "Maybe you're right. I suppose when a man does something like that it shouldn't be kept a secret." She faltered, trying to break it gently, but found herself at a loss for words. "I don't know how else to say it except straight out. Mike never ran from anything in his life and he probably wouldn't have this time either. But there was more to it. The reason he stayed, I mean. He was willing to take on Anderson and that bunch so you wouldn't think bad of him. I tried to talk him out of it, but he had his mind set."

"Oh, Jesus." Kinch seemed to stagger and his face went ashen. "He didn't have to get himself killed to prove nothin'. I would've understood."

"Mike thought it was important enough that he wasn't willing to take a chance. He did it the only way he knew how." The boy was badly shaken, worse than Belle had expected, and she tried to soften the blow. "Maybe it's not much consolation, but Mike was sure he could trick Anderson into making it a fair fight. I think he really believed he could pull it off and walk away without a scratch."

"Yeah, it was fair awright." The muscle at the back of his jawbone twitched in a hard knot. "Six to one. With him backed up against a wall."

There was a sharp rap at the back door and the room went deathly still. Kinch's arm moved and the Colt appeared in his hand. Stepping back beside the stove, he drew a bead on the window shade, then nodded for Belle to open the door. She threw the bolt and jerked the door open, moving quickly out of the line of fire. Dr. Gass Boyd stepped through the entrance and stopped, looking first at the two women and finally at the gun barrel centered on his chest.

"Youngster, it would be a serious error in judgment for you to shoot me. I'm about the last friend you have left in this town."

Belle slammed the door and bolted it. Something in Boyd's voice alarmed her, more the tone than the words themselves. But as she turned to question him, Kinch holstered his pistol and stepped away from the stove.

"Sorry I threw down on you, Doc. Guess I'm a little jumpy tonight."

"Save your apologies, son." Boyd set his bag on the table and smiled. "After what you did tonight you have every right to a case of nerves."

"I don't understand." Belle shot him a puzzled frown. "What's Kinch done?"

The doctor looked from her to the boy and one eyebrow arched quizzically. "You mean to say you haven't told them?"

"Just about Mike." Kinch ducked his head. "Didn't see that it'd do any good to tell 'em about the rest."

"What do you mean, the rest?" Belle moved around the table and faced Boyd squarely. "Doc, will you please explain what's going on here?"

"Perhaps you ladies had better sit down. Our young friend seems to have omitted a few rather salient details."

Sugar obediently took a chair but Belle remained standing. "Quit hedging, Doc. Let's have it."

"Very well. I have just come from the hardware store, which is temporarily serving as a funeral parlor. As of this moment there are five dead and four wounded. In my opinion one of the wounded will die before morning. The others have a fair chance of pulling through."

"You're still beating around the bush. What does that have to do with Kinch?"

Boyd glanced over at the kid and his sober expression deepened. "Belle, it seems you are harboring a paragon of modesty as well as a fugitive. According to a hundred or so eyewitnesses, Kinch personally accounted for four of the dead and two wounded. One of whom is as good as dead right now."

"Oh, my God." Belle sank into a chair.

Sugartit stared unblinkingly at the boy, her eyes glazed

over with shock. Belle was aghast, unable to get her breath for a moment, and finally she looked up at the little physician in complete bafflement.

"He didn't say a word."

"Precisely." Boyd treated the kid to a benevolent smile. "Along with unerring aim, he has the virtue of modesty."

"Five men." Sugartit's statement came in a dazed whisper.

"And a sixth wounded," Boyd noted in a clinical undertone.

Belle shook her head in numbed disbelief, and at last her gaze settled on the boy. "Why didn't you tell us?"

Kinch gave her a hangdog look and shrugged. "I figured you had enough on your mind. Hearin' about Mike, I mean."

"But how in God's name did you do it?"

"I dunno. It all happened so fast I ain't real sure." The kid mulled it over a little, trying to sort it out in his mind. "Mike and Anderson went down just as I come through the door. Then the rest of them Texans ganged around for a looksee and I started shootin'. Funny thing is, they just stood there. Didn't try to run or duck or nothin'. It was sorta like knockin' over tin cans, the way Mike showed me when we used to practice."

Silence descended on the kitchen, and for a moment everybody stared at him in dumbstruck wonder. Presently the doctor cleared his throat and tugged reflectively at his ear. "I'm not much of a shot myself, but offhand, I'd say you had a damned good teacher."

"Best there ever was," Kinch agreed. They exchanged glances and the boy frowned. "Something you said bothers me, though, Doc. I ain't no slouch with a pistol, but Mike never taught me how to get six men with five shots. Y'see, he believed in carryin' the hammer on an empty chamber, and I only had five loads. That's what throws

me. There was only five of them Texans and I drilled
ever' one of 'em dead center."

Boyd eyed him speculatively. "What about the trainmen?"

"What trainmen?"

"There were two Santa Fe men seated at the table next
to Mike's."

"I don't know what you're talkin' about, Doc. All I
saw was that bunch of Texans standin' over Mike and
Anderson."

Belle gave the physician a keen sidewise scrutiny.
"Doc you're hinting at something. That's why you snuck
in the back door, isn't it? You didn't want anybody to see
you coming here."

"I'm afraid so," Boyd admitted. "One of those killed
was Pat Lee, a Santa Fe engineer." He paused and looked
at the boy. "Anderson swears it was your shot that
killed him."

"Anderson?" Kinch spit the word out, glaring thun-
derstruck at the doctor.

"Why, yes. Perhaps I forgot to mention it, but Anderson is going to live. Despite a very serious chest wound
he'll make it with any luck—"

Kinch kicked a chair out of his way and headed for
the door. Boyd surprised even himself by darting across
the room and blocking the boy's path.

"Now wait a minute, son. Don't go running off in cir-
cles like a bee had stung you."

"Get out of my road, Doc."

"You're going after Anderson, is that it?"

"Damn right! He killed Mike, didn't he?"

"And I suppose Mike taught you how to walk in and
shoot a wounded man while he's laid up in bed. Was that
one of the lessons?"

The kid just stood there a moment, half mad with rage,

then he wheeled around and started pacing the kitchen. Belle and Sugar looked at one another, unnerved and not a little frightened by what they had seen in his face. After a moment Boyd regained his composure and came back to the table.

"Kinch, the night Mike McCluskie carried you to his hotel room I promised him I would look after your health. In a way, that's what I'm still doing. Now suppose we all remain calm and I'll explain what brought me down here."

When no one objected, he went on. "There are a number of things happening in Newton at this very moment. First off, Bob Spivey has telegraphed to Topeka for a U.S. marshal. He means to put the fear of God into this town, and there is already talk that a swift hanging would be just the thing to turn the trick. Secondly, Anderson's statement against Kinch is backed up by one of his cowhands. The one who's going to live. Son, from where I sit, that makes you the prime candidate for a necktie party."

Kinch stopped pacing and glowered back at him. "I didn't kill no Santa Fe men. All I shot was Texans."

"I don't doubt that for an instant. But it's your word against theirs. Now, you're in no danger from the Texans. From what I heard at the dancehall they don't think much of the way Anderson and his crew ganged up on Mike. Unfortunately, the same can't be said for the townspeople. Or the U.S. marshal, for that matter."

"What about Anderson?" the kid demanded. "Hadn't somebody better charge him with murder for what he did to Mike?"

"Probably they will. But from the little I've overheard, I suspect his men intend to sneak him out of town before morning. That won't change a thing, though. Anderson's statement will still hold, and when the U.S. marshal arrives, he'll come looking for you. Whether or not you actually killed the engineer would be a moot question at that point. The townspeople are in an ugly mood. They want to make an example out of somebody, and I'm afraid you're it."

The logic of Boyd's argument was hard to dispute. Everybody looked back and forth at one another for a while and there was silent agreement that the boy had worked himself into a bad spot.

At last Belle turned to face the doctor. "What you're saying is that we have to get Kinch out of town before some drunk gets busy and organizes a lynching bee."

"That's correct," Boyd nodded. "The sooner, the better. Oddly enough, there happens to be a horse out back right now. With a bill of sale in the saddlebags."

Belle turned her attention to the kid. "Kinch, I'll try to tell you what Mike would say if he was sitting here instead of me. He was a gambling man, but he always knew when to fold a losing hand. That's what you're holding right now. It's time to call it quits and find yourself a new game. Otherwise Sugar's liable to be burying her man the same as I'll have to bury mine."

That struck home and the boy swallowed hard. "Maybe so, but I'd feel like I'm runnin' out on Mike. I sorta had it in mind to finish what he'd started with them Texans."

"You're not running! Get that out of your head. If you had it to do over, you'd have told Mike to leave. Wouldn't you? Well this is the same thing. Sugartit and me, we're asking you to go for our sake."

Sugartit flew out of her chair and rushed into the kid's arms. "Please, honey, do it for me. Just this once. Wherever you go, you let me know and I'll be there with bells on. I promise."

Boyd cleared his throat and looked away. "Son, I suspect there's little time to waste. You had best be off while you have the chance."

"Yeah, sorta looks that way, don't it?"

Kinch pulled Belle into a tight hug and afterward shook the doctor's hand. Then Sugartit threw herself in his arms again and gave him a kiss that was meant to last. Finally she let go and he headed for the door. But half-way out he turned and looked back.

"You want to hear something funny? I ain't never been on a horse in my life. This oughta be a real circus."

The door closed and they just stood there staring at it. Somehow the whole thing seemed a bad dream of sorts. A nightmare that would pass with the darkness and leave their lives untouched. But moments later the spell was broken and reality came back to stay.

Hoofbeats sounded outside and slowly faded into the night. Like a drummer boy tapping the final march, they heard a faint tattoo in the soft brown earth.

Kinch Riley would return no more.

CHAPTER 16

THE KID often came to a grove of cottonwoods along the riverbank. There was something peaceful about the shade of the tall trees and the sluggish waters gliding past in a silty murmur. Yet it was only within the past week that the Red had settled down and started to behave itself. Spring rains had been heavy, and the snaky, meandering stream had crested in a raging torrent for better than a fortnight. A mile wide in some places, roiling and frothing in its turbulent rush southward, it had been a watery graveyard of uprooted trees, wild things dead and bloated, and a flotsam of debris collected in its wandering rampage.

Kinch hadn't cared much for the river in flood. It reminded him somehow of an angry beast, hungry and drooling, devouring everything in its path. Watching it had disturbed him, almost as if the river and the thing gnawing on his lungs were of a breed. Kindred in the way of things carnivorous and lurking and ever ready to fatten themselves on the flesh of the living. That the thought was far-fetched—a figment of the nagging fear which shadowed his thoughts these days—made little difference. It was no less real, and in some dark corner of his mind he was obsessed with but one thing.

He must not die. Not yet.

But as the flood waters receded, and the warmth of spring came again to the land, he found a measure of hope. The prairie turned green as an emerald sea, and overnight bright clusters of wild flowers seemed to burst from the earth. New life, borne in on soft southerly breezes, was everywhere he looked. He drew strength from its freshness and vitality, and with it, the belief that he might, after all, hold on till his work was completed.

While his thoughts still turned inward, he dwelled not so much on himself these days as on the happier times of a summer past. That brief moment when he'd had it all. The excitement and laughs, friendship and love. When the Irishman and Belle and Sugartit had given him something that neither time nor space could erase.

Seated beneath the leafy cottonwoods, soaking up the warming rays of a plains sun, his mind often wandered back. There, in a bright little cranny far off in his head, McCluskie still lived. Tall and square-jawed, alert and tough and faintly amused. Busted nose and all. Kinch could summon forth at will the tiniest detail. How the Irishman walked and talked and knocked back a jigger of whiskey. The hard-as-nails smile and the quick grin and that soft grunt of disgust. The deliberate way he had of rolling a smoke and flicking a match to life with his thumbnail. Every mannerism and quirk acquired on the long hard trail from Hell's Kitchen to the dusty plains of Kansas. It was all there, shiny bright and clear as polished glass, tucked neatly away in the back of his mind. Etched boldly and without flaw, indelible as a tattoo.

Still, the kid wasn't fooling himself. The image existed only in his mind's eye. Along with it persisted the certain knowledge that the man he summoned back so easily was dead and long buried. Mike McCluskie, that part of him which was flesh and bone, had been under ground some nine months now. The other part, what the preachers always made such a fuss over, was somewhere else. Though just exactly where, nobody had ever nailed down for sure.

Kinch had given that considerable thought. Particularly at night, when he came to sit beneath the trees and listen to the river. Head canted back, searching the starry skies, he wondered if there was a heaven. Or a hell. And if so, the further imponderable. Which place would the spirit of Mike McCluskie most likely be found? Somehow he had a feeling that the Irishman had made it to the Pearly Gates. Probably fighting every step of the way, too. Heels dug in and squawling like a sore-tailed bear.

The kind of people McCluskie had enjoyed most in life were the rascals and the highrollers. Being separated from them in the hereafter was something he wouldn't have counted on. If he had gone up instead of down, it had doubtless taken some mighty hard shoving on somebody's part.

Which way he had gone didn't mean a hill of beans, though. Not to the kid, anyhow. He himself wasn't all that hooked on religion, and so far as he could see, one way looked about as good as another. Just so he could tag along with the Irishman when his time came, he didn't give a tinker's damn whether it was heaven or hell or somewhere in between. When he checked out for good, finally gave up the ghost, he meant to make himself heard on that score. Anybody that tried to punch his ticket a different direction than McCluskie was going to have a stiff scrap on his hands.

Kinch chuckled to himself and slowly climbed to his feet. For someone living on borrowed time, he sure had some powerful notions about the hereafter. Like as not, when a fellow passed on, they just gave him his choice, and there wasn't any big rhubarb about it one way or another.

Squinting at the sun, he made it a couple of hours before noon. Time he got off his duff and swamped out the saloon. Quitting the cottonwoods, he headed up the bluff toward the station.

The town wasn't much. Aside from the saloon, there

was a ramshackle hotel, two general stores, and perhaps
a dozen houses scattered about the surrounding prairie.
While the township had been officially designated Salt
Creek, honoring a nearby tributary which flowed into the
larger stream, it was known simply and universally as
Red River Station. Situated on a high limestone bluff
overlooking the river, it was as far as a man could go and
still say he was in Texas. Once across the Red, he entered
Indian Territory.

The reason for the station's existence lay just west of
town. There, a wide natural chute, boxed in by limestone
walls, sloped down to the water's edge. Starting in late
spring and continuing into early fall, herds of longhorns
were driven down the chute and pushed across the river.
A sandbar ran out from the northern back, and when the
cattle reached it, they had begun the long haul up the
Chisholm Trail. Some two hundred fifty miles farther
north, after passing through Indian Territory, the trail
ended at the Kansas railheads. Abilene, Newton, and the
reigning cowtown this particular spring, Wichita.

Small as it was, it seemed likely that Red River Station would thrive and prosper forever. Though the cowtowns faded into obscurity as quickly as rails were laid
south and west, the station depended on nothing but itself. It was the gateway to the Chisholm Trail, the only
known route through the red man's domain, and this stra-
tegic location guaranteed its prosperity.

The trail herds passing the station had been sparse
thus far this spring. Cattlemen were reluctant to ford the
Red, and the latticework of rivers crisscrossing Indian
Territory, until the flood waters had receded. But the billowing plume of dust on the southern horizon steadily
grew larger, and over the past week, better than three
herds a day had made the crossing. Soon, as many as
ten herds a day, numbering upward of twenty thousand

longhorns, would be stacked up waiting their turn. Red River Station made not a nickel's profit off the cattle themselves, but its little business community grew fat and sleek off the cowhands. After fording the river, the Texans wouldn't again see civilization for close to a month. The station was their last chance, and in the way of thirsty men doing dirty work, they made the most of it.

Kinch came through the back door of the Alamo Saloon and started collecting his gear. Broom and featherduster, mop and pail. Tools of the trade for a swamper. He didn't care much for the job, emptying spittoons and swabbing drunken puke off the floor, but beggars couldn't be choosers. The way he looked at it, Roy Oliphant had been damned white to take him on, and he felt lucky to have a bunk in the back room, three squares, and a little pocket change. More importantly, it allowed him to straddle the jaws of the Chisholm Trail while he watched and planned and waited.

Hugh Anderson would pass this way, as did all Texas cattlemen, sooner or later. When he finally showed, the kid had a little surprise in store. An early Christmas present, of sorts.

After sweeping the floor, he started mopping the place with a practiced, unhurried stroke. Nine months on the end of a mop had taught him that there was no fast way. Slow and sure, that was the ticket. It left the floor clean and his lungs only slightly bent out of shape. He was nearing the rear of the saloon when Roy Oliphant came down from his room upstairs.

The boy paused, breathing hard, and leaned on his mop. "Mornin', Mr. Oliphant. All set for another day?"

Oliphant stopped at the bottom of the stairwell and gave him a dour look. The saloonkeeper was a gruff bear of a man, widowed and without children, and early morning generally found him foul-tempered and vinegary.

But in his own way, rough and at times blistering, he had a soft spot for strays. The ones life had shortchanged and left discarded along the wayside. There were occasions when he reminded the kid just the least little bit of McCluskie.

"Bub, ever' now and then I get the notion you haven't got a lick of sense. Look at the way you're huffin' and puffin'. Goddamnit, how many times I got to tell you? Slow down. Take it easy. The world ain't gonna swell up and bust if you don't burn the end off that mop."

Kinch grinned and took another swipe at the floor. "Aw, cripes, Mr. Oliphant. Workin' up a sweat is good for me. Gets all the kinks ironed out."

"Why sure it does," Oliphant observed tartly. "That's why you're wheezin' like a windbroke horse, ain't it?"

"Well, I always say if a job's worth doing it's worth doing right. Besides, you got the cleanest saloon in town, so what're you always hollerin' about?"

Oliphant grunted, holding back on a smile. "Don't give me none of your sass. This here's the only saloon in town and you damn well know it."

"Yeah, but it's still the cleanest."

"Real funny, 'cept I ain't laughin'. You're not foolin' anybody, y'know?"

"What d'you mean?"

"C'mon, don't play dumb." Oliphant headed toward the bar, talking over his shoulder. "You buzzsaw that mop around so you can get back down to the bluffs and start bangin' away at tin cans."

The kid blinked a couple of times, but he didn't say anything.

Oliphant drew himself a warm beer and downed half the mug in a thirsty gulp. He wasn't a man who liked riddles, and the boy had been a puzzle of sorts from the day he walked through the door. Looking back, he often wondered why he'd taken the kid on in the first place. He knew galloping consumption when he saw it, and a smoky saloon didn't exactly qualify as a sanatorium. Which was what the youngster needed. When he rode into town, he'd been nothing but skin and bones, pale and sickly and wracked with fits of coughing. The saloon-keeper would have laid odds that he'd never make it through the winter. But the kid had hung on somehow, and never once had he shirked the job.

Still, after all these months, Oliphant had to admit to himself that he really didn't know the kid. Like this deal with the tin cans. He had sneaked down and watched the boy practice a few times. What he saw left him flabber-gasted. Kinch made greased lightning look like molasses at forty below. Moreover, he rarely ever missed, and he went through the daily drills as if his life depended on every shot. The saloonkeeper was baffled by the whole thing, plagued by questions that seemingly defied any reasonable answer.

Where had he learned to handle a gun that slick? Who taught him? And most confusing of all, why in the name of Christ did he practice so religiously, day in and day out?

But Roy Oliphant wasn't the kind to stick his nose in other people's business. He ruminated on it a lot, watch-ing silently as the kid spent every spare nickel on pow-der and lead, yet he had never once allowed his curiosity to get the better of him. Not until today.

Kinch was still staring at him as he drained the mug and set it on the bar. "That's what I like about you, bub. You're closemouthed as a bear trap."

"You mean the gun?"

"Hell, yes. What did you think I was talkin' about? You work at it like your tail was on fire, but I never once seen you wear the damn thing. Sorta gets a fellow to wonderin' after a while."

"Aw, it's just a game somebody taught me. Y'know, something to help pass the time."

Oliphant gave him a skeptical look, but decided to let it drop. He hadn't meant to bring it up in the first place, and why he'd picked this morning to get nosy puzzled him all the more. Live and let live was his motto, and he'd never lost any skin minding his own business. If the kid had some deep dark secret, that was his privilege. Most times, what a man didn't know couldn't hurt him, and it was best left that way.

"Well, I guess you'd better finish up and get on back to your game. Only do me a favor, will you? Don't wear out my mops so fast. Them goddamn things cost money."

Kinch grinned and went back to swabbing the floor. Presently he disappeared into the storeroom and after a while the rusty hinges on the alley door groaned. Oliphant listened, waiting for it to close, then smiled and drew himself another beer.

Some more tin cans were about to bite the dust.

The kid's routine varied little from day to day. Swamp out the saloon, put in an hour or so working with the Colt, then return to his room and clean and reload the pistol. Afterward, he would stroll around town, always keeping his eye peeled for horses with a certain brand, and generally end up back at the saloon not long after noontime. There, he took up a position at the back of the room, supposedly on hand in case Oliphant needed any help. But his purpose in being there had nothing to do with the job. Whenever a fresh batch of Texans rode into town they made straight for the Alamo, and he carefully scrutinized each face that came through the door. While the long hours sapped his strength, and breathing the smoke-filled air steadily worsened his cough, he seldom budged from his post till closing time. Sooner or later the face he sought would come through the door, and he wasn't about to muff the only chance he might get.

Time was running out too fast for that.

Hardly anyone paid him any mind. He was just a skinny kid with a hacking cough who cleaned up their messes. That was the way Kinch wanted it. He kept himself in the background, and since coming to town, he had made it a habit to never wear a gun. With the Colt on his hip, there was the ever present likelihood he might become involved in an argument and wind up getting himself killed. That was one chance he wasn't willing to risk. Not until he'd performed a little chore of his own.

Yet there were times when he despaired of ever pulling it off, and this was one of those days. His cough was progressively growing worse, and the only thing that kept it under control was the bottle he had stashed in the storeroom. It was something to ponder. Nine months he had waited, and unless something happened damned quick, he'd cough once too often and that would be the end of it. Which wasn't what he'd planned at all, and personal feelings aside, it seemed unfair as hell to boot. Justice deserved a better shake than that. But then, as the Irishman had once observed, life was like a big bird. It had a way of dumping a load on a man's head just when he needed it least.

This was a thought much on his mind as he returned from the storeroom. He had developed quite a tolerance for whiskey the past few months, and the fiery trickle seeping down through his innards right now felt very pleasant. With any luck at all it would hold his cough at bay for a good hour. Not that an hour was what he needed,

though. The way things were shaping up he had to figure out a cure that would hold him for a month, or more.
Maybe the whole damn summer. Then he chuckled
grimly to himself, amused by the absurdity of it.

There wasn't any cure, and if that big bird didn't dump
all over him, he might just luck out with a couple of more
weeks. But as he came through the door the laugh died,
and his throat went dry as a bone.

Hugh Anderson and his crew were bellied up to the
bar.

Kinch couldn't quite believe it for a minute. After all
this time they had finally showed. He stood there, watching Oliphant serve them, and it slowly became real. The
waiting had ended, at last, and for the first time in longer
than he could remember, he felt calm and rested and cold
as a chunk of ice. Stepping back, just the way he'd planned
it, he simply vanished in the doorway and headed for his
room.

Moments later, he reappeared and the Colt was
cinched high on his hip. Walking forward, he stopped at
the end of the bar, standing loose and easy, just the way
the Irishman had taught him.

"Anderson."

The word ripped across the saloon and everyone
turned in his direction. Somebody snickered, but most of
the crowd just gawked. The hard edge to his voice had
fooled them, and they weren't quite sure it was this rag-
gedy kid who had spoken. Then they saw the gun, and
the look in his eye, and the place went still as a church.
Kid or not, he had dealt himself a man's hand.

Anderson took a step away from the bar and gave him
a quizzical frown. The Texan had slimmed down some
from last summer, but other than that, he looked mean
as ever.

"You want somethin', button?"

"Yeah. I want you."

"That a fact?" Anderson eyed him a little closer. "I don't place you just exactly. We met somewheres?"

"It'll come back to you. Tuttle's Dancehall in Newton. The night you murdered Mike McCluskie."

"Sonovabitch!" Anderson stiffened and a dark scowl came over his face. "You're the one that shot up my crew."

Kinch nodded, smiling. "Now it's your turn."

"Sonny, you done bought yourself a fistful of daisies."

"You gonna fight, yellowbelly, or just talk me to death?"

The Texan grabbed for his gun and got it halfway out of the holster. Kinch's arm hardly seemed to move, but the battered old Navy suddenly appeared in his hand. Anderson froze and they stared at one another for an instant, then the kid smiled and pulled the trigger. A bright red dot blossomed on the Texan's shirt front, just below the brisket, and he slammed sideways into the bar. Kinch gun-shot him as he hung there, and when he slumped forward, placed still a third slug squarely in his chest. Anderson hit the floor like a felled ox, stone cold and stiffening fast.

There was a moment of stunned silence.

Before anybody could move, Roy Oliphant hauled out a sawed-off shotgun from beneath the bar. The hammers were earred back and he waved it in the general direction of Anderson's crew. "Boys, the way I call it, that was a fair fight. Everybody satisfied, or you want to argue about it?"

One of the cowhands snorted, flicking a glance down at the body. "Mister, there ain't no argument to it. The kid gave him his chance. More'n he deserved, I reckon. Leastways some folks'd say so."

Kinch turned, holstering the Colt, and walked back

toward the storeroom. His eyes were bright and alive, and oddly enough, his lungs had never pumped better. He felt like a man who had just settled a long-standing debt.

What the Irish would have called a family debt.

Late that afternoon Kinch stepped aboard his horse and leaned down to shake hands with the saloon-keeper. "I'm obliged for everything, Mr. Oliphant."

"Hell, you earned your keep. Just wish you'd have give me the lowdown sooner, that's all. Not that you needed any help. But it don't never hurt to have somebody backin' your play."

"Yeah, that's the same thing I used to tell a friend of mine." The kid sobered a minute, then he grunted and gave off a little chuckle. "He was sort of bullheaded, too."

"You're talkin' about that McCluskie fellow."

"Irish, his friends called him. You should've known him, Mr. Oliphant. He was one of a kind. Won't never be another one like him."

"Well, it's finished now. You ever get back this way, you look me up, bub. I can always use a good man." They both knew it wasn't likely, but it sounded good. Oliphant suddenly threw back his head and glared up at the boy. "Say, goddamn! I ain't ever thought to ask. Which way you headed?"

"Wichita. Just as fast as this nag'll carry me."

"That's a pretty fair ride. Sure you're in any kind o' shape to make it?"

"I'll make it." The kid went warm all over, and in a sudden flash, Sugartit's kewpie-doll face passed through his mind. "Got somebody waitin' on me."

Oliphant leered back at him and grinned. "Yah, what's her name?"

"Mr. Oliphant, you wouldn't believe me if I told you."

Hickok & Cody

A Knight in Buckskin

"You have something I want," Richter said. "I'm willing to pay quite generously for an exchange. Enough to put you and Cody on easy street."

"What makes those kids worth so much? Why you after 'em anyway?"

"I'm not at liberty to say."

"Guess that's your tough luck."

Hickok grabbed Richter by the collar and the seat of his pants and bodily threw him off the train. Richter hit the roadbed on his shoulder, tumbling head over heels, and rolled to a stop in a patch of weeds.

The conductor slammed open the door. "What in God's name happened?"

"That feller hadn't bought a ticket. He was so ashamed, he just up and jumped off the train."

The conductor gawked. "Why on earth would he jump?"

"You know, it's funny, he never said. Some folks are mighty strange."

Praise for Spur Award-Winning Author Matt Braun

"Matt Braun is one of the best!"
> —Don Coldsmith, author of the Spanish Bit series

"Braun tackles the big men, the complex personalities of those brave few who were pivotal figures in the settling of an untamed frontier."
> —Jory Sherman, author of *Grass Kingdom*

NOVELS BY MATT BRAUN

WYATT EARP
BLACK FOX
OUTLAW KINGDOM
LORDS OF THE LAND
CIMARRON JORDAN
BLOODY HAND
NOBLE OUTLAW
TEXAS EMPIRE
THE SAVAGE LAND
RIO HONDO
THE GAMBLERS
DOC HOLLIDAY
YOU KNOW MY NAME
THE BRANNOCKS
THE LAST STAND
RIO GRANDE
GENTLEMAN ROGUE
THE KINCAIDS
EL PASO
INDIAN TERRITORY
BLOODSPORT
SHADOW KILLERS
BUCK COLTER
KINCH RILEY
DEATHWALK
HICKOK & CODY
THE WILD ONES
HANGMAN'S CREEK
JURY OF SIX
THE SPOILERS
THE OVERLORDS

Hickok & Cody

MATT BRAUN

St. Martin's Paperbacks

These novels are works of fiction. All of the characters, organizations, and events portrayed in them are either products of the author's imagination or are used fictitiously.

KINCH RILEY / HICKOK & CODY

Kinch Riley copyright © 1975 by Matthew Braun.
Hickok & Cody copyright © 2001 by Winchester Productions, Ltd.

All rights reserved.

For information address St. Martin's Press, 175 Fifth Avenue, New York, NY 10010.

ISBN: 978-1-250-29398-5

Our books may be purchased in bulk for promotional, educational, or business use. Please contact your local bookseller or the Macmillan Corporate and Premium Sales Department at 1-800-221-7945, ext. 5442, or by e-mail at MacmillanSpecialMarkets@macmillan.com.

Printed in the United States of America

Kinch Riley St. Martin's Paperbacks edition / June 2000
Hickok & Cody St. Martin's Paperbacks edition / May 2001

St. Martin's Paperbacks are published by St. Martin's Press, 175 Fifth Avenue, New York, NY 10010.

10 9 8 7 6 5 4 3 2 1

To

Macduff

Who gave of himself unstinting loyalty and
unconditional love.

AUTHOR'S NOTE

A WRITER and historian once observed, "When fact becomes legend, print the legend."

Hickok & Cody is based on historical fact. The Grand Duke Alexis of Russia actually traveled to America for a buffalo hunt on the Western Plains. There was an Orphan Train operating out of New York, carrying street urchins to adoptive homes in the West. All of this happened.

William F. "Buffalo Bill" Cody appeared in stage productions long before the advent of his Wild West Show. The plays were written by Ned Buntline and presented at theaters in New York and other Eastern cities. The success of the plays ultimately convinced Cody that "the show business" was the life for him.

James Butler "Wild Bill" Hickok did, in fact, go East to appear in Cody's stage productions. One season on the stage convinced him that acting was a sham, false heroics for the gullible masses. He discovered as well that Eastern cities left him longing for the endless skies and grass-scented winds of the plains. He returned, all too gladly, to the West.

All that is true, and all the rest is legend. In 1872, the Grand Duke Alexis and the Orphan Train converged with Hickok and Cody on the Western Plains. Heroic in fact as well as legend, Cody and Hickok became the paladins of desperate orphans. Their quest took them to New York, and the Broadway stage, and a murderous confrontation with underworld czars. New York was never the same again.

Hickok & Cody is fiction based on fact. A story of knights in buckskins who brought their own brand of justice to the streets of New York. A tale of mythical feats by legendary plainsmen.

Allegory in which West meets East—with a bang!

CHAPTER 1

A BROUGHAM carriage clattered along Irving Place shortly after midnight. The driver turned the corner onto Twentieth Street and brought his team to a halt. The horses snorted frosty puffs of smoke beneath a cobalt winter sky.

The brougham was a four-wheeled affair, with the driver perched on a seat outside. A gas lamppost on the corner reflected dully off the windows of the enclosed cab. Otto Richter shifted forward inside the cab and wiped condensation off the window with his coat sleeve. He slowly inspected the streets bordering Gramercy Park.

The park was a block long, centered between Lexington Avenue on the north and Irving Place on the south. Darkened mansions lined the perimeter of what was an exclusive enclave for some of the wealthiest families in New York. The whole of Gramercy Park was surrounded by an ornate eight-foot high wrought-iron fence.

"Looks quiet," Richter said. "Let's get it done."

Turk Johnson, a bullet-headed bruiser, followed him out of the cab. Richter glanced up at the driver.

"Stay put till we get back."

"I'll be waitin' right here, boss."

Richter led the way along the sidewalk. A few houses down, he mounted the steps to a three-story brick mansion. Johnson was at his elbow, standing watch as he halted before a stout oak door with stained glass in the top panel. He took a key from his overcoat pocket and inserted it into the lock. The door swung open.

A light snow began to fall as they moved into foyer.

Johnson eased the door closed, and they waited a moment, listening intently for any sound. On the left was an entryway into a large parlor, and on the right was the family sitting room. Directly ahead, a broad carpeted staircase swept grandly to the upper floors.

The silence was disturbed only by the relentless tick of a grandfather clock. Richter motioned with his hand, stealthily crossing to the bottom of the staircase. They took the stairs with wary caution, alert to the creak of a floorboard underfoot. Their movements were wraithlike, a step at a time.

A single gaslight burned on the second floor. Still treading lightly, they paused to get their bearings at the stairwell landing. Neither of them had ever before been in the house, but they knew it well. There were two bedrooms off the head of the stairs and another along a hallway to the right. The master bedchamber, which overlooked Gramercy Park, was at the front of the house. The servants were quartered on the top floor.

Richter nodded to the doorway on their left. "Careful now," he whispered. "The old woman's a light sleeper."

The remark solicited a grunt. Johnson was burly, robust as an ox, his head fixed directly on his shoulders. He grinned around a mouthful of teeth that looked like old dice. "Whyn't fix her wagon, too?"

"*Quiet!*" Richter hissed sharply. "Try to keep your mind on the job."

"Whatever you say, boss."

"Come along."

Richter turned toward the front of the house. A moment later, they stopped outside the master bedchamber. He gripped the doorknob, twisted it gingerly, and stepped inside. Embers from the grate in the fireplace faintly lighted the room. He moved closer to the bed.

A man and a woman lay fast asleep. The man was

strikingly handsome, the woman a classic beauty, both in their early thirties. Her hair was loose, fanned over the pillow, dark as a raven's wing. He snored lightly, covers drawn to his chin.

In the glow of the fireplace, Richter's features were hard and angular. He was lean and wiry, with muddy deep-set eyes, and a razored mouth. He stared at the couple for an instant, his expression implacable. Then he pulled a bottle of ether from his overcoat pocket.

Johnson moved forward with two rags. Richter doused them with ether, quickly stoppered the bottle, and returned it to his pocket. He took one of the rags from Johnson and they walked to opposite sides of the bed. Neither of them hesitated, Johnson working on the man and Richter the woman. They clamped the rags down tight, covering nostrils and mouth.

The man arched up from the bed, his hands clawing at the rag. Johnson grabbed him in a headlock, immobilizing him with brute strength, and forced him to breath deeply. The woman's eyes fluttered open and she gasped, inhaling raw ether; she struggled only briefly in Richter's arms. Hardly a minute passed before they were both unconscious, sprawled on the bed.

Richter stuffed the rag in his pocket. He removed the pillow from beneath the woman's head and placed it over her face. Johnson, working just as swiftly, buried the man's face in a pillow. There was no resistance from the couple, for they were anesthetized into a dreamlike state, incapable of fighting back. The men slowly smothered them to death.

When it was over, Richter arranged the woman's head in a comely pose on the pillow. Johnson followed suit, and they stepped back, admiring their handiwork. "Well now," Richter said with a note of pride. "They look quite peaceful, don't they?"

Johnson grinned. "Damn good way to kick the bucket. Never felt a thing."

"Yes, all very neat and tidy. Let's see to the children, Turk."

Richter hurried out the door. At the staircase landing, he once again saturated the rags with ether. Then they separated, Johnson moving to the bedroom on the right and Richter proceeding along the hallway. Some moments later they returned, each of them carrying a child bundled in a blanket. Richter gave Johnson a sharp look.

"Everything all right?"

"Went off smooth as silk."

Johnson was holding a boy, perhaps nine or ten years old. The girl in Richter's arms appeared to be a year or two older. She was a mirror image of her mother, just as the boy favored his father. They were both unconscious, breathing evenly.

"Time to go," Richter said, darting a glance at the other bedroom door. "Take it easy on the stairs."

Johnson trailed him down the staircase. They moved quietly through the foyer just as the grandfather clock chimed the half hour. Richter paused outside the house, juggling the girl with one arm, and locked the door. The snow was heavier now, thick white flakes swirling across Gramercy Park. They turned upstreet toward the waiting carriage.

One at a time, the children were loaded into the cab. Richter was the last to clamber aboard, signaling the driver to move out. The horses lurched into motion, heads bowed against the squalling snow. The carriage rounded the corner at the far end of Gramercy Park.

"Whatta night!" Johnson said, motioning to the huddled forms of the children. "Who are these kids, anyhow?"

"Augustus and Katherine."

"They got last names?"

Richter permitted himself a thin smile. "Not any-more."

The carriage trundled off toward the Lower East Side.

Manhattan was an island. Some two miles by fifteen miles in mass, it was connected to the outside world by railroad bridges along the northern shoreline. The only other outlets were ferries that plied the Hudson River.

The settled part of the island, more commonly called New York City, was a five-mile stretch at the southern tip of Manhattan. With the population topping a million, there were a hundred thousand people for every square mile, a teeming cauldron of humanity. Worldly men called it the Bagdad of North America.

Delancey Street was located in the heart of the Lower East Side. There, in tenements wedged together like rabbit warrens, the working class of the city struggled to outdistance squalor and poverty. New Year's was just a week past, but the people of Delancey Street found no reason to celebrate 1872. Their days were occupied instead with putting bread on the table.

The brougham carriage halted at the intersection of Delancey and Pitt. A faded sign affixed to the building on the southeast corner identified it as the New York Juvenile Asylum. The two-story structure was worn and decrepit, a battered wooden ruin much like the rest of the neighborhood. It was a warehouse for the flotsam of the city's young.

The driver hopped down to open the carriage door. Richter emerged first, carrying the girl, followed by Johnson with the boy. Heavy wet snow clung to their greatcoats as the driver hurried to jerk the pull-bell outside the entrance to the asylum. A pudgy man with wispy hair and dewlap jowls opened the door on the third ring. He waved them inside.

"I was getting worried," he said. "Thought maybe something had gone wrong."

"Nothing went wrong," Richter replied. "Just this damnedable snow, that's all. The streets are a mess."

"Hardly the night for an abduction, hmmm?"

"Your mouth will be the death of you, Barton. Let's hear no more about abduction."

Joseph Barton was the director of the Juvenile Asylum. He was a man of small stature, and corrupt to the core. He spread his hands in a lame gesture. "No harm intended. I was just making talk."

"Don't," Richter warned. "All the talk stops tonight."

The anteroom of the asylum was warmed by a potbelly stove stoked with coal. There was a tattered sofa and a grouping of hard straight-back chairs meant for the infrequent visitor. The children were placed on the sofa, still wrapped in their blankets. Richter took a moment to check the pupils of their eyes.

"Marvelous invention, ether," he said with some satisfaction. "They'll be out for at least another hour."

"I'd hoped for longer," Barton said in a piping voice. "The train's scheduled to depart at eight. What if they make a fuss when they wake up?"

"How many brats do you have in this sinkhole?"

"At the moment, probably five hundred or so. Why do you ask?"

Richter stared at him. "You ought to know how to handle hard-nosed kids. Get them some clothes out of your stockroom, nothing too fancy." His gaze shifted to the children. "Turn 'em into regular little orphans."

"Yes, but—" Barton hesitated, undone by his nerves. "What if they resist being put on the train?"

"I'm sure you'll think of something clever. That's what you're being paid for."

There were hundreds of men and women in New York who devoted their lives to homeless children. Most of them were affiliated with religious organizations, or charitable foundations. There were, as well, men without scruple or conscience who looked upon indigent children as a means of lining their own pockets. Joseph Barton was just such a man.

The opportunity for graft stemmed from the fact that youngsters under fifteen represented one-third of the city's population. At any given moment, upward of a hundred thousand homeless children were roaming the streets of New York. Some were orphans, their mothers and fathers dead from the ravages of disease and overwork. Others, children of the poor, were simply turned out by their parents to fend for themselves. To survive, they raided garbage bins and learned to live by petty crime.

The crisis brought swift action by the state legislature. The Truancy Law, enacted at the close of the Civil War, authorized police to arrest vagrant children ages five through fourteen. Some were brought to the House of Refuge, operated by a coalition of religious concerns. Others, particularly the troublemakers, were packed off to a secular facility, the Juvenile Asylum. The latter institution was dedicated to discipline, instilling the virtue of daily toil. The children were then indentured as apprentices to tradesmen.

Those youngsters considered beyond redemption were shipped West on the Orphan Train. Farmers and ranchers on the distant plains welcomed them with a mix of Christian charity and a profound belief in the values of hard work. All of which nicely solved the problem of delinquents and mischievous street urchins. The Orphan

Train departed New York's Grand Central Station every Friday.

"I'll certainly do my best," Barton said now. "None of the children especially like the thought of being sent West. We're sometimes forced to restrain them until the train leaves."

"I don't want them harmed," Richter told him. "The whole idea is to get them adopted. The farther West, the better."

"Oh, yes, I understand completely."

"Make sure you do, for your own good."

There was a veiled threat in Richter's tone. He pulled out a wad of greenbacks and started peeling off bills. "There's the thousand we agreed on," he said stiffly. "A thousand more once they're adopted."

Barton thought it unwise to count the bills. "How will I satisfy you the adoption has actually taken place?"

"You've no need to worry on that score. I'll know."

"Very well, just as you say."

"One last thing," Richter said. "You'll likely read about some missing children in tomorrow's papers. Don't try to put two and two together and get four."

"How could I not put it together?" Barton asked guilelessly. "Were there all that many children abducted tonight?"

"Pretend you're deaf, dumb and blind. Otherwise . . ."

Richter motioned casually to Johnson. The bruiser fixed Barton with a cold, ominous look. Barton quickly averted his gaze.

"Otherwise—" Richter went on, "Turk will pay you a visit some dark night. I doubt you'd recover."

"There's no reason to threaten me. I'm quite good at keeping a confidence."

"Then I predict you'll live to a ripe old age."

Richter walked to the door. Johnson gave Barton an

evil grin, then turned away, closing the door as he went out. On the street, the two men crossed to the curb, where Richter paused before entering the carriage. He looked up at the falling snow.

"I'm afraid we'll have to sleep fast, Turk."

"Why's that, boss?"

"We have a train to catch."

Otto Richter was a man who left no stone unturned.

CHAPTER 2

THE CAMPSITE was something on the order of a bivouac. Tents were aligned with military precision, forming a boxlike square fronting the waters of Red Willow Creek. Cavalry troopers stood guard at the cardinal points of the compass.

Wild Bill Hickok and Buffalo Bill Cody stood with a group of army officers in the center of the compound. Cody, with a flair for showmanship, was resplendent in pale buckskins, a crimson shirt worn beneath his fringed jacket. Hickok wore a stained buckskin jacket, his woolen trousers stuffed into the tops of mule-earred boots. A brace of Colt Navy pistols, carried cross-draw fashion, were wedged into a wide belt around his waist.

The weather was uncommonly mild for January on the Nebraska plains. Though the mercury hovered around forty, patches of snow still dotted the landscape from a recent storm. The campsite was located some forty miles south of Fort McPherson, headquarters for the Fifth Cavalry Regiment. Among the officers present were Lieutenant General Phil Sheridan, Major General George Armstrong Custer, and four brigadier generals. The officers were attired in field dress, their gold braid sparkling in an early morning sun.

A burly Russian Cossack snapped to attention as the flap opened on the largest tent in the compound. The Grand Duke Alexis, son of Alexander II, Czar of all the Russias, strode from the tent. He was tall and stout, with dark muttonchop whiskers and a regal bearing. He wore a fringed buckskin jacket, ivory in color and elaborately decorated with quillwork and shiny beads. The jacket was a gift, presented to him by Sheridan only yesterday.

"Good morning," he said, addressing the group in a heavy accent. "Excellent day for a hunt, is it not?"

"Excellent indeed," Sheridan replied. "I trust you slept well, Your Highness."

"Oh, yes," Alexis beamed, favoring Cody and Hickok with a broad smile. "You gentlemen will teach me how the buffalo are killed. *Da*?"

"Yessir, we will," Cody assured him. "You'll get the hang of it in no time. Won't he, pardner?"

"Why, shore he will," Hickok agreed. "'Specially with you to show him the ropes. You're in good hands, Duke."

The Grand Duke chose to overlook his truncated title. He was fascinated by the similarity between the two men. They were both solid six-footers, ruggedly handsome, their hair spilling down to their shoulders. Yesterday, when they met his train in North Platte, he'd been surprised to find Hickok in the party. From conversation, he gathered that Hickok was between jobs as a lawman and had been invited along by Cody. He felt fortunate to have them both on the hunt.

The Wild West was all the vogue with European nobility. Every year, royal sportsmen crossed the Atlantic to hunt buffalo on the wind-swept plains. The hunt for the Grand Duke had been orchestrated by the State Department in concert with the army brass. Russia was a friendly power, having aligned itself with the Union during the bloody turmoil of the Civil War. Five years ago, in 1867, the Grand Duke's father had ceded the territory of Alaska to the United States, further cementing the relationship between two great powers. All of which accounted for six generals in attendance on today's hunt.

Phil Sheridan motioned to where troopers waited with saddled horses. "You're in luck, Your Highness," he said with an expansive gesture. "Cody insists that you use his personal horse, Buckskin Joe."

"Finest buffalo horse on the plains!" Custer interjected, ever eager to display his expertise. "I can truthfully say I've never seen his equal."

"I am honored," Alexis said, looking at Cody. "How did you arrive at such an unusual name for your horse?"

"Well, don't you see, he's a buckskin. I just tacked on 'Joe' to give him a handle."

"A handle?"

"Yessir, a handle . . . a name."

"Ah, of course, now I understand."

The men walked toward the horses. Cody got Alexis mounted on Buckskin Joe, and the nobleman told himself he'd made a wise choice. Through the Russian ambassador, he had requested that Buffalo Bill Cody act as his personal guide. Cody was hailed by the press and the public alike as the most formidable buffalo hunter on the Western Plains. In 1867, while working as a contract hunter for the Kansas Pacific, he had killed 4,280 of the shaggy beasts. The tracklaying crews, grateful for the bounty, tagged him with a sobriquet that stuck. He became Buffalo Bill.

Wild Bill Hickok was no less a legend to the Grand Duke Alexis. On and off a scout for the army, Hickok's greater fame stemmed from his years as a lawman. His notoriety had little to do with buffalo and everything to do with Western desperadoes. His name was known on the steppes of Russia just as it was throughout the capitals of Europe. The world doted on his adventures, awed by tales of his speed and deadliness with a pistol. There was, in the lore of the West, only one Wild Bill. He was the most renowned mankiller of the day.

The hunting party rode south from the Red Willow Creek camp. They were trailed by a troop of cavalry, acting as escort in the event they encountered a hostile band of Sioux. An hour or so out, with Cody and Alexis in the lead, they topped a low rise on the rolling plains. Spread out before them, grazing on the umber grasses of winter, was a herd of some three hundred buffalo. Alexis was determined to take one of the great beasts with his new pistol, a Smith & Wesson .44 presented to him before he entrained from New York for the West. Cody explained how to place the shot from horseback.

Hickok and the generals waited on the knoll. Cody led the way onto the prairie, approaching the herd at a sedate trot. He cut out a woolly-coated cow grazing at the edge of the herd, and forced her into a lumbering lope. Then, twisting in the saddle, he motioned Alexis forward. The Grand Duke spurred Buckskin Joe into a gallop and bore down on the cow. His arm extended, he fired six shots from the Smith & Wesson, raking the cow with lead. She swerved away, seemingly unfazed, and rejoined the herd. A moment later she went back to cropping grass.

From the knoll, Hickok grunted with mild amusement. Sheridan cursed, and Custer shook his head, and the other generals held their silence. They watched as Cody took Alexis aside for a short lecture on the craft of hunting buffalo. Finally, with Alexis nodding, Cody pulled a Springfield .50 rifle from his saddle scabbard. Like his horse, he had named his rifle, and he fondly called it "Lucretia." The name derived from a Victor Hugo drama entitled *Lucretia Borgia*, the story of an ancient Italian noblewoman noted for her venom. The rifle was as deadly as its namesake.

Cody selected a mammoth bull from the herd. He rode off to the left of Alexis, urging Buckskin Joe into a gallop with a hard swat across the rump. The bull snorted, whirling away from the horsemen, quickly separated from the herd. Alexis kneed Buckskin Joe alongside, matching the bull stride for stride, the reins in one hand, the butt of Lucretia pressed to his shoulder. The rifle boomed and the bull went down headfirst, his horns plowing furrows in the dark earth. Alexis vaulted from the saddle, tossing the rifle to Cody, and pulled an evil-looking knife from his belt. He cut off the bull's tail, thrusting it overhead with a jubilant shout.

Before the day ended, the Grand Duke of all the Russias killed six times more.

The regimental band played a lively air. A celebration was in progress, with the royal party seated in the dining tent. Waiters in white jackets scurried around lighting coal-oil lamps as a vermilion sunset slowly faded into dusk. The menu for the evening featured buffalo hump aux champignons.

"A toast," Sheridan said, raising his wine glass. "To the Grand Duke Alexis. Seven buffalo in a single day!"

"Hear! Hear!"

The men were seated around a long table covered with white linen. They chorused the toast in loud voices, quaffing wine from crystal goblets. Alexis, who was savaging a slab of buffalo hump with the exuberance of a man who reveled in the kill, accepted their praise with regal modesty. He raised his own glass.

"I, too, make a toast," he said in an accent thickened by wine. "To Buffalo Bill, who must surely have Russian blood. A man among men!"

"Hear! Hear!"

Their shouts rang out across the compound. Fully five hundred men were camped along the banks of Red Willow Creek. There were four troops of the Fifth Cavalry, the regimental band, and a train of sixteen wagons to haul provisions. Major engagements against hostile tribes had been fought with fewer men and no supply train at all. But the troopers encamped by the creek found no fault with the royal hunt. Tonight, they feasted on buffalo as well.

The guest of honor insisted that Cody and Hickok be seated at his end of the table. He was aware that Sheridan, commander of the military division, and Custer, the fabled Indian fighter, felt somewhat slighted. Yet he'd been feted by generals since childhood, for he was, after all, the successor to the Russian throne. He wanted to learn more of the plainsmen, the storied heroes of the frontier.

Hickok, he discovered, was the mentor of Cody. At thirty-five, Hickok was nine years older and already a legend before they met. In 1867, a New York journalist traveling the West wrote an article for *Harper's New Monthly Magazine*. The article dealt with Hickok's exploits during the Civil War, when he'd infiltrated behind Confederate lines, operating as a Union spy. The journalist proclaimed, with attendant gory details, that Hickok had killed over a hundred men. He anointed him "The Prince of Pistoleers."

Other publications jumped to follow Hickok's adventures. He worked as a scout for the army, serving under Custer in the Seventh Cavalry. Then, after a stint as a deputy U.S. marshal, he was elected sheriff of a Kansas hellhole. From there, he went on to serve as city marshal of Abilene, the roughest cowtown on the plains. Abilene, where he'd killed two men, was his last assignment, ended less than a month ago. He was the scourge of outlaws, reputed to have dropped nine men in gunfights.

Dime novels, the craze of Eastern readers, immortalized him forever in the minds of the public. General George Armstrong Custer, penning an article for *Galaxy*

Magazine, labeled him the perfect specimen of physical manhood, unerring with rifle or pistol, a deadly adversary. Henry M. Stanley, better known for locating Dr. David Livingstone in darkest Africa, also wrote an article for *Harper's*. He portrayed Hickok in herculean terms, a plainsman and peace officer who had never killed a man without good cause. Wild Bill Hickok was enshrined into the pantheon of American folklore.

Cody, by contrast, had never killed a white man. His path to glory began in 1860, when at the age of fourteen he rode into history for the Pony Express. That same year, he met Hickok, who became his friend and mentor in the days ahead. When the Civil War erupted, he served with the Kansas Volunteer Cavalry, operating as a scout for the Union forces. Following the war, he sometimes worked with Hickok as a deputy U.S. marshal, and later found fame as Buffalo Bill with the Kansas Pacific Railroad. Later still, Hickok obtained a position for him as a scout with Custer's Seventh Cavalry.

From there, after gaining the attention of General Sheridan, Cody was assigned to the Fifth Cavalry. Over time, he was promoted to Chief of Scouts, operating out of Fort McPherson, deep in Sioux country. His three years of service resulted in a record unequaled by any scout on the frontier. He engaged in nine expeditions against the Sioux, and fought in eleven pitched battles. At twenty-six, he was a seasoned veteran, having killed ten warriors in personal combat. His courage in the field brought a commendation for valor by direct order of the Secretary of War.

Cody, like Hickok, attracted Eastern journalists. In 1869, Ned Buntline traveled West to Fort McPherson, under contract for a series of stories in the *New York Weekly*. His first installment, entitled *Buffalo Bill, the King of the Border Men*, catapulted Cody into national fame. He depicted Cody as an intrepid scout and fearless Indian fighter, and generally sensationalized every aspect of Cody's life. Following the series, he churned out four dime novels in two years, each more heroic than the last. To an entranced public, Cody became the Galahad of the Plains, a knight in buckskin.

"Now, you must indulge me," Alexis said, as intoxicated by the men as the wine. "What were your grandest adventures?"

Cody wagged his head. "I don't know as I'd call 'em grand."

"Don't be coy," Sheridan admonished from the other end of the table. "Tell him about the Battle of Summit Springs."

"Well—" Cody tugged at the small goatee on his chin. "You reckon he wants to hear that old chestnut?"

"Of course!" Alexis thundered. "I insist."

Cody launched into a windy tale of blood on the plains. A band of Cheyenne led by Tall Bull had taken two white women captive and fled north toward the Powder River country. The Fifth Cavalry gave chase, and several days into the pursuit Cody located the hostile camp. The cavalry charged, overrunning the village, killing fifty-two warriors and recapturing one of the women captives. The other was clubbed to death during the battle, and Cody in turn shot Tall Bull in a pitched fight. The death of their chief put the Cheyenne to flight.

Alexis was round-eyed. "And you scalped him? *Da*?"

"Shore did." Cody pulled a thatch of dried hair from inside his jacket and tossed it on the table. "Peeled the bugger's top knot clean off."

There was absolute silence at the table. Cody kept a hunk of beaver pelt handy to palm off on pilgrims and complete the joke. Everyone watched Alexis as he stared at what he believed to be a Cheyenne scalp, taken in the heat of battle. Custer was on the verge of a braying laugh when Sheridan shut him down with a cold look. Before anyone could spoil the joke, Sheridan glanced over at Hickok.

"Wild Bill, it's your turn," he said quickly. "Tell the Grand Duke about that fracas in Springfield. The time you shot Dave Tutt."

"Not much to tell," Hickok said, knuckling his sweeping mustache. "Maybe he'd sooner inspect Cody's scalp."

"No! No!" Alexis commanded, averting his gaze from the beaver pelt. "I want to hear of this shooting, Wild Bill. You must tell me."

Hickok spun a wry tale of love and death. In 1865, shortly after the Civil War, he'd drifted into Springfield, Missouri. A classic love triangle developed, with he and a gambler named Dave Tutt vying for the attentions of the same woman. Finally, over a poker table one night, he and Tutt exchanged insults of the worst kind. The next morning, on the Town Square, Tutt accosted him and fired the first shot. Hickok, deliberate even in a fight, drilled him through the heart. There, on the Springfield square, he'd coined the term that speed's fine, but accuracy is final.

"You left out a salient detail," Sheridan prompted. "What was the range when you fired?"

Hickok smiled. "A measured seventy-five paces."

"Astounding," Alexis exclaimed. "Why did he fire on you at such a distance?"

"Well, Your Highness, he'd never seen me shoot before. I reckon you could say he was a mite surprised."

"Champagne!" Alexis roared. "We make a toast to Wild Bill and Buffalo Bill. We get drunk!"

Hickok and Cody exchanged a look. They'd told the tales so often that by now it was like a vaudeville act.

Cody reclaimed his Cheyenne scalp as the waiters popped the corks. Hickok smiled at the fun of it all.

Alexis, Grand Duke of all the Russias, hoisted his glass with a booming laugh.

CHAPTER 3

THE LAND was stark and flat. Cornfields stood struck dead by winter, their slender stalks gone tawny with frost. The train sped westward under a dingy sky.

Katherine stared out at the bleak landscape. Thick clouds of black smoke from the engine swirled past the window. Augustus was asleep beside her on the seat, huddled within his coat against the chill of the passenger coach. She watched the fleeting cornfields with a forlorn expression.

There were six coaches on the train. Five were for orphans, and the sixth, the last in the string, was for fare-paying passengers. On each of the orphan coaches there were two attendants, a man and a woman, to look after the children. Their duties seemed more that of wardens than guardians.

Over the past week the train had followed the Union Pacific tracks westward. Slowly, with stops at every hamlet along the line, the train had made its way through Ohio, Indiana, Illinois, and finally into Iowa. The landscape became flatter and bleaker with every mile, somehow desolate. A sense of abandonment hung over the orphan coaches.

Katherine felt dazed, curiously hollow inside. The day the train left New York, she and Augustus had fought and kicked and screeched until they were forcibly carried onto the coach. They continued to protest they were not orphans, until finally Mr. Crocker, the agent for the Children's Aid Society, had threatened to bind and gag them in their seats. Their rebellion, stilled by the threat, turned to sullen apathy.

The helplessness of their situation was overwhelming. Katherine was ten, Augustus a year younger, and they'd never before been separated from their parents. At first, reduced to whispers, they wondered why they had been taken from their home in the dark of night. Even more, they were distressed that their parents had not intervened, somehow prevented their abduction. There seemed no good answers, only hard questions.

Yet, ever so slowly, they pieced together fragments of their ordeal. Katherine vaguely remembered a face, the face of a man, caught in the light of the lamp from the hallway, who had clamped a bitter-smelling rag over her face. Augustus recalled a huge man, unbelievably strong and quilted with muscle, holding him tight until he succumbed to a stinky rag. The men were shadowy figures, dim specters but nonetheless real.

Their terror the next morning was all too vivid. They found themselves at the mercy of workers at what was called the Juvenile Asylum. A man everyone addressed as Mr. Barton supervised their being dressed in clothing that was threadbare and tattered, obviously used. Then, after being manhandled onto an enclosed freight wagon, they were carted off to Grand Central Station. All their protests, like those of other children on the platform, went unheeded. They were dragged onto the train.

By the end of the first day, their spirits were at a low ebb. From talk among children in the coach, they learned they were aboard what was called the Orphan Train. There were five coaches, each packed with a hundred children, all destined to be adopted somewhere out West. For a brief moment, Katherine and Augustus were appalled by the thought that their parents had forsaken them, put them up for adoption. All their lives they had known love and affection, and their hearts broke to think their mother and father were involved. But then, flooded with memories of their rough abduction, they knew it wasn't true. They had been stolen from their parents.

"What are you looking at?"

Katherine turned to find Augustus rubbing sleep from his eyes. He was a sturdy youngster, with the square jaw-line and pleasant features of their father. She shook her head with a woebegone expression.

"Nothing, really," she said, studying the dismal countryside. "Everything seems so much the same."

Augustus yawned. "Where are we?"

"I think this is still Iowa. I don't really know."

"Doesn't make any difference, does it?"

"No," Katherine said sadly. "Not unless they turn the train around."

"How far is Iowa from New York?"

"Very, very far. Why do you ask?"

"Oh, you know." Augustus shrugged, his features downcast. "I was thinking about Mother and Father. They must be looking for us."

"Not in Iowa," Katherine said. "I'm sure they're worried sick. But who would ever dream of Iowa?"

"Maybe we ought to try to escape. Next time they stop and put us out on the platform for the farmers, we could just run. Hide somewhere until the train leaves."

"Yes, I suppose we could try. Although, where would we go? How would we ever get back to New York?"

"We could find a policeman," Augustus offered. "All he'd have to do is telegraph Mother and Father. We'd be on our way home in no time."

"You two got bats in your belfry. Go ahead, holler cop and see what it gets you."

In the seat opposite them were two young boys. One

was asleep, but the other was watching them with open mockery. Over the past week they had learned that he was twelve, a tough little Irish scrapper from the Hell's Kitchen section of New York. His name was Jimmy Callaghan.

"What do you mean?" Katherine asked. "Why wouldn't a policeman help us?"

"Wake up for chrissake," Jimmy said with a wiseacre sneer. "You think a cop's gonna believe all that crap about your dear ol' mom and dad? You got another think comin'."

Augustus bridled. "Don't talk to my sister that way. Watch your language."

"And you watch your mouth, boyo, or I'll box your ears."

"Stop it!" Katherine said haughtily. "We are not orphans, and I think Augustus is right. A policeman would too help."

"Whatta laugh," Jimmy chided her. "You're on the Orphan Train and a copper wouldn't buy a word of it. He'd turn you over to Crocker quick as a wink."

"Quiet down," Augustus said, darting his eyes up the aisle. "Here he comes."

Thadius Crocker was a large, portly man with a perpetual scowl. "Breakfast time, boys and girls," he called out in a bogus jolly voice. "Let's rise and shine to a glorious new day."

The attendants followed him along the aisle. One passed out sandwiches while the other ladled milk into battered tin cups from a canister. The sandwiches were jelly and bread, served for breakfast, lunch, and supper. The milk was, as always, lukewarm.

"Look alive," Crocker said cheerily, moving away. "We're stopping in Council Bluffs this morning. Today's your day to find a home."

Augustus opened his sandwich. "Aww, wouldn't you know, it's jelly. I can't eat this again."

"Hand it over then," Jimmy said eagerly. "Anything's better'n nothin'."

"Jimmy's right," Katherine ordered. "You eat that now, Augustus. And drink your milk, too."

Jimmy Callaghan was right about many things. He was crude and foul-mouthed, a product of the impoverished Irish who inhabited Hell's Kitchen. But he had lived on the streets for almost half his life, and he was wise beyond his years. He'd told her all there was to know about the Orphan Train.

The Reverend Charles Loring Brace was the moving force behind the adoption program. A Methodist minister, he believed that vagabond children placed in Christian homes would turn out to be respectable citizens. The solution was to ship them off to the hinterlands, which also removed thousands of urchins from the streets of New York. The Truancy Law gave him the authority and wealthy do-gooders supported the plan with generous donations. He established the Children's Aid Society.

Printed circulars were sent to religious organizations from Ohio to Wyoming. In church meetings, ministers throughout the Midwest and across the Western Plains urged their parishioners to adopt displaced children. The Orphan Train quickly became a rolling adoption agency, the weekly schedule posted in churches and railroad stations at every stop along the way. There were no legal documents involved with a child's placement, but rather a simple verbal agreement by the new parents to provide a good home. Some twenty thousand children were shipped west every year.

Over the past week almost all the children on the train had been adopted. Some went along reluctantly, but others, resigned to their fate, played to the prospective parents and tried to find decent homes. Katherine noticed that boys were more acceptable than girls, and she quickly concocted a plan with Augustus. At every stop, they acted quarrelsome and unruly, passing themselves off as troublemakers. So far, their plan had worked, and they were among the less than fifty children left on the train. No one seemed partial to adopting them.

Shortly before noon, the train chugged into Council Bluffs. The engineer set the brakes, and the train ground to a halt before the depot. A crowd of farmers and towns-people were gathered outside the stationhouse, there to inspect the orphans. Some of the farmers had traveled twenty miles or more by wagon, looking for stout young boys to perform chores and work the fields. Whether moved by Christian charity, or merely drawn by the pros-pect of cheap labor, they edged forward as the train rolled to a stop. Everyone wanted first chance at the pick of the litter.

Thadius Crocker and his attendants ushered their charges off the coaches. The children were herded onto the depot platform, where they were formed into irregu-lar ranks. Katherine, who was still weighing the possi-bility of escape, nudged Augustus and warned him off with a look. There were now ten attendants for fewer than fifty children, and the attendants were posted on the outer ranks of the group. Any thought of escape, at least in Council Bluffs, was clearly out of the question. They would be run down before they reached the end of the platform.

"Brothers and sisters!" Crocker addressed the crowd in a sonorous voice. "Allow me to welcome you on be-half of the Children's Aid Society. We invite you to provide a Christian upbringing for these poor tykes."

The invitation drew blank stares. The crowd was un-certain as to how they should proceed with inspecting the

children. "Let me introduce some of the little darlings,"
Crocker said, like a carnival barker working a midway
show. "Here's a bright lad with a head on his shoulders.
Tommy Noonan, step forward for these good people."

By now, many of the children were anxious to be
adopted. The farther west the train went, the land became
increasingly bleak and inhospitable. Iowa was worse than
Illinois, and no one doubted that Nebraska would be even
more barren. There was talk as well that wild Indians still
roamed the plains of Nebraska. Today seemed a good day
to find a family.

Tommy Noonan was a freckle-faced red-head with a
winning smile. He marched to the front of the group and
recited the Gettysburg Address word for word. One of the
farmers, figuring anyone who could quote Abe Lincoln
was a bargain, quickly latched onto the boy. Crocker took
them aside to settle the arrangements.

A girl stepped forward. She looked to be about thir-
teen, with small, budding breasts, and golden hair that
gave her an angelic appearance. She gulped a deep breath
and sang a stirring rendition of "Onward Christian Soldiers" in a quavering soprano. Some of the crowd thought
she had been coached, but they were nonetheless impressed. She was adopted by a childless couple who
operated the local hardware store.

Katherine and Augustus stood toward the rear of the
group. A farmer and his wife approached, apparently
uninterested in singers or aspiring scholars of Abe Lincoln. They studied the children with a critical gaze, as
though sizing up livestock at an auction. They scarcely
glanced at Katherine, who was obviously too delicate for
farm work. But they thought Augustus looked promising,
and the farmer moved a step closer. He took hold of Augustus, prodding with thorny fingers for shoulder muscle and strength. Katherine jumped between them.

"Leave him alone!" she shrieked, her eyes blazing. "He's not for sale!"

"Out of the way, girlie," the farmer growled. "I'm lookin' at this here boy."

"You keep your filthy hands off my brother!"

One of the attendants, an older man with spectacles, swiftly intervened. "You'll have to excuse her, sir," he said to the farmer. "They're brother and sister, and they prefer not to be separated. She's really a very nice girl."

"Don't want no girl," the farmer grumped. "Got my mind set on a boy."

The farmer selected Jimmy Callaghan instead. Walking away, the Irish youngster looked back over his shoulder at Katherine and Augustus. He gave them a sly grin and a slow wink, as if to say the farmer had made the mistake of his life. They disappeared into the crowd.

Within the hour, eleven children had been adopted. The farmers and townspeople gradually drifted away, leading the new additions to their families. Crocker and his staff herded the remaining children back aboard the train. The engineer tooted his whistle and the station-master signaled from the end of the platform. The loco-motive lurched forward with a belch of steam.

Otto Richter was standing at the rear of the train. He swung aboard the last passenger coach just as the con-ductor was about to shut the door. He moved through the vestibule and into the coach, and found Turk Johnson eating a bag of peanuts. He slumped wearily into the seat.

Johnson cracked a peanut shell. "Any luck, boss?"

"No," Richter said stiffly. "They pulled their usual brother-and-sister act. That girl's enough to scare anyone off."

"What if nobody adopts 'em?"

"We have our orders, Turk."

"Be a shame," Johnson said, munching absently on a peanut. "You know, after we've brought 'em all this way."

Richter nodded. "Let's hope it doesn't come to that."

The Orphan Train crossed the line into Nebraska.

CHAPTER 4

THE LAST day of the royal hunt was an extravaganza of bloodsport. The Grand Duke Alexis was sated with killing, having downed thirty-three buffalo in five days. Cody arranged entertainment of a different sort.

The Indians rode into camp late that morning. Spotted Tail, chief of the Brule Sioux, led a hundred warriors mounted on fleet buffalo ponies. His band was currently at peace with the government, but he trusted no white man beyond certain limits. His warriors pitched camp on the opposite side of Red Willow Creek.

Phil Sheridan was of a like mind. He ordered Custer to turn out the troops, and two companies were kept on alert at all times. Custer's reputation was that of a man who could start a war simply for his own amusement. Yet the Sioux respected his ability as a field commander, and even more, his physical courage. The Grand Duke was safe with Custer in the role of watchdog.

Cody thought the vigilance unwarranted. Late yesterday, with the day's hunt ended, he'd sensed that Alexis was bored with killing buffalo. He talked it over with Hickok, and together, they'd convinced Sheridan to make the last day a memorable day. Cody knew that Spotted Tail's band was camped on the Republican River, some thirty miles to the west. After dark, he had made the ride aboard Buckskin Joe and counseled with the Brule chief. The upshot was a hundred Sioux braves gathered opposite the army compound.

Spotted Tail was intrigued by the idea of a great chief from a distant land. He had some vague notion of a vast water to the east, what the whites called the Atlantic Ocean. Cody impressed on him that Alexis was somewhat like the Great White Father in Washington. Though Spotted Tail was mystified about the faraway place known as Russia, he nonetheless grasped that the Grand Duke was the ruler of a powerful tribe. Still, it was Cody's skill at bartering, rather than Spotted Tail's curiosity, that brought the Sioux to Red Willow Creek. He had promised the Brule leader a hundred pounds of tobacco.

Sheridan considered it extortion. "For God's sake!" he fumed. "How am I going to justify a wagonload of tobacco?"

"All in a good cause," Cody said. "President Grant wanted the Grand Duke looked after. Today'll be the icing on the cake."

"Well, it's expensive icing, Mr. Cody."

"No more so than turnin' out the regiment for escort duty. Besides, Spotted Tail and his boys wouldn't have come otherwise. I'd say we got ourselves a bargain."

"Damn the bargain," Custer interrupted waspishly. "We should have ordered him in and had done with it. He could hardly refuse."

"Don't bet on it," Hickok countered. "I wouldn't exactly call the Brule tame Injuns."

Custer, like Hickok and Cody, wore his hair shoulder-length. He was the most flamboyant general in the army, not to mention the youngest, and overly proud of his reputation as an Indian fighter. He cocked his head with a haughty smirk.

"Hostile or tame, who cares?" he said derisively. "Give me a regiment and I'll ride through the Sioux nation. Brule, Hunkpapa, Oglala, the whole lot!"

"Gen'ral, you might be surprised," Hickok said. "They're a pretty scrappy bunch."

"Wild Bill, I'm disappointed in you. I thought you enjoyed a good fight."

Sheridan silenced them with a look. "Gentlemen, I suggest we defer that discussion for another day. Our mission at the moment is to entertain the Grand Duke." He glanced at Cody. "How do you propose to go about this?"

"Let's have a powwow," Cody said lightly. "The Grand Duke's never met a real live redskin. We'll let him palaver with Spotted Tail for a while. That'll make a story when he gets back to Russia."

"No doubt," Sheridan said dryly. "And after their . . . powwow?"

"Got it all fixed. Spotted Tail and his boys will show him how the Sioux hunt buffalo. Ought to be a regular lollapaloosa."

"All right, Mr. Cody, bring on the vaunted leader of the Brule. Tell him I expect him to earn all that tobacco."

"Yessir."

Cody swung into the saddle. He forded the creek atop Buckskin Joe and returned some ten minutes later with the Brule chief. Spotted Tail was in his early fifties, with flat, dark features, and an eagle feather affixed to his coal-black hair. He rode a magnificent chocolate-spotted pinto.

Alexis, along with Hickok and the generals, waited by an open fire in the center of the compound. Cody, acting as interpreter, introduced the Grand Duke and the Brule chief with great fanfare. Once they were seated on the ground, a camp orderly served everyone coffee in galvanized mugs. Spotted Tail laced his coffee with four heaping spoons of sugar.

"Perhaps he would prefer vodka," Alexis suggested. "I think he does not like our coffee."

"Not that, Your Highness," Cody said. "Injuns have

just got a powerful sweet tooth, that's all. Liquor wouldn't be a good idea, anyhow."

"Oh, why not?"

"Well, no tellin' what a drunk Injun might do. Tends to make 'em a little loco."

Spotted Tail drained his mug. He smacked his lips with satisfaction and rattled off a guttural question to Cody. The scout turned to Alexis.

"I told him last night where you're from. He wants to know if you have red men in Russia."

"None quite like him," Alexis observed thoughtfully. "The Tatars from the east overran Mother Russia in ancient times. My ancestors drove them back perhaps three centuries ago. Some still live in the province we call Siberia."

Spotted Tail listened to the translation with great interest, nodding sagely. Then he spoke at length, gesturing off to the east, and Cody repeated his words. "He says his country has also been overrun from where the sun rises. Only in his case, it was white men who took the land. He says the whites are as leaves on the trees—too many to fight."

"Is he not a warrior chief?"

"One of the worst there ever was. 'Course, now he's what's called a 'peace chief.'"

"I do not understand this . . . peace chief?"

Cody briefly explained. Spotted Tail was a famed war chief who had fought the encroachment of white men on Sioux lands from 1854 to 1868. But finally, convinced it was a fight that could not be won, he signed a peace treaty and led the Brules onto a reservation in southern Dakota Territory. He had kept the peace for almost four years.

The Brules, Cody went on, were allowed to leave the reservation and hunt buffalo along the Republican River. Among army men, Spotted Tail was considered the wisest of the old war chiefs, for the people of his band would survive the deadly conflict on the Western Plains. Yet, despite having yielded to the whites, he remained exalted as a warrior among all the Sioux, even with tribal leaders who continued the struggle. One of those was his nephew, the young war chief of the Oglala band, Crazy Horse.

"What a strange name," Alexis remarked. "Why is he called Crazy Horse?"

"I don't rightly know. Maybe it's because he's always on the prod. He does like a fight."

"Would Spotted Tail ever join his nephew in battle?"

Cody smiled. "Well, sir, I just suspect not. You see, he's crazy like a fox."

Spotted Tail, who understood more English than he pretended, nodded wisely. The Grand Duke caught the sly look, and the two men exchanged a quick glance. Then Spotted Tail held out his mug for more coffee.

Alexis thought the Brule leader was indeed crazy as a fox. Old and crafty, a man who fought no fight he could not win. And in doing so, won.

The hunting party forded Red Willow Creek early that afternoon. Spotted Tail and the Grand Duke, flanked by Hickok and Cody, rode out front. Sheridan and the generals were a short distance behind.

To the rear, perhaps a hundred yards off to the west, were the Brule warriors. They rode in a loose phalanx, their lances and carbines glinting in the afternoon sun. Off to the east, two troops of cavalry rode parallel with the Indians. Their orders were to provide a protective escort for the Grand Duke.

Some while later the party topped a low hogback ridge. Spread out before them was a wide plain bordered on the south by a broad, steep-walled arroyo. A herd of a thousand or more buffalo dotted the prairie, grazing on winter grass the color of coarse straw. The arroyo appeared to be a mile or so beyond the herd.

The purpose of today's outing was to present a spectacle few white men had ever seen. The Grand Duke Alexis was to witness the manner in which the Plains Tribes traditionally hunted buffalo. Even more, he was to observe the skill with which ancient weapons were used to down the shaggy beasts. The Brule Sioux prided themselves on being great hunters.

"Watch close now, Your Highness," Cody said, pointing off to the band of warriors. "See that short, stumpy feller on the chestnut stallion? His name's Running Dog and he's a holy terror with a bow and arrow. Keep your eye on him."

Spotted Tail waved his coup stick overhead, then motioned forward. The warriors urged their ponies off the ridge and rode out onto the grassy plain. They split into two columns, kicking their mounts into a steady trot. One column fanned east of the herd and the other angled off to the west They gigged their horses into a gallop.

The herd wheeled away from the headlong charge of yipping horsemen. Running Dog rode in the vanguard of the western column, maneuvering his pony with the pressure of his knees. As he pulled alongside a large cow, he drew his heavy ashwood bow to full curve and released a steel-tipped arrow. The arrow sliced into the cow behind her right shoulder and drove clean though, exiting below her left leg. The cow faltered in mid-stride, wobbling to a stop. She collapsed onto the ground.

"*Amazing!*" Alexis bellowed, standing in his stirrups. "The arrow passed all the way through."

"Told you he was a terror," Cody said, grinning. "Now keep your eye peeled for a tall feller on a bay gelding. Goes by the name of Black Elk. He's hell with a lance."

The herd swerved west as the lead buffalo neared the arroyo. The warriors yipped louder, still hugging the flanks at a gallop, and drove the herd back toward the ridge. Black Elk kneed his gelding into position, singling out a huge bull. His lance was ten feet long, with a steel head honed to a daggerlike point. He leaned forward, adding the momentum of a charging horse to the weight of the lance, and thrust the point into the bull's heart. He reined aside, leaving the lance planted to the hilt as the bull slowed to a walk. Then, already dead on its feet, the bull crashed to the earth in a thick puff of dust.

"Stuck him good," Hickok said with some admiration. "Never saw it done better."

Alexis looked astounded. "There is a majesty in such a feat. To kill . . . savagely."

"Sight to behold," Cody agreed. "Not one I'd want to try. Takes some powerful doing."

The balance of the afternoon was spent watching warriors attempt to outdo one another. Their horse-back skills were a thing of wonder, almost magical, and not one in five missed with the bow or lance. Yet none of them were able to match the hunting powers of either Running Dog or Black Elk. They downed forty-nine buffalo, and unlike white men, who killed for sport, nothing would be wasted. The winter robes and freshly butchered meat would be hauled back to their village on the Republican River.

By sundown the evening meal had been served to the royal party in the dining tent. Troopers stacked logs on the firepit in the center of the compound, and presently a blazing bonfire lit the camp. Orderlies rushed to arrange a row of chairs outside the dining tent, with a commanding view of the area around the fire. The evening's entertainment was to be an authentic scalp dance,

performed by Spotted Tail and his Brule Sioux. Alexis
was given the place of honor.

"You're in for a treat," Cody said, leaning closer to the
Grand Duke. "The Sioux set some store by the scalp
dance. Pretty near a holy thing."

"This ritual?' Alexis asked. "Do I understand they
perform it to celebrate killing their enemies?"

"Yessir, that's a good part of it," Cody replied.
"'Course, there's times they'll honor the bravery of the
poor devils that got their scalps took. Ought to be quite
a show."

Sheridan laughed. "You can credit what he's saying,
Your Highness. Cody knows the show business."

"Show business?" Alexis said doubtfully. "I am not familiar with the term, General."

"Stage show," Sheridan explained. "Something like an
opera without the music. Our Mr. Cody is a bit of an
actor."

"How interesting." Alexis said, turning to Cody. "I see
you are a man of many parts. Where do you perform
these stage shows?"

"New York City, mostly," Cody informed him. "The
hostiles hole up during the winter and scouting gets a
little slow. I generally go back East a couple months."

Ned Buntline, the dime novel writer, also penned
plays based on Cody's frontier exploits. Last year, for the
first time, Cody had gone East to appear in a stage production. He was a scout by profession, but he enjoyed
what he thought of as a dalliance with the stage. He liked
the money as well.

Alexis glanced over at Hickok. "Are you also a showman, Wild Bill?"

"No, sir, it ain't my callin'," Hickok said with a sardonic smile. "I leave all the playacting to Cody. He's the
Shakespeare of the bunch."

Cody groaned. "You'll have to excuse him, Your Highness. He's just a mite jealous."

Before Alexis could reply, Spotted Tail and his Brule Sioux appeared at the edge of the compound. Their faces were streaked with war paint, and they were armed with tomahawks and stone-headed war clubs. Drums throbbed ominously in the distance and several of the warriors loosened blood-curdling howls. They began stomping around the fire to the beat of the drums.

Alexis idly wondered if Buffalo Bill had orchestrated the performance.

CHAPTER 5

A HAWK floated past on smothered wings, briefly silhouetted against a bright forenoon sun. The weather was
crisp, creeks rimed with patches of ice, a brisk wind out
of the north. The rolling plains swept onward like a saf-
fron ocean of grass.

Cody held the reins of four spirited cavalry horses.
The open carriage was double-seated, with the heavy
springs designed for cross-country travel. Hickok shared
the driver's seat, and like Cody, wore a high-collared
mackinaw. Sheridan and the Grand Duke were in the
back seat, bundled in greatcoats and woolen scarves. A
buffalo robe was thrown across their legs.

Alexis was still nursing a hangover. Two nights ago,
to celebrate the end of the hunt, he'd over-indulged himself on champagne. To the delight of everyone in camp,
he had joined Spotted Tail and the Brule Sioux in their
scalp dance. He proved to be agile, despite his size, and
he'd introduced some Cossack leaps and whirls that fascinated the warriors. Spotted Tail pronounced him a
great chief.

The next morning, the army broke camp. North Platte,
a town some fifty miles to the north, was the nearest railhead. A private train awaited Alexis, and the trip to the
depot would consume the better part of two days. From
North Platte, he would travel to New York City, where
wealthy socialites planned a formal ball in his honor. The
Russian battle fleet, which had escorted him to America,
was anchored off Manhattan Island. He was to sail for
his homeland in a week's time.

Today, their second day on the trail, Alexis seemed somewhat improved. Last night, when they camped thirty miles north of Red Willow Creek, he had switched from champagne to vodka. All morning he'd been sipping from a flask, and the stronger spirits worked a curative effect. Champagne, he explained without irony, was an insidious drink, whereas vodka restored fire to a man's soul. His rosy cheeks seemed to prove the point.

"Unusual weather," Sheridan said, trying to make conversation. "We've had only one snowfall of any significance this winter. Not typical of the plains."

"Come with me to Moscow," Alexis said with wry good humor. "I daresay there is several feet of snow on the ground. We Russians pride ourselves on the harshness of our winters."

"We could certainly use some of that here. A hard snow would drive the hostiles into winter camp. They'll continue to raid as long as the weather holds."

Phil Sheridan was a soldier who believed in taking the fight to the enemy. During the Civil War, his cavalry had laid waste to the Shenandoah Valley, routing Confederate forces in a brilliant campaign. He was frustrated by the will-o'-the-wisp tactics of the Sioux and the Northern Cheyenne. Hit-and-run was not his idea of a war.

"These hostiles," Alexis said, as though testing the word. "What do they hope to accomplish by raiding farmers and transport lines? How can they defeat your army unless they force a battle?"

Sheridan barked a harsh laugh. "Your Highness, you've put your thumb on the problem. Indians will avoid a full-scale battle at all costs. They harass us instead with these damnedable raids."

"The general's right," Cody said from the front seat. "Not their way to stand and fight, even when you track 'em down. They're skirmishers, strictly hit-and-run."

"Tough buggers, all the same," Hickok added. "I recollect somebody called 'em the finest light cavalry in the world. Wasn't them your words, Gen'ral?"

"Yes, that's correct," Sheridan said curtly. "But the Grand Duke made the salient point a moment ago. Light cavalry will never win a war unless they come to battle."

Hickok shrugged. "Well, maybe they don't figure to win. Maybe they're just tryin' to hold their own."

Sheridan fell silent. He turned in the seat, looking back at Custer and the other generals, their horses held to a walk behind the carriage. Beyond them, the companies of the Fifth Regiment were strung out in a long column. Not once, in all his years on the plains, had he been able to engage the Indians in battle with a full regiment. Hickok, he told himself, saw the problem with a certain finite clarity. The hostiles were fighting a holding action.

Sometimes he slept poorly, his dreams a stew of misgiving. He admired the Indians in many ways, and indeed, he believed them to be the finest light cavalry ever seen by man. All too often he felt personally sullied by the government's record of broken treaties, lies piled upon lies. But history was a litany of one people conquering another, frequently for spoils and inevitably to claim the land. However much he admired the Indians, he was a soldier no less than the Roman generals of ancient times. The Western Plains were his Egypt.

Alexis was also impressed by Hickok's insightful remark about the hostiles. He leaned forward in his seat. "I have been meaning to ask, Wild Bill. What are your plans now that our hunt has concluded?"

"Likely back to Kansas," Hickok said, twisting around. "There's a cowtown I just suspect will be needin' a marshal. Place called Ellsworth."

"Yes, of course," Alexis said, intrigued by the thought.

"I have read a good deal of your Texas cowboys. Are they as ferocious as reported?"

Hickok chuckled. "I don't know as I'd call 'em ferocious. Texans ain't got sense enough to come in out of the rain. That and liquor puts 'em crosswise of the law."

"So, then, you will return to marshaling. *Da*?"

"Well, cattle season don't start till June. I doubt Ellsworth will be hirin' much before May."

Alexis considered a moment. "Would you be offended if I asked you a personal question?"

"No, I reckon not," Hickok said. "Go ahead, ask away."

"Have you ever found it necessary to kill a cowboy?"

"I shot a Texan last summer in Abilene. Gamblin' man by the name of Phil Coe. But to answer your question— no cowboys."

"I see," Alexis said. "May I ask why?"

"Not worth the trouble," Hickok observed. "I generally just toss 'em in the hoosgow. They sober up by mornin'."

"We're there," Cody broke in. "North Platte just ahead."

The carriage crested a small hill. Though it was the county seat, North Platte was a community of less than two thousand people. The town was largely an extension of the railroad tracks, a center of trade for farmers and ranchers. The Union Pacific depot was south of the tracks, with fewer than a dozen buildings scattered at random nearby. The business district was north of the tracks, surrounded by a grid of streets dotted with houses. A train, chuffing smoke, stood on a siding by the depot.

"How about it, General?" Cody called out. "Want to deliver the Grand Duke in style?"

Sheridan appeared uncertain. "What do you have in mind?"

"Let's take 'em by storm!"

Cody popped the reins with a sharp snap. The horses jumped in the traces and took off at a pounding lope. The carriage jounced and swayed as they careened down the hillside, the wheels striking the ground every ten feet or so. Custer pumped his arm overhead, signaling the troop commanders at the rear. The cavalry broke into a gallop.

They roared into North Platte at a full charge.

The private coach was elegance on wheels. The interior was paneled in rosewood, with plush armchairs and a massive leather sofa. A Persian carpet covered the floor, and to the rear was a private bedroom and lavatory. Directly forward was a single passenger coach, and beyond that a dining car. The kitchen was ruled by a French chef.

James Gordon Bennett, publisher of the *New York Herald*, owned the private coach. Bennett was a man of immense wealth and power, and he had provided the train for the Grand Duke's hunting trip. Hickok was nonplussed by the lavish accommodations, but Cody took it all in stride. A year ago he'd served as guide on a buffalo hunt for Bennett and several of New York's more prominent businessmen. He recalled only too well that the rich liked to travel in style.

The train was ready to roll. Sheridan and Custer and the other generals were to accompany the Grand Duke as far as St. Louis. Headquarters for the Division of the Missouri, Sheriden's command, was located there, and the generals would return to duty. Alexis, now playing the role of host, turned his attention from the officers to Cody and Hickok. His Cossack manservant appeared with wrapped boxes and he presented each of them with gifts. For Cody there was a bag of gold coins and jeweled cufflinks. Hickok opened his box to find a diamond stickpin.

"Well, now," Cody said, hefting the bag of gold.

"That's mighty generous, Your Highness. I'm plumb obliged."

"Same goes here," Hickok said, clearly surprised. "Didn't expect nothin' like this."

Alexis beamed. "Consider it a token of my appreciation. You have given me a hunt I will never forget. I return to Russia with many fond memories."

The Grand Duke walked them to the rear of the coach. He embraced each of them with a backslapping bear hug and shook their hands in farewell. As they started down the steps, a westbound train ground to a halt outside the depot. The royal train got underway, waiting for a switchman to throw the bar on the siding, and pulled onto the main tracks. Alexis waved to them from the door of the private coach.

"Fine feller," Hickok noted as the train gathered speed. "Never once put on any airs, did he?"

Cody nodded. "Not all that bad a shot, either. Got the hang of it pretty quick."

"You came away like a Mexican bandit. How much you got in that bag of gold?"

"Looks to be five hundred or so. I'm buyin' the drinks."

"Let's find ourselves a saloon."

The troopers of the Fifth Cavalry were ordered to mount their horses. Fort McPherson was some fifteen miles southeast of town, and the major in charge of the detail wanted to arrive there by nightfall. Cody spoke with him briefly, indicating that he planned to stay over in North Platte a couple of nights. A trooper was assigned to drive the carriage at the end of the column.

Cody and Hickok started across the tracks, leading their horses. As they rounded the locomotive of the westbound train, they saw a group of farmers on the platform outside the depot. Their attention was drawn to six bedraggled children, lined up and standing apart, as though on display. A large portly man was addressing the farmers in a mellifluous voice.

"Brothers and sisters!" Thadius Crocker said to the farmers. "Welcome on behalf of the Children's Aid Society. These poor little orphans"—he paused, gesturing to the children—"are here looking for good homes. We ask you to open your hearts in Christian charity."

Their curiosity whetted, Cody and Hickok stopped to watch. They had heard of the Orphan Train, but they'd never seen one until today. The children appeared to them somehow pitiful, dirty and plainly disheartened, dressed in tattered clothing. Hickok noticed a girl and boy standing slightly apart from the other children. He thought they looked like wild young colts ready to bolt.

Augustus was no less aware of the two plainsmen. His eyes darted over their buckskin outfits, their shiny pistols, and their broad-brimmed hats. Then, his gaze drawn to their shoulder-length hair, something snapped in his mind. He studied their faces, one with a mustache and the other with a mustache and goatee, and suddenly he knew. He'd seen those faces many times before, in pen-and-ink drawings. On the covers of dime novels!

"*Look,*" he hissed to Katherine, barely able to contain himself. "It's Wild Bill Hickok and Buffalo Bill Cody. The Heroes of the Plains!"

Katherine glanced at him with no great interest. "How on earth could you know that? You're imagining things."

"No, I'm not either. It's them."

"All right, then, it's them. Who cares?"

Katherine was beside herself with fear. For the past two days the Orphan Train had steamed westward through Nebraska. With each stop at some barren depot, more and more of the children had been adopted. There were only six left, herself and Augustus included, and she had no idea how far they were from New York. She felt lost and deserted, and ached desperately for the sight of her parents. She bit her tongue not to burst out in tears.

There were more farmers than children on the platform. The moment Crocker stopped talking, the farmers surged forward, intent on leaving with a child. One of them, a rawboned man with beady eyes and hard features, roughly elbowed the others aside and strode directly to Augustus and Katherine. He clapped a hand squarely on the boy's shoulder.

"I'll take this one," he said, motioning to Crocker. "Make him into a farmer in no time. Give him a good home, too."

"You will not!" Katherine screeched in a shrill voice. "You leave him alone!"

Thadius Crocker rushed to intervene. "You'll have to excuse the outburst. May I ask your name, sir?"

"Homer Ledbetter."

"Well, you see, they're brother and sister, Mr. Ledbetter Perhaps you would consider taking both. I assure you they are hard workers."

"I dunno—" Ledbetter stared at Katherine a moment, then bobbed his head. "Yeah, sure, I'll take 'em off your hands. My missus needs a girl in the kitchen, anyways."

"You won't regret it," Crocker said, pleased to be rid of the obstreperous girl and her brother. "All I require is your solemn vow that you will give them a Christian upbringing and never mistreat them. Do you so swear?"

"We are not orphans!" Katherine squalled. "Why won't you believe me?"

"Feisty, ain't she?" Ledbetter with a sour smile. "Well, don't make no nevermind. My missus'll straighten her out."

"Bless you, brother," Crocker said hurriedly. "You've done the Lord's work here today."

The farmer took hold of Augustus. When he reached for Katherine, she resisted and he grabbed her by the wrist. He dragged her kicking to the end of the platform and lifted her unceremoniously into a wagon. Then he hefted Augustus aboard and climbed into the driver's seat, clucking to his team as he gathered the reins. The boy stared back at Hickok and Cody as the wagon disappeared around the side of the depot.

"Damn shame," Hickok said, his eyes cold. "That sorry bastard will work 'em into the ground. He come here to find cheap labor."

"No Christian charity there," Cody agreed. "Don't think I'd want to be an orphan."

"You can say that again."

"Well, let's get ourselves a drink. I'm still buyin'."

"Lead the way, ol' scout."

They walked off toward the center of North Platte.

CHAPTER 6

HICKOK AND Cody emerged from the Cedar House shortly after sundown. The hotel was located at the intersection of First and Locust, a block north of the train station. Directly across the street was the town's only livery stable.

The plainsmen had taken a room at the hotel earlier that afternoon. Fortified by several rounds of rye whiskey, they felt the need to refurbish themselves. A scalding bath removed the trail dust, and a shave at the tonsorial parlor left them smelling of bay rum. They were prepared for a night on the town.

Their first stop was the Bon Ton Café. Hickok lived by the maxim that a full stomach offset the deleterious effects of John Barleycorn. Years ago, he'd taught Cody that a balance of solid food and snakehead whiskey was the secret to steady nerves. They ordered blood-red beefsteak with fried potatoes, canned tomatoes, and sourdough biscuits. A toothpick finished off the meal.

Outside again, they stood surveying their options. Locust Street was the main thoroughfare, crowded with shops and stores, and at the north end, was the county courthouse. The nightlife revolved around three saloons, one of which they'd sampled that afternoon, and a smaller dive devoted solely to the town's drunks. The third establishment was a gaming den and watering hole with hurdy-gurdy girls. They turned upstreet.

The Tivoli occupied the northeast corner of Locust and Fourth. The strains of a banjo and a rinky-dink piano were mixed with the squealing laughter of women.

Opposite a mahogany bar were faro layouts, dice, roulette, and three tables reserved for poker. Flanking the backbar mirror were the ubiquitous paintings of nude voluptuaries romping through pastoral fields. A small dance floor at the rear was crowded with couples who stomped about in time to the music.

Cody was a regular patron of the Tivoli. Everyone in town was aware of the royal hunt for the Grand Duke Alexis, which had been widely reported in the local newspaper. They were aware as well that Wild Bill Hickok, the deadliest pistol shot in the West, had been a member of the hunting party. Several men at the bar greeted Cody by name, and after ordering drinks, he introduced them to Hickok. The men shook hands as though a lion tamer had suddenly dropped into their midst.

Three girls joined them at the bar. The women wore peekaboo gowns, cut short on the bottom and their breasts spilling out of the top. Cody, who was handsomer than Hickok, and a better talker, invariably attracted women. He possessed all the social graces and casually presented himself as an educated man. In truth, his education had been gleaned from reading Chaucer and everything written by Charles Dickens. He'd learned how to spin a tale by studying the masters.

Hickok, by contrast, seemed almost coarse. He was taciturn, with a saturnine wit, and given to pungent language. Certain women were attracted to him in the way a cobra uncoils from a basket, drawn by the danger. But he begrudged his younger friend nothing, and even took amusement in watching the byplay. Cody was married, though he seldom advertised the fact, and boyishly faithful to his wife. For all his appeal to the ladies, it never went beyond talk. He was simply a born showoff.

"You've never seen anything like it," he said, the girls hanging on his every word. "The Grand Duke of all the Russias and a whole passel of Sioux. What a sight!"

"Tell us," a buxom brunette trilled. "Were the Indians on the warpath?"

Cody, an audience at hand, plunged into a wild tale of derring-do. Hickok figured the story would hold the crowd spellbound for a good part of the evening. He lit a cheroot, puffing a thick cloud of smoke, and wandered across to the poker tables. His own education ran more to the pasteboards than to books, and he freely admitted he'd never read Charles Dickens. Yet where cards were concerned, he considered himself something of a scholar. He knew all the tricks of the trade.

One of the first tenets was that every game was assumed to be crooked. A poker table served as a lure to cardsharps, ever on the lookout for an easy score. One of their favorite dodges was to introduce a marked deck into a game, "readers" with secret symbols on the backs of the cards. Another trick was shaved cards, trimmed along the sides, or cards with slightly rounded corners, employed by those with the dexterity to deal from the bottom. A tinhorn, no less than a magician, relied on sleight of hand.

Hickok stopped at one of the tables. There was an empty chair and he nodded to the other players. "You gents mind fresh money?"

The men exchanged glances, and one of them grinned around a cigar wedged in the corner of his mouth. "We're honored to have you in the game, Mr. Hickok. Pull up a chair."

The rules were dealer's choice, restricted to five-card stud and five-card draw. Ante was five dollars, with a twenty-dollar limit and three raises. Check and raise was permitted, which made it cutthroat poker and a game perfectly suited to Hickok's style. He prided himself that other men seldom knew what he held.

"Everybody ante," the man with the cigar said. "Draw poker, jacks or better to open."

Hickok, inscrutable as a sphinx, caught three queens on the deal.

The night was clear and bitterly cold, a bone-white crescent moon floating on the horizon. Augustus paused in the shadows, where the rutted wagon road merged with the street in front of the train station. He slowly scanned the depot for any sign of life.

A single lamp burned in the window of the office. He saw a man slouched in a chair, chin on his chest, fast asleep. Somewhere in the distance a dog barked, setting off a chorus of howls on the west side of town. He waited, listening, until the commotion died down.

"All right," he said. "Let's go on."

Katherine stepped from the shadows. She was shivering, the wind cutting through her threadbare coat. "Are you sure it's safe?"

"I got you this far, didn't I?"

She couldn't argue the point. Augustus seemed to have some sixth sense for direction, even in the dark of night. The faint moonglow afforded little light, and yet he had found the crossroads some miles to the east, and instinctively turned west. He'd brought them again to North Platte.

Their escape was no less the work of Augustus. Late that afternoon, upon arriving at Homer Ledbetter's farm, they'd discovered that he lived in a sod house. Neither of them had ever heard of a house constructed from grassy chunks of soil cut from the earth. Nor were they prepared for what they found inside the house.

Ledbetter's wife was a crone with a sharp tongue and a nasty disposition. She had immediately put Katherine to tending a cookstove in the windowless, one-room sod house. Katherine just as quickly became queasy from the stench of unwashed bodies in a confined space. Her mind reeled when she realized she was standing on a *dirt* floor.

The Ledbetter's only child, a son, was a chunky twelve-year-old with a mean streak. He took charge of Augustus and put him to work unharnessing the team of horses. Afterward, he supervised as Augustus carried firewood from the wood pile to the house, all the while bullying him in a hectoring voice. By suppertime, Augustus was ready to crown the boy with a stick of firewood.

Homer Ledbetter proved to be a petty tyrant. He sat at the head of the table, and his wife dutifully served his plate before anyone else. The boy acted cowed in his father's presence, as though he expected a beating if he opened his mouth. Supper was a tasteless stew, thick with grease, and a platter of fried cornmeal dodgers. Katherine and Augustus wished again for the jelly sandwiches on the Orphan Train. They picked at their food.

All during the meal Ledbetter lectured them on their new duties. Augustus would muck out the barn, split and haul firewood, and take care of general chores. Katherine would tend to the henhouse, work in the kitchen, and keep the house itself in order. Their duties were those of servants, and Ledbetter was a man who tolerated nothing less than obedience. His mouth stuffed with food, he pointed to a leather razor strop hanging on the wall. The penalty for disobedience was a proper hiding.

There was too little room in the house for Katherine and Augustus. After supper, Ledbetter showed them their sleeping quarters, a storage shed near the barn. They were given moldy quilts and told to be ready to start work at daylight. Almost as an after-thought, Ledbetter motioned to a rickety privy behind the house, and explained that dried corn shucks were a farmer's toilet paper. He seemed amused by the expression on their faces, and left them to arrange their bedding. Katherine promised herself she would burst before she went near the privy.

The lamps were extinguished in the house shortly after a sickle moon rose in the sky. Augustus, who was wrapped in one of the quilts, watched through a crack between the boards of the shed. His voice shaky with bravado, he informed Katherine that he wouldn't be held in slavery; he was determined to escape. She was frightened, fearful they would be caught and punished, even more fearful of the life awaiting them if they didn't run. They waited only long enough to ensure that the homesteader and his family were asleep. Then they took off.

The track leading from the house eventually connected with a crossroads several miles to the south. Augustus, following some inner compass, confidently turned onto the road to the west. They had no idea how far they'd walked, or for that matter, where they were. They were cold, exhausted by their ordeal, but driven by the urge to escape. Some hours later, almost miraculously, they saw the light of the lamp in the North Platte depot. Their relief was momentary, for their journey was not yet over.

"I'm so cold," Katherine said wearily. "Couldn't we stop and get warm in the train station?"

Augustus squared his shoulders. "We have to find Buffalo Bill and Wild Bill. They'll know what to do."

"But how on earth will we find them? They might be anywhere."

"We just have to look and keep on looking, that's all."

The town was dark, forbiddingly still. The only lights visible were those from a few buildings along the main street. Augustus took Katherine's hand and they walked north toward the lights. There was no-where else to turn.

Faintly, off in the distance, they heard the strains of a piano.

Cody was in his glory. The crowd around the bar listened raptly as he regaled them with yet another whopper. The hour was approaching midnight, and he'd held them mesmerized throughout the evening. They kept him supplied with whiskey and he spun tales, real and imagined, from his days on the plains. He thought he could talk forever.

Hickok was on a streak. A mound of double eagles and assorted gold coins was piled before him on the table. All night he'd drawn unbeatable hands, edging out players who themselves held strong cards. On those occasions when he bluffed, the other players were so snake-bit that they folded, convinced he had the goods. He calculated he was ahead by at least three hundred.

The piano player suddenly trailed off in the middle of a tune. Beside him, the banjo player strummed on a moment then hit a jarring chord. The few couples left on the dance floor skittered to a halt, caught off balance as the music ended. Cody stopped talking, and Hickok paused in the midst of a bet, and the crowd at the bar abruptly drew back in surprise. Their eyes were fixed on the door.

Augustus and Katherine stepped into the saloon. For an instant, caught in the wondering stares and tomblike quiet, they stood frozen in place. Then a light of recognition flashed over the boy's features and his mouth parted in a sappy smile. He tugged Katherine forward.

"Buffalo Bill! Wild Bill!" he shouted vigorously. "We thought we'd never find you!"

Hickok and Cody exchanged a bewildered look. After a moment, Hickok rose from the poker table and moved to the bar. He stopped beside Cody.

"Well, young feller," he said softly. "What brings you and the little lady out on a cold night? Why're you lookin' for us?"

"We saw you at the train station," Augustus said in a fit of agitation. "This morning, when that farmer took us off in his wagon. Don't you remember, Wild Bill?"

"By golly, that's right," Cody chimed in, staring down at the boy. "You're the brother and sister that got off the Orphan Train."

"We are *not* orphans," Katherine said stridently. "You have to believe us."

Cody knelt down, on eye level with her. "What's your name, little missy?"

"I am Katherine Stanley. And this is my brother, Augustus. We are from New York City."

"So how'd you come to be on the Orphan Train? I mean, if it's like you say, that you're not orphans."

"We were abducted from our parents."

"Abducted?" Hickok said, watching her closely. "You was stole from your folks?"

"We were!" Augustus yelped. "I swear we were!"

Katherine suddenly became aware of the saloon girls. Her eyes went round as she stared at their exposed bosoms and their legs revealed by the short skirts. Cody failed to notice, his gaze still fixed on the boy. He leaned closer.

"Would you swear it on a stack of Bibles, young feller?"

"Yes, sir," Augustus said solemnly. "You know I wouldn't lie to you, Buffalo Bill."

"How would I know that?"

"Because you and Wild Bill are the Heroes of the Plains. Cross my heart and hope to die before I'd lie to you."

Cody flushed with pride. He stood, glancing at Hickok. "I think they're tellin' the truth."

"Yep," Hickok grunted. "So do I."

"What do we do now?"

"I reckon this here's a matter for the law. We'll let these tads tell their story to the proper authorities."

"Try the courthouse," the bartender suggested. "Two of Sheriff Walker's deputies are down with the grippe. He's tending the jail himself tonight."

Hickok nodded. "Sounds like he's our man. That suit you, young Mr. Stanley?"

"Yes, sir, Wild Bill," Augustus said quickly. "You and Buffalo Bill know what's best."

"How about you, little Miss Stanley? You willin' to have a talk with the sheriff?"

Katherine tore her eyes away from the breasts of a tall brunette. Her features went crimson and she shyly looked down at the floor. "Oh, yes, thank you so much, Wild Bill."

Hickok glanced at the bartender. "Collect my stake off that poker table. I'll be back directly."

"I'll look after it, Mr. Hickok."

"Obliged," Hickok said, turning to Cody. "C'mon, Hero of the Plains, let's go do our duty."

Cody grinned. "What the boy said was 'Heroes.' You're rowin' the same boat."

"Don't remind me."

They led Augustus and Katherine from the saloon.

CHAPTER 7

SHERIFF JACK Walker stared at the two men seated before his desk. His office was in the basement of the courthouse, with a holding pen for drunks and four jail cells down the hall. The clock on the wall opposite his desk moved steadily toward midnight.

The purpose of the late-night call was as yet unclear. But the man named Otto Richter was well dressed and well spoken, and obviously the one in charge. The other man, introduced simply as Mr. Johnson, was just as plainly a toughnut, the muscle rather than the brains. Which made the sheriff wonder why Richter needed a bodyguard.

"What can I do for you?" Walker asked. "We don't get many visitors from back East. Especially this late at night."

Richter smiled. "You're quite observant, Sheriff. I assume my accent gave me away."

"Yeah, I've known a few Easterners in my time. You don't talk like folks out here."

"We've come on a matter of business. I hoped we might speak in confidence."

"Depends on whether or not it's official business. What's on your mind?"

Earlier that day Richter had watched from inside the depot as the children were unloaded from the Orphan Train. A casual conversation with one of the attendants revealed that Katherine and Augustus had been adopted by a farmer named Homer Ledbetter. Their new home was some miles northeast of town.

Richter and Turk Johnson had then engaged rooms in the Platte City Hotel. The balance of the afternoon was devoted to discreet inquiries about the county's chief law enforcement officer, Sheriff Jack Walker. Richter discovered that the sheriff was popular with voters, but nonetheless a man of questionable character. He routinely took payoffs from the bawdy houses on the south side of town.

The call on Sheriff Walker was purposely late. Richter wanted the conversation conducted in private, and equally important, the courthouse would be deserted well before midnight. The secrecy of his mission was uppermost, and the proposition he planned to offer might be refused. In that event, the only alternative was for Johnson to kill the sheriff. The late hour ensured there would be no witnesses.

"What I have in mind," Richter said now, "might be termed a personal business arrangement. A rather generous fee for your services."

Walker looked interested. "What sort of services?"

"You're familiar with the Orphan Train?"

"I know it stops here pretty regular."

"Today, two young orphans were adopted by a farmer named Homer Ledbetter. Do you recognize the name?"

"Mr. Richter, I know everybody in Lincoln County. Ledbetter homesteaded a quarter-section about five miles outside town. What's your interest in him and these orphans?"

"I'm an attorney," Richter lied smoothly. "I've been retained to oversee the adoption of these children, a boy and a girl. My client wants periodic reports as to their well-being—and their treatment."

"That a fact?" Walker said skeptically. "Why's your client so keen on two particular kids?"

"I'm afraid that is privileged information. Let's just say the fee would make it worth your while."

"How much?"

"A thousand now and a hundred a month for the next year."

Walker's salary as sheriff was a hundred and fifty dollars a month. He thought there was something decidedly fishy about Otto Richter and the story about the orphans. Still, short of murder, there was little he wouldn't do for a thousand in cash. Not to mention the extra hundred a month.

"Mr. Richter, you've got yourself a deal. I'll keep a sharp eye on Ledbetter and those kids."

Turk Johnson pulled out a leather pouch and spilled fifty double eagles onto the desk. Richter waved his hand with idle largess. "I know Westerners prefer gold to greenbacks. I believe you'll find the count correct."

"Looks right to me," Walker said, scooping up a handful of double eagles. "I like a man who pays on the spot."

"One other thing."

"What's that?"

"When I buy a man, I expect him to stay bought. As the saying goes, come hell or high water, you're mine."

"You care to spell that out?"

"Certainly," Richter said. "Your absolute silence and loyalty are part of our bargain. Anything less is not acceptable."

Walker frowned. "You threatenin' an officer of the law?"

"A word to the wise should be sufficient."

There was a moment of profound quiet. Then Walker opened the center drawer of his desk and raked the coins in with a sweep of his arm. He looked up with a shifty grin.

"I just suspect you're some kind of crook, Mr. Richter. But what the hell, I'm no angel myself."

"I think we'll work well together, Sheriff."

"So where do you want those reports sent?"

"General delivery," Richter said without expression. "New York City."

Walker chuckled as he wrote it down in a laborious scrawl.

"You kids say you're from New York City?"

"Yes, sir, Wild Bill," Augustus replied. "We live in a house on Gramercy Park."

"Never heard of it," Hickok said. "Wasn't your folks in the house when you got carried off?"

"Well, yes, sir . . . they were."

"Then how come they didn't stop it?"

"We don't know," Augustus said in a wistful voice. "Katherine and I talked about it lots on the train. We just don't know."

Cody shook his head. "I thought Injuns was the only ones that carried kids off. Never figured New York for a dangerous place."

"Oh, it is, Buffalo Bill," Katherine assured him earnestly. "How else could we have been abducted?"

"Guess that's the question beggin' an answer."

Hickok led the way, Augustus at his side, as they crossed the intersection of Sixth and Locust. The courthouse was straight ahead, a two-story frame building that occupied half a city block. In the faint moonlight, Hickok spotted a sign for the sheriff's department above a flight of stairs leading to the basement. He turned in that direction.

A moment later they came through the door of the sheriff's office. Hickok saw a man seated behind the desk with a badge pinned on his shirt. There were two other men, on their feet as though preparing to leave, standing in front of the desk. Their manner of dress indicated to

Hickok that they were probably city folk, and he wondered what business they had with the law at midnight. He nodded to the man with the badge.

"I reckon you'd be Sheriff Walker."

"That's me," Walker said, rising from his chair. "I heard you were in town, Mr. Hickok. 'Course, everybody knows Bill Cody."

"Evenin', Sheriff," Cody said. "You busy with these gentlemen?"

"No, we're all done," Walker announced. "Mr. Richter and Mr. Johnson were just leaving."

Hickok noticed that the two men appeared stunned. They were staring at the children, and though they tried to hide it, their shock was evident. A visceral sense of danger came over Hickok, and he'd learned never to ignore the feeling. He survived on instinct and quick reflexes.

Cody stepped aside as the two men edged toward the doorway. He nodded to them, then looked back at the sheriff. "Figured you ought to talk with these children. Appears they were abducted from New York City and put on the Orphan Train."

Walker's mouth dropped open. "I—" he faltered, struggling to regain his composure. "You say they're orphans?"

"Not exactly," Cody said. "Way it sounds, somebody tried to pass 'em off as orphans."

Katherine was watching the two men with a strange expression. As they sidled toward the door, Richter's features were caught in the shadowy light from the lamp on the sheriff's desk. She suddenly gasped, clutching desperately at Cody's arm. Her eyes were wide with terror.

"Oh, nooo—" Her voice quavered, barely audible. "He's the man . . ."

"How's that?" Cody glanced down at her with bemused surprise. "What man?"

"He . . . he's the one."

"The one what?"

"He's the one who took me from my bedroom! I remember his face from the hallway light."

"That's absurd," Richter protested loudly. "I've never seen this girl in my life."

"Katherine's right!" Augustus blurted, pointing an accusing finger at Johnson. "The man who got me was big, great big strong hands. That's him!"

Hickok seemed to move not at all. The Colt Navy revolvers appeared in his hands and he earred back the hammers. He trained one on Richter and the other on Johnson. His eyes were like stone.

"Don't move," he ordered. "Stand real still."

"How dare you!" Richter said in an offended tone. "Whatever's going on here, we know nothing about these children. The sheriff will vouch for us, won't you, Sheriff?"

Walker quickly assessed the situation. He knew Richter would expose him unless he went along. The thousand dollars in his desk drawer was a dead giveaway. He opted for the lie.

"Holster your guns," he said harshly, glaring at Hickok. "Mr. Richter and Mr. Johnson are respectable businessmen. You're out of line, Hickok."

Hickok ignored the outburst. "Tell me something, Richter," he said evenly. "Whereabouts you boys from?"

Richter stiffened. "What does that have to do with anything?"

"Lemme guess," Hickok said. "You're New York born and bred—ain't you?"

"Where I'm from is no concern of yours."

"See there, you just answered my question."

"Hold on now." Walker started around his desk. "You put those guns away or I'll place you under arrest."

Cody pulled his Colt Army. "Just stay where you are, Sheriff. You're not arresting anybody."

"Goddamn you, Cody!" Walker bridled. "I'll report you to Colonel Reynolds. He'll have you up on charges."

"Likely the other way 'round," Cody said. "You're in cahoots with a couple of child abductors. I doubt you'll be wearin' that badge much longer."

"Time to make tracks," Hickok said in a commanding voice. "Bill, you go ahead and get the kids outside. I'll keep these gents covered."

Cody ushered the children through the door. Katherine darted a last hateful glance at Richter as she stepped into the night. Hickok wagged the snout of first one pistol and then the other at the three men. His mouth was set in a hard line.

"Any of you jokers follow me out, I'll stop your ticker."

No one moved as he backed through the door.

The night clerk at the Cedar House was nodding off. The bell over the door jarred him awake, and he looked up to see Hickok and Cody with two small children. His brow furrowed in a question mark.

"Don't ask," Hickok said, as they crossed the lobby. "Pretend you dreamt the whole thing."

"Yessir, Mr. Hickok, I didn't see nothin'."

"That's the spirit, bub."

Upstairs, Cody unlocked the door to their room. The children followed him inside, trailed by Hickok, and he quickly locked the door. He tossed his hat on the bed with a troubled look.

"Some kettle of fish," he said. "Got a dangblasted crook for a sheriff."

Hickok snorted. "I'd wager we've seen the last of him. He ain't got the stomach for a fight."

"Think I'll pay a call on the county judge. High time somebody heard the truth."

"Whole courthouse might be full of polecats. Let's chew on that awhile."

"So what's our next move?"

Katherine and Augustus were seated on the edge of the bed. They appeared spent, their shoulders slumped with exhaustion. Hickok crossed the room and sat down next to them. He looked at Katherine.

"Need you to think real hard," he said. "Are you plumb certain about that feller they called Richter? No mistakes?"

"I couldn't forget his face." Her eyes puddled with tears, her features bunched tight. "How will we ever get back to Mother and Father now?"

Hickok put an arm around her shoulders. She leaned into him, snuffling tears, and he gently stroked her hair. "Don't fret yourself," he said. "We'll figure something out."

"Wild Bill won't let us down." Augustus sniffed, wiping his nose, and took his sister's hand. "Didn't you see the way he pulled his guns? I mean wow, fast as lightning! Just like it says in the dime novels."

Hickok seemed acutely embarrassed. Cody smothered a smile and looked at him with a deadpan expression. "Well, you heard the youngster, Wild Bill. Where do we go from here?"

"You know the U.S. Marshal for Nebraska?"

"Yeah, his name's Omar Drake. Headquartered at the state capitol."

"That's our play," Hickok said firmly. "We'll telegraph him first thing in the mornin'. A federal lawman will have these sprouts home in no time."

"Durn right he will!" Cody marveled. "Why didn't I think of that?"

Hickok smiled. "'Cause there's only one Wild Bill."

The children were given the bed. They were sound asleep in seconds, feeling safe for the first time since their abduction. Hickok and Cody stretched out on the floor, saddlebags beneath their heads, their mackinaws for covers. Cody was asleep when he closed his eyes, but Hickok lay awake staring into the dark. A worrisome thought kept surfacing in the back of his mind.

He wondered why children with parents had ended up on the Orphan Train. It was a question he intended to put to the one named Richter. Tomorrow.

Just as soon as the kids were off his hands.

CHAPTER 8

A GENTLE wind chased puffy clouds around an azure sky. The sun crested the tops of buildings and stood lodged like a brass ball on the eastern horizon. All throughout town the smell of woodsmoke eddied on the breeze.

Shops and stores opened for business at eight o'clock. By then Locust Street was already jammed with freight wagons and the lighter wagons of farmers. The boardwalks were crowded with early shoppers about their errands and teamsters unloading all manner of goods. North Platte hurried to greet another day.

Hickok and Cody, followed by the children, came out of a café next door to the hotel. Katherine and Augustus were stuffed, having been treated to their first decent meal since boarding the Orphan Train. The plainsmen, hearty eaters themselves, had ordered steak and eggs, with a platter of flapjacks on the side. The children consumed an entire pitcher of milk.

From the café, they walked upstreet to Zimmerman's Mercantile. Hickok and Cody, talking about it over breakfast, decided the children were in desperate need of new outfits. Their threadbare clothing was by now soiled and unkempt from their journey west on the train. Nathan Zimmerman, elated to have Buffalo Bill Cody and Wild Bill Hickok in his store, personally waited on the children. He brought out his best stock.

Augustus was outfitted with corduroy trousers and a blue flannel shirt, sturdy boots and a pint-sized mackinaw, and a black slouch hat. Katherine, with Zimmerman's coaxing, selected a ruffled calico dress, a woolen mantle coat, a chambray bonnet, and high-topped calfskin shoes. They changed in the fitting room, leaving their old clothing to be thrown out. Their appearance as well as their spirits were measurably improved. They felt decently attired for the first time since their abduction.

When they emerged from the store, Augustus seemed particularly proud of his Western duds. He imagined himself a courageous scout or a bold lawman, and put a swagger into his step. Katherine was simply thrilled to be clean and presentable, no longer a wretched little ragamuffin. She shyly planted a kiss on Cody's cheek and then kissed Hickok as well. Her eyes were bright with happiness.

"Thank you, thank you," she said gaily. "You're both so wonderfully kind."

Augustus stuck out his chest. "Boy, I wish Mother and Father could see us now. Wouldn't that be something!"

"That reminds me," Hickok said. "What's your pa's name?"

"Henry," Katherine said. "Henry Morton Stanley."

"And I recollect you live on a park?"

"Yes, Number 24 Gramercy Park."

"We'll telegraph your pa when we wire the U.S. Marshal. Let him know you're safe and sound."

"Oh, thank you, Wild Bill." Katherine took his hand with sudden affection. "Mother and Father must be frantic with worry."

"There you rascals are!"

Homer Ledbetter reined his team to a halt. He hopped down from the wagon and strode toward them with an angry scowl. He stopped on the boardwalk.

"You little scutters!" he said hotly. "Thought you'd run off, did you?"

"No need to shout," Cody said, stepping forward. "I remember you from yesterday, at the train depot."

"Outta my way," Ledbetter growled. "I adopted them brats fair and square. I'm here to collect 'em."

"Well, way it turns out, they're not orphans. So your adoption don't hold."

"Mister, you ain't foolin' nobody. You're not gonna make off with kids I done took in."

"You've got the wrong idea," Cody told him. "We're fixin' to send 'em back home. That's the God's honest truth."

"Don't gimme none of your gawddamn horseshit. Stand aside!"

"No, I don't think so."

Ledbetter launched a looping haymaker. Cody slipped the blow and hit him with a splintering left-right combination. The farmer staggered off the boardwalk and Cody hammered him with a solid right to the jaw. He went down with a thud, out cold.

"Wow." Augustus's eyes were round as saucers. "What a punch!"

"Yessir," Hickok said wryly. "Buffalo Bill is one fine pugilist."

Cody sucked on a skinned knuckle. "Sorry half-wit wouldn't listen to reason. What was I supposed to do?"

"Why, just what you done. What else?"

They left Ledbetter sprawled in the dust. A block downstreet they paused outside the hotel. Hickok motioned off toward the railroad tracks.

"You go on to the depot and send them wires. I'll take the kids up to the room."

Cody nodded. "What was that New York address again?"

"Henry Morton Stanley. Number 24 Gramercy Park."

The drumming sound of hoofbeats brought them

around. A cavalry trooper skidded his horse to a halt and swung down out of the saddle. The horse was caked with sweat and the trooper was breathing hard. He hurried toward them.

"Mr. Cody!" he said stoutly. "The colonel wants you double-quick. There's been an Injun raid."

"Damn," Cody cursed. "Whereabouts?"

"Farnum relay station. Hostiles made off with the horses and killed both the handlers. Burned the station to the ground."

"Has the colonel put a unit in the field?"

"Cap'n Meinhold's company," the trooper said. "They're trackin' the Injuns somewhere off to the northeast. Colonel says you'll find 'em up around the Loup River."

Cody turned toward the hotel. He saw the desk clerk watching them from the doorway. Then, abruptly, he turned back to Hickok.

"I've got no choice but to skedaddle. Can you manage the kids?"

Hickok considered a moment. "Don't care much for the odds. Richter and his bully-boy might come at me with the sheriff and a bunch of deputies. I doubt I could hold 'em off without you and your army connections."

"So what are you sayin'?"

"I haven't had a scrap with the Injuns in a spell. Let's take the kids along."

"You serious?"

"They'd be a damnsight safer on a patrol than here in town. If I was to get arrested, we'd never see 'em again."

"You're sure?"

"You got a better idea?"

"Soldier!" Cody barked. "Hightail it over to the livery and get our horses saddled. Tell 'em we'll be rentin' their two best horses."

The trooper took off running. Cody swapped a look with Hickok, then glanced at the children. He shook his head with a dubious frown.

"Hope you kids can stay on a horse."

Augustus gave him a nutcracker grin. "We are trained equestrians, Buffalo Bill."

"Equestrians?" Hickok said. "What the devil's that?"

"Why, how to stay on a horse, Wild Bill."

Ten minutes later they rode north out of town.

The Platte City Hotel was a half block north of the Cedar House. All morning Richter and Johnson had posted themselves at the plate-glass window fronting the lobby. From there, they had a clear view of the street.

Richter as yet had no concrete plan. A confrontation was out of the question, for he and Johnson was no match against Hickok and Cody. But he had to resolve the matter of the children, and soon. Things were starting to spiral out of control.

From the lobby, Richter had watched as the children were taken to breakfast and then to Zimmerman's Mercantile. He'd seen the dispute with Homer Ledbetter, and the conference between Cody and Hickok following the arrival of the cavalry trooper. And now, thoroughly baffled, he watched as the plainsmen rode off with the children.

Some minutes later Richter and Johnson entered the Cedar House. The desk clerk was properly intimidated by Johnson's scowl, and even more persuaded by a hundred dollars in gold. He told Richter everything he'd overheard in the cavalry trooper's report, and the conversation between Hickok and Cody. He was then sworn to an oath of silence, which was not taken lightly. Turk Johnson was clearly the penalty for a breach of trust.

The news was better than Richter had hoped. A plan

crystallized as he emerged from the hotel and turned up-town. To a large extent, the success of the scheme was dependent on the cooperation of the sheriff. But Richter was reasonably confident that Walker could be made to see the light. Any man whose livelihood was decided at the ballot box jealously guarded his good name. All the more so if he was a crook.

At the courthouse, Richter and Johnson caught the sheriff as he was leaving his office. One of his deputies had recovered sufficiently from the grippe to relieve him, and he was headed home. His features knotted, for he devoutly wished he'd seen the last of the two men. Some inner voice told him the situation had gone from bad to worse.

"We have a problem," Richter said without preamble. "Hickok and Cody just rode out of town with the children."

"Not my problem," Walker countered. "Our agreement was for reports on a couple of orphans. Turns out those kids aren't orphans."

"Whatever their status, you're still at some personal jeopardy."

"How do you figure that?"

"Consider the consequences," Richter said impassively. "You took a bribe, which in itself is a felony. Cody will inevitably raise the issue with army officials and someone will report it to the newspapers. Voters tend to believe what they read, and corruption is a dirty word." He paused for emphasis. "You wouldn't stand a chance in the next election."

Walker felt like a man who had dipped a toe in quicksand only to have his leg entrapped. To extricate himself he somehow had to ensure that Richter prevailed in the matter of the so-called orphans. Only then would Richter catch a train back to New York.

"All right," he said at length. "What do you want from me?"

"An introduction," Richter informed him. "Every town has its rougher element, and someone who's cock-'o-the-walk. Who would that be in North Platte?"

"Axel Bohannon," Walker said. "Him and his men are hide hunters part of the time and general hell-raisers all the time. Why do you ask?"

"Would you consider Bohannon a mercenary? Will he take pay to commit violence?"

"Hell, he might do it for free. He's kissin' kin to a mad dog. What is it you're plannin'?"

"Do you really want to know?"

"Now that you mention it . . . forget I asked."

"Where might I find Mr. Bohannon?"

"Him and his boys have got a cabin south of the tracks. The one with a corral out back."

"I'll tell him you send your regards."

Some while later Richter knocked on the door. The man who answered it wore filthy longjohns and a sullen expression. "What d'you want?"

"Axel Bohannon," Richter said. "I'm here on a matter of business."

The inside of the cabin smelled like a wolf's den. There were three double-bunk beds, with worn clothing, saddles and camp gear strewn about the room. Four men were still in bed and a fifth sat at a table by the stove. He spilled tobacco into a rolling paper, waiting for the one who answered the door to move aside. He popped a match on his thumbnail.

"Who're you?" he said, lighting his cigarette. "How'd you get my name?"

Bohannon was lean and muscular, with brutish features. Richter left Johnson to guard his back and walked to the table. He took a chair.

"Otto Richter," he said simply. "How I came by your name isn't important. I understand your services are for hire."

"Do you?" Bohannon exhaled a wad of smoke. "What sorta services you lookin' for?"

"Wild Bill Hickok and Buffalo Bill Cody have something that belongs to me. In point of fact, two children."

"And?"

"I want you to get them back."

"Hickok and Cody," Bohannon said, flicking an ash with his little finger. "Nobody to mess with even when you're sober. Tell me why I'd do a thing like that?"

"A thousand dollars," Richter said. "Half now and half when the job is finished."

"Do you want 'em dead?"

"Only if it comes to that."

Bohannon stared at him. "What're these kids to you?"

"Does it matter?" Richter said equably. "We're talking about Hickok and Cody—and a thousand dollars."

"You cut right to the bone, don't you? Awright, let's say I'm interested. What's next?"

Richter briefly explained the problem. Cody and Hickok were riding even now to join a company of the Fifth Cavalry. Their destination, according to his information, was somewhere along the Loup River. The children were with the plainsmen.

"I'll be go-to-hell," Bohannon said, mildly amused. "Took kids off huntin' hostiles. That's what you're sayin'?"

"I'm afraid so."

"Well, now it ain't just Hickok and Cody no more. You're tellin' me a troop of cavalry and Christ knows how many hostiles. A thousand ain't enough."

"How much?"

"Double oughta get it."

"Very well," Richter agreed. "Two thousand."

"Done." Bohannon puffed his cigarette. "How you want this handled?"

"I have no interest in either the cavalry or the Indians. Once we find them, your job is to trail them without being seen. I want to catch Hickok and Cody alone—with the children."

"You're comin' with us?"

"That's correct."

"Sounds like a barrel of laughs." Bohannon motioned across the room. "You and your strongarm boy horsemen, are you?"

Johnson held his gaze with a stoic expression. "Horsemen or not," Richter said, "we're along for the ride. That's part of the deal."

Bohannon grinned. "Well, like they say, money talks."

Richter began counting out double eagles.

CHAPTER 9

THE CAVALRY troop was camped along the South Fork of the Loup River. As the sun dipped toward the western horizon, the river was transformed into a rock-studded ribbon of gold. A sharp wind rattled through the cottonwoods lining the banks.

There were forty troopers in Company B. Veterans of the Indian wars, their bivouac was tightly contained, with their horses picketed along the river. Four pack horses carried rations and grain, and small fires for cooking warded off the chill. Sentries were posted on the perimeter of the camp.

Cody sighted the fires just as sunset gave way to dusk. The children were lined out behind him, and Hickok brought up the rear. Katherine was mounted on a gentle mare and Augustus rode a blaze-faced roan gelding. Though they were trained to English saddles, they had fallen into the rhythm of Western rigs with natural ease. The plainsmen were increasingly impressed by the spunk of the youngsters.

Augustus was beside himself with excitement. To be rescued by Hickok and Cody, the Heroes of the Plains, was beyond his wildest dreams. To be included in a scout for hostile Indians pursued by the cavalry was an adventure that fired his imagination. Katherine, by contrast, was enthralled by the chivalry and valorous manner of the two plainsmen. She dreamily imagined herself the Guinevere of a grand quest into forbidden lands, fraught with danger. She wasn't yet sure whether Hickok or Cody would be her Lancelot.

The troopers were squatted around fires, cooking salt pork and softening hard tack in the fatty juices. Cody wondered how the children would take to the spartan rations that sustained the cavalry on a chase. He thought Augustus would tough it out, and Katherine, too polite to complain, would subsist on nibbles. As he stepped out of the saddle, Captain Charles Meinhold, the company commander, hurried forward. Then, looking past him, Meinhold saw the children. His face set in a glowering frown.

"What's the meaning of this, Mr. Cody? Who are these children?"

Cody ducked his head. "Cap'n, I know it's against regulations. But we didn't have a whole lot of choice."

"Tommyrot!" Meinhold railed. "You made a choice, but it was the wrong one. The worst choice!"

"Well, sir, it's a long story."

"Give me the abbreviated version."

Cody covered the details in a rapid-fire monologue. When he finished, he raised his hands in a lame shrug. "Like I said, we didn't have any choice."

Meinhold appeared stupefied. "Let me understand this. These children were abducted in New York, rescued by you and Mr. Hickok in North Platte, and now you've brought them on a sortie against hostiles. Did I miss anything?"

"No, sir, that pretty well covers it."

Cody knew he was in hot water. Meinhold was a soldier's soldier, and operated strictly by the book. A German immigrant, Meinhold had joined the army in 1851 and advanced through the ranks to sergeant major. During the Civil War, he was commissioned and awarded two brevets for valor in battle. After the war, he was assigned to the Fifth Cavalry, with the permanent rank of captain. He was widely regarded the top field commander in the regiment.

"Consider yourself on report," he said bluntly. "When we return to post, you will answer directly to Colonel Reynolds. Do I make myself clear?"

Cody nodded. "Guess that's plain enough."

"Get those children settled and then report to me."

"Yessir."

Augustus and Katherine seemed wounded by the severity of the tongue-lashing. From the nature of the reprimand, they realized they were responsible for placing Cody at risk. He smiled, rolling his eyes, as if to say it was a matter of no consequence. With Hickok trailing along, he walked them to one of the fires, where several troopers were gathered. The corporal in charge of the packhorses agreed to look after them and get them fed. One of the troopers began slicing extra rations of salt pork.

"You should've laid it on me," Hickok said as they walked back through the camp. "Tell the cap'n I'm the one that brought the kids along."

"Don't worry about it," Cody said. "Wasn't like you twisted my arm."

"All the same, you're the one with your tit in a wringer."

"Well hell, it's not like it's the first time."

Meinhold waited by a fire. He nodded genially to Hickok, seemingly recovered from his fit of temper. "Good to have you with us, Mr. Hickok. Another scout is always welcome."

"Glad to be of service, Cap'n. How many hostiles we trailin'?"

"Difficult to say," Meinhold admitted. "They stole twenty horses, all of which are shod. Otherwise, I doubt we could have trailed them this far."

"Still headed north?" Cody asked. "Anybody check across the river?"

"Sergeant Foley rode ahead while it was still light. He found their tracks."

"I just suspect we'll overtake 'em come mornin'."

"What makes you think so, Mr. Cody?"

"Cap'n, they pushed them horses real hard for a day and a night. I doubt they figure anybody's still on their trail."

"I see." Meinhold was thoughtful a moment. "You think they may have stopped, is that it?"

Cody nodded. "Wouldn't be surprised but what they took a breather. We'll find out come first light."

Meinhold stared off into the dark. "Do you agree, Mr. Hickok?"

"Yessir, I do," Hickok said. "You'll have your fight."

"You sound quite confident."

"Well, don't you see, Cody and me know our Injuns. We ain't all that civilized ourselves."

Captain Charles Meinhold thought the statement only partially true. The presence of the children in camp seemed to him the opposite side of the coin. Though he would never say so out loud.

He preferred his scouts on the rank side.

Cody was in charge of the scouting party. Sergeant John Foley and six troopers were placed under his direct command. Hickok went along for the ride.

The detail rode out as the sky paled with the dinge of false dawn. A cursory inspection of the tracks by Cody and Hickok revealed that there were twenty-three shod horses and eleven unshod Indian ponies. The trail, as though on a compass heading, was dead north.

The main command was to follow at first light. Cody's orders were to locate the hostiles and send a trooper back with directions. Captain Meinhold would then advance with Company B and move into position for attack.

The children, secure with the pack train, would follow the main command.

Not quite an hour later the scouting party topped a low knoll in the prairie. The sun slowly crested the horizon, and below them, a tributary creek fed eastward into the South Fork of the Loup. A tendril of smoke drifted from the embers of a fire, and blanketed forms were scattered about the campsite. The horse herd was guarded by a lone warrior.

Cody signaled the men to dismount on the reverse slope of the knoll. He wormed forward on his belly, removing his hat, flanked by Hickok and Sergeant Foley. They carefully scrutinized the camp, which was perhaps a hundred yards beyond their position. The mounted warrior sat watching the herd on a grassy flatland near the creek. Cody kept his voice to a whisper.

"I count eleven," he said. "Look to be Sioux."

"Not Cheyenne," Hickok added. "Likely some young bucks off on a raid."

"Got a hunch we ought to hit 'em now. They're liable to be on the move before we get the captain up here."

"You got my vote. Catch 'em by surprise while they're still in their blankets. Wouldn't hardly be a fight."

"Not so quick," Sergeant Foley interjected. "Captain's orders were to locate 'em and report back. Didn't say nothin' about attacking on our own."

"First rule of engagement," Cody said confidently. "Take the fight to your enemy before he has a chance to escape. Says so in the Officers Handbook."

Foley appeared skeptical. "You're the one that answers to the captain. He's gonna ream you a new asshole."

"I'll worry about that when the time comes."

Cody outlined his plan of attack. Foley slithered back down the slope and began briefing the troopers. Hickok fell in beside Cody as they walked toward their horses. He arched an eyebrow in question.

"You a student of the Officers Handbook?"

Cody grinned. "Don't recollect I ever read it."

"Meinhold's liable to wet his drawers."

"Not if we bring him them horses."

Cody led them east into the sunrise. The knoll gradually dropped off onto the flatland near the creek. His plan was to capture the horse herd and leave the Sioux warriors afoot. They rounded the end of the knoll, holding their mounts to a walk, and turned upstream. The attack would be made with the sun at their backs.

The sound of their approach was muffled by the dry grassland. They were within fifty yards before the horse guard turned, shielding his eyes with his hand, and stared into the sun. He suddenly whooped a warning cry and charged them, firing a Henry repeater on the run. Cody and Hickok were armed with Winchester '66 rifles, and the crack of their shots was almost simultaneous. The warrior tumbled over the rear of his mount.

The horse herd stampeded. Three of the troopers swung west at a gallop and circled most of the herd back to the south. Some of the Indian ponies, terrified by the smell of white men, broke away and forded the creek. Cody and Hickok, with Foley and the other three troopers, charged the encampment. Four of the warriors fought a rear guard action, while the others splashed across the creek in an effort to catch the ponies. The four who stayed behind went down under a volley from the charging horsemen.

On the opposite side of the creek, five of the six warriors managed to clamber aboard their ponies. The one left on foot turned to fight as Cody and Hickok swerved toward the creekbank. Hickok abruptly reined to a halt,

the Winchester at his shoulder, and fired. The slug struck
the warrior in the chest and he stumbled sideways, collapsing onto the ground. Cody spurred ahead, fording the
stream, and gave chase after the fleeing Sioux. Outdis-
tanced, he finally skidded to a stop, jumped off his horse,
and fired from a kneeling position. A warrior at the rear
of the pack fell arms akimbo off his pony.

Cody mounted and rode back to the campsite. Hickok
rose from inspecting the trappings of one of the fallen
warriors. He indicated the painted markings on an arrow.
"Oglala," he said. "You reckon Crazy Horse was one of
them that got away?"

"Tend to doubt it," Cody remarked. "He's the big au-
ger of the Oglalas. Got other fish to fry."

Hickok tossed the arrow aside. "I count seven with the
one you just shot. They're liable to give you a medal."

"That horse herd counts more than a bunch of dead
Sioux. Folks do prize their livestock."

"Not to mention we didn't lose nobody."

None of the troopers had been wounded. Sergeant
Foley got them busy hazing the herd back over the knoll.
Hickok and Cody paused for a last look at the bodies of
the fallen Sioux. Neither of them felt any great pride
about the outcome of the fight. Nor did they feel remorse.

The Oglala lived by a code that sustained any warrior
in battle. Today was a good day to die.

Axel Bohannon took a small brass telescope from his
pocket. He extended the telescope to its full length and
scanned the distant column. The troopers were dismounted, and he watched as Hickok and Cody talked
with the cavalry commander. A detail of soldiers drove
a herd of horses to the rear of the column.

"Turned out to be more'n a scoutin' party." He collapsed the telescope, nodding to himself. "Appears

Cody and Hickok jumped the redsticks and took back them horses. Wonder how many they killed."

"I'm not interested in Indians," Richter said. "Are the children still with the pack train?"

"Yep, nothin's changed there."

A noonday sun stood lodged in the sky. Bohannon and Richter were hidden in a copse of trees bordering one of the many creeks that emptied into the South Fork of the Loup. Johnson and the other men waited with the horses a short ways downstream. They had trailed the cavalry column all morning.

Bohannon was a seasoned plainsman. Late yesterday, after a hard ride from North Platte, he'd found the military encampment. By skirting south, they had avoided detection and taken shelter along the wooded river. Early that morning, they had observed the scouting party ride off to the north. Richter elected to shadow the main column, rather than follow Hickok and Cody. His principle interest was in the children.

Richter was in some discomfort. He was far from an accomplished horseman, and Johnson had never been aboard a horse in his life. Their buttocks were galled from long hours in the saddle, and Richter found himself walking like a spraddle-legged duck. He watched now as the cavalry column wheeled about and turned south. He looked at Bohannon.

"Where are they headed?"

"Fort McPherson," Bohannon said. "That's where the soldier-boys are headquartered."

"The question is," Richter stared off at the column, "will Cody and Hickok go with them to the fort?"

"That'd be anybody's guess. We'll have to tag along and find out."

"How far is it?"

"Well, as the crow flies, I'd judge about thirty miles."

"Jesus Christ," Richter groaned. "It might as well be in China."

Bohannon chortled slyly. "Your backsides must be hurtin' powerful bad. Sure you're up to it?"

"I'll manage somehow, Mr. Bohannon."

"Mebbe we'll get lucky. Cody and Hickok might split off from the soldiers. Head back to North Platte."

"That would certainly simplify things."

"Wouldn't it?" Bohannon said, waving his arms. "There's a half-dozen places between here and there where I could bushwhack 'em easy as pie. Everybody'd figger the Injuns done it."

Richter exhaled heavily. "I haven't said anything about killing them . . . yet."

"No, not just yet, but you will."

"What makes you think so?"

"You got no choice," Bohannon said pointedly. "Only one way you're gonna get them kids away from Hickok and Cody. You gotta kill 'em."

A strange look came over Richter's face. He was silent a moment, as though weighing some quandary known only to himself. Then he seemed to gather himself with grudging effort. He nodded to Bohannon.

"I regret to say we'd best get mounted."

"You're a brute for punishment, ain't you? Bet you wish you'd never seen a horse."

"All in a good cause, Mr. Bohannon."

"Tell me that after another twenty miles."

They walked off downstream under the dappled shade of the trees.

CHAPTER 10

FORT MCPHERSON was located on a broad plain of rolling grassland. Cottonwood Creek snaked out of the north and curled around the southern perimeter of the post. On the far side of the creek steep bluffs guarded a range of broken hills.

Company B rode into the fort shortly before ten o'clock the next morning. As the column passed through the main gate, the regimental trumpeter sounded Boots and Saddles. The troopers of the Fifth Regiment hurried into formation on the parade ground for drill call. Guidons of the assembled companies fluttered on a crisp northerly breeze.

Hickok was always impressed by the size of the garrison. One of the larger military posts on the frontier, it was spread over nearly forty acres. There were some thirty buildings, including barracks, stables, quartermaster depot, and the hospital. The regimental headquarters, a sprawling frame structure, was located on the north side of the parade ground.

Sergeant Foley and his detail drove the horse herd to a large corral at the southwest corner of the compound. Captain Meinhold brought the company on line near the flagpole in the center of the parade ground. There, he turned over command to the First Sergeant, and once the troopers were dismounted, they led their horses to the company stable. An orderly rushed to take the captain's horse.

Meinhold swatted dust off his uniform with his gloves. He waited by the flagpole while Cody and Hickok collected the children and their horses and walked

forward. Katherine and Augustus seemed no worse
for their expedition with the cavalry, and they gawked
round-eyed as troops wheeled around the parade ground
in close order drill. Meinhold adjusted his campaign hat.

"Let's report in, Mr. Cody," he said brusquely. "I'm
sure the colonel will be interested in hearing about these
children."

Cody winced. "I'd think he'd be more interested in the
hostiles, Cap'n."

"Yes, that, too."

Meinhold marched off toward regimental headquarters.
In the orderly room, Sergeant Major Daniel O'Meara and
four clerks snapped to attention. The children were parked
on a bench by a potbellied stove, and O'Meara rapped on
the door of an inner office. He swung it open, stepping
aside as Meinhold, Cody, and Hickok filed through. His
eyes touched on Cody with a glint of amusement.

"Colonel, sir!" he barked. "Captain Meinhold, and
scouts Cody and Hickok."

Colonel John Reynolds was an austere man with
chiseled features and a neatly trimmed mustache. He remained seated at his desk, the national flag and the regimental flag draped from standards behind his chair.
Through the open door, his gaze settled momentarily on
the children. He nodded to O'Meara.

"Thank you, Sergeant Major."

O'Meara went out, closing the door. Reynolds stared
across his desk with a curious expression. "Gentlemen,"
he said amiably. "May I inquire who those children belong to?"

"To me, sir," Cody blurted. "Me and Mr. Hickok."

"Indeed?" Reynolds said. "Would you care to explain
yourself, Mr. Cody?"

Cody told him the story. As he related the odyssey of
the children, Reynolds's features ran the gamut from

amazement to anger. There was a moment of leaden silence when Cody finally wound down.

"You surprise me, Mr. Cody," Reynolds said curtly. "Your duty was to the mission. Those children are a civilian matter."

"Beg your pardon, Colonel," Hickok interrupted. "Cody was responsible for seven hostiles bitin' the dust and he recovered them stolen horses. Cap'n Meinhold will bear me out."

Meinhold cleared his throat. "Apart from the children, Colonel, I'd be forced to agree. Mr. Cody performed in an exemplary manner."

"What am I to do with you, Cody?" Reynolds asked in a bemused voice. "You redeem yourself even in the midst of willful disobedience."

Cody looked abashed. "I'll go along with whatever you say, Colonel."

The door swung open. Sergeant Major O'Meara stepped inside, shoulders squared. "Colonel, sir!" he boomed. "Telegraph for Mr. Cody just come over the wire."

"How providential," Reynolds said dryly. "Don't let me stop you, Mr. Cody. Go right ahead."

O'Meara handed over the telegram. Cody unfolded the form and quickly scanned the message. He read it through again.

HAVE CONTRACTED THREE-MONTH RUN OF STAGE SHOW IN NEW YORK'S GRANDEST THEATER. YOUR PRESENCE REQUIRED HERE POSTHASTE. TELEGRAPH DATE OF ARRIVAL.

NED BUNTLINE

Cody looked up. "It's from my stage partner in New York. Says I've got to come right away. He's contracted a theater."

"Come now, Mr. Cody," Reynolds said. "Your leave of absence doesn't start for another week. You know that."

"Yessir, no argument there. But what's a week more or less? He wouldn't ask if it wasn't important."

Cody's arrangement with the army permitted him a leave of absence for the months February through April. The hostile tribes seldom broke winter camp before early May, and the raiding season was usually delayed for a spring hunt. By then, he would have returned to duty as Chief of Scouts.

"Perhaps you're right," Reynolds conceded. "Quite frankly, I'd rather not consider the thought of disciplinary action. We'll leave it that the success of your mission offsets the matter of the children. You have your extra week, Mr. Cody."

"I'm obliged, Colonel," Cody said gratefully. "I'll make it up to you come spring."

"Just don't return with any children."

"No, sir, I shorely won't."

There was a sense of relief all around. After a round of handshakes, Cody and Hickok collected the children from the orderly room. Outside headquarters, they walked toward the hitch rack where their horses were tied. Hickok gave Cody a sideways glance.

"I take it you're headed East."

"There's an evenin' train out of North Platte. Got plenty of time to make it."

"You're forgettin' something, ain't you?" Hickok said. "What are we gonna do with these kids?"

Cody grinned. "How'd you like to see New York City?"

The sun dropped steadily westward. Up ahead was a creek lined with trees, and Cody thought it a good spot to allow the horses a drink. He figured they would make North Platte with time to spare.

Earlier, before leaving Fort McPherson, he and Hickok had gathered their gear from his quarters. They were prone to travel light, and their war bags were strapped behind their saddles. Yet the matter of New York still hung between them like a gaseous shroud. Cody decided to broach it from a new angle.

"Look here now," he said. "We're dutybound to see that these kids get home. What better way than to take 'em ourselves?"

"You're wastin' your breath," Hickok said gruffly. "I ain't going to New York, and that's that."

"What've you got against New York?"

"Too damn many people to suit my style."

"You've got nothin' else to do," Cody persisted. "They won't be hiring a marshal for Ellsworth till May at the earliest. You said so yourself."

"Yeah?" Hickok grumped. "So what?"

"So what's your plans between now and then?"

"There's lots of gamblin' dives between here and Kansas. You might recollect I'm a fair-to-middlin' poker player."

"Dollar here, dollar there," Cody said dismissively. "Why not make yourself some real money?"

Hickok squinted at him. "What exactly are we talkin' about here?"

"Couple of hundred a week, steady work. That's a sight more than you make wearin' a badge."

"What kind of work?"

"There's a spot for you in my stage play. The show business pays mighty good."

"You must've popped your cork. Whatever gave you the notion I'd go on the stage?"

"You're a natural," Cody insisted. "All you have to do

is stand up there and talk. Somebody else even writes the lines."

"Thanks all the same," Hickok said doggedly. "Think I'll stick to poker."

"What about the kids? You started this and you ought to see it through. Never knew you to be a quitter."

Katherine and Augustus were listening intently. From talk among the cavalry troopers, they'd heard how Cody and Hickok routed the Sioux raiders and killed seven warriors. By now they idolized the plainsmen in the way of saints or mythical dragon slayers. Augustus squirmed around in his saddle.

"Won't you please come with us, Wild Bill? Even if you never go on the stage, you'll like New York. I just know you will!"

"Yes, please do," Katherine urged. "Going home wouldn't be the same without you, Wild Bill. We so want you to meet Mother and Father."

Hickok suddenly sat straighter. The treeline bordering the creek was some three hundred yards to their direct front. His eyes narrowed.

"We got trouble," he said solemnly. "There's somebody in them trees."

"You sure?" Cody said.

"Damn right I'm sure. Somebody's fixin' to ambush us. Might be Injuns."

"We can't take any chances with the kids. We'll have to run for it."

"You kids listen to me," Hickok ordered. "When I give you the word, boot your horses and take off. Got that?"

The children nodded, their features taut with fear. Hickok barked a command and the four of them wheeled their horses west at a gallop. The distant treeline spurted flashes of smoke, followed an instant later by the rolling crack of rifles. Katherine's saddlehorn exploded, and

Augustus's hat went sailing in the air. The angry buzz of slugs whistled past Hickok and Cody. They pounded off at a dead lope.

Otto Richter watched them from the trees. On the ride south, trailing them to Fort McPherson, he'd realized that all his options had been foreclosed. Army officials were now aware of the situation, and simply killing Cody and Hickok solved nothing. There was only one solution that would end the problem. He'd instructed Bohannon to kill the children.

"Gawdammit!" Bohannon raged. "Something must've tipped them off."

"Let's get mounted," Richter told him. "We have no time to lose."

"What's your hurry?"

"I think we can assume they're headed for North Platte. Do you agree?"

"Yeah, that'd be my guess."

"I've just upped the price," Richter said. "Five thousand if those children are dead by nightfall."

"Uh-huh," Bohannon said, his eyes inquisitive. "What about Hickok and Cody?"

"I'm interested only in the children."

"And I did hear right—five thousand?"

"Precisely."

Bohannon ordered his men to get mounted.

Cody came out of the livery stable. He had returned the rented horses, and without telling Hickok, arranged to stable their horses. Hickok was waiting with the children on the boardwalk.

"We'd better eat," Cody said. "Never know what kind of vittles you'll find on a train."

"Good idea," Hickok commented. "Wouldn't want to send you off hungry."

Augustus looked at him. "Aren't you coming with us, Wild Bill?"

"I'm still thinkin' on it, sport. Haven't made up my mind."

They crossed the street to the Bon Ton Café. A waitress took their orders and a sense of gloom settled over the table. Cody finally broke the silence.

"You think it was Injuns that tried to bushwhack us?"

"Maybe," Hickok said thoughtfully. "'Course, that'd be a helluva coincidence, wouldn't it? Tangle with one bunch yesterday and stumble across another today."

"So what are you sayin'?"

"I got to wonderin' about that Richter feller. Could be he's still after these here kids."

Cody studied on it a moment. "Way it sounded, there was at least six rifles, maybe more. Where would Richter get all them guns?"

"Don't know," Hickok admitted. "Unless he's trailin' us with the sheriff and a pack of deputies. They was in pretty thick, you'll recollect."

"I suppose stranger things have happened."

The children seemed to cringe at the mention of Richter. The waitress returned with their orders, and the men let the subject drop. When they came out of the café, dusk had fallen over North Platte. They walked toward the train station.

At the depot, Cody purchased four tickets. The eastbound train ground to a halt as he emerged onto the platform. He handed one of the tickets to Hickok.

"You're all set."

Hickok exhaled heavily. "Haven't said I was going to New York."

"I don't think you'll let the kids down. They're dependin' on you."

"You shore know how to twist the knife."

"Oh, please, Wild Bill," Katherine pleaded, tugging at his sleeve. "Won't you please do it for us?"

"Well, little missy—"

Hickok abruptly pushed her aside. He saw a group of riders step down from their horses at the west end of the platform. In the spill of light from the depot windows, he counted eight men. One of them was Otto Richter.

"Do what I tell you," he said roughly to Cody. "Get the kids on the train. Now!"

Cody obeyed without question. He grabbed each of the children by the arm and rushed toward the center coach. They were the only ones boarding the train, and the debarking passengers were already moving through the stationhouse. As they neared the coach, the men at the end of the platform went for their pistols. The conductor ducked back onto the train.

A ragged volley of shots whistled across the platform. The slugs pinged off the side of the coach, one plucking at Augustus's coatsleeve and another nipping the hem of Katherine's skirt. Hickok pulled a Colt Navy with either hand, thumbing the hammers as the barrels came level. He opened fire in a drumming roar, the shots blending together. Two men pitched forward on their faces.

The train lurched into motion. Hickok backed across the platform, alternately firing his Colts with methodical precision. Axel Bohannon staggered, drilled through the chest, and slumped to the ground. Another man spun away, spurting blood from his throat, and collapsed in a heap. Hickok fired again, then stepped aboard as the train got under way. Cody and the children were waiting in the vestibule.

"You hit?" Cody demanded. "You all right?"

Hickok shrugged him off. "Looks like you shanghaied me after all."

The train gathered speed. As it pulled away from the

depot, Richter and Turk Johnson darted from the shadows. They sprinted along the track bed and Johnson leaped onto the observation deck of the last passenger coach. He dragged Richter aboard.

The train sped through the night from North Platte.

CHAPTER 11

CODY WAS his own best press agent. He quickly befriended the conductor and set about making arrangements for their trip East. A sizable gratuity ensured they would travel in style.

The conductor hardly needed his palm greased. He was almost euphoric to have Buffalo Bill Cody and Wild Bill Hickok aboard his train. An avid reader of dime novels, he accorded them the courtesy reserved for dignitaries. They were shown to a parlor car forward of the passenger coaches.

Hickok had never heard of a parlor car. The conductor explained that it was something new, a car with four private compartments. The Union Pacific was testing the cars between New York and San Francisco, providing luxury accommodations for wealthy travelers and businessmen. Three of the four compartments were already occupied.

The plainsmen agreed that it was a godsend. With a little planning, the compartment was spacious enough for four. There was a double bunk bed, similar to the Pullman sleeping cars, and a small sitting area by the window. There was even a private lavatory, with running water and a commode. They would have no problem keeping an eye on the children.

Katherine and Augustus were still shaken by the gunfight at the train station. Yet, however great their fear, they were awed by the memory of Hickok blazing away with a pistol in either hand. The reality was far more exciting, and frightening, than anything they might have

imagined from dime novels. Hickok told them to get settled in, and wisely dodged their questions about the
shootout. He motioned Cody into the passageway outside
the compartment.

"Need to talk," he said, waiting for Cody to close the
door. "What happened back there at the depot don't make
sense."

"I know," Cody said. "Where the deuce did Richter
find himself an army?"

"That's not what I'm getting at. Them bastards wasn't
shootin' at me, or you. They was shootin' at the kids."

"What makes you say that?"

"There wasn't a bullet come anywhere near me. Them
kids was drawin' all the fire."

"You serious?"

"Hell, yes, I'm serious. You don't believe me, take a
look at their clothes. Them holes is bullet holes."

"I'll be jiggered," Cody said, dumbfounded. "Why
would Richter want to kill the kids?"

Hickok nodded soberly. "Told you it don't make any
sense."

"We're missin' something here somewheres. Richter
was the one that abducted them from New York—"

"And sent 'em West on the Orphan Train."

"—plannin' all along they'd be adopted by some
farmer off in the middle of nowhere."

"So when that got bollixed, he switched tactics. Set
about tryin' to kill 'em."

"Yeah, but why?"

They muddled on it a moment. "There's things we
don't know," Hickok finally said. "How'd the kids get stole
from their folks in the first place? Sounds like Richter
pulled it off mighty easy."

Cody tugged at his goatee. "You think their folks hired
Richter?"

"I reckon that'd be one answer. All we know for sure is that Richter was bound and determined they'd never return East."

"Which means there's liable to be somebody in New York that feels the same way. Somebody willin' to kill them."

Hickok grimaced. "Hate to think it's their folks, but who the hell knows? Stranger things have happened."

"You're right," Cody said gravely. "We've got to be real careful when we hit New York City. Nobody's to be trusted."

"Meanwhile, we don't say nothin' to the kids. Let 'em think everything's hunky-dory."

"I'm mighty glad you're along for the ride."

"Guess there wasn't no choice when the shootin' started."

In the compartment, they found the children seated on the lower bunk. Hickok suddenly thought of something he'd overlooked. He shot Cody a quick glance.

"Hope you wasn't plannin' to stop off and see Lulu. Doubt it'd be wise to lay over in St. Louis."

Cody caught the warning in his voice. "No, we'll go straight through to New York. I'll see Lulu another time."

Augustus was overcome with curiosity. "Who is Lulu, Buffalo Bill?"

"Why, she's my wife, young feller. Her and the children live in St. Louis."

"You're married?" Katherine said, visibly shocked by the news. "You have children?"

"Shore do," Cody acknowledged. "Arta, that's my daughter, she's just turned six. Kit, that's the boy, he's two now."

"Kit—?"

"Well, he's named after another famous scout, Kit Carson. He was a mite before your time."

"How long have you been married?"

"Going on seven years, come March. Time flies when you're not lookin'."

Hickok seated himself on an upholstered bench across from the bunks. He took a powder flask and a pouch of lead balls from his war bag and began reloading his pistols. Katherine continued to question Cody, and as he listened, he thought again that it was a strange marriage. But then, Lulu was a strange woman.

Her given name was Louisa, though everyone called her Lulu. She was originally from St. Louis, a religious girl educated in a convent. Cody married her shortly after the Civil War, and she'd followed him West on his first posting as a scout. Yet she was appalled by army life, and with the birth of their daughter, she returned to St. Louis. She tolerated an occasional visit by Cody.

Hickok was often amused by what passed for marital bliss. Lulu was content with the children and her home in St. Louis, and in their entire married life, Cody had never spent longer than a month at a time in her bed. As he reflected on it, Hickok thought his friend was home only long enough to sire children. Cody much preferred to be off with the cavalry, chasing Indians.

"Do you miss your wife?" Katherine asked. "How long has it been since you were home?"

Cody wasn't sure. "Well, near as I recollect, it was last summer sometime. June, maybe July."

"Goodness," Katherine said, surprised. "Augustus and I don't mind if you stop in St. Louis. Wouldn't it make your wife very happy?"

"Just bet it would." Cody exchanged a furtive look with Hickok. "But I've got business in New York with this stage play. I'll stop by next time through."

Katherine saw the look pass between them. Her attention turned to Hickok. "Are you married too, Wild Bill?"

Cody laughed. "Wild Bill's not the marryin' kind. Scared he'll get his wings clipped."

"I don't understand," Katherine said. "What does he mean, Wild Bill?"

"Guess it's like this . . ." Hickok paused, placing percussion caps behind the chambers on his pistol. "A feller shouldn't get married till he finds the right girl. Just any old girl won't do."

"And you've never found the right girl?"

"I can truthfully say that's a fact."

Katherine thought there was no question that Buffalo Bill was the handsomer of the two men. But she was strangely drawn to the danger that lurked behind every syllable of every word spoken by Wild Bill. All the more so since she'd now discovered that he wasn't married.

"I've been thinking . . ." she hesitated, then rushed on, certain he was the one to ask. "Why were those men shooting at us, Wild Bill?"

Hickok stuffed the loaded pistol in his belt. "Buffalo Bill and me don't rightly know. We figure to find out what's what when we get to New York."

"Mother and Father will be able to tell us. I just know they will."

"Maybe so." Hickok deftly changed the subject. "Speakin' of New York, Scout Cody, what in tarnation have you got me into with this show business?"

"Told you before," Cody said. "You get up on a stage and talk. Buntline writes the words you say. He calls it a script."

Ned Buntline advertised the production as the *Buffalo Bill Combination*. In stage terms, a combination was a theatrical troupe that presented the same play for the run of the show. A stock company, by contrast, offered a repertory of plays, often changing from night to night. The bigger difference, however, was that a stock company production was the work of professional actors. Buntline's plays relied solely on the fame of the star.

"No need to worry," Cody went on. "You'll do just fine on the stage, Jim. Just fine."

Augustus appeared startled. "Wild Bill, why did Buffalo Bill call you 'Jim'?"

"I reckon he just slips every now and then. You see, my name's really James Butler Hickok. But that sort of got lost in the shuffle."

"I think that's a nice name," Augustus said. "Why don't people call you Wild Jim?"

"That'd suit me," Hickok said, tamping powder and ball into his other pistol. "I've been tryin' to ditch Wild Bill ever since I got hung with it."

"Then why do they call you Wild Bill?"

"Well, it happened durin' the war. One of them flukes that never makes much sense."

"What is a fluke?"

"Oddball things that happen to a man."

Hickok explained that he'd been a scout during the Civil War. On one assignment, operating as a spy behind Confederate lines, he had been caught out. He fought off a swarm of Rebels in a running gun battle and finally swam his horse to safety across a river. The Union troops on the opposite shore saw the last of the fight and his miraculous escape. Someone dubbed him Wild Bill and the name stuck.

"So that's a fluke," Hickok concluded. "Feller that tagged me with the handle didn't even know me. I ain't outrun it yet."

Augustus averted his eyes. "Will you get mad at me if I tell you something?"

"'Course I won't get mad at you. Go ahead, speak your piece."

"Well—it's just that . . . ain't is not a word."

Hickok looked up from his pistol. "What do you mean, it ain't a word?"

Augustus gave him a shy glance. "We were taught in school that it isn't . . . a proper word."

"There's more to life than school learnin'. Take your name for example."

"My name?"

"Augustus," Hickok said slowly. "That's purely a mouthful, ain't it?"

"I guess it is."

"So wouldn't you like to have your own handle? Something easier to swallow?"

"Like what?"

Hickok grinned. "From now on, I'm gonna call you Gus. How's that sound?"

"Gus," Augustus repeated, testing the word. "I think I like it."

"Now, about your sister." Hickok nodded to him with a sly smile. "Katherine's sort of a mouthful too. Maybe we'll just call her Sis."

"You *will* not," Katherine shrieked. "I am not a— Sis!"

Hickok gave the boy a conspiratorial look. "What do you think about that, Gus?"

"Well," Augustus went along, struggling not to laugh. "When no one can hear us, I call her Katie."

"What does she call you?"

"Auggie."

"Auggie and Katie." Hickok deliberated on it a moment, abruptly smiled. "I'd sooner call you by special names. How about Gus and"—he winked drolly at the girl— "Kate."

Katherine thought she would melt. She blushed bright as a beet, certain she would love him forever. "A special name," she said in a throaty voice. "Oh, yes, thank you, Wild Bill."

"Don't mention it, Kate." Hickok stuck the second pistol in his belt. "Think I'll step out and have a smoke. Little stuffy in here for cigars."

Katherine simpered. "I love the smell of cigars."

Cody grunted a laugh. Hickok ignored him, moving through the door into the passageway. He lit a cheroot, and then, deciding to stretch his legs, walked back to the passenger coaches. The train hurtled eastward across the plains, the dark of nightfall upon the land. The coaches were dimly lighted by coal-oil lamps.

Hickok thought he might catch a breath of fresh air. There was an observation deck at the rear of the train, and he made his way to the last passenger coach. As he moved along the aisle, he suddenly squinted, hardly able to credit his eyes. Richter and his hooligan, the one named Johnson, were seated at the rear of the coach.

Richter was seated by the window. Johnson was dozing, his chin resting on his massive chest. Hickok stopped in the aisle, and Richter turned from the window, his features abruptly guarded. He poked Johnson in the ribs with his elbow.

Richter stared at him. "We're not looking for trouble, Hickok."

"Well, you done found it, you sorry sonsabitches. Why're you after them kids, anyway?"

Johnson started out of his seat. Hickok pulled one of his Colts, thumbed the hammer. He hooked the blade of the front sight in Johnson's nose.

"Sit real still," he said. "All I need's an excuse."

"Take it easy, Turk," Richter said, placing a hand on Johnson's arm. "We have as much right on this train as he does. He won't do anything."

Hickok's eyes went cold. "Here's the way it works,

Richter. You or your gorilla come anywhere near them kids and I'll kill you. Take it as gospel fact."

"You don't frighten me," Richter scoffed. "I'll come and go as I please."

"You're already talkin' like a dead man."

Hickok ripped the blade of the sight out of Johnson's nostril. Johnson clutched at his nose, a jet of blood pouring over his hands. Lowering the hammer, Hickok backed away, the Colt still leveled on them. His voice was pleasantly ominous.

"Don't let me see you boys again."

Johnson watched him with a murderous glare. Hickok turned in the aisle and walked back through the train. A few minutes later he opened the door of the compartment, motioning Cody into the passageway. He waited until the door was closed.

"We've got company," he said. "Richter and Johnson are on the train."

Cody went ashen. "You talked to them?"

"After a fashion. I warned 'em off, but it won't do no good. They'll make a try for the kids."

"Judas Priest! You got any bright ideas?"

"Just one," Hickok said. "We ain't gonna let them kids out of our sight."

They decided the children would not be allowed out of the compartment. Once they were back inside, the door was locked and the sleeping arrangements were quickly settled. Katherine and Augustus shared the upper bunk, and Cody stretched out on the lower bunk. Hickok, seated on the upholstered bench, took the first watch.

Katherine smiled down at him from the top bunk. "Good night, Wild Bill."

"Get some sleep, Kate. Don't let the bedbugs bite."

She giggled. "I promise I won't."

Hickok leaned back against the bench. Cody would spell him at midnight, and until then, he had plenty to occupy his mind. Somewhere before New York, Richter and Johnson would make a play for the children. The question that wouldn't go away was *Why?*

He thought about it as the train barreled through the night.

CHAPTER 12

CHICAGO WAS the midcontinental shipping center of the nation. The city was located at the southern tip of Lake Michigan, and served as a major port on the Great Lakes. Yet it was the railroads that transformed Chicago into a metropolis. The city by the lake was in the midst of a boom.

The good times were all the more remarkable because of the fire. Three months ago, on a Sunday night in October, Mrs. O'Leary's cow became known around the world. The cow kicked over a lantern, which set the barn afire, and within hours a holocaust raged through the streets. The city's buildings, constructed of timber and slats, went up like kindling.

By the following night, the Great Chicago Fire had burned itself out. Three hundred people were dead, half the buildings in the city were destroyed, and one hundred thousand were homeless. But Chicago, like the phoenix of ancient myth, was reborn from the ashes. The city arose anew to the sound of hammers pounding nails into rip-sawed lumber.

Hickok smelled the stockyards when he stepped off the train. The longhorns trailed from Texas to the Kansas cowtowns ended up in the slaughterhouses of Chicago. By some estimates, upward of seventy thousand longhorns had been shipped north from Abilene last summer. The sweetish smell of manure permeated the railroad district.

Cody and the children joined Hickok on the depot platform. The stationhouse was immense by Western standards, and hundreds of travelers scurried from train to train. Hickok scanned the crowds, searching the sea of faces for some glimpse of Richter and Johnson. His every instinct told him they were out there. Watching. Waiting.

Chicago was the terminus for Western trains. Hickok and Cody were forced to lay over for the night, and catch a morning train to New York. They were all too aware that the danger to the children increased a hundredfold in a large city. Oddly enough, even among the jostling throngs, they felt more exposed than on the open plains. The hustle and bustle of the jammed railway station merely set their nerves on edge.

A porter directed them to a nearby hotel. The sun smoldered on the western horizon as they came out of the depot. For a moment, they stood marveling at the renaissance of a city virtually leveled by flame. Just three months ago, the Great Chicago Fire had been headlined in every newspaper in America. They expected to see a city in ruin, and instead they saw a forest of buildings in every direction. The transformation was startling.

The Dearborn Hotel still smelled of raw lumber. Located a block north of the railway station, the three-story structure had been hammered together within a month of the fire. The hotel was unpretentious and cheap, a stopover for travelers stranded between trains. A lone settee positioned on a nondescript carpet provided the sole amenity in the lobby. The desk clerk looked like a bartender in a workingman's saloon. He wore red garters on his shirtsleeves.

"Afternoon," Cody said. "We'd like to engage rooms for the night."

The clerk scrutinized the children with an inquisitive look. "Will that be one room or two?"

"Two," Cody answered. "Adjoining rooms with a connecting door."

"We have one set of adjoining rooms on each floor. Any preference?"

"First floor," Hickok said. "Hear you're prone to fires in this town."

The clerk sniffed. "We refund in case of a fire. That will be ten dollars—in advance."

"Godalmighty," Hickok groaned. "We don't aim to buy the place."

"Do you want the rooms or not?"

Hickok bristled at the man's tone. Cody intervened before his friend could instruct the clerk in manners. Too often, he'd seen the instruction result in broken noses and missing teeth, or worse. He slapped a gold eagle on the counter and signed the register "William F. Cody." The clerk handed him two keys.

The rooms were spartan as a monk's cell. The beds were hard as planks, with dingy sheets and coarse woolen blankets. Along one wall was a washstand with a chipped basin and a faded mirror. On the opposite wall were wooden pegs for clothing and a straight-backed chair, and beneath the bed was a stained johnnypot. A lavatory at the end of the hall served the entire floor.

"Highway robbery," Hickok fumed. "Leave it to city slickers to pick your pocket."

Augustus put on a smile. "It's only for one night, Wild Bill. We'll be on our way to New York tomorrow."

"I like a man who looks on the bright side, Gus. Guess it could've been worse."

Hickok went into the adjoining room. He took the wooden chair and wedged it beneath the knob of the door leading to the hall. Katherine and Augustus watched him with puzzled expressions. She finally gave way to curiosity.

"Why did you do that, Wild Bill?"

"No harm in being careful," Hickok said. "Anybody

rattles that door knob tonight, I want you to yell out real loud. You understand?"

"Do you think someone would try to come in our room?"

"Kate, it's like they say, an ounce of prevention."

Hickok glanced back at the adjoining door and Cody gave him a cryptic nod. Words were unnecessary, for they each read the other's mind. They were thinking the same thing.

Richter and Johnson were out there somewhere.

A short while later they returned to the lobby. Hickok and Cody were carrying bundles of wrinkled clothes taken from their war bags. Cody left Hickok with the children and carried both bundles to the desk. He showed the clerk a five-dollar gold piece.

"We need to get these things pressed. Think you could arrange that?"

"There's a Chinese laundry around the corner. I'll take care of it."

"Have to be back tonight."

The clerk accepted the gold piece. "How's an hour sound?"

"Just about right."

Outside the hotel, Cody and Hickok fell in on either side of the children. The streetlamps were lit and the sidewalks were crowded with people. They turned north from the hotel and went off in search of a place to have supper. Hickok kept looking over his shoulder.

Three blocks upstreet they found O'Malley's Steakhouse. The restaurant had red-checkered tablecloths and sawdust on the floor, and a small bar at the rear of the room. The waiter recommended the twelve-ounce ribeye, with mashed potatoes and gravy, and winter squash. Hickok and Cody ordered rye whiskey, and a pitcher of milk for the children. The waiter scurried off to the kitchen.

Not quite an hour later they emerged from the restaurant. Augustus and Katherine were stuffed, hardly able to finish half of their steaks. The plainsmen once again flanked them and they turned back toward the hotel. There were fewer people on the streets, and they loafed along at a leisurely pace. On the corner they passed a saloon and Hickok spotted card tables through the tall plate-glass window. He paused, drawn to a gaming den in the way metal finds a magnet, and the others stopped with him. Cody suggested it was not the night for poker.

Hickok, reluctantly, was forced to agree. He was about to turn away when a reflection in the window caught his attention. He hesitated, fishing a cheroot from inside his jacket, and struck a match on his thumbnail. The wind was out of the north, and he turned slightly, shielding the match in his cupped hands. As he puffed on the cheroot, he glanced over the flame.

Richter and Johnson were on the opposite side of the street. They were halfway up the block, standing before a haberdashery, feigning interest in the window display. He thought they were likely watching him in the shop window, and he snuffed the match, quickly looked away. All in an instant, he knew he had to end it here, tonight. He turned back to Cody.

"Everybody keep their eyes on me," he said firmly, nodding to the children. "Don't let on what I'm about to tell you. Our friends are across the street, back a little ways."

Cody held his gaze. "Any chance we could shake them?"

"We're long past that. I'm gonna go in this saloon to play poker, and I want you to get mad as hell. Then you take the kids and go on back to the hotel. Don't argue with me, just do it."

"What am I supposed to say?"

"You're the actor, think of something."

"The devil you are!" Cody shouted, inventing dialogue to suit the role. "You're not fixin' to stick me with these kids while you play poker all night!"

"I'll do what I please," Hickok said loudly. "You're the one that signed on as nursemaid, not me. You don't like it, lump it."

"You got some brass!"

"Just leave me the hell be."

Hickok wheeled through the door of the saloon. He walked to the poker tables, which were across from the bar. Through the window, he saw Cody turn downstreet with the children. Upstreet, he saw Richter and Johnson glance at the saloon as they neared the opposite corner. He took a chair at one of the tables, certain they would follow Cody. They, to the surprise of the other players, he pushed back out of the chair. He hurried toward the door.

Outside, he saw Richter and Johnson angling across the street. Cody and the children were approaching the next intersection, walking in the direction of the hotel. Hickok lengthened his stride, closing the distance as the two men dodged around a horse-drawn coal wagon halfway down the block. There was no one else in sight and he quickened his pace. He caught them as they stepped onto the curb.

"Look who's here," he said tersely. "You boys don't know good advice when you hear it."

"Hickok!" Richter spun around "I thought—"

"Defend yourselves," Hickok ordered. "I mean to kill you."

"No, wait!"

"Defend yourselves."

Richter backed away, hands thrown up as if to ward off bullets. Johnson's hand snaked inside his coat and came out with a stubby bulldog revolver. Hickok was a beat faster, leveling a Colt Navy even as he cocked the hammer. He fired two shots in rapid succession, the roar reverberating off buildings. The slugs struck Johnson over the sternum, not a handspan apart, and he buckled at the knees. He toppled off the curb and into the gutter, the revolver slipping from his grasp. His eyes rolled back in his head.

A short distance downstreet, Richter ducked into an alley. Hickok rushed forward, flattened himself against a storefront, and cautiously looked around the building. The alleyway was black as a tunnel, the far end dimly illuminated by lamplights from the next street over. He saw Richter, a shadow against the fuzzy aureole of light, sprinting headlong for the opposite end. He sighted and fired, the bullet whistling harmlessly through the night. Richter disappeared around the far corner.

Hickok started to follow. Then, aware that the gunshots would draw the police, he turned away from the alley. He couldn't afford to be arrested, much less explain to a court the convoluted tale of why he'd killed a man. His overriding concern remained the safety of the children.

He hurried off toward the hotel.

The depot was mobbed with an early morning crowd. The train for New York was scheduled to depart at seven o'clock, and people waiting to board were already congregated on the platform. Cody and Hickok, with the children in tow, threaded their way through the crush. Their passage drew stares.

Hickok was attired in a handsomely tailored Prince Albert frock coat. A brocaded vest and striped trousers were set off by a colorful tie and a diamond stickpin. He wore a scarlet embroidered silk sash around his waist, with the brace of ivory-handled Colts carried crossdraw fashion. He looked somewhat like an armed peacock.

Cody was himself a dashing spectacle. His bone-white buckskin jacket was decorated with fringe and elaborate quillwork. A royal-blue shirt and gaily colored kerchief complimented the outfit, with nankeen trousers stuffed in the tops of dark oxblood boots. His Colt Army was carried in a holster at waist level.

Earlier, when they arrived at the station, Cody had again booked space on a parlor car. Their dapper attire, and the children's animated manner, attracted the conductor's eye. He personally escorted them on board, insisting a porter take their war bags, and got them settled in their compartment. The train pulled out a short time later.

All morning Hickok had kept a wary lookout for Richter. He and Cody were in agreement that they couldn't let their guard down. So long as Richter was alive, the children were still in imminent peril. Yet, for all their watchfulness, they'd seen nothing of Richter in the station or among the passengers on the platform. They were nonetheless convinced he'd somehow managed to board the train.

Last night, after the children were asleep, Hickok had related details of the fight. Cody already suspected someone was dead, for he'd heard three gunshots as he rushed Katherine and Augustus into the hotel. Upon learning that it was Johnson, he had expressed concern that their problem was far from solved. Richter was a formidable adversary, a zealot of sorts, staunch in his resolve to kill the children. His narrow escape would hardly deter him from another try.

Some miles east of Chicago, Hickok got to his feet. He commented that he needed a smoke, trading a hidden look with Cody. Outside the compartment, he moved through the passageway and proceeded to the first passenger coach. Every seat was full, and he methodically searched the faces as he walked along the aisle. There were five coaches on the train, and he went through each on like a hunter patiently stalking prey. He found Richter in the last seat of the last coach.

There was no one sharing Richter's seat. He kept his hands in plain sight, nodding to Hickok. "Won't you join me, Mr. Hickok. Perhaps it's time we had a talk."

Hickok stopped in the aisle. "What's there to talk about?"

"Let me ask you a question. Are you a wealthy man?"

"Get to the point."

"You have something I want," Richter said. "I'm willing to pay quite generously for an exchange."

"Yeah?" Hickok said without inflection. "How much?"

"Ten thousand."

"Lot of money."

"Enough to put you and Cody on easy street."

"What makes those kids worth so much? Why you after 'em anyway?"

"I'm not at liberty to say."

"Guess that's your tough luck."

"What?"

Hickok took him by the collar. Richter tried to resist and Hickok jerked him into the aisle and waltzed him to the rear door. Outside, on the observation deck, Hickok grabbed him by the collar and the seat of his pants and bodily threw him off the train. Richter hit the roadbed on his shoulder, tumbling head over heels, and rolled to a stop in a patch of weeds. He lay motionless as the train chugged eastward.

The conductor slammed open the door. "What in God's name happened?"

"Would you believe it?" Hickok said guilelessly. "That feller hadn't bought a ticket."

"How do you know that?"

"Why, he told me so himself. He was so ashamed, he just up and jumped off the train."

The conductor gawked. "Why on earth would he jump?"

"You know, it's funny, he never said. Some folks are mighty strange."

Hickok left the conductor to ponder the riddle. He walked back through the coaches and stepped into the compartment. Cody looked up with a quizzical expression.

"Enjoy your smoke, Jim?"

"There you go again, slipping up on names. You got to remember I'm the one and only Wild Bill."

Cody chuckled. "I take it you had yourself a good time?"

"That little problem we was talkin' about?" Hickok said. "We won't be bothered with it no more."

"You handled it, did you?"

"You shore as hell got that right."

"Honestly!" Katherine admonished prettily. "Why do you curse so much, Wild Bill?"

"Well, Kate." Hickok knuckled his mustache. "I reckon it's the bad company I keep. Buffalo Bill taught me all the wrong words."

"But he almost never uses curse words."

"You just ain't been listenin' real close."

"Who cares!" Augustus laughed happily. "We're on our way to New York!"

Hickok grinned. "Gus, we'll have you there in no time."

CHAPTER 13

THE TRAIN arrived in New York on January 29.

Grand Central Station was a sprawling five-acre complex that served over a hundred trains a day. The railyard was covered by an immense overstructure of iron sheds, the most spacious enclosure on the North American continent. New Yorkers were quick to boast that it rivaled London's St. Pancras as the largest train station in the world.

Hickok and Cody stepped off the train with the children. Augustus was practically hopping with excitement, and Katherine was radiant, hardly able to contain herself. Their long ordeal on the Orphan Train, and their adventures on the Western Plains, were now at an end. Their protectors had brought them once again to Manhattan Island. They were almost home.

Ned Buntline and Texas Jack Omohundro were waiting on the platform. Buntline was a short, stout man with a game leg and a winning smile. He limped forward like a toy soldier no longer in good working order. Texas Jack was a leathery, rawboned plainsman with a soupstrainer mustache. A former scout, he was close friends with both Cody and Hickok.

"Welcome, welcome!" Buntline said with a moon-like grin. "How was your trip?"

Cody accepted his handshake. "Ned, it'd make the best dime novel you ever wrote. This here's Bill Hickok."

"Indeed?" Buntline said gleefully. "Wild Bill Hickok in the flesh. You are just as I imagined you, Mr. Hickok."

Hickok nodded. "Glad you got what you expected, Mr. Buntline."

"Call me Ned!"

Cody and Hickok warmly shook hands with Omohundro. He ducked his chin at the children. "Who's your friends?"

"Katherine and Augustus," Cody said proudly. "These youngsters are long on grit, Jack. I'll tell you about it on the way to the hotel."

"Hotel?" Katherine echoed. "Aren't you taking us home, Buffalo Bill?"

"Well, not just yet. Wild Bill and me got a couple of things to check out first."

Her face crumpled. "But we want to go home."

"Kate, listen to me." Hickok gently touched her shoulder. "You remember the man that was after you and Gus? We've got to make sure he don't have friends waitin' for you here in New York. You understand me?"

"I think so." Her bottom lip trembled with fright. "Would they try to steal us again?"

"That's a chance we ain't gonna take. We'll have a talk with your folks and see what's what. No need to rush into things."

"Wild Bill knows best," Augustus chimed in. "Him and Buffalo Bill have brought us this far. You have to trust them, Katie."

"Oh, Augustus, you're such a ninny sometimes. I trust them with all my heart."

"Then everything will be all right. You wait and see."

Buntline and Omohundro exchanged a puzzled glance. But Cody had promised the story in good time, and they held their silence. Omohundro led the way along the platform as Buntline went into a rhapsodizing monologue about the theater he'd contracted. A few moments later they climbed the stairway from the railyard and entered the main terminal. Hickok stopped in his tracks.

Grand Central Station was the masterwork of railroad

baron Cornelius Vanderbilt. The beaux-arts architecture, a mass of brick and granite, was an airy colossus completed in 1871. The central chamber rose majestically, nearly two hundred feet high, with vaulted arches above massive stained-glass windows. The marble floor stretched onward forever and the constellations of the zodiac, gold against blue on the ceiling, gave it a kaleidoscope effect. The impression was not unlike that of a vast amphitheater reaching for the stars.

"Godalmighty," Hickok breathed, looking upward. "You could put most of Kansas in here."

Omohundro chuckled. "Floored me the first time I saw it, too. These New York folks, they think big."

"Jack, it purely beats all. Damned if it don't."

"Wait'll you see the city."

Outside the terminal they emerged onto Forty Second Street. Buntline had a landau carriage waiting and they squeezed into the enclosed cab. Two blocks over they turned south onto Fifth Avenue and the traffic abruptly became chaotic. The broad thoroughfare, as far as the eye could see, was jammed with wagons and carriages of every description. All of them horse drawn.

Even inside the cab, the air festered with the stench that was unique to New York. A ripe blend of rotting garbage, horse manure, and noxious coal smoke pouring from chimneys. Hickok wrinkled his nose, unable to hold his breath and yet overpowered by the smell. He suddenly longed for the crisp, clean winds of the plains.

"Takes getting used to," Omohundro said, noting his expression. "Couple of days, you won't even notice it."

"Jack, it'd gag a dog off a gut wagon."

"Well, mostly, it's all them horses."

Buntline, like many New Yorkers, was prone to brag on the enormity of the city in all its facets. He merrily recounted the gist of an article he'd read in the *New York*

Times only yesterday. There were forty thousand horses in the city, and every day they unloaded four hundred tons of manure and twenty thousand gallons of urine. He slapped his knee with a ripsnorter of a laugh.

"You can imagine, it keeps the street-sweepers busy!"

"Jack's right," Cody remarked. "I'd forgot what it smells like here. Does take getting used to."

"Yeah, it's odoriferous," Omohundro said. "A whiff of fresh air would likely kill me now."

Texas Jack Omohundro was a Westering man who had come East. By birth a Southerner, he had served with J.E.B. Stuart's Cavalry Corps during the Civil War. Afterward, he migrated to Texas, where he'd gained his nickname and a reputation as an Indian fighter. He knew Hickok from a sojourn through Kansas, and until last year, he had worked as a scout at Fort McPherson. Cody had talked him into joining the Buffalo Bill Combination.

New York, curiously enough, agreed with Omohundro. One season on the stage seemingly turned a roughhewn plainsman into a citified dandy. All the more important, he had fallen for a beautiful Italian actress and married her in the spring of 1871. When Cody returned to duty at Fort McPherson, Omohundro had elected to remain behind with his bride. He was now a professional actor, appearing in occasional stage plays until Cody came East for the new season. These days, he acted the part of a plainsman.

Hickok thought Omohundro had taken leave of his senses. The idea of forty thousand horses in one town boggled his mind; he considered their daily droppings too great a sacrifice for the love of any woman. Yet, as he stared out the window of the carriage, he was nonetheless impressed by the sheer magnitude of the place.

They drove past buildings seven and eight stories high, so tall he had to crane his neck to see the sky. Three stories was the tallest building he'd ever seen, and now he was looking at structures that towered like mountains. He told himself he was a long way from Kansas.

Too damn far for comfort.

The Fifth Avenue Hotel was located on the southwest corner of a busy intersection. Broadway angled across Fifth Avenue directly in front of the hotel, and on the opposite side of the street was Madison Square. The landscaped seven-acre square was lined with such fashionable shops as Tiffany's and F. A. O. Schwarz.

A liveried doorman greeted the carriage. Bellmen rushed to collect the scant baggage, and Buntline led the entourage into the hotel. The lobby was a sea of pink marble, with glittery chandeliers and plush seating arrangements, and an air of decadent opulence. The hotel manager welcomed them with an obsequious smile.

Buntline had reserved a suite for Cody and Hickok. There were two bedrooms, each with its own lavatory, and a sitting room with an onyx marble foreplace. A lush Persian carpet covered the sitting-room floor, and grouped before the fireplace were several chairs and a chesterfield divan. The view from the third-floor windows overlooked Madison Square.

Giuseppina Morlacchi, Omohundro's wife, was waiting for them in the suite. She was small and svelte, with youthful breasts, a stemlike waist, and nicely rounded hips. Her features were exquisite, somehow exotic and doll-like, with a lush, coral mouth that accentuated her high cheekbones. Her hair was the color of dark sable, and she spoke with a pronounced Italian accent.

"Beeel!" she squealed, dragging Cody into a tight embrace. "We are sooo happy to see you again!"

"Same here." Cody said with a loopy grin. "You're lookin' mighty fine, Giuseppina."

"Oh, you were always the flatterer!"

Hickok quickly learned that Morlacchi was her stage name. Buntline explained that every Western play required an Indian maiden, and Giuseppina, with her flawless olive complexion, perfectly fit the part. She graced Hickok with a dazzling smile and bold, flirtatious eyes, and he abruptly changed his mind. He thought perhaps Omohundro was wise to stay in New York.

"Pleasure, ma'am," Hickok said, offering her a courtly bow. "Texas Jack's a lucky feller."

"How gallant!" she trilled. "All of you scouting men have such a way with words."

"Well, ma'am, that's easy enough where you're concerned."

She looked at the children. "And who are these beautiful leettle darlings?"

Hickok smiled. "This here's Kate and Gus. They've been travelin' with us a spell."

"Giuseppina, my love," Buntline broke in smoothly. "We have business matters to discuss. Would you be a dear and entertain the children? We won't be long."

"But of course!" she exclaimed. "I weel tell them a story."

Hickok laughed. "You might like to hear their story. It's a real humdinger."

"Come along, then, we weel all tell stories."

Giuseppina took the children into one of the bedrooms. Augustus looked smitten by her sloe-eyed sensuality, and Katherine watched her with the alert expression of one woman studying another's worldly allure. The door to the bedroom closed with Giuseppina's spirited laughter.

On the way to the hotel, Cody had briefly explained the situation with the children. He dropped into one of the easychairs as Buntline and Omohundro seated themselves on the divan. Hickok stood staring out the widow at Madison Square.

"We got 'em here safe and sound," Cody went on where he'd left off. "But we're not just exactly sure how their folks fit into all this. You ever hear of a Henry Morton Stanley?"

"Stanley?" Buntline mused aloud. "I seem to recall there is a Stanley involved with the Guaranty Trust Bank. Old New York money and lots of it. Could be your man."

"You recollect whether he lives on Gramercy Park?"

"That would certainly be an address for a banker. Gramercy Park is old money and old New York."

Hickok turned from the window. "I ain't got the least goddamn interest in what he does for a livin'. We don't trust nobody till we get a handle on things."

Omohundro looked at him. "You sound a mite tetchy about these kids."

"Yeah, I reckon so," Hickok said evenly. "Bill and me done planted a slew of jaybirds that was tryin' to kill Gus and Kate. Somebody wants 'em dead awful bad."

"Planted?" Buntline appraised the word. "Are you saying you killed men to protect the children?"

Hickok shrugged. "No more'n we had to."

"So what's your move?" Omohundro asked. "You mean to contact the family?"

"Think I'll handle that," Cody said quickly, glancing at Hickok. "You'd barge in like a bull in a china shop. What we need's a tactful approach. You agree?"

"Why shore," Hickok said dryly. "You always was the diplomat of the bunch. Just don't let the cat out of the bag."

"I'll drop around to Gramercy Park tomorrow mornin'. We'll keep the kids here till things come clear."

"You've no time to lose," Buntline observed. "We open in Philadelphia day after tomorrow."

"Philadelphia?" Cody said, astounded. "What happened to New York?"

"Bill, it's a new show," Buntline said defensively. "We'll play Philadelphia for a week and work out the kinks. I want it perfect when we open here in New York."

"Well, you're the boss when it comes to the show business. Guess we're headed to Philadelphia."

Buntline was indeed the maestro. His real name was Edward Zane Judson, but he had adopted the *nom de plume* Ned Buntline. A character himself, he'd had six wives and once fought a duel over a dalliance with another man's wife. Some years ago he had been jailed for instigating a theater riot against an English actor who was in competition with Edwin Forrest, America's greatest Shakespearean. He was renowned for his dime novels, and now he'd made his name as a playwright. The Buffalo Bill Combination was his entrée into the theater.

"Forgot to ask," Cody said. "What's the name of the new show?"

Buntline swelled with pride. *"The Scouts of the Plains!"*

"Yeah, that's us," Cody said, glancing around at Hickok and Omohundro. "What's the story?"

"You might say it is *The Three Musketeers* taking battle to the warlike tribes."

Cody looked blank. "Who's the three musketeers?"

"Who—" Buntline laughed deep in his belly. "Only the grandest novel ever written by Alexander Dumas. One of the immortals!"

"Never heard of him," Cody said. "Funny name for a feller that writes dime novels."

"No, no, he was a Frenchman. Dead now scarcely two years. A genius!"

"I'll take your word for it, Ned."

Hickok crossed the room. He took a firebrand from the fireplace and lit a cheroot. His gaze fixed on Cody.

"Maybe we ought to talk about Philadelphia."

"What about it?"

Hickok exhaled smoke. "Day after tomorrow's pretty damn quick. Don't give us much time to get things settled with Kate and Gus."

"Time enough," Cody said. "I'll get the lowdown from their folks in the mornin'. We'll go from there."

"What if the lowdown ain't all we need to know? What then?"

"C'mon now, don't go borrowin' trouble. Wait and see what I ferret out."

"Just so's we're clear on things," Hickok said. "Them kids are our first order of business. Not Philadelphia."

"Hold on!" Buntline protested. "We're booked into a theater. We must be there!"

Hickok pointed the cheroot at him. "I'm not talkin' to you. This here's between me and Cody."

Buntline deflated back onto the divan. Texas Jack Omohundro, who knew a warning when he heard one, stared off into space. Cody raised his hands in mock surrender.

"The kids first," he said. "That satisfy you?"

Hickok puffed a wad of smoke. "Just wanted to hear you say it."

Buntline wondered how many men they had killed over the children. Then, on second thought, he decided he didn't want to know. His one imperative was to get them to Philadelphia.

The Scouts of the Plains must go on.

CHAPTER 14

CODY LEFT the hotel at eight o'clock the next morning. The doorman whistled up a hansom cab and gave the driver the address. The cab trundled south on Broadway into the theater district, where traffic was in a state of bedlam even at the early hour. Farther downtown, the driver turned east onto Twentieth Street.

The sky was overcast, dull pewter clouds obscuring the sun. Cody sat back in the seat, staring out at brownstones that were the current architectural vogue. His thoughts raced over the surface of the last few weeks like a dragonfly skimming the still waters of a pond. He found himself incapable of penetrating the mystery of the children's abduction, and the attempts on their lives. He wondered what revelation might be provided by their parents. Or then again, perhaps none at all.

A short while later the cab rolled into Gramercy Park. Once a marshland, the area had been reclaimed by real-estate developer Samuel Ruggles in 1831. The original square was inspired by London's St. John's Park, and required the removal of a million wagonloads of earth. Ruggles built his own mansion there in 1839, and shrewdly deeded the square to buyers of the other sixty-five plots. The neighborhood quickly became the enclave of New York aristocrats.

Gramercy Park itself was enclosed by a tall wrought-iron fence with ornate filigree. The manicured landscape was filled with sundials and cozy benches, and the surrounding residents were given gold keys to the entrance gates. The mansions, expressing the taste of their owners, were an eclectic mix of Greek Revival, Italianate, and Victorian Gothic. The elite who resided there included William Steinway, of piano fame, railroad baron Samuel Tilden, and industrialist Peter Cooper. The park, even in the dead of winter, smelled of old money.

The cab stopped at 24 Gramercy Park. Cody paid the driver and climbed a short flight of steps to the mansion. He rapped the brass door-knocker and tugged the lapels of his buckskin jacket. A butler attired in black opened the door with a neutral smile. He examined Cody's outfit at a glance.

"Yes, sir," he said formally. "May I help you?"

"I'm William Cody. I'd like to see Henry Stanley."

"Who?"

"Henry Morton Stanley. I was told he lives at 24 Gramercy Park."

The butler appeared flustered. Then, stepping aside, he motioned Cody inside. "Would you wait here, sir?"

Cody removed his hat. His gaze swept the foyer and the broad, carpeted staircase. The butler walked to a set of sliding doors and disappeared inside. He returned a moment later.

"This way please, sir."

Cody entered a lushly appointed sitting room. A strikingly handsome man was seated before the fire-place in a leather wingback chair. He was in his early thirties, with dark hair and quick gray eyes. He dropped the *Wall Street Journal* on a nearby table.

"Mr. Cody?" he said tentatively. "How may I assist you? I'm Leland Stanley."

"Your man must've misunderstood. I'm lookin' for Henry Stanley."

"May I ask the purpose of your visit?"

"You might say it's personal," Cody replied. "Maybe you could tell him I'm here."

"Actually, no," Stanley said soberly. "I'm afraid my brother passed away some three weeks ago."

"I'm powerful sorry to hear that. How'd he die?"

"Well, in point of fact, he was murdered. He and my sister-in-law, murdered in their beds. What is your interest in my brother, Mr. Cody?"

Cody abruptly put it together. Three weeks ago dovetailed with the time Katherine and Augustus had been placed on the Orphan Train. His expression betrayed nothing.

"You'll pardon my askin', Mr. Stanley. Was your brother killed the night Katherine and Augustus got abducted?"

"Why, yes—" Stanley stopped, his eyes suddenly guarded. "What do you know about Katherine and Augustus?"

"I know they're alive and well. They got put on the Orphan Train to Nebraska."

"Nebraska?"

"That's where they ended up."

"They're alive?" Stanley sounded as if he were choking on a fish bone. "You've seen them?"

"Saw 'em with my own eyes."

"Where are they now?"

Cody was a clever liar when the situation demanded. Some visceral instinct warned him that the truth would better await another time. He spread his hands in all innocence.

"They're with a friend of mine. He's on his way here now, bringing them by train. His name's Wild Bill Hickok."

"Hickok?" Stanley stared at him. "By any chance are you *that* Cody? Buffalo Bill Cody?"

"Some call me that," Cody acknowledged. "Do the

children have any relatives besides yourself, Mr. Stanley?"

"Their grandmother."

"That would be your mother?"

Stanley nodded. "She's still distraught over Henry's death. She hasn't been out of her bed since the night he died. I'm afraid grief has made her quite ill."

"Any other relatives?"

"Not on our side of the family. Amanda, Henry's wife, has family in Connecticut. Why do you ask?"

Cody shrugged. "Just wondered who'd look after 'em now that their folks are gone."

"I will," Stanley said. "I *am* their uncle."

"Any idea why they were abducted?"

"Until today I didn't know what to think. The police are at their wits' end."

Cody thought it rang false. Stanley should have been rejoicing over the news of the children. Instead, he seemed somehow on edge, oddly nervous. Lots of questions and no smiles.

"I'll get word to you," Cody said. "Just as soon as Hickok arrives with the children."

Stanley's eyes were alert. "Where are you staying, Mr. Cody?"

"The Victoria Hotel."

The lie came easily. Something told Cody to beware of revealing too much. On the way out, he assured Stanley he would be in touch no later than tomorrow. The minute Hickok's train arrived in New York.

He lied all the way to the door.

Hickok and Omohundro were seated before the fireplace. They were old friends, and Omohundro felt no qualms about asking questions others would avoid. He listened as Hickok related his deadly tenure as marshal of Abilene.

The story abruptly ended. Cody barged into the suite and the look on his face brought them out of their chairs. They knew him too well not to realize that the visit to the Stanley mansion had gone awry. Hickok cocked an eyebrow.

"What was it lit your fuse?"

"Where are the kids?"

"They're changin' clothes," Hickok said. "Giuseppina figured they wasn't outfitted proper to see their folks. She went out and bought 'em some city duds."

"Their folks are dead," Cody said, lowering his voice. "Murdered the very same night the kids were abducted. Killed in their beds."

"I'll be go to hell. How'd you find out?"

"Talked with their uncle, feller name of Leland Stanley. He wasn't exactly overjoyed to hear they're alive."

"What'd he say?"

Cody recounted the gist of the conversation. He went on to note that something about Leland Stanley raised a red flag. Nothing specific but nonetheless there.

"Just a gut hunch," he concluded. "You know the feelin'."

"Damn right," Hickok said. "We're still wearin our topknots 'cause we got good instincts. I'd trust a gut hunch any day."

"Figured it was best to keep my trap shut. None of it makes any sense."

"No, it don't, and that's a fact. Why'd Richter abduct 'em in the first place?"

"Why not kill 'em the night he killed their folks? No doubt in my mind he's the one that done it."

"'Course he was," Hickok said. "But why'd he try to get 'em adopted? No rhyme nor reason to it."

Cody looked baffled. "All the more so since he tried to kill 'em once they got un-adopted. Somebody didn't want them kids back here in New York."

"You think their uncle's tied into it?"

"I think there's something mighty fishy there. Told me their grandma was sick with grievin' and confined to her bed. But he was plumb disappointed to learn about the kids."

"Don't sound natural, does it?"

"What about the kids?" Omohundro interrupted. "Somebody'll have to tell them about their folks."

Hickok appeared chary. He shot a glance at Cody. "You got kids of your own. You understand 'em better than me."

"God," Cody sighed. "What'll I say?"

"Guess there ain't no way around the truth."

"Ta-dah!"

Giuseppina swept into the middle of the room. Her eyes were bright with merriment and her arms were out-flung in a dramatic pose. On cue, Katherine and Augustus appeared simultaneously from the two bedrooms. Katherine wore a taffeta knee-length dress and Augustus was attired in a serge suite and a foulard tie. Their faces beamed with the fun of their new outfits.

"Aren't they darling!" Giuseppina said happily. "Have you ever seen anything so precious?"

The men stared at them with stoic expressions. The children looked confused, their smiles suddenly down-turned. Katherine stepped forward.

"What's wrong?" she said shyly. "Don't you like our new clothes?"

"No, it's not that," Cody said. "You look fine. Just fine."

"What is it, then, Buffalo Bill?"

"Well, honey, we have to tell you something . . . about your folks."

"Mother and Father?" she asked. "You've talked with them?"

Cody swallowed hard. "Katherine. Augustus. I want you to be brave—" He faltered, his voice choked. "Your folks have gone to heaven."

"Heaven?" Katherine watched him with the look of a wounded fawn. "You mean they—they are . . ."

"I'm afraid so. God's took them to the Promised Land. They're at peace now."

"Nooo!" Augustus screamed. *"Noooo!"*

Katherine's eyes flooded with tears. She threw herself into Hickok's arms, burying her head against his shoulder. Augustus sobbed with a low, strangling sound, tears spilling over his cheeks. Cody pulled him into a tight hug.

Giuseppina's features went rubbery with shock. Jack rose from his chair, his expression grave, and put his arm around her shoulders. The children wept and moaned, their pitiful, broken cries filling the room. Hickok gave Katherine his handkerchief, his eyes sorrowful and oddly moist. She looked up at him with sudden terror.

"Grandmama?" she murmured timorously. "Is Grandmama . . ."

"She's fine," Hickok reassured her. "Buffalo Bill says she's still mourning your folks and not feelin' all that spry. But she'll be up and about before you know it."

"I met your Uncle Leland," Cody added, alert to her reaction. "He's taking care of your grandmother and lookin' after the house. Maybe you'd like to go stay with him?"

"No!" Katherine wailed. "Mother hates Uncle Leland!"

Augustus blinked back tears. "Father doesn't like him, either. He always calls him the black sheep."

"Well, don't you worry," Hickok said in a soothing tone. "We'll wait till your grandma's feelin' herself again."

The softly spoken pledge opened a new floodgate of tears. Cody motioned to Giuseppina and she gently collected the children. She led them into one of the bedrooms, cooing at their wretched sobs, and closed the door. A glum silence settled over the room.

"Out of the mouths of babes," Cody finally said. "Their father didn't have no use for his own brother. Guess I was right about Uncle Leland."

Hickok grunted. "There's just one way to keep them kids safe. We're gonna take 'em with us to Philadelphia."

"We'll only be there a week. What happens when we come back to New York?"

"I reckon we'll figure something out. We've got to."

Cody thought Buntline wouldn't like it. But just as quickly he decided to hell with it. The matter was settled.

The children were going to Philadelphia.

Otto Richter looked like he'd walked into a buzzsaw. His right cheekbone was skinned raw and an ugly, purple bruise darkened his forehead. His greatcoat was ripped at the shoulder, and his left trouser leg hung in shreds. He was caked with filth.

The butler showed him into the sitting room. The gaslights were lit for the evening, and Leland Stanley was seated before the fireplace, reading the *New York Times*. He folded the paper, placing it on a table, and rose from his chair. He watched Richter cross the room with thinly veiled distaste. His features were cold.

"What happened to you?"

"Fell off a train," Richter said vaguely. "Finally caught

another one outside of Chicago. I came straight from the station."

"I see," Stanley remarked. "Did your accident have anything to do with Cody and Hickok?"

"How do you know about them?"

"Cody paid me a call this morning. He told me Hickok is on the way to New York with the children."

"That's pure bunkum," Richter said. "They're both already here and they have the children. I've been trailing them from Nebraska."

Stanley frowned at him. "How did Hickok and Cody become involved?"

Richter briefed him on the last three weeks. Stanley was not wholly without conscience, and he'd always preferred that no harm come to the children. He silently commended Richter for following orders, and waiting until there was no alternative to killing. Yet he was infuriated by Richter's failure to complete the assignment.

"Why didn't you telegraph me while all this was going on?"

"I had it under control," Richter said. "Things went to hell there toward the end."

"You are a master of understatement, Otto."

"I'll handle it, Mr. Stanley. They're in my territory now."

"Not for long." Stanley gestured at the newspaper. "I was just reading an article in the *Times*. You're familiar with Cody's stage show?"

Richter nodded. "I know he's involved with Ned Buntline."

"From what I read, Buntline intends to take the show on the road before bringing it to New York. They open in Philadelphia tomorrow night."

"I assume your orders haven't changed. You still want me to take care of the children?"

Stanley considered the euphemism for murder. He wished there were another way, for he really didn't want the blood of children on his hands. But there was simply too much at stake.

"How very unfortunate," he said quietly. "But the answer to your question is yes. Take care of the children."

"I'll leave for Philadelphia in the morning."

"Otto."

"Yes?"

"You musn't fail me this time."

"Consider it done, Mr. Stanley."

Richter turned toward the door. When he was gone, Stanley stared into the fireplace a moment. His expression was contemplative, curiously saddened as he reflected on the unalterable nature of events. Finally, gathering himself, he walked into the foyer and went upstairs. He knocked lightly on his mother's bedroom door.

Elizabeth Stanley was propped up on a bank of pillows. Her features were drawn, her complexion sallow in the flickering gaslight. She managed a faint smile.

"Have you come to tuck me in, Leland?"

"I wanted to say good night, Mother. How are you feeling?"

"Oh, you shouldn't worry," she said. "I believe I'm actually a little better."

"Well, then." Stanley bent down, kissed her on the cheek. "Get a good night's sleep."

"Leland."

"Yes, Mother?"

"Have you learned anything more of Katherine and Augustus?"

"I have a first-rate detective on the job. You rest now and try not to worry yourself too much. I feel confident we'll find them."

"I pray to God they're all right."

"I'm sure they are, Mother."

Stanley lowered the flame on the gaslight. He moved from the bedroom into the hall and closed the door. His face was set in a somber cast.

He thought things would be better when the children were dead.

CHAPTER 15

THE PENN Hotel was located on the corner of Sixth Street and Chestnut. Ned Buntline, ever anxious to display his expertise, noted that it was named after the founder of Pennsylvania. King Charles II of England had bestowed a large land grant on William Penn in 1682.

Hickok was deaf to the lecture. As they walked from the hotel to the theater, he was in a highly agitated state of mind. He had faced armed men and hostile Indians and survived the bloody killing ground of the Civil War. All of that he had done with equanimity but now his nerves fairly jangled along his backbone. Tonight he would face a live audience on stage.

Cody and the others were attentive to Buntline's dissertation. The children were all eyes as they passed the most hallowed ground in the nation's history, Independence Square. Buntline explained that the Continental Congress had convened there in 1775, and appointed George Washington General of the Army. A year later, on July 4, the Declaration of Independence had been adopted.

Buntline was a fount of information. He went on to note that Philadelphia was a Greek word for "brotherly love." Thus it had become known as the City of Brotherly Love, the birthplace of American freedom. The children hung on his every word, peppering him with questions about the Liberty Bell and the Constitution. Ever the ham, Buntline basked in their wide-eyed wonder, playing the scholar to eager young acolytes. His initial displeasure at having them along had long since disappeared. He found them a receptive audience.

Cody was gladdened by the children's animated manner. Yesterday, on the train from New York, they had withdrawn into despair and heartsick torment over their loss. Then, drained of tears and emotionally exhausted, they had fallen into a troubled sleep. Late last night, when the train arrived in Philadelphia, the resilience of youth had seemingly restored their spirits. They were by no means recovered, and moments of grief still shadowed their eyes. Yet they had bounded back remarkably well.

A good part of their invigorated manner had to do with the show. The play was to be staged at the Arch Street Theater, and Buntline had assembled the cast early that morning. Local actors had been hired for the roles of savage Indians, and there was a full complement of lighting men and stagehands. The entire day had been spent in rehearsal, with Buntline coaching the actors, sometimes berating them, as they struggled to memorize their lines. Buntline's frenzied energy had at last brought vitality to the production.

Katherine and Augustus were exhilarated by the sound and fury of the play. The lights and action and bloodcurdling war cries left them agog with marvel. Neither of them had ever seen a stage production, and they spent the day watching the madness of a rehearsal unfold in the theater. Buntline was seemingly everywhere at once, and they were all but mesmerized by his stage directions and his leather-lunged exhortations at the actors. By day's end they saw chaos and confusion transformed into some semblance of orderly stagecraft. They were bewitched by the wonder of it all.

The children's turnaround eased Cody's concern for their welfare. But the burden of putting on a stage play was measurably increased by his distress at Hickok's wooden performance. Hickok seemed incapable of memorizing lines, and thoroughly bewildered by the dazzling lights and Buntline's stage directions. There were times when Buntline's frustration, expressed in shrill anger, put Hickok on the verge of throttling the voluble showman. Cody intervened, warning Buntline to calm down, and counseling Hickok to simply be himself rather than act the role. Yet he worried that Hickok and Buntline were a volatile mix. One the gunpowder and the other the match.

The Arch Street Theater was emblazoned with lights. The top line on the backlit marquee proclaimed in foot-tall letters THE SCOUTS OF THE PLAINS. The lines directly below, equally bold, announced the stars of the show: BUFFALO BILL CODY, WILD BILL HICKOK, and TEXAS JACK OMOHUNDRO. Buntline whizzed past as though he were a whirligig on course with momentous events. Hickok, startled to see his name in lights, felt a chill ripple along his spine. Cody thought it a fine display, with perhaps one exception. He wondered if his name might have been bigger.

The stage door was through an alleyway beside the theater. When they came through the door, the backstage area was in a state of pandemonium. The prop man was scurrying around with tomahawks and feathered lances, and stagehands were putting the final touches on the scenery. The ten actors playing Sioux warriors were decked out in black wigs with braids and tawny costumes meant to resemble fringed buck-skin. They were applying nut-brown greasepaint to their faces and hands in an effort to counterfeit the look of redskins. Buntline waded in like an evangelist exhorting the faithful

"Godalmighty," Hickok woofed, halting just inside the door. "I've done joined the circus."

Cody laughed. "It'll all come together when the curtain goes up."

"I ain't sure I've got the gall for this, Bill."

"Jim, you're just a little nervy, that's all. The show business people call it 'opening-night jitters.'"

"I'd sooner hunt bears with a switch."

"Stop carryin' on so. You'll be fine."

"Says you."

The show was sold out. Every seat in the house was full and a lucky few got standing room at the rear of the theater. As the audience leafed through the playbill, they saw that the show would be presented in three acts. The subtitles fairly fired the imagination.

ACT 1. THE SCOUTS AND THE RENEGADES

ACT 2. THE SCOUTS' OATH OF VENGEANCE

ACT 3. THE TRIUMPH OF THE SCOUTS

The playbill also indicated an opening number by Mlle. Giuseppina Morlacchi. Under her resume, the audience discovered that she had studied dance at La Scala, in Milan, Italy. Her debut was in Genoa, and from there she had appeared throughout Europe and England before immigrating to America in 1869. She was the toast of New York, and her legs were insured for $100,000 by Lloyds of London. The audience fully expected to see a classical ballerina.

The curtain rose at eight o'clock. The orchestra blared to life and Giuseppina exploded out of the wings in a knee-length peekaboo gown and sheer net stockings. She pranced around the stage, her eyes bright with laughter, flapping her skirts ever higher. Then, as the tempo of the music quickened, she whirled to center stage, squealing and kicking in a rousing exhibition of the French cancan. She ended the number by leaping high in the air and landing on the stage in a full-legged split. The audience broke out in cheers.

Giuseppina blew them kisses as she skipped offstage. The curtain dropped as the orchestra segued into a stirring rendition of "The Battle Hymn of the Republic." When the number was finished, the orchestra fell silent and the curtain rose on Act One of the play. The set was designed to replicate grassy plains with majestic mountains and an endless azure sky painted on the backdrops. A campfire, constructed of orange and red crepe paper, was positioned at center stage. Cody and Hickok stood warming their hands by the fire.

The audience gave them a thunderous ovation. There were shouts from all around the theater of *"Buffalo Bill!"* and *"Wild Bill!"* Cody beamed a jack-o'-lantern grin and Hickok looked everywhere but at the crowd. After a minute, Cody finally raised his arms and stilled the applause. He struck a dramatic pose and cued Hickok with the opening line.

"Glad you found my camp, Bill. What've you been up to lately?"

Hickok froze. He opened his mouth but nothing came out. His line in the script had to do with renegade Sioux warriors raiding settlers. But his mind went blank, and he was acutely aware of the audience waiting for him to speak. Cody cued him again.

"What've you been up to lately, Bill?"

Hickok nervously cleared his throat. He said the first thing that popped into his mind. "I've been out on the hunt with the Grand Duke Alexis."

Cody blinked, momentarily thrown. But the royal hunt had been widely reported by newspapers, and he figured

the audience would think it was all part of the play. He
quickly improvised, feeding Hickok questions about the
Grand Duke and the hunt. Once they started talking,
Hickok, little by little, recovered from his stage fright.
Cody gradually steered their dialogue back to the script.

The story revolved around a hostile band of Sioux.
Texas Jack Omohundro next appeared onstage, to complete the trio of scouts. Shortly afterward, Giuseppina
made her entrance, costumed in a wig and braids and
buckskin dress. She played the part of Dove Eye, a Sioux
maiden in love with Cody, offering to help the scouts
thwart the renegades. The audience was held rapt by the
love interest.

Act One closed with Dove Eye being captured by the
hostiles. Cody, with Hickok and Omohundro at his side,
swore an oath of vengeance. Throughout Act Two there
were a series of running skirmishes, as the scouts pursued the renegades back and forth across the plains. The
actors disguised as Sioux warriors were slaughtered
wholesale, only to crawl offstage and reappear in the next
battle scene. At the close of Act Two, the scouts were
wearied from killing but had yet to rescue Dove Eye.
They stood talking at center stage.

"We go forward," Cody emoted, dramatically thrusting an arm overhead. "I will not cease the fight until
Dove Eye is safe again."

Omohundro postured. "We are with you unto the
death. Isn't that right, Wild Bill?"

A calcium spotlight from high above the balcony
swung onto Hickok. He shielded his eyes, suddenly
blinded, and took a step aside. The spotlight trailed him,
and his temper, already frayed by an hour onstage,
abruptly snapped. He shouted at the operator. "Turn the
durn thing off!"

The dazzling light held him pinned in place. One of

his pistols was charged with blanks, but the other was fully loaded. He cursed under his breath, jerking the loaded Colt, and fired. A shattering of glass exploded above the balcony and the spotlight went dead. He grinned at Cody.

"Guess that jaybird'll listen now."

The audience roared with laughter. The curtain fell, ending the scene, and Buntline rushed onto the stage. Hickok waved him off, ignoring his outrage, and Cody kept them separated until the curtain rose on Act Three. The story played out in a final volcanic battle, which left the ten renegade Sioux sprawled in death. Dove Eye was saved, the scouts emerged triumphant, and the packed house erupted with applause. The cast took four curtain calls.

Otto Richter was seated at the rear of the theater. He watched as Cody and Hickok came center stage for a standing ovation. The play seemed to him more farce than drama, and quickly forgotten. His thoughts turned instead to the children, how to finish the job. A plan would evolve once he trailed them from the theater, located the hotel where they were staying. All he needed from there was a fix on their habits, their daily schedule.

A way to separate them from the Scouts of the Plains.

Buntline hosted a breakfast for the cast the following morning. The reviews were in and his pudgy cheeks were cherry-red with excitement. He passed out copies of the *Philadelphia Journal* to everyone seated around the table. The talk stopped as they fell to reading.

Last night at the Arch Street Theater was the scene of a most extraordinary drama. The occasion was Ned Buntline's new play with the very appropriate title of *The Scouts of the Plains.* Buffalo Bill Cody

and Wild Bill Hickok, noted Western characters of
national fame, were presented in a hair-raising tale
of blood on the plains. They played their own original selves with considerable élan.

"Élan?" Hickok said dubiously. "What the devil's that
mean?"

Buntline chortled. "You gentlemen have been highly
complimented. It means spirited and with great self-
assurance."

"Well now," Cody said with a broad smile. "I like the
sound of that."

"Keep reading," Buntline said. "There's more!"

Texas Jack Omohundro, a frontier figure in his own
right, played a stalwart scout with dash and skill.
Mlle. Giuseppina Morlacchi, the Italian danseuse,
essayed the part of a beautiful Indian maiden with a
weakness for scouts. She sustained the dramatic interest from first to last, captivating the audience.

"You are beautiful!" Katherine bubbled. "I loved
watching you, Giuseppina."

Giuseppina blushed. "You are a leetle dear to be so
kind."

Augustus jiggled in his chair. "Don't forget Buffalo
Bill and Wild Bill, and Texas Jack, too. They were all
wonderful."

"We have a hit!" Buntline announced grandly. "We'll
take New York by storm!"

"Thanks to you," Cody said. "You wrote another
corker, Ned."

"Casting modesty to the winds"—Buntline preened—
"I have to say I outdid myself."

"So then," Cody said, holding his gaze. "How'd we do at the box office?"

Buntline briskly rubbed his hands together. "We'll easily clear twenty-five hundred for the week. We're in the chips!"

Cody did a quick mental calculation. Buntline, the writer and producer, received the lion's share, fifty percent. Texas Jack and Giuseppina, who were worth every penny, jointly shared twenty percent of the proceeds. By rough estimate, he and Hickok would pocket close to four hundred dollars apiece for the week. He gave Hickok a sly grin.

"How do you like them apples? Told you we'd have ourselves a payday."

"No complaints," Hickok said amiably. "Long as you keep that damn spotlight out of my eyes."

Buntline's cheery manner evaporated. He pulled in his neck and puffed up like a toad. "So far as I'm concerned, we should deduct that from your share of the receipts. Do you have any idea how much calcium lights cost?"

"Who the hell cares?" Hickok said with open scorn. "That thing was so bright I couldn't see ten feet. I won't have it."

"Which raises another matter. Why were you carrying a loaded pistol? You were instructed to use blanks."

"For openers, I don't go nowhere without a loaded gun. And you don't *instruct* me to do anything. Got it?"

"Hold on now," Cody intervened. "Ned, I wanted to talk to you about that spotlight, anyway. I'm glad you brought it up."

Buntline pursed his mouth. "What about it?"

"Well, you saw for yourself, the audience went for it in a big way. I think we ought to let Wild Bill shoot out the light in every show."

"You must be joking."

"What's more important?" Cody said. "A calcium light or a nifty piece of showmanship? You stop and think about it."

Buntline thought about it. His forehead squinched with concentration and he seemed to drift off. He finally looked up. "By golly, you're right," he conceded. "The show's the thing and showmanship's the game. Wild Bill can shoot out the light."

"Figured you wouldn't let a good idea slip by."

"Of course, we'll have to have an extra spotlight. Dramatic effect is vital to the show."

"I reckon so," Cody agreed. "Just don't put the spare on Wild Bill."

"Why not?"

Hickok smiled. "'Cause then I'd shoot out two a night."

Everyone laughed except Buntline. The humor of it escaped him, for the show business was serious business. Nothing to be ridiculed.

He thought the Prince of Pistoleers was going to be a handful.

CHAPTER 16

TWO DAYS later Hickok stepped off the train at Grand Central Station. He walked through the terminal, again dazzled by the zodiac painted on the ceiling. He wondered how the hell painters worked that high in the air.

Outside the terminal, he flagged a hansom cab. The driver was a gnome of a man, with a dented derby hat and the apple-red nose of a drinker. He stared down at Hickok's Western garb with watery, bloodshot eyes.

"Where to?"

"The police station."

"Which one?"

"How many you got?"

"Last count there was seven, maybe eight."

"Try the one for Gramercy Park."

"That'd be the Twenty Ninth Precinct."

Hickok climbed into the cab. He settled back in the seat, wishing he'd slept more on the overnight train from Philadelphia. Yesterday, when he announced he was going to New York, Buntline had been livid. He'd told the fat man to stuff it.

The purpose of the trip was Katherine and Augustus. They were still in the dark about the children's family, and the show was scheduled to open in New York in five days. Cody agreed that it was prudent to investigate the family before returning with the children. Particularly their uncle, Leland Stanley.

The show was the least of Hickok's concerns. After two performances of *The Scouts of the Plains*, he'd never felt more the fool. Strutting about the stage, spouting ridiculous lines, seemed to him far too much humiliation for a grown man. His attention turned instead to the safety of the children, and who wanted them dead. He planned to start with the police.

The precinct house was located off Broadway on Twenty Second Street. Hickok began with the desk sergeant, insisting that he would talk only with the precinct commander. He was directed to the office of Captain Alexander Williams, located on the second floor. Williams was a square-jawed man with dark salt-and-pepper hair and the powerful build of a dockworker. His gaze fixed on Hickok's pistols.

"I see you're armed, Mr. Hickok. We have an ordinance against carrying firearms."

"Most towns do," Hickok said, taking a chair before the captain's desk. "Don't you make an exception for fellow lawmen?"

"From your dress, I take it you're a Westerner."

"Last job was marshal of Abilene, Kansas. I work off and on as a deputy U.S. marshal."

"Hickok?" Williams said in a quizzical tone. "I think I've read about you in the *Police Gazette*. Wild Bill Hickok?"

Hickok rocked his hand. "Don't believe everything you read."

"Well, it's an honor to have you in New York, Mr. Hickok. Anybody asks you about those pistols, you tell them to come see me."

"I'm obliged, Cap'n."

"Don't mention it."

Captain Alexander "Clubber" Williams was an institution in New York. As a patrolman, he had averaged a fight a day for four years, clubbing street hoodlums cold with his nightstick. In the Twenty Ninth Precinct, he formed a squad devoted to bashing neighborhood thugs senseless, with or without provocation. Newspapers quoted him as saying, "There is more law in a policeman's nightstick then in a decision of the Supreme Court." Hickok was his kind of lawman.

"Well now, what can I do for you, Mr. Hickok?"

"I'm lookin' into a matter," Hickok said. "Has to do with the murder of a New York man. Henry Morton Stanley."

Williams gave him a measured stare. "Stanley and his wife were murdered in their home, smothered to death. What's your interest in the case?"

"You done answered the first question. That's a tough way to get killed."

"We haven't got the first lead in their murders. Do you know something I don't?"

"I know their children were abducted. That's why I'm here."

"What about the children?"

Hickok told him the story. He ended with his concern about returning them to New York. Someone, he observed, meant to see them dead.

"I'd say you're right," Williams ventured carefully. "What makes you suspect their uncle?"

"Well, like I said, he wasn't exactly tickled to hear they're alive. That makes a man wonder."

"The family could force you to return the children, Mr. Hickok. That's the law."

"Yeah," Hickok conceded. "'Course, they'd have to find 'em first. I don't aim to let that happen."

"So what do you want from me?"

"Anything you can tell me about this Leland Stanley."

Williams debated a moment. Tammany Hall, the ruling force in politics for decades, had been brought down in the 1871 elections. William "Boss" Tweed, the leader of Tammany Hall, had been exposed by the *New York*

Times and indicted on charges of corruption. The reform party was now in control of the city, and wealthy businessmen were at the forefront of the movement. The Stanleys were one of the most prominent families in New York.

"I've got kids of my own," Williams said. "I'd like to help you, but it would be political suicide. I'd be kicked off the force before you could blink."

Hickok frowned. "You're sayin' the family's got political muscle?"

"They own the Guaranty Trust Bank. In this town, money talks."

"I was dependin' on the police to lend a hand. Hell, Cap'n, we're talkin about murder."

"Here's a name." Williams jotted something on a scrap of paper. "If you turn up anything solid, I'll back your play. Otherwise, we never met."

Hickok studied the name. "Who's Charlie Phelan?"

"The best private investigator in New York."

CHARLES M. PHELAN
INVESTIGATIONS

The lettering on the door was faded and chipped. The office building was located on Sixteenth Street, a block east of Union Square. Hickok rapped on the door.

"It's open!"

The voice carried the wisp of a brogue. Hickok stepped through the door and found himself in a cubbyhole of an office. There was a battered desk, a single chair for visitors, and a row of filing cabinets along one wall. A grimy window overlooked the street.

"What can I do for you?"

Charlie Phelan rose from behind the desk. He was a broad-shouldered Irishman of considerable girth and

blunt edges. His eyes were a crackling blue and he had
the flattened nose of a pugilist. He extended a meaty
hand.

"I'm Charlie Phelan."

"Hickok," Hickok said, accepting his handshake. "I
got your name from Cap'n Williams, over at the police
station."

"Did you now?" Phelan said. "You must have a delicate problem indeed, Mr. Hickok. Clubber doesn't often
send business my way."

"Clubber?"

"That's his moniker. Clubber Williams, the toughest
cop in the city."

"How'd he get the name?"

Phelan warmed to the subject of crime in New York.
The underworld operated in three principle districts of
the city. Satan's Circus, where theaters and fine restau-
rants were mixed with bordellos and gambling dens, was
between Fifth Avenue and Eighth Avenue. Hell's Kitchen,
controlled largely by the Irish, was west of Satan's Circus and dealt in every vice known to man. The Bowery,
with its saloons, dance halls, and brothels, was on the
Lower East Side. The gangs extorted tribute from merchants, pulled daring robberies, and performed mayhem
for a price. Murder for hire was a specialty among the
Bowery toughs.

"Clubber gives 'em rough justice," Phelan concluded.
"They avoid him like the devil dodges Holy Water."

Hickok nodded. "Never thought of New York as a dangerous place. Sounds worse than Kansas."

"Kansas?" Phelan studied him intently. "By the Christ,
I thought you looked familiar. I've seen your picture on
dime novels."

"Yeah, guess you have."

"You're Wild Bill Hickok!"

"Guilty."

Phelan laughed. "I'm proud to have you in my office, Mr. Hickok. Why'd Clubber send you to see me?"

"Murder and child abduction."

Hickok again recounted the story. He added the gist of his conversation with the police captain. When he finished, he appeared puzzled. "What's Tammany Hall, anyway?"

"Just a building," Phelan said. "Headquarters for Boss Tweed and his political cronies. In New York, Tammany Hall and dirty politics are spoken in the same breath."

"Never saw politics that wasn't dirty. Cap'n Williams acted plumb spooked about these new reformers."

"Indeed, you're talking about one of the oldest families in the city. Any investigation of the Stanleys might well put you at loggerheads with the reformers."

"Don't bother me," Hickok said. "You willin' to take the case?"

"I'm expensive," Phelan replied. "Twenty dollars a day plus expenses."

"Consider yourself hired. I want everything you can turn up on this Leland Stanley."

"And the children's grandmother? I happen to know her name is Elizabeth Stanley. She's one of the grand dames of New York society."

Hickok shrugged. "Might as well check her out, too."

"Anyone else?"

"From what Cody learned, the uncle and the grandma are the only family. I reckon that's it."

"Hmmm." Phelan steepled his fingers, thoughtful. "That raises an interesting point, Mr. Hickok."

"Like what?"

"The family fortune must be in the millions. The mother and father were murdered, which made the children the natural heirs. Sound right so far?"

"Yeah," Hickok said. "So what's your point?"

"A little known law," Phelan said. "In New York, once a person has been missing for seven years, he's declared legally dead. Maybe that's why the children were abducted, put out for adoption. To make them disappear."

"The uncle and the grandma inherit everything after seven years. That the idea?"

"There's motive enough with so much money involved."

Hickok reflected a moment. "Guess that'd explain why Richter tried to kill 'em after the adoption fell through. Except for one thing."

"Which is?" Phelan asked."

"Why not kill 'em the night their folks was murdered? Why wait seven years?"

"Killing the parents *and* the children might have tipped the police. So they were shipped off on the Orphan Train instead."

"I suppose it's possible."

"Something else to consider," Phelan added. "Maybe the grandmother—or the uncle—didn't have the heart to kill them. Not until the adoption fell through."

"Too many 'maybes,'" Hickok said. "Wish now I hadn't thrown Richter off that train. A dead man don't make much of a witness."

"Well, as they say, water under the bridge. How would you like me to handle the investigation?"

"Trail this Leland Stanley night and day. One way or another, we've got to get the goods on him."

"I'll do my best," Phelan said. "But I have to tell you, it won't be easy. So far he's kept his hands clean."

"That's the whole idea," Hickok informed him. "Way it looks, Stanley ain't much for doing his own killin'. He'll need somebody to replace Richter."

"By all the saints, you're right! A hired killer."

"Get me a name and I'll do the rest."

"What do you mean—the rest?"

Hickok smiled. "I won't throw this one off a train."

Union Square was a madhouse. The sidewalks were lined with men, and north and south on Broadway, the street was mobbed with women carrying placards. The women marched ten abreast, forcing traffic to the curbs by sheer weight of numbers. Their voices rang out in a strident chant.

"We want the vote! We want the vote now!"

Hickok heard the roar as he approached the corner. The men on the sidewalks jeered back with catcalls and ribald shouts. The women waved their placards, drowning out the men with the shrill vibrato of their chant. Union Square pulsated with the riotous clamor.

Policemen were stationed all along the street. On the near corner, Hickok saw Captain Clubber Williams watching the crowds with a jaundiced eye. He bulled his way through knots of men bellowing to make themselves heard over the women. He stopped beside Williams at curbside.

"Howdy, Cap'n," he said, gesturing at the women. "What the hell's all this?"

"A suffragette parade," Williams said dryly. "The ladies think they're entitled to the vote."

"I never heard of such a thing." Hickok seemed shocked. "Women and politics ain't . . . natural."

"You don't have suffragettes out West?"

"None I've ever seen."

"Well, I estimate you're looking at three thousand or more today. There's their leader. Victoria Woodhull."

Hickok saw a woman in a skirt and mannish jacket, wearing a floppy tie. "I'll be jiggered," he said in amazement. "Looks like she's tryn' to be one of the boys."

Williams snorted. "Well she should, Mr. Hickok. She's running for president."

"You're joshing me."

"No, sir, it's no joshing matter."

Williams went on to explain. The National Women's Suffrage Association and its sister organization, the American Woman Suffrage Association, advocated the right of women to vote. Victoria Woodhull, the radical of the movement, agitated for legalized prostitution, birth control, and the ballot. Her crusade for the enfranchisement of women led to an open challenge against Democrats and Republicans. She was the presidential candidate of the new People's Party.

"Think about it," Williams said. "How'd you like to have her in the White House?"

"Plumb scary," Hickok grumped. "A president in bloomers ain't no way to run a country."

"Not to worry yourself, Mr. Hickok. Hell will freeze over before women get the vote."

"Yeah, I suspect you're right, Cap'n."

Williams lowered his voice. "Did you have that talk with Charlie Phelan?"

"Shore did," Hickok said. "I've just come from there. He's on the case."

"Where will he start his investigation?"

"Told him to stick to Leland Stanley like a tick on a dog."

"Charlie knows his business. If there's anything shady, he'll get to the bottom of it. You're in good hands."

"I'm obliged for the introduction."

"Afraid I have to move on, Mr. Hickok. Let me know how things work out."

Williams walked off as the suffragettes marched north on Broadway. Hickok waited until the crowds thinned out and street traffic was restored to normal. He flagged a cab and told the driver to take him to Grand Central Station. He planned to be back in Philadelphia by morning.

On the ride uptown Hickok fell into a reflective mood. He couldn't shake the thought of three thousand women parading in their crusade for the vote. Nor could he fathom a woman candidate for president.

New York, he told himself, was a strange place. Damn near another country, and a world apart.

He longed yet again for the Western Plains.

CHAPTER 17

OTTO RICHTER took three days to formulate a plan. He worked on the premise that Hickok and Cody were immune to offers of money, however great the amount. Nor would they surrender the children when confronted by violence and violent men. He needed something to offer in exchange.

A trade.

The first step was to organize a gang. He'd wired Billy McGlory, the underworld boss of New York's Bowery district. McGlory was the undisputed czar of vice and criminal enterprise on the Lower East Side. Theft, robbery, even murder for hire fell under his domain. His word was law.

Their friendship went back to childhood. Richter was the son of German immigrants, and McGlory was third-generation Irish-American. Despite their cultural differences, they were drawn together in youthful paroxysms of muggery and violence. They grew to manhood by ruling the streets.

McGlory, with Machiavellian ruthlessness, became the kingpin of the Lower East Side. He bought corrupt politicians and bribed cops, and operated with impunity from the law. Richter, with an aptitude for intrigue and violence, became the enforcer. His trademark was murder for hire.

Within hours after his wire to New York, Richter had a reply, and a name. McGlory's counterpart in Philadelphia was Teddy Ryan, overlord of crime in the City of Brotherly Love. A meeting with Ryan resulted in the loan of four hooligans for whatever purpose Richter saw fit. The men were seasoned thugs, adept with knife or gun.

Richter put them to work the same day. He couldn't afford to be seen, for both Hickok and Cody knew him on sight. So he established an around-the-clock surveillance, employing the four thugs as his eyes and ears. From morning till night, the men shadowed the movements of everyone in the stage troupe. No one went anywhere without being followed.

The first two days, the problem became apparent. The children were constantly accompanied by Hickok and Cody, either at the hotel or the theater. A direct confrontation would have resulted in a gunfight, and Richter was wary of violence in a strange town. Even more, he was wary of Hickok and Cody. He'd seen them in action.

Then, after the second performance of the show, Hickok had boarded the night train for New York. The move caught Richter by surprise, and he was at a loss as to the purpose of the trip. But Hickok's departure improved the odds, and he thought he'd at last gained the edge. The notion was quickly dispelled.

Texas Jack Omohundro stepped in to fill the void. He assumed Hickok's role as bodyguard, and along with Cody, escorted the children to and from the theater. Omohundro carried a Colt six-gun strapped to his hip, and there was small doubt he would use it if the occasion demanded. His reputation as an Indian fighter was second only to Cody.

Richter felt stymied at every turn. Time was dwindling away, for he had to complete the job before the end of the week. The show was scheduled to open in New York next week, and he'd given his word to Leland Stanley. He was a godless man, unburdened by conscience or scruple; but he prided himself on always keeping his word. He would somehow ensure that the children never returned to New York.

The four thugs routinely kept him abreast of their surveillance. Last night, sifting through all he'd learned, he suddenly came up with the masterstroke. Texas Jack Omohundro, his tastes refined by city life, was apparently fond of brioche for breakfast. Yet he clearly couldn't be bothered to run his own errands. He sent his wife instead.

Giuseppina, though a star of the stage, was nonetheless a dutiful spouse. Every morning she walked to a French bakery on Seventh Street, to fetch a bag of the buttery, freshly baked rolls for her husband. One of the thugs had followed her three days running, and her errand never varied by more than a few minutes. She was there when the brioche came out of the oven.

Early that morning a closed carriage parked at the corner of Seventh and Walnut. One of the thugs occupied the driver's seat and the other three were inside the cab. Marcel's French Bakery was a half block north of their position, on the west side of Seventh. The sky was bright and clear, and they watched as Giuseppina hurried along the street. She ducked into the bakery.

The driver snapped the reins. The matched set of bays leaned into the traces and the carriage slowly rolled north along Seventh. A moment later Giuseppina emerged from the bakery, carrying a bag of piping-hot brioche. The carriage swerved across the street, the driver timing it perfectly, and skidded to a halt before the bakery. The three thugs jumped from the cab.

Giuseppina screamed as they grabbed her. But she was overpowered, lifted off her feet, one of the men clamping a hand over her mouth. They quickly wrestled her into the cab, forcing her onto the floorboard, and slammed the door. Several passersby watched helplessly, frozen by the swift and brutal efficiency of the attack. The carriage rounded the corner onto Sansom Street.

Some ten minutes later the carriage rolled through the doors of a warehouse on the Delaware River. One of the thugs closed and barred the doors, and Giuseppina was unloaded from inside the cab. Richter walked forward as she shook free, straightening her coat, and looked at him with a terrified expression. His mouth crooked in an evil grin.

He had his hostage.

Hickok entered the hotel shortly before eleven o'clock that morning. Upstairs, he proceeded to the suite that he shared with Cody and the children. He unlocked the door and stopped dead in the entryway. His eyes swept the room.

Cody stood at the window, staring out over the city. Buntline was seated on the sofa, his gaze fixed on the crackling flames in the fireplace. Omohundro was hunched forward in a chair, head in his hands, his eyes hollow. They looked like three men at a wake.

Hickok closed the door. "What's going on here?"

"Jim!" Cody turned from the window, rushed forward. "God, I'm glad you're back."

"That makes two of us. Why the long faces?"

"They've got Giuseppina!"

"Who's got Giuseppina?"

"We don't know." Cody snatched a sheet of paper off the table by the sofa. "Here, read this."

We have Mrs. Omohundro. She is safe for now, but dead unless you follow orders. Bring the children to Penn's Landing at midnight, the park by the river. We will exchange Mrs. Omohundro for the children. Try anything smart and she dies.

Hickok looked up. "Where'd you get this?"

"A bellman delivered it," Cody replied. "He said a man walked in and gave him a dollar to bring it up. He couldn't tell us much about the man."

"Let's hear it, anyway."

"Stoutly built, medium height, rough-looking. Wearing a cheap suit."

"You called in the police?"

"We talked it over and decided it's not a good move. Jack's afraid it'd hurt Giuseppina's chances."

"How do we know somebody's actually got her? You're sure she's missing?"

Cody explained about Giuseppina's morning trip to the bakery. When she failed to return, Omohundro went looking for her and discovered that she'd been abducted off the street. The note had arrived shortly after his return to the hotel.

"No question they've got her," Cody said at length. "The question is who's 'they'?"

"Probably the kids' uncle," Hickok said. "If we're right, he's the one that Richter feller was workin' for. Like as not, he hired somebody to replace Richter."

Omohundro rose from his chair. His features were a mask of tightly constrained fury. "Whoever the hell it is, I'd like to get my hands on him. What sort of slimy bastard steals women and kids?"

"Don't worry, Jack," Cody said, trying to calm his fear. "We'll get Giuseppina back."

"Damn sure will," Hickok said, nodding agreement. "Where are the kids, anyway?"

"In their bedroom," Cody said. "They're pretty upset about Giuseppina. Got it in their heads it's their fault."

Omohundro grimaced. "I tried to tell 'em it wasn't so. Guess they're too young to understand."

"Not anybody's fault," Hickok said tersely. "We're dealin' with the sorriest sonsabitches I ever run across."

Cody pulled at his goatee. "You find out anything in New York?"

"Hired us a private investigator."

Hickok related how he'd come to retain Charlie Phelan. The political situation, he noted, made it difficult, for the Stanleys were one of the most influential families in New York. He was nonetheless confident.

"Got a good feelin' about this Charlie Phelan. Whatever's to be found, he'll root it out."

A knock sounded at the door. Buntline scooted off the sofa and hurried across the room. When he opened the door, two midgets stood in the hallway. He greeted them effusively.

The midgets were in their late thirties. They were dressed in pint-sized business suits, and appeared to be somewhere around three feet tall. Buntline ushered them into the suite.

"Gentlemen," he said, turning to the others. "This is Orville Beatty and Noah Foster. They're headliners over at the Orpheum Vaudeville Theater."

Hickok looked baffled. Cody laughed and slapped him on the shoulder. "Orville and Noah have agreed to help us rescue Giuseppina. They're gonna impersonate Katherine and Augustus."

"Yeah?" Hickok said hesitantly. "How you figure to pull that off?"

"We're actors," Beatty said in a piping voice. "Noah will wear a dress and I'll wear boy's clothes. We'll look— and *act*—the part of children."

Cody nodded. "Nobody'll be able to tell the difference in the dark. We'll fool 'em pretty as you please."

"Might just work," Hickok said, studying the midgets more closely. "Whose idea was it?"

"Ned come up with it," Cody said, grinning. "Leave it to a showman when you need a little magic."

Hickok thought he might revise his opinion of Buntline. His gaze shifted to the midgets. "What is it you gents do in vaudeville?"

"Song and dance men." Noah Foster straightened to his full height. "We're the best in the business."

"Well, I have to hand it to you, you've got guts. There's liable to be some fireworks tonight."

Foster proudly cocked his chin. "Giuseppina Morlacchi is a fellow actor. How could we not help her?"

"Exactly!" Beatty chimed in. "One for all and all for one in the show business. It's a matter of honor."

Hickok thought the midgets were taller than they looked.

A brisk wind whipped in off the river. The indigo sky glittered with stars, flooding the park grounds in a spectral light. The eerie moan of the wind echoed through the trees.

Penn's Landing fronted the shoreline of the Delaware River. There, in 1682, William Penn first stepped ashore to claim his land grant. The park, named in his honor, comprised nearly forty acres of trees, with a broad meadow in the center. From north to south, the park stretched almost a half mile.

Not long before midnight a carriage halted along Delaware Avenue. The wide thoroughfare bordered Penn's Landing on the west, and the carriage stopped almost midpoint with the park. The door opened and Hickok stepped out, the brace of ivory-handled Colts wedged in his sash. Cody was next, followed by Omohundro and Buntline, and the two midgets. They stood scanning the expanse of trees.

Cody and Omohundro wore gun belts with holstered

pistols. Buntline, game for a fight and armed with a bulldog revolver, tried to keep his hands from shaking. Orville Beatty was attired in a knee-length coat and a slouch
hat, which obscured his features. Noah Foster was tricked
out in a dress and shawl, and a long, black wig taken from
the theater. In the dark, without close inspection, they
would pass for the children.

North of Penn's Landing, the masts of ships moored
at wharves were framed against the sky. The men waited
a moment longer, wary of trickery, alert to any movement
in the trees. Earlier that evening Cody, Hickok and
Omohundro had managed a stilted performance in *The
Scouts of the Plains*. Beatty and Foster, their minds else-
where, had mechanically plodded through their act at
the vaudeville theater. But now, waiting by the carriage,
their focus was on the show ahead. They were about to
give the performance of their lives.

Hickok led the way. He walked along a pathway
through the trees, followed by Cody and the costumed
midgets. Omohundro and Buntline, their guns drawn and
leery of every shadow, brought up the rear. The pathway
ended at the edge of the treeline, opening onto a grassy
meadow dimly lighted by the stars. The men paused on
the verge of the meadow, where Hickok, Omohundro, and
Buntline melted into the trees. Cody stepped forward.

"This is Bill Cody!" he shouted. "Anybody out there?"

"We're here," a voice called back. "Do you have the
kids?"

"Look for yourself." Cody put his arms around the
midgets. "Do you have Mrs. Omohundro?"

"Here she is." A man stepped from the trees across
the way, holding Giuseppina's arm. "We'll meet in the
middle and make the trade."

"I warn you, don't try any dumb stunts. I have men
covering me with guns."

"That goes both ways, Cody. My boys have got you in their sights right now."

"Then we've got ourselves a standoff. Let's get this business done."

Cody walked forward with the midgets. On the opposite treeline, the man moved out, still holding Giuseppina by the arm. They were on a direct line, and some moments later, they came together in the center of the meadow. Giuseppina looked terrified, and Cody, peering closer, was astounded by what he saw. The man before him was a man he'd thought dead—Richter!

Richter squinted in the pale starlight. He looked from one midget to the other, visibly startled. "What the hell—"

Their plan went off like clockwork. Cody tackled Giuseppina, throwing her down, and the midgets dropped to the ground. Hickok opened fire from the trees, followed an instant later by Omohundro and Buntline. The air sizzled with the whine of slugs.

Richter took off running. The opposite treeline blossomed with flame as the roar of four pistols split the night. Hickok sighted on a muzzle flash and lightly feathered the trigger. A man screamed, stumbling from the trees, and pitched to the ground. Omohundro, aiming at a streak of muzzle blast, wounded another man. Richter disappeared into the trees.

Cody opened fire. Hickok, along with Omohundro and Buntline, sprayed the opposite treeline with lead. Orville Beatty and Noah Foster pulled Giuseppina to her feet and scuttled back across the meadow. Cody retreated, firing as he moved, covered by a rattling volley from Hickok and the other men. He made it into the trees unscathed.

The meadow went silent. Giuseppina fell into Omohundro's arms, and Hickok stood vigilant as the gunfire abruptly ceased from the opposite treeline. Omohundro led his wife back through the darkened pathway, trailed closely by Buntline and the midgets. Cody and Hickok acted as rearguard.

Cody huffed. "You're not gonna believe it when I tell you."

"Tell me what?"

"That jasper back in the meadow—it was Richter."

"Richter!" Hickok parroted. "You know damn well I threw him off that train. I killed the bastard."

"Well, Jim, he's done riz from the dead."

"Sonovabitch!"

CHAPTER 18

HICKOK HURRIED through Grand Central Station. His mind was focused on other matters, and he scarcely glanced at the colorful zodiac on the ceiling. He hopped into a cab on Forty Second Street.

The buildings of New York's skyline rose stark against overcast clouds. Hickok had caught the milk-run train from Philadelphia, departing at three that morning. He was tired and still confounded by Cody, who had argued against his leaving. He decided he'd taught Cody more about scouting than about trailing desperadoes. He knew he was right about Richter.

The cab dropped him at Union Square. He hadn't eaten since last night, and he stepped into a café, where he wolfed down a quick order of hash and eggs. Outside again, he felt somewhat restored, and took a moment to light a cheroot. He checked his pocket watch and saw that it was approaching two o'clock. He crossed the square to Sixteenth Street.

Charlie Phelan was seated at his desk. He looked up as Hickok came through the door. "You're a regular gadabout, Mr. Hickok. I hadn't expected to see you so soon."

"Have to stay on the move," Hickok said, taking a chair. "Things are happening fast."

"Are you talking about Philadelphia?"

"You recollect me mentioning a feller named Richter?"

"Why sure, the one we thought was working for Stanley."

"Appears he's come back from the grave."

"He's alive?"

"'Fraid so."

Hickok briefed him on the abduction and rescue of Giuseppina. Phelan appeared dumbstruck as he listened to the role played by the midgets, and openly impressed by the outcome of the shootout. He wagged his head.

"I see why they call you Wild Bill," he said humorously. "That's the damnedest story I ever heard."

Hickok waved it off. "Thing is, I think Richter's headed back to New York. Maybe he's already here."

"What leads you to believe that?"

"Well, he made his play in Philadelphia and he lost. I've got a hunch his next try will be on home ground. Just figures he'd know the show opens here in two days."

"Let me understand," Phelan said. "He botched the job there, and two days gives him time to hatch a plan for New York. Is that the idea?"

"Yep." Hickok puffed his cheroot, sent eddies of smoke curling toward the ceiling. "Way I've got him pegged, he don't do nothin' on the spur of the moment. He plans it out first."

"Sounds reasonable to me."

"On top of that, he'd likely want to check in with Stanley. We might just catch 'em with their pants down."

Phelan smiled. "Wouldn't that make our case!"

"Damn tootin'," Hickok said, almost jovial. "How're you doing with your investigation?"

"Not to brag, but I've uncovered enough dirt to plant a garden."

Phelan recounted the details. Leland Stanley was a wastrel and a spendthrift, heavily in debt to many of New York's classier casinos. His livelihood was derived from a trust fund established by his long-deceased father, and the principle was badly depleted. Until his brother's death, he had been living in a modest flat, and to all appearances, practically broke. To top it off, he reputation was that of a dissolute libertine.

"Never worked a day in his life," Phelan said sardonically. "He's what New Yorker's call a playboy."

"Playboy?" Hickok repeated. "What's that mean?"

"A term coined by the social crowd. Someone who spends his time chasing after showgirls. Our Mr. Stanley is out on the town every night."

"You work fast. How'd you find out all this?"

"Last night I tailed Stanley to John Morrissey's casino. I've done Morrissey a favor here and there over the years. He gave me the lowdown on Stanley."

"What about the bank?" Hickok asked. "Stanley spend any time there?"

"Not much," Phelan said. "When his brother died, he took over as president of Guaranty Trust. But the rumor's about that he's little more than a figurehead. His work day is usually eleven to three."

"So he'll be leavin' pretty quick, won't he?"

"You can set your watch he's out the door at three sharp."

"Let's go." Hickok got to his feet. "We'll just tag along and see what happens. We might get lucky."

"How long do you plan to tail him?"

"Till he leads us to Richter."

Twenty minutes later they were posted at the lower end of Fifth Avenue. A block south of their position was the tall marble archway that opened onto Washington Square. Directly across the street was the granite façade of the Guaranty Trust Bank. Everything about the building reeked of old money.

Leland Stanley emerged from the bank at two-fifty-nine. He was nattily attired in a chesterfield topcoat with a velvet collar and a silk stovepipe hat. A carriage waited at curbside, and the driver jumped down to open the door.

Stanley tipped his hat to a lady as he crossed the sidewalk.

"Handsome devil, ain't he?" Hickok joked. "Bet he's hell with the women."

"God loves a sinner," Phelan joked. "First time you've see him?"

"Yeah, but it won't be the last time. We're gonna stick to him like a burr under a saddle."

"I take it that's fairly tight."

"Charlie, it don't get no tighter."

Phelan flagged a hackney cab. He held the door for Hickok, then ordered the driver to follow the carriage. As he stepped inside, he smiled to himself, struck by the vagaries of a detective's life. He was actually on the chase with Wild Bill Hickok.

He wondered if he would earn his spurs tonight.

Gaslights flickered like fireflies around Gramercy Park. The overcast sky made the night dark as pitch, and there was a sharp bite to the air. Hickok and Phelan sat huddled in a hackney cab.

Their vigil was now into its fourth hour. After following Stanley from the bank, they had parked just off the corner of Twentieth Street and Irving Place. Their stomachs groaned with hunger and the collars of their coats were turned up against the chill of the night. They watched the mansion through the foggy cab window.

"Wish we'd got supper," Hickok said, staring at the mansion. "You sure he'll come out again?"

"Quite sure," Phelan said with conviction. "Our Mr. Stanley is a night owl. He always goes out."

"Guess a man in your line of work gets used to waitin'. How long you been a detective?"

"I worked with the Pinkertons during the war and a

year or so after the peace. I finally decided to go on my own."

The Pinkerton Detective Agency, operating out of Chicago, was the largest investigative agency in the world. Under the direction of founder Allan Pinkerton, the agency had organized a spy network for the Union during the Civil War. The Pinkertons were currently involved in tracking the Missouri bandit leader, Jesse James.

"I done a little spy work myself," Hickok said. "'Course, out West, we wasn't as organized as the Pinkertons."

"I remember reading about it," Phelan said. "Your adventures have been well-documented in the dime novels."

"Half that stuff is pure beeswax. Damn writers invent—"

Hickok stopped. A carriage rolled to a halt outside the mansion. The front door opened and Stanley came down the steps. He was dressed in white tie and tails and a long evening cape. He crossed the walkway to the carriage.

"Look at that outfit," Hickok said. "He's a regular dandy, ain't he?"

Phelan laughed. "A man about town has to look the part. The showgirls expect it."

"Does he have a special girl?"

"Our Mr. Stanley likes to spread his charms around. A different girl every night."

They followed the carriage to the Strand Theater on Broadway. The feature attraction was the Lydia Thompson Burlesque Company, fresh from England. The company consisted of eight buxom blondes who sang wicked ballads and performed high-stepping dance routines. Their act flaunted conventional morality with gleeful satire.

The advent of showgirls in burlesque theaters gave rise to the playboy. Wealthy businessmen, the majority of them married, vied for the attentions of tartish singers and dancers. The men lavished jewelry and flowers on the girls, and openly squired them around to New York's after-hours nightspots. The girls, accustomed to bartering their wares, offered love for sale.

Leland Stanley was considered a prize. Unlike most playboys, he was a wealthy bachelor, and perhaps susceptible to marriage. Late that evening, he left the burlesque theater with the star of the show, Lydia Thompson. She was voluptuous, with an hourglass figure, and seemingly entranced by his urbane wit. He took her to a concert saloon on the west side of Union Square.

A theatrical variety hall, the concert saloon was a New York institution. The nightspots presented comedians, half-nude chorus lines, and singers who belted out raunchy tales to the accompaniment of a small orchestra. There were tables and chairs on the main floor, and private booths on the balcony overlooked the stage. The waitresses wore high tasseled red boots and dresses that covered hardly anything.

Stanley and his British showgirl were escorted to a booth on the balcony. Hickok and Phelan took a table downstairs, which afforded a direct view of the booth. The room was packed with a boisterous crowd laughing and cheering at the rowdy antics of the performers. The orchestra segued into a high-stepping number and a bevy of chorus girls pranced out of the wings. The audience greeted them with giddy applause.

Hickok ordered a whiskey and Phelan a beer. The chorus line was still jiggling around the stage when the waitress returned with their drinks. Hickok sipped his whiskey, then suddenly tensed, lowering his glass to the table. He nodded at the balcony.

"Take a peek," he said. "There's our boy."

Phelan glanced at the booth. "That's Richter?"

"In the flesh."

Richter tapped Stanley on the shoulder. Stanley turned, acknowledging him with a curt look, then said something to the British showgirl. She smiled engagingly, and Stanley rose from his chair, joining Richter at the rear of the booth. Their conversation appeared heated, with Richter subjected to a sharp grilling. Stanley's features were flushed with anger.

"No doubts now," Hickok said. "Stanley was behind it the whole time."

Phelan nodded. "Doesn't look too happy, does he?"

"I'd just guess he expected better news from Philadelphia."

Stanley abruptly ended the conversation with a jerky wave. Richter turned away, his mouth clamped tight, and disappeared through a curtain at the back of the booth. Hickok dropped a double eagle on the table. "Let's go."

"You mean to follow Richter?"

"I aim to capture the bastard. He don't know it but he's gonna give us Stanley."

They rose from their table. As they started forward, they were blocked by a crush of people watching the show from the rear of the room. Hickok cleaved a path through the crowd and spotted Richter hurrying out the entrance. He cursed, roughly shoving people aside.

On the street, they saw Richter step into a hansom cab. Phelan whistled another cab to a stop and jerked open the door. Hickok clambered aboard beside the driver, ordering him to move out. Phelan jumped inside.

They trailed Richter's cab down Broadway.

The Bowery glittered with clusters of varicolored glass globes lighted by gas. The streets were alive with

working-class theaters presenting flea circuses, eques-
trian acts, and blackface minstrel shows. One marquee
boasted the risqué attraction of *Fifty Nice Girls in
Naughty Sketches*.

Billy McGlory's Armory Hall was located on Hester
Street. Headquarters for McGlory and his gang of hooligans, Armory Hall was infamous throughout the Bowery. The establishment was a saloon and dance hall, with
the dance floor occasionally converted to an arena for
prizefights. No one went there expecting light entertainment. Richter's cab let him off in front of Armory Hall.
As he pushed through the door, Hickok ordered his driver
to stop at the corner. He gave the driver a gold eagle and
hopped down to the curb. Phelan stepped out of the cab.

"Let's not rush into anything," he said, as the cab
pulled away. "You're probably not familiar with Billy
McGlory."

Hickok looked at him. "Who's Billy McGlory?"

"The boss of all that's unholy on the Lower East Side.
He's nobody to mess with."

"You think Richter's tied in with him?"

"I do now," Phelan said. "He leaves Stanley and comes
straight to McGlory's dive. I'd say there's a connection."

"One way to find out," Hickok observed. "I'm going
in there and get Richter. You coming along?"

"Well never get out of there alive."

"You armed?"

"Yes."

"Just follow my lead."

Hickok walked directly to Armory Hall. As he went
through the door, Phelan fell in at his side. A long mahogany bar was at the front of the room, with tables and
chairs along the opposite wall. The dance floor was at the
rear, with a piano, a fiddle player, and a trumpeter. The
place was jammed with a late-night crowd.

Richter was seated at a table toward the rear. He was talking to a beefy, thick-shouldered man with the face of a cherub and the eyes of a stone-cold killer. He glanced up and saw Hickok by the door and his face went chalky. He spoke to the man, who gave Hickok a look that could have cracked a rock. Then he pushed back his chair and hurried across the dance floor. He disappeared through a door at the rear of the room.

Hickok started forward, Phelan a pace behind. Billy McGlory stood, circling the table, and walked to the end of the bar. He motioned to four men ganged around the counter and they quickly formed a phalanx behind him. He moved to block Hickok's path.

"Far enough," he said, hooking his thumbs in his vest. "You and your friend get while the getting's good."

Hickok stared at him. "Hand over Richter and we won't have any trouble."

"Otto's out the back door and well gone by now. You've come up short this night."

"I'll just have a look in that back room."

"I think not," McGlory said in a rumbling voice. "I'm told you're none other than Wild Bill Hickok. Is it true?"

"You were told right," Hickok said. "You and your boys stand aside. I'm comin' through."

McGlory gestured with his head. The four hooligans started around him, three armed with blackjacks, and one with brassknuckles. Hickok pulled his Colts in a blurred motion, thumbing the hammers. His eyes went cold.

"Which one of you peckerheads wants to die first?"

The men shuffled to a stop. A muscle ticced at McGlory's jawline and his features went flat. Phelan edged closer to Hickok.

"Time to leave," he said. "There's a bunch of his men behind us. Not the best of odds."

"Cover my back."

Hickok waited for the detective to draw his revolver and turn to face the crowd. Then he nodded to McGlory. "Tell Richter he's dead the next time I see him."

McGlory laughed. "You're out of your league, Hickok. Don't come back to the Bowery."

"You got it bassackwards, bub. Don't make me come back."

Phelan cleared a path through the crowd. Hickok slowly backed away, one Colt still trained on McGlory as they went out the door. On the street, they turned north toward Union Square.

"Whew!" Phelan let out a gusty breath. "There for a minute, I almost wet my drawers."

Hickok wasn't amused. "That goddamn Richter's got more lives than a cat."

"You think he'll show up again?"

"I shorely do hope so, Charlie."

"What do you mean?"

"Richter's the key to Leland Stanley."

"You don't quit, do you?"

"Not while I can fog a mirror."

They walked off into the night.

CHAPTER 19

THE BUFFALO Bill Combination arrived in New York the morning of February 7. The show was scheduled to open that night, and everyone in the troupe was in high spirits. The Philadelphia engagement had played to sold-out houses.

Hickok met them at the platform. He was accompanied by Charlie Phelan, who was now retained as a full-time bodyguard for the children. Their dustup in the Bowery had convinced him the detective was reliable in a tight situation, and willing to use a gun. He thought the children would be safe in Phelan's care.

Katherine ran ahead of the others. "Oh, Wild Bill!" she squealed, throwing herself into his arms. "I've missed you so!"

"Missed you, too," Hickok said, holding her with one arm as he reached for Augustus with the other. "How's tricks with you, Gus?"

"I'm fine, Wild Bill." Augustus hugged him tightly. "Why didn't you come back to Philadelphia?"

"Well, I had business that needed tendin' here. Figured I'd just wait till Buffalo Bill brought you along."

Cody gave him a look. "Got that business tended to, did you?"

"Tell you about it later," Hickok said. "Shake hands with Charlie Phelan."

"Glad to," Cody said, clasping the detective's hand. "Heard good things about you, Charlie."

Hickok exchanged handshakes with Buntline and Omohundro, and Giuseppina gave him a big kiss. Three porters appeared with large steamer trunks loaded onto carts. The trunks were packed with the show's costumes and assorted paraphernalia. Buntline told them he'd wired ahead for a delivery wagon.

"I have to run," he said, fidgeting with excitement. "I'll arrange everything at the theater for this afternoon's rehearsal. Remember, one o'clock sharp!"

"We'll be there," Cody assured him. "I just suspect Wild Bill needs a little rehearsal."

"Yes, I daresay he does!"

Buntline dashed off after the porters. The children clung to Hickok as the party mounted the stairs to Grand Central Station. Phelan fell in behind the children, his eyes searching the throngs of passengers as they walked through the main terminal. They emerged onto Forty Second Street.

A horse hooked to a cab relieved itself as they crossed the sidewalk. "How's your nose holding out?" Omohundro inquired of Hickok. "You got used to all these horses yet?"

"Tell you what, Jack," Hickok said, deadpan. "Day I do, that's the day to move on. I'll know my sniffer's ruint for good."

Giuseppina giggled. "I must say I love it anyway. It is so—New York!"

"Yeah," Hickok agreed. "Ain't roses, that's for shore."

Some while later they were again settled into the suite at the Fifth Avenue Hotel. Giuseppina took the children into their bedroom to unpack, and closed the door. Hickok dropped into a chair by the fireplace and the other men got themselves seated. He looked across at Cody.

"How's Gus and Kate holdin'up?"

"Pretty fair," Cody said. "They get weepy now and then, but that's to be expected. It's only been a week."

"Seems more like a month," Hickok allowed. "Fightin'
Injuns ain't nothin' compared to the savages hereabouts."

"Had your hands full, have you?"

"Yeah, and then some."

Hickok gave him a quick account of the past two days.
He established the connection between Richter and Stan-
ley, and went on to relate the Bowery standoff with Billy
McGlory. He ended by nodding to Phelan.

"Charlie will bear me out. There ain't no bottom to
this goddamn sinkhole."

Cody shook his head. "You're sayin' this McGlory
will back Richter's play?"

"No doubt about it," Hickok said firmly. "We're up
against a whole passel of the bastards."

"You're the expert on cutthroats and desperadoes.
How do we handle it?"

"For openers—" Hickok pointed to Phelan. "I've hired
Charlie to guard the kids while we're busy with the show.
He'll stick with 'em like a mustard plaster."

"Sounds like a good start. What else?"

"Jack and Giuseppina," Hickok said. "I want 'em
moved into this hotel today. Jack can spell Charlie when
need be, and we'll know Giuseppina's safe. I don't see
no other way."

Cody turned to Omohundro. "That all right with you,
Jack?"

"Bet your boots," Omohundro affirmed. "We can't
have her abducted again. Once was enough."

"Buntline will pay for the room," Cody said. "He'll
squeal like a pig, but the hell with it. We're through taking chances."

"Let's understand," Hickok told them. "Here in the
hotel, at the theater, wherever we are—them kids ain't
never left alone."

Cody considered a moment. "You got any idea a'tall how Richter will come at us?"

"Nope," Hickok admitted. "Forgot to tell you we learned his first name. He's called Otto."

"Sorry scutter," Omohundro cursed. "I'd sooner call him dead."

"Jack, you mark my word," Hickok said. "You'll get a bellyful of killin' before it's over."

Charlie Phelan thought it the words of an oracle.

The theater district was known simply as The Rialto. To New Yorkers, the term alone implied the very heart of American theater. The world's greatest actors were to be found there.

Lawrence Barrett was starring in *Julius Caesar*. Edwin Booth, brother of Lincoln's assassin and the country's foremost tragedian, was in a year-long run of *Hamlet*. Joseph Jefferson, one of the most popular actors of the day, was playing in *Rip Van Winkle*.

The Rialto was situated along Broadway. A half-mile stretch, from Union Square to Madison Square, encompassed virtually the whole of New York's legitimate theater. The term "legitimate" was commonly used to distinguish traditional theater from burlesque and vaudeville. The wealthier class considered The Rialto fashionable in any season.

The Lyceum Theater, located at Broadway and Twenty Second, was a modern showcase along The Rialto. The marquee was emblazoned with THE SCOUTS OF THE PLAINS, and the crowds began arriving shortly after seven o'clock. A long line of landau and brougham carriages deposited the city's aristocracy outside the theater.

The opening night show was sold out. Buffalo Bill Cody and Wild Bill Hickok, and to a lesser extent, Texas Jack Omohundro, were all the rage among New York's elite. The mythical wilderness of the Western Plains, where knights in buckskin rode forth to battle warlike tribes, captured the imagination of theatergoers. The Wild West was the allegorical Arthurian legend of America.

The audience might have been disabused of their romantic notions had they been allowed backstage. Buntline was in the midst of a raging tirade, shouting at prop men, stagehands, and the cast. His most scathing remarks were directed at the ten actors who had been hired to play the Sioux warriors. The rehearsal that afternoon had left him all but apoplectic.

"This is *not* Shakespeare!" he railed. "You are playing Indians. Indians!"

Cody and Hickok watched from the door of their dressing room. They were attired in buckskins, with broad hats and colorful shirts, and suitably armed with pistols and bowie knives. Hickok shook his head.

"Buntline would've made a good drill sergeant. He's hell on givin' orders."

"Don't fault him too much," Cody said. "It's just that he wants everything perfect. He's got a lot at stake."

"Christ, he's pullin' in a ton of money. You'd think he'd be tickled pink."

"Well, the money's not everything. Ned's lookin' to make his mark in the show business. That'll open all kinds of doors."

Hickok squinted. "Doors to what?"

"The swells," Cody said with a rueful smile. "Ned wants a foothold into the New York social set. He aims to use the theater to get there."

"Might as well teach a pig to waltz. He ain't got the breedin' for it."

"Yeah, but it's a barrel of fun watchin' him try. Never saw a man with his spring wound so tight."

Hickok glanced back into the dressing room. Phelan was seated on a lumpy couch with Katherine and Augustus. He'd found a ball of string and held them fascinated as he fashioned a cat's cradle with his fingers. The affinity between the children and the detective was already apparent, and Hickok thought he'd made a wise choice. Phelan was a man of many talents.

"Places, everybody!" the stage manager yelled. "Five minutes till curtain!"

"Jumpin' Jesus," Hickok grouched. "Time to kill them make-believe Injuns."

Cody laughed. "We'll make an actor of you yet."

The curtain went up at eight o'clock. Giuseppina performed the opening number, a dance involving gossamer veils and balletic twirls, more suitable for sophisticated New Yorkers. The opening scene of the play, with Cody and Hickok around the campfire, had been revised to include the bit about the Grand Duke Alexis. Hickok got over his jitters with a recounting of the royal hunt.

In Act Two, Hickok shot out the spotlight. The audience thought it a delightful touch of stagecraft and roared with laughter. Hickok was so pleased with himself that he hammed it up even more in one of the skirmishes with the Sioux warriors. Instead of killing them, as called for in the play, he fired blanks at their heels. The powder burns caused a riotous departure from the script.

Taken unawares, the greasepaint Indians hopped and screeched, frantically gyrating around the stage. Hickok kept them dancing, firing with a devilish grin, until his pistol ran dry. Then, singed and furious, but actors to a man, the bewigged warriors toppled helter-skelter in feigned death. The audience broke out in hilarious applause and Hickok took a bow.

Act Three played out with a final, tumultuous battle scene. The warriors were massacred en masse, and Dove

Eye, the delectable Indian maiden, was reunited with that stalwart of the plains, Buffalo Bill. The cast took five curtain calls, and Cody and Hickok were called back for a standing ovation from the crowd. Buntline was waiting in the wings when they came offstage, surrounded by the powder-burned actors. He looked like he could chew nails.

"Are you mad?" he ranted at Hickok. "How dare you fire at these men!"

"What're you yellin' about?" Hickok said with a crooked grin. "That crowd ate it up."

"Wild Bill's right," Cody interceded. "Why not add it to the show, Ned?"

"Now you've gone mad!"

"Hear me out. Wild Bill could fire at the floor instead of their legs. The boys could do all that hoppin' and wailin', and the audience wouldn't know the difference. We'd still get the laughs."

"Well—"

"You know it'd work."

"Perhaps."

"Think of all them laughs . . . and the publicity."

Buntline put it in the show.

James Gordon Bennett, publisher of the *New York Herald,* hosted an opening-night party. The affair was held at Delmonico's, the preeminent dining establishment in the city. The guest list included the luminaries of the New York aristocracy.

Among those in attendance were Commodore Cornelius Vanderbilt, William Waldorf Astor, and Jay Gould. They were the robber barons of the day, shrewd financiers who had plundered railroads, the stock exchange, and assorted industries with piratical zeal. Their combined wealth was second only to the United States Treasury.

Their excesses gave rise to what was commonly known as the Gilded Age. The era was marked by galvanized capitalism, industrial expansion, and ostentatious displays of wealth. The leisure hours of the social set were consumed by the opera, the theater, and lavish parties unrivaled by European nobility. One financier threw a party to honor his cocker spaniel, who arrived sporting a collar studded with diamonds.

The party tonight was to honor Cody and Hickok. Yet the titans of industry, no less than the masses, were captivated by plainsmen who had braved a wilderness as exotic as darkest Africa and fought the savage tribes to the death. Hickok, even more than Cody, was phantasmal, a sorcerer of armed conflict. He was death astride a pale horse, the Prince of Pistoleers.

Cornelius Vanderbilt, a heavyset man with muttonchop whiskers, cornered him while drinks were being served. "I say, Mr. Hickok," he inquired with wily curiosity. "Are these reports in the press to be taken literally?"

"Depends," Hickok said, sipping the finest whiskey he'd ever tasted. "Which reports was that?"

"Why, the allusion to you having killed a hundred men in the war. I ask you, sir, a *hundred*?"

James Gordon Bennett and William Waldorf Astor were drawn closer by the question. Hickok quaffed his whiskey, letting them hang on his reply. "Well, don't you see," he said with a straight face, "some men, God rest their souls, was born to be killed. Just happened I was their grim reaper."

"Grim reaper, indeed!" Vanderbilt's wattled features creased with a jolly smile. "You have a droll sense of mortality, Mr. Hickok."

"What's life without a few laughs?"

Hickok was amused by the conversation. He thought

the mythical stature accorded to Cody and himself was
a gem of a joke. These men, citified Easterners, were
never able to separate the truth from what they read in
the papers or saw on the stage. So in the end, the joke
was on them.

Dinner was an elaborate affair. The meal began with
imported salmon, a confection of sweetbreads and pâté
de foie gras, followed by a rich terrapin soup. The main
course was canvasback duck, accompanied by asparagus,
savory mushrooms, and artichokes. A different wine was
served with every course.

Mrs. Jay Gould was seated beside Cody. Her gown
was Parisian, with a breast-heaver that swelled her bosoms, and she wore a diamond necklace with an emerald pendant the size of a peahen's egg. She smiled at him
over a bite of duck.

"I'm simply overcome with curiosity, Mr. Cody. Do
you enjoy fighting the savages?"

"No, ma'am," Cody said without hesitation. "Fact is,
I admire the Injuns. They're good fighters and fine
people."

She looked confused. "Then why do you fight them?"

"Why, ma'am, we're buildin' ourselves a nation here.
Some folks have to move aside so others can move on.
The Injuns just got in the way."

"You sound as though you sympathize with them,
Mr. Cody."

"Don't know about that, ma'am. But I shorely do
respect 'em."

Cody glanced across the room, his attention drawn to
Buntline. The showman was seated beside Alexander
Stewart, one of the richest men in New York. Katherine
and Augustus, who had been passed off as Phelan's
children, were at a table with the Omohundros and several social lions. He looked back at Mrs. Gould.

"Talkin' about Injuns," he said breezily, "how'd you like the show?"

She tittered. "May I ask you a question, Mr. Cody?"

"Shore thing."

"Are all Indian maidens as ravishing as Mlle. Morlacchi?"

"Yes, ma'am, they're the fairest flowers of the plains."

"Oh, my, do tell me more."

Cody spun a titillating tale of love in the Wild West.

CHAPTER 20

THERE WERE rave reviews in the morning paper. Cody, beside himself with pride, poured over the critics' words. He read the *New York Times* aloud to Hickok.

"*The Scouts of the Plains* is an extraordinary production with more wild Indians, scalping knives, and gun powder to the square inch than any drama ever before seen on a theater stage. Buffalo Bill Cody and Wild Bill Hickok are the epitome of valiant frontiersmen."

"Epitome?" Hickok said. "What the hell's that mean?"

"Don't know," Cody said absently. "Think it's a compliment."

"They say anything about me shootin' out the lights?"

"Yeah, you wowed 'em with that one. Called you the 'finest pistol marksman extant.'"

"Extant?"

"Way it sounds, that means still livin'."

"Still livin', huh?" Hickok knuckled his mustache. "Well, I reckon they got that right."

Cody held out a copy of the *New York Herald*. "Wait'll you read this. Glory be!"

The play is beyond all precedent in the annals of stage lore. It has all the thrilling romance, treachery, love, and revenge of the richest dime novels ever written. The subject is so popular with readers of border tales that the temptation to see the real actors cannot be resisted.

Hickok snorted. "Helluva way to make a livin'. I'd be a red-faced baboon if anybody out West saw me on that stage."

"They'd be pea-green with envy," Cody said. "We're in high clover and no end in sight. How many of them earns what we do?"

"That ain't the point. I'm talkin' about all the phony claptrap we spout. I feel like an impostor."

"Well, that's the show business. You mix a little fact and a little fancy, and folks are entertained. Where's the harm in that?"

"I ain't no entertainer," Hickok said dourly. "I'd sooner be an organ grinder with a monkey. Nothin' phony about that."

"Tell you what's a fact," Cody confided. "There might come a day when I'd go full-bore into the show business. I have to admit I like the stage."

"You sayin' you'd give up scoutin'?"

"I'm sayin' I like the applause. Don't matter that it's play actin' and mostly nonsense. There's worse places than standin' in the limelight."

A log crackled in the fireplace. Hickok stared out the sitting room window, as though some profound revelation were to be found in the sunny sky. He finally looked around.

"I always figured it for a joke. You know, like April Fool's."

"April Fool's?" Cody said blankly. "What're you talkin' about?"

"All this hurrah they make about you and me. We fed 'em some guff and they printed it up in them dime novels, and folks swallowed it whole. But that don't make us the Heroes of the Plains."

"Who's the heroes, then?"

"Hell's bells, I don't know," Hickok barked. "I'm just

sayin' we invented most of what we told 'em. All a load of hogwash."

Cody took his fame seriously. "I don't recollect I ever bent the truth out of shape. Besides, there's nothing wrong with spinnin' a tale. Folks want to believe that stuff."

"Maybe you was made for the show business. April Fool's every night of the week."

"Well, like I said, there's worse things than the limelight. The money's not bad, either."

The door burst open. Katherine and Augustus hurried into the suite, followed by Phelan. Their faces were animated and they seemed themselves again. Whatever they were thinking about their parents, they rarely spoke it out loud. Their grief, if not diminished, was somehow suppressed.

"Have fun?" Cody asked.

"Oh, yes!" Katherine said gaily. "Giuseppina has such wonderful gowns. And her jewelry . . . !"

"A pretty lady needs fancy things. We'll buy you something nice over at Tiffany's."

"Will you—*truly*?"

The children had grown antsy cooped up in the suite. They'd spent the morning visiting Giuseppina and Omohundro, in their room down the hall. Phelan, the youngsters' constant shadow, had accompanied them.

"Who cares about Tiffany's?" Augustus scoffed. "Texas Jack showed me how his gun works. Even let me hold it!"

Hickok frowned. "Guns ain't boy's toys, Gus."

"No harm done," Phelan said. "Jack unloaded it and let me check it. He was careful."

"Pow! Pow!" Augustus shouted, his thumb and forefinger cocked like a pistol. "I bet I could shoot the lights out, too, Wild Bill."

Hickok exchanged a look with Cody. Then his gaze shifted to Phelan. "Bill and me got an invite to the racing heats this afternoon. You and Jack stick close till we get back. Don't let Gus and Kate out of here."

Phelan nodded. "We'll be on our toes."

"Well, foo!" Katherine pouted. "We have to stay here and be bored silly. It isn't fair, Wild Bill."

"Think so?" Hickok said with a teasing smile. "What if me and Buffalo Bill stop by that store, Tiffany's? How's that sound?"

"Honestly, you promise?"

"Cross my heart."

Harlem Lane was north of Central Park. The area was largely countryside, some five miles north of the theater district. The terrain was flat and open, perfect for racing horses. A few farmhouses were scattered along the broad, dirt lane.

The elite of New York adopted ducal pastimes during the Gilded Age. Every afternoon, when the weather permitted, men of prominence gathered at Harlem Lane for the racing heats. Their presence signified that they could afford to curtail their working day to the mornings. Their rivalry was yet another display of their wealth.

Dexter, a champion trotter owned by Robert Bonner, was reportedly purchased for thirty-three thousand dollars. Leonard Jerome, another racing enthusiast, quartered his horses in a stable paneled in walnut and floored with wall-to-wall carpet. Gould and Vanderbilt, even the Reverend Henry Ward Beecher, were known for their prize racing stock. Everyone who was anyone in the New York aristocracy came to Harlem Lane on a sunny afternoon.

Their ladies spent the afternoon at Central Park. No less than the men, the women of high society flaunted their wealth on a carriage promenade. Decked out in sable and gaily feathered hats, they were driven through the park in stately broughams, or an occasional barouche, the carriage favored by European nobility. The coaches were hauled by sleek steeds and piloted by liveried drivers in brass-buttoned uniforms. Pedigree, in New York, was often mirrored by pageantry.

Cody and Hickok prided themselves on their knowledge of horseflesh. On the Western Plains, where the warlike tribes bred superb mounts, a scout's horse was often the margin between life and death. Last night, during the party at Delmonico's, the robber barons had openly bragged on the bloodlines of their racing stock. Jay Gould had extended an invitation to today's heats, and Cody and Hickok had readily accepted. They were curious to see if New Yorkers knew anything about horses.

Cody, in particular, considered himself an authority on the subject. His favorite mount, Buckskin Joe, was fleet as the wind, descended from stock brought to the New World by the Conquistadors. He had raced Buckskin Joe against the prize mounts of army officers and Indian chiefs, and he'd never lost. Yet the horses paraded around Harlem Lane today were almost beyond his ken, and certainly beyond his means. He quickly revised his opinion of New Yorkers.

Dexter was a stallion imported from Kentucky. He was a barrel-chested animal, all sinew and muscle, standing sixteen hands high and well over a thousand pounds in weight. A blood bay, with black tail and mane, his hide glistened in the sun like dark blood on a polished redwood. He whinnied a shrill blast and pawed the earth as though he spurned it and longed to fly. His nostrils flared in anticipation of the first race.

A horse named Copperdust was his opponent. Tall and

powerful, the rangy chestnut looked like Dexter cast in
a different color. Jay Gould, who owned Copperdust, was
confident his fiery-eyed stallion could not be beat. Like
all robber barons, he thought of any endeavor in terms
of money, including a sporting event. He casually offered
Robert Bonner, Dexter's owner, a gentleman's wager of
ten thousand dollars. Bonner, as though dealing in spare
change, accepted the bet with an insouciant nod. The
challenge match was on.

Cody and Hickok were floored. Neither of them had
ever seen ten thousand dollars, much less possessed such
a princely sum. In a time when the daily wage for the av-
erage working man was two dollars or less, ten thousand
was a veritable fortune. The nonchalance with which
the wager had been made convinced the plainsmen that
they were in rarified company, and out of their element.
Except for their celebrity, they would have never been
invited.

Cornelius Vanderbilt joined them as the race got under
way. He was in his seventies, a mogul among moguls
who had recently endowed a university, to be named in
his honor. Yet, for all his years, he was still a feisty com-
petitor, all the more so where it involved Jay Gould.
Though Gould was in his middle thirties he had wrested
control of the Erie Railroad from Vanderbilt in a brutal
financial struggle. Vanderbilt blithely wagered Gould another ten thousand on the race.

The heat was set for a mile along the country lane. The
horses were attached to sulkies, light two-wheeled carriages with a flimsy seat for the driver. The drivers were
professionals, on salary to the owners and paid handsomely for their services. On signal, the drivers snapped
their reins, exhorting the stallions with crisp shouts, and
surged across the starting line. Copperdust jumped to an
early lead, the wheels of the sulkies leaving a rooster-tail

of dust in their wake. Dexter quickly narrowed the lead to a single length.

A crowd of some two hundred men lined Harlem Lane. The robber barons comprised perhaps a quarter that number, with the rest divided between socially prominent businessmen and hangers-on. The betting was heavy, and their voices were raised in rollicking cries as the stallions pounded along the road. The race was neck and neck most of the way, and the drivers began popping their whips as the sulkies blasted past the three-quarter mark. At the finish line, Dexter put on an explosive burst of speed and took it by a nose. The crowd shouted themselves hoarse.

Gould was magnanimous in defeat. He boasted that Copperdust would prevail next time, and amiably congratulated Bonner and Vanderbilt on their victory. Gentlemen never settled wagers with cash, and the winners knew they would receive a check by messenger sometime tomorrow. The hubbub died down as grooms hurried forward to attend the sweat-lathered stallions. Gould walked off to have a word with his driver.

The crowd retired to their carriages to await the next heat.

Vanderbilt invited Cody and Hickok to join him for refreshments. A manservant rushed to unfold a storage compartment at the rear of the carriage. He set out whiskey and brandy, an assortment of meats and cheese, and a basket of seasonal fruits. Cody thought he'd seen a regiment subsist on less.

"By Godfrey," Vanderbilt crowed. "It does my heart good to trim Jay Gould. A little comeuppance will do wonders for his soul."

"That was some race," Hickok said, accepting a whiskey. "You and Mr. Gould longtime rivals, are you?"

"Yes, it would be fair to say we are rivals, But understand, I have the utmost respect for Jay. He is brilliant in matters of business and finance."

Cody tried the brandy. "Never been much of a businessman myself. High finance tends to make me dizzy."

"To each his own," Vanderbilt observed. "You and Mr. Hickok are scouts and Indian fighters without peer. I seriously doubt I could survive as much as a day on the Western Plains."

"That's mighty good brandy," Cody said, holding his glass to the light. "Got a nice bite to it."

"Napoleonic Brandy, imported from France. I'll have a case sent over to you."

"Well now, I'm obliged, Mr. Vanderbilt."

"No need to stand on ceremony. All of my friends call me Commodore."

"You a navy man?"

"Hardly anything so dashing." Vanderbilt paused, accepting cheese on a wafer from his manservant. "More of an honorary title from business and charitable works. I'm quite active in civic affairs."

"Civic affairs?" Cody mused. "You talkin' about politics?"

"Actually, I'm more involved in projects to benefit the city. The new museum is our latest effort."

"What sort of museum?"

"One more ambitious than the Louvre in Paris."

Vanderbilt warmed to the subject. In league with the Astors and other members of the social hierarchy, he had set about to create the finest art museum in the world. Over the generations wealthy New York families had amassed impressive private art collections. Their goal was to establish a museum and donate their art treasures for public display. The project, in the end, would further exalt the status of New York.

The Metropolitan Museum of Art opened in 1870. The temporary quarters were on Fourteenth Street, near Union Square. But ground had been broken for a permanent home, a granite colossus to be built uptown on Fifth Avenue. Even now, a drive was underway to expand the collection with the works of Rembrandt, Van Dyck, Vermeer, and the contemporary master, Albert Bierstadt. Upon completion, the museum would be the standard for all the world.

"Imagine, if you will," Vanderbilt concluded. "A museum grander than any edifice known to man. Here in New York."

"Sounds big," Cody said, more interested in the brandy than the art. "Bet it'll cost a bundle."

"Before we're through, in the tens of millions."

Hickok was scarcely listening. He was thinking instead that Cornelius Vanderbilt had been around a long time. The financier was elderly, rich beyond reckoning, and doubtless privy to the darkest secrets of New York's social elite. On the spur of the moment, Hickok decided to take a chance. He tried to edge into it sideways.

"Talkin' about money," he said vaguely. "I was readin' in the *Police Gazette* about a wealthy family that got murdered. Think the name was Stanley."

"Dreadful thing," Vanderbilt commented gravely. "I've known the Stanleys for thirty years, perhaps more. One of the finest families in New York."

"I recollect the paper mentioned a name—Leland Stanley?"

Vanderbilt's features clouded. "Leland would be the exception. I haven't much use for him."

Hickok looked curious. "How's that?"

"To put it charitably, the man is a cad. He lived off his brother—Henry, the one who was murdered—and devoted his time to debauchery and loose women. I closed my account when he assumed control of the family bank."

"What about his mother?" Hickok asked casually. "The paper said she wasn't murdered. I forgot her name."

"Elizabeth Stanley." Vanderbilt's tone softened. "A saint of a woman, in every sense of the word. I wonder that she ever gave birth to Leland."

"Know her well, do you?"

"As I said, thirty years or more. What prompted your interest in the Stanleys?"

"Well, you know, once a lawman always a lawman. Never like to see a murder go unsolved."

Cody sensed it was time to end the conversation. He deftly diverted the financier's attention. "Are you racin' a horse today, Commodore?"

Vanderbilt went off on a fervent soliloquy about his prize trotter. The stallion's name was Midnight.

CHAPTER 21

"I TEND to buy it."

"Why's that?"

"Vanderbilt's nobody's dummy. He's known the woman for thirty years."

Cody waved a hand. "I've been married to Lulu near on seven years and I still don't know her. Women have got a way of foolin' a man."

"Not Vanderbilt," Hickok said with conviction. "He didn't get rich as Midas on bad judgment. We can forget about the grandma."

"Jim, I shorely do hope you're right. That'd mean the kids have some family that's not tryin' to kill'em."

"I think we're safe there."

"Well, just for the sake of argument, let's say it's so. We've still got Leland Stanley to worry about . . . and Richter."

"Yeah, I've been ponderin' on Richter."

A shaft of sunlight spilled through the window of the sitting room. Last night, after the show at the theater, they'd returned directly to the hotel. Hickok had been moody and thoughtful, and this morning he was still somewhat withdrawn. They were alone in the suite, seated before the fireplace. He stared into the flames.

"And?" Cody prompted. "What about Richter?"

Hickok's features were serious. "Much as I'd like to kill the bastard, that won't work. Billy McGlory would just replace him with another hired gun."

"You think Stanley's dealin' directly with McGlory?"

"That'd be my guess."

"So what's our move?"

"We ain't got a helluva lot of choice. We've got to capture Richter."

Three days had passed since Hickok's encounter with Billy McGlory. Though he hadn't spotted a tail, he was confident their movements were being shadowed night and day. He sensed Richter was watching and planning, awaiting an opportune moment. The children's lives were still in peril.

"Richter's slippery," Cody said absently. "How you figure to collar him?"

"Don't know the how or where just yet. I want to talk with Phelan."

There was a rap at the door. Cody answered it and Charlie Phelan walked into the suite. He guarded the children from morning till night, leaving once they were safely returned from the theater. His bloodshot eyes indicated he wasn't getting much sleep.

"Morning," he said, doffing his hat and coat. "Hope you haven't had breakfast. I could use some coffee."

"The kids are getting dressed," Cody remarked. "Soon as they're ready, we'll go downstairs."

"Sounds good." Phelan crossed to the sofa, took a seat. "Anything special on for today?"

Hickok lit a cheroot. "We've just been talkin' about Richter. We need to track him down."

"Does that mean you're back to the original plan? Take him into custody and turn him against Stanley."

"I don't see no other way to end this mess."

"Any ideas where we start?"

"Armory Hall," Hickok said, exhaling a streamer of smoke. "I want you to mount a watch on McGlory's place and get a line on Richter. Find out where he lives, or when he's alone. Somewhere we can grab him off the street."

"Easier said than done," Phelan informed him. "A

stakeout on Armory Hall wouldn't last ten minutes. Somebody would tip McGlory."

"You sayin' it can't be done?"

"The Bowery's no place to pull a surveillance. Everybody knows everybody else, and I'd stick out like a sore thumb. Probably get myself killed."

Hickok's gaze became abstracted. He was in Phelan's town, and he was forced to accept the detective's word that surveillance wasn't the answer. Yet he couldn't afford to wait for Richter to make still another attempt on the children's lives. All along, from Nebraska to New York, he'd been reacting to Richter's moves, ever a step behind. It was time to take the initiative.

"Let's go at it another way," he said. "Anybody you know who could act as a go-between with McGlory?"

"John Morrissey," Phelan replied. "You'll recall he gave me the inside dope on Stanley."

"The feller that owns a casino?"

"That's the one."

"Tell me about him."

Morrissey, Phelan explained, operated the finest casino in New York. For years, always playing the angle, he'd been aligned with Boss Tweed and Tammany Hall. But with the shift in political winds, his allegiance had shifted to the wealthy reformers, many of whom patronized his casino. He was, nonetheless, an Irishman, a product of Hell's Kitchen, and never far from his roots. He still maintained his ties to the underworld.

"You might say he walks the fence," Phelan went on. "He hobnobs with the swells and he's pals with all the gang bosses. Nobody in this town ignores Johnny Morrissey."

"So McGlory would trust him?"

"Probably more than he'd trust the Pope. What do you have in mind?"

"Charlie, we're fixin' to run ourselves a bunco game. I want you to set up a meetin' with Morrissey."

Phelan squinted. "What reason do I give him?"

"Tell him Wild Bill Hickok aims to do a helluva favor for one of his pals."

"You're talking about McGlory?"

"None other."

"You lost me," Cody interjected. "What's this got to do with Richter?"

Hickok grinned. "We're gonna trap the son-of-a-bitch."

The Savoy Club was on Twenty Fourth Street, east of Madison Square. The location was within walking distance of the theater district, and the clientele comprised the male aristocracy of New York. Women were not allowed in the Savoy.

The main salon was heavily carpeted, with dark paneled walls and crystal chandeliers. A collection of Old World art the envy of any museum was scattered about the room. The club was divided by an aisle, one side of which was devoted to chemin de fer and roulette. On the opposite side, an equal number of tables were covered with faro layouts.

Faro was a game originated by French kings and currently all the rage from New York to San Francisco. At the far end of the salon were a dozen poker tables, covered with baize cloth and lighted by overhead Tiffany lamps. There was a small afternoon crowd, almost lost in the baronial magnificence of the room. The club was pervaded by the decorous atmosphere considered *de rigueur* among gentlemen gamblers.

The ambience of the salon was an elegance far beyond Hickok's experience. Phelan led him to a door at the rear of the room, which was guarded by a strong-arm thug in a fashionable suit. Down a hallway, they were admitted to an office lushly appointed with leather chairs and walnut furniture. John Morrissey rose from behind his desk.

"Mr. Hickok," he said pleasantly, extending a hand. "A pleasure to meet you."

"Same here." Hickok accepted his handshake. "Appreciate you takin' the time to see me."

"Not at all, not at all. Any friend of Charlie's is welcome in the Savoy."

Morrissey motioned them to chairs. He exuded a sort of patrician assurance, as though his profile might once have graced an ancient coin. He was impeccably attired, his hair flecked with gray, and he spoke in a resonant, organlike voice. Yet, despite a ready smile, his eyes were sharp and alert, filled with craftiness. He nodded across the desk with a benign look.

"I've read the reviews on your show. You and Mr. Cody are the toast of the town."

Hickok played along. "We'd like you to be our guest. I'll send around some tickets."

"That's very nice of you." Morrissey hesitated, still smiling. "Now, how can I be of service? Charlie tells me it has to do with Billy McGlory."

"I reckon McGlory and me got off on the wrong foot. I was hopin' you might act as peacemaker."

"Yes, I heard about that unfortunate incident at Armory Hall. What would you like me to say to Billy?"

Hickok leaned forward with a conspiratorial air. "I've got something he wants. You know, that business Charlie asked you about—Leland Stanley."

"No, I don't know," Morrissey said smoothly. "And quite frankly, I don't want to know. Let's leave it that I'll try to broker a truce."

"Whichever way you want to handle it. Just tell him I'm fed up with this stage nonsense and ready to head back West. I'm willin' to strike a deal."

"When would you like to meet with him?"

"The sooner the better so far's I'm concerned."

Morrissey reflected a moment. "I could probably have Billy here in an hour or so. Are you a gambling man, Mr. Hickok?"

"I'd have to say I'm partial to poker."

"I believe there's a game going on now. You can amuse yourself while you're waiting."

"Don't mind if I do."

Morrissey led them back into the club. Five men were seated at a poker table and he made the introductions. He insisted Hickok's marker was good, ordering a houseman to bring a thousand dollars in chips. Once Hickok was settled into a chair, he nodded amiably. His gaze shifted to Phelan.

"Take good care of our friend, Charlie. I shouldn't be long."

"We'll be here," Phelan said. "Thanks again, Johnny."

"Think nothing of it."

Morrissey returned to his office. Hickok quickly discovered that poker was played differently in Eastern casinos. The traditional rules had been revised to include straights, flushes, and the most elusive of all combinations, the straight flush. The highest hand was now a royal flush, ten through ace in the same suit. The rules gave the game an added dimension.

Poker out West was still played by the original rules. The top hand was four aces, drawn by most players only once or twice in a lifetime. The other cinch was four kings with an ace, which precluded anyone holding four aces. For Hickok, the Eastern rules altered the perspective of the game, but not the game itself. His style was to read the players rather than their cards.

He bluffed them out of three pots in a row.

Billy McGlory arrived at the club shortly before four o'clock. Hickok excused himself from the game, ahead by some three hundred dollars. Morrissey, who wanted nothing to do with the meeting, ushered them into his private office. He then walked Phelan out to the bar for a drink.

McGlory tossed his hat on the desk. He seated himself in one of the chairs, his eyes narrow with suspicion. "I'm told you're after making a deal. What's on your mind?"

Hickok stared at him. "The kids for twenty thousand."

"Richter offered you ten thousand once before and you turned him down. Why the switch?"

"Cody swore I'd make my fortune in the show business. Turns out it's him and Buntline stuffing their pockets. All I've seen is peanuts."

"Horseshit." McGlory's gaze bored into him. "You and Cody have been protecting those brats like you was on a crusade. What's changed?"

"The price has changed," Hickok said impassively. "Cody was the one all hearts-and-flowers about them kids. I was just along for the ride."

"That why you shot Turk Johnson and threw Richter off the train?"

"I was lookin' after my investment. Cody all but took a blood oath I'd get rich in the show business."

"So now you're ready to ditch Cody and hand over the kids. That it?"

"Yeah, for twenty thousand simoleons. Way I see it, money talks and bullshit walks."

"Why should I pay you a red cent? Only a matter of time till Richter gets hold of those kids."

Hickok paused like a magician reluctant to reveal his last best trick. "Why fight a war when it ain't your money? Leland Stanley's the one payin' the freight."

McGlory tugged thoughtfully at his ear. "You tried your best to kill Richter in Philly. Maybe this is just another setup."

"I ain't plannin' to harm him. I'm strictly in it for the money. You've got my word."

"I'll hold you to it. You kill him and that's egg on my face. Understand me?"

"Nothing wrong with my hearing."

"So how do we work this exchange?"

"I recollect Richter's partial to midnight. We'll meet on the pathway west of the zoo."

"Why the zoo?"

The idea was Phelan's. Late that morning, scouting for out-of-the-way locations, they had walked through Central Park. The zoo fitted Hickok's plans perfectly.

"Neutral territory," he said. "Nobody's in the park at midnight."

McGlory shrugged. "All right, the zoo it is."

"Just Richter and me," Hickok warned him. "I see anybody else and the deal's off."

"You'll have the kids there?"

"They'll be close at hand. Once Richter shows me the money, I'll deliver the kids. Won't take ten minutes."

"You have a helper, then." McGlory gave him a cagey look. "Charlie Phelan's in it with you, is he?"

Hickok smiled. "Don't ask and I won't tell you no lies."

"You remember one thing, Mr. Wild Bill Hickok."

"What's that?"

"No tricks," McGlory said with blunt vindictiveness.

"Otto Richter walks out of that park alive or you'll answer to me. Got it?"

"Got it," Hickok said evenly. "Richter will leave there alive and kicking. I guarantee it."

"Then we're on for midnight."

Neither of them offered to shake hands. Hickok left him in the office and walked back into the club. He found Phelan at the bar with Morrissey.

"Well, Mr. Hickok," Morrissey said. "Everything work out to your satisfaction?"

"You might say things never looked better. I appreciate all you done."

"You're welcome at the Savoy anytime, Mr. Hickok. Drop around whenever you'd like a poker game."

"I'll do that."

Morrissey walked them to the door. On the street, Hickok and Phelan turned toward Madison Square. The detective was brimming with curiosity.

"You really pulled it off?"

"Slicker'n a whistle."

"How the Christ did you convince him?"

"Charlie, there's nobody easier to con than a con man."

Phelan appeared confused. "What's that mean?"

"McGlory thought he gaffed me," Hickok said, amused by it all. "He'll rig it for Richter to grab the kids and keep the money. Likely try to kill me, too."

"You talk like you knew it all along."

Hickok chuckled. "Tell you, these New York desperadoes give me a laugh. They think they invented the game."

"What game?"

"The one we're gonna play tonight."

CHAPTER 22

THE SHOW was standing-room-only that night. Hickok's shooting out the spotlight again brought down the house, and Giuseppina, as Dove Eye, enthralled the audience when she was reunited with Buffalo Bill. The cast took five curtain calls.

By now, the drill following the show had become routine. Katherine and Augustus, surrounded by Cody, Hickok and Phelan, were escorted out the stage door. Tonight, Giuseppina and Omohundro were accompanied by Buntline, and they trailed close behind. Two carriages, hired for the run of the show, awaited them on the street. They stepped aboard for the short ride back to the hotel.

Katherine snuggled close to Hickok as the carriage pulled away. Cody and Phelan, with Augustus between them, settled back on the opposite seat. Though the children now considered themselves troupers, their energy invariably began to flag each night when the show ended. Hickok, one arm around Katherine, checked his pocket watch with the other hand. In the light from the street, he saw that it was a few minutes after ten. He thought they had little time to spare.

A short while later they all trooped into the suite. The children went to their bedroom, to change into their night clothes. Hickok and Cody, with Phelan in the middle, took a seat on the sofa. The others, their faces solemn, found chairs by the fireplace. Phelan extracted a hand-drawn map from his inside jacket pocket, and spread it on the table before the sofa. Earlier, during the stage show, he had rendered the sketch from memory. The map was of Central Park.

"Go ahead, Charlie," Hickok said, then glanced across at Cody. "Bill, you need to pay close attention to the layout. I got a look this mornin' when Charlie and me scouted the park."

Cody nodded. "I'm all ears. Let 'er rip."

"Here's Fifth Avenue," Phelan said, pointing with his finger. "The building closest to the street is the old Arsenal, and directly behind it is the zoo. This dotted line west of the zoo is a footpath."

"Over here?" Cody tapped the map. "What're these scratchy marks?"

"Trees," Phelan noted. "They wind around south of the zoo and thin out along the pathway. You can see they get heavier between the pathway and this road back of the zoo. That's East Drive."

The map covered a relatively small area in the southeast corner of the park. A large pond was indicated north and west of where Fifty Ninth Street, a broad thoroughfare, crossed Fifth Avenue. East Drive followed a serpentine line between the pond and the western perimeter of the zoo. The Arsenal, which fronted the zoo, was at the intersection of Fifth Avenue and Sixty Fourth Street.

"Looks clear enough," Cody said. "How do we pull it off?"

Hickok leaned over the table. "We'll drop Charlie off here." He jabbed at a spot on the map. "Once he works his way through them trees, he'll take a position to cover me on the path. You and me will drive on to the Arsenal, and you'll stay there. I'll head for the zoo to meet Richter."

Cody frowned. "You mean to leave me in the carriage?"

"Richter's got to believe you're waitin' in the carriage with the kids. I don't see no other way."

"You know good and well he's gonna jump you with a bunch of thugs. I'd feel a sight better if I was with you."

"Bill, we've got to bamboozle him into thinkin' the kids are there. Nothin' for it but that you stick with the carriage."

"I don't like it," Cody said. "You and Charlie are liable to have a fight on your hands."

Hickok ignored the objection. "You just let me worry about Richter."

The bedroom door opened. Katherine hurried across the room, having changed into a flowery nightgown. Augustus, who wore a billowy nightshirt, looked asleep on his feet. They made the rounds, hugging everyone good night, saving Hickok and Cody for last. The youngsters went from one to the other, kissing the plainsmen on the cheek, lingering a moment in their arms. Then they scampered off to the bedroom.

"So touching," Giuseppina sighed, her eyes moist. "How those leetle darlings love you both."

Cody wagged his head sadly. "Guess they figure we're all the family they've got."

"Jack. Ned." Hickok stood, again checking his pocket watch. "We're dependin' on you to look after the kids. Don't open that door for nobody."

Omohundro and Buntline were both armed. They exchanged a glance, then Omohundro nodded. "You take care of Richter," he said stoutly. "We'll hold down the fort here."

"Indeed!" Buntline added with an air of bravado. "You needn't worry yourselves. The children are in good hands."

"Do take care," Giuseppina said softly. "Come back safely."

Cody pulled a grin. "Nothin' more certain in the world, Dove Eye."

Hickok led the way out of the suite. Cody and Phelan followed him to a staircase at the end of the hall, a narrow passageway normally used by maids and servicemen. On the ground floor, they went through the kitchen and exited into a darkened alley. None of them doubted that Richter had someone watching the front of the hotel.

Outside, they walked through the alley and turned west on Twenty Fifth Street. One of the carriages retained for their nightly trips to the theater was waiting for them at the corner of Sixth Avenue. The driver was trustworthy, sworn to secrecy, and paid handsomely for tonight's venture. They clambered aboard with a last look along the street.

The carriage trundled north toward Central Park.

Some twenty minutes later the carriage stopped at the corner of Sixth Avenue and Fifty Ninth Street. They were not quite two miles north of the theater district, and directly across the street lay Central Park. The wide thoroughfare was virtually deserted so late at night.

Hickok stepped from the carriage. He stood for a moment inspecting the T-shaped intersection in all directions. Finally, satisfied they had not been followed, he motioned smartly to Phelan. The detective hopped down to the pavement and without a word hurried across the street. He disappeared into the park.

Central Park was the masterwork of Calvert Vaux, a London-born architect transplanted to New York. Five years ago, in concert with Superintendent of Parks Frederick Olmsted, he broke ground on the project. A vast expanse of raw countryside was remolded in his vision, with landscaped hills, open meadows, and rolling copses

of trees. Thousands of laborers and stonemasons literally
sculpted the earth.

Vaux's dream was a pastoral sanctuary away from the
congestion and demonic rhythm of the city. The end result was 843 acres of meandering paths, tranquil lakes,
and sprawling meadows that stretched north from Fifty
Ninth Street to Harlem Lane. The park was over two
miles long and a half mile wide, crisscrossed by carriage
lanes, sunken transverse roads, and forty stone bridges.
There was nothing to rival it in all the world.

Charlie Phelan paused inside the treeline. He watched
the carriage round the corner onto Fifty Ninth Street and
some moments later turn north on Fifth Avenue. Directly
ahead of him lay the Pond, a horseshoe-shaped basin that
froze over in the winter and became a natural skating
rink. The Pond was illuminated by calcium lights, and a
solitary pair of skaters, a man and a woman, glided
gracefully about the icy surface. He idly thought they
were lovers, immune to time or the frosty chill.

The moon hung high and cold, diamond-hard in the
dead-of-night sky. Phelan ghosted through the trees,
skirting the Pond, and several minutes later paused before the Inscope Arch. The ornate bridge was constructed
of pink and gray granite, with a spacious underpass to
accommodate a bridal path. The archway supporting the
bridge was fourteen feet wide and twelve feet tall, and
the bridge itself was a hundred feet long. Beyond lay the
westerly bend of East Drive.

Somewhere in the distance the mournful hoot of an
owl floated eerily through the night. Phelan hesitated,
surveying the terrain in all directions, and darted across
East Drive. On the other side he vanished into the shel-
terbelt of the trees and cautiously made his way north in
the dappled moonlight. He was alert to sound and movement, for he was certain that Richter and his men were

even now infiltrating the park. His every instinct told him they were not far ahead.

The trees thinned out over the slope of a stunted, rock-studded hill. Phelan warily watched his footing, moving step by step, and halted in the shadow of a tall oak. His position overlooked the footpath west of the zoo, and beyond, not thirty yards away, was another stand of trees. He slowly scanned the treeline, and some inner voice told him that there were men, guarded and silent, waiting in the darkened timber. He pulled a Colt New Model Police revolver from his waistband and hooked his thumb over the hammer. His eyes continued to search the trees.

On Fifth Avenue, the carriage rolled to a halt on the east side of the street. The aristocracy of New York, ever determined to outdistance the lower classes, were moving farther and farther uptown. Several mansions were under construction across from Central Park, towering monuments to the robber barons and merchant princes of the city. Opposite the construction sites was the Arsenal, built prior to the Civil War as a storage facility for munitions. The building now housed the Museum of Natural History.

Lampposts along Fifth Avenue cast aureoles of light on the cobblestone sidewalks. Hickok opened the carriage door and subjected the Arsenal to long, careful scrutiny. All looked quiet, and his gaze shifted a block upstreet, where a lone carriage was parked by the curb bordering Central Park. Beneath the glow of a nearby lamppost, he made out the form of the driver, sitting motionless, wrapped in a heavy great-coat. He gestured to Cody.

"I'm layin' odds," he muttered sourly. "Dollar to a donut says that coach belongs to Richter. He's already here."

Cody looked out the door. "You think him and his gang are waitin' in there now?"

"Nope," Hickok said shortly. "I figure they're somewheres over by the zoo. Waitin' for me to show."

"Goddarnit, it's just like I told you before. You're gonna walk straight into a hornet's nest."

"Wouldn't be the first time."

"Damn well might be the last," Cody fumed. "I still say I ought to come with you."

"No dice," Hickok said. "You stick here and shoot anybody that comes within shoutin' distance. Only way Richter's gonna believe you've got the kids."

"You're hell on givin' orders. Who made you the general?"

"Somebody's got to brace Richter and I reckon that's me. I shoot straghter'n you, anyhow."

"Jim, I have to tell you, that's a mighty lame excuse."

"Well, it's the only one I've got. Guess it'll have to do."

"You always was a hardhead."

"Just sit tight and I'll see you directly."

Hickok stepped out of the door. One eye on the carriage upstreet, he crossed Fifth Avenue at a measured stride. The Arsenal loomed before him like an ancient monolith.

He walked into Central Park.

The zoo was dark. A flagstone walkway wound past cages that housed grizzly bears, sea lions, monkeys, and other exotic species. The cages were heavily barred, with enclosed dens at the rear for protection against the cold. The quiet was deafening.

Hickok felt his nerves shut down. A strange calm, something akin to fatalism, came over him whenever he went in harm's way. Yet he was acutely aware of his surroundings, vision inexplicably sharper and sounds magnified. His senses notched upward to a finer pitch.

A wakeful monkey chattered as he moved past a darkened cage. The pungent odor of dung and the ripe blend of animal smells hung over the zoo. In another cage, a boar grizzly, disturbed by the monkey, woofed a guttural warning. The bear's yellowed eyes glowed like embers behind the steel bars.

Hickok was not alarmed by the sounds. The element of surprise had never entered into his plans for tonight's encounter. He wanted Richter to believe that it was on the square, a straight business deal, the children in exchange for money. Even more, it was important that Richter believed he had the edge. There was weakness in overconfidence.

The pathway beyond the zoo was lighted by a silvery moon now at its zenith. Hickok resisted the impulse to look at the trees on his left, trusting that Phelan was already in position. His gaze fixed instead on a dense stand of trees to his right, obliquely north of the path. He felt certain that was the direction by which Richter had entered the park. He stopped in a patch of moonlight.

Otto Richter seemed to materialize from the treeline. One moment there was nothing, and the next moment he was moving forward at a deliberate pace. He carried a small leather satchel, and his eyes darted back toward the zoo, wary someone else might step from the shadows. He halted on the pathway.

"Hickok," he said in a guarded voice. "After Philadelphia, I have good reason not to trust you. Are you alone?"

"Are you?" Hickok countered. "Let's get down to it, Richter. You got the money?"

"Twenty thousand." Richter hefted the satchel in his left hand. "Do you have the children?"

"Charlie Phelan has them."

"Where?"

"Here in the park," Hickok said. "You show me the money and let's make sure the count's right. Then I'll take you to them."

"Yeah, you'll take me," Richter said roughly. "Not just the way you planned, though. All right, boys!"

Three men stepped out of the treeline. The glint of moonlight on metal reflected off the pistols in their hands. Hickok considered them with a level stare, then glanced back at Richter. "You sure you want it this way?"

Richter's features went cold as a stone adder. "You'd better have those kids, Hickok. Otherwise you're a dead—"

A split second was all Hickok needed. His hands moved even as Richter was still talking. The three men, caught off guard, were a beat behind. He produced the Colts, and shot one of the men in the chest. Phelan appeared from behind the tall oak and drilled another one through the stomach. The third man got off a hurried snap-shot that went wide.

Richter slammed Hickok upside the head with the satchel. Hickok stumbled, knocked off balance, and Richter sprinted toward the zoo. The third hooligan fired again, the slug plucking at the sleeve of Hickok's coat. His attention focused on the gunman, Hickok was vaguely aware of chattering monkeys as Richter disappeared along the zoo walkway. His arm came level and the Colt bucked in the same instant Charlie Phelan fired. The thug went down as though he legs had been chopped off.

Richter dashed out of the zoo. He saw Cody hurrying across Fifth Avenue and abruptly forgot about the carriage waiting upstreet. His hand dipped inside his coat, frantically drawing a revolver, and he snapped off a shot. The slug whistled harmlessly through the night, and

Cody stopped, clawing at a Colt holstered on his hip. As the pistol came to bear, Richter's nerve deserted him and he dropped the satchel. He turned back into the park.

A mounted policeman, drawn by the gunshots, clattered up from Fifty Ninth Street. He skidded to a halt, aware of one man in the middle of Fifth Avenue and another bolting headlong through the park. He glowered down at Cody.

"What the hell's going on here?"

"Officer, I don't have time to explain."

Cody jerked him off the horse. The policeman hit the pavement with a thud and Cody vaulted into the saddle. He sawed at the reins, booting the horse in the ribs, and took off at a lope. Off in the distance, the landscape bathed in moonlight, he saw Richter running south through the trees. He urged the horse into a gallop.

Richter barreled across East Drive. He ducked into the underpass beneath Inscope Arch and darted out the other side on the bridal path. He heard the drum of hoofbeats and glanced over his shoulder at the rider bearing down on him. His legs pumped as he put on a burst of speed and bore off in the direction of the Pond. Cody leaped from the saddle, collaring him around the neck, and drove him to the ground. His lungs exploded with a whoosh of air.

"Gotcha now!" Cody shouted jubilantly. "You dirty rotten bastard!"

Otto Richter collapsed in the moonlit earth of Central Park.

CHAPTER 23

HICKOK EMERGED from the trees by East Drive. Phelan was a step behind and trailed him across the roadway. They were following Cody.

On the far side of Inscope Arch, they found him at the edge of the bridal path. He was standing over Richter, whose hands were bound behind his back with his neck-tie. A horse was cropping brittle winter grass at the verge of the treeline.

"Where you been?" Cody said jovially. "You missed our little wrestlin' match."

"We started into the zoo," Hickok said. "Heard a shot and saw you jerk that cop off his horse. Figured you was after Richter."

"I rode him down pretty as you please. How'd he slip past you and Charlie?"

"We was busy with them pistoleros he brought along. They're back there pushin' up daisies."

"Thought as much when I heard the shootin'. Then our boy here come bustin' out of the zoo. Say hello for yourself, Richter."

"Go to hell," Richter said. "The whole lot of you."

Hickok stared down at him. "We're fixin' to find out how tough you are, sport. I want some questions answered."

"You won't get anything out of me."

"Don't bet on it."

"We can't take him to the hotel," Cody broke in. "The kids are there and that wouldn't rightly do. Not if you're thinkin' what I'm thinkin'."

"Charlie, you got any ideas?" Hickok said, glancing at Phelan. "We need somewheres that's private. Somewheres we won't be disturbed."

"Sheep Meadow." Phelan pointed off to the northwest. "One of the biggest meadows in the park. Should be deserted this time of night."

"Things are liable to get a little loud."

"No one will hear us out there."

"Good enough," Hickok said. "Bill, you'd better get rid of that cop's horse. We don't want nobody doggin' our trail."

Cody led the horse to the end of the bridge. He swatted it on the rump and the horse clattered off toward Fifth Avenue. Hickok hoisted Richter to his feet and followed Phelan deeper into the park. Cody fell in behind.

Sheep Meadow was a quarter mile or so to the northwest. Once a grazeland for sheep farmers, it was now a spacious field where families gathered for picnics in the summertime. The meadow was ringed by trees washed in the silvery glitter of the moon. There was no one in sight.

Hickok halted near the trees on the southern fringe of the meadow. He looked at Richter. "Here's the deal," he said. "You're gonna tell us about McGlory and Stanley, and there ain't no other way. Not if you aim to leave this place alive."

"You won't kill me," Richter said with a cocksure laugh. "I'm no good to you dead."

"Friend, you got it bassackwards," Hickok informed him in a hard voice. "You're no good to me alive—unless you talk."

"Let me have him," Cody snorted gleefully. "I'll make him squawk like a duck."

"What've you got in mind?"

"A little trick the Injuns taught me. Works everytime."

Cody untied Richter's hands. He slammed him up against a leafless birch and bound his hands behind the tree. Hickok seemed to get into the spirit of things, and helped Cody collect armloads of fallen branches from the woods. Phelan watched them with a bemused look, wondering it they were serious. The stacked branches were soon piled higher than Richter's knees.

Hickok provided the matches. Cody built a teepee of twigs beneath the branches and lit the fire. He fanned it with his hat and the dried wood caught with a sharp crackle. Flames licked around the tops of Richter's shoes.

"You're crazy!" Richter shouted, his expression suddenly frenzied. "You can't burn me alive!"

"Why shore we can," Cody said breezily. "I've seen the Injuns burn a man to a crisp. Stinks something awful."

"For God's sake, it's not human!"

"Well, we can stop it anytime you say. All you gotta do is start talkin'."

The cuff of Richter's trousers caught fire. Flame lapped about his ankles and his mouth opened in a banshee howl of terror. Phelan looked no less terrified, his eyes wide with horror. He grabbed Hickok's arm.

"Jesus, call it off," he blurted anxiously. "We're not savages."

"Turns your stomach, don't it?" Hickok said. "But you know, you're right, Charlie. This ain't a fit way for any man to die."

Hickok kicked the fiery branches aside, smothering the flames on Richter's trousers. He gave Cody a rueful look. "Bill, you been around them heathen red-sticks too long. Damned if it ain't just a little savage."

Cody sulked. "You want him to talk, don't you?"

"Yeah, but you can tell he ain't fixin' to squeal. The man's got brass balls."

"So what're you gonna do?"

"Just have to kill him."

Hickok pulled one of his Colts. He thumbed the hammer and pressed the muzzle between Richter's eyes. "You got any last prayers, get 'em said. You're on your way."

"Wait," Richter croaked pitifully. "I'll tell you everything, all of it. Just don't kill me."

Charlie Phelan was never sure whether it was all an act. Later, reflecting on it, he suspected Hickok and Cody might have staged a mock execution. But there was no doubt they'd broken their man.

Otto Richter told them everything.

A bright morning sun flooded Gramercy Park. There was a snap in the air and the horses snorted steamy puffs of frost. The carriage stopped before the Stanley mansion shortly before eight o'clock.

Inside the cab, Hickok and Cody, with Richter wedged between them, occupied one seat. Omohundro and Phelan were crowded into the other seat with Augustus and Katherine. The children seemed to have lost their fear of Richter, who was singed around the ankles, his hands bound behind his back. His eyes were empty with defeat.

Hickok crawled out of the carriage. He assisted Richter down and waited until Cody stepped onto the sidewalk. Late last night they had returned to the hotel, where Richter was held under guard in the suite. The children, upon awakening, greeted the news of Richter's capture with a sense of deliverance. Their long ordeal was nearly at an end.

"Charlie. Jack." Hickok looked back into the carriage at Phelan and Omohundro. "You boys keep a sharp lookout till this business is finished. I doubt it'll take too long."

Omohundro bobbed his head. "Charlie and me will take care of the kids. Don't worry about a thing."

"Wild Bill," Katherine said in a plaintive voice. "Aren't you taking us with you? We want to see Grandmama."

"You and Gus sit tight," Hickok said gently. "We'll come get you directly. I promise."

Hickok and Cody walked Richter toward the mansion. During the night, they had decided to confront Lelend Stanley with Richter's confession. They were wary of contacting the police until all the loose ends had been tied together. Richter, who feared Billy McGlory more than he feared them, had refused to implicate the underworld czar. They hoped Stanley would break under pressure.

The butler answered the door. Hickok shoved past him, with Richter and Cody in tow. They proceeded along the central hall, checking rooms as they went. Halfway down the hall, they came upon the dining room. Stanley and his mother were seated at the breakfast table.

"Stanley, the jig's up," Hickok said bluntly. "You remember Otto Richter, don't you?"

All the color leeched out of Stanley's features. Elizabeth Stanley, by now recovered from her illness, appeared confused. "How dare you!" she protested. "Leland, who are these men?"

"Ma'am," Cody said, doffing his hat. "I'm Bill Cody and this here's Bill Hickok. We've got some bad news."

"Don't get no worse," Hickok said, halting at Stanley's end of the table. "Richter spilled the beans, gave us the whole story. Ain't that right, Richter?"

"Yeah," Richter mumbled with a hangdog look. "I told them."

Stanley struggled to regain his composure. "I don't know this man and I want you out of this house. Now!"

"Won't wash," Cody said. "Richter put your neck in a

noose hopin' to save himself. You're headed for the gallows."

"Unless you get smart, real fast," Hickok added. "You testify against Billy McGlory and we'll ask the judge for leniency. That's your only out."

Richter stiffened. "Don't say a—"

Hickok cuffed him upside the head. "Keep your trap shut."

"Stop that!" Elizabeth Stanley rose from her chair. "I demand to know the meaning of this. Instantly!"

Cody wished there were another way. "Ma'am, I hate to be the one to tell you," he said, moving a step closer. "Your son—Henry—and your daughter-in-law?"

"Yes, what about them?"

"This feller—" Cody motioned to Richter. "Well, he's the scoundrel that done them in. And much as it's gonna hurt you, Leland hired him to do it."

"How absurd!" she said, outraged, casting a glance at Stanley. "Leland, tell them there has been some mistake."

"Mother . . ." Stanley's voice trailed off. "You musn't believe these men. I've done nothing wrong."

Elizabeth Stanley stared at him. His features were waxen and he was unable to hold her gaze. She saw the desperate look and she suddenly gasped, a hand to her mouth. "My God," she said, collapsing into her chair. "How could you?"

"Mother, you have to believe me . . ."

"I see it in your face." Her eyes welled over with a sudden rush of tears. "The mark of Cain on my own son. Henry and Amanda and . . . the children."

"No, ma'am," Cody said hurriedly. "Augustus and Katherine are gem-dandy, just fine. We've got'em waitin' outside."

"Mr. Cody, was that your name? I'm so confused by all this. Where have they been?"

"Well, ma'am, it's sort of a long story. Why don't we let them tell you?"

A few moments later Katherine and Augustus rushed into the dining room. "Grandmama!" they squealed in unison and threw themselves into her arms. Elizabeth Stanley clutched them to her bosom, her face wet with a mixture of tears and joy. The children hugged her as though they would never let go.

"Would you look at that," Cody said, absently swiping at his nose. "Guess it was worthwhile after all."

"'Course, it was," Hickok said vigorously. "Knew that from the very start."

"Appears they've got some catchin' up to do. Maybe we ought to get on about our business."

"Bill, I just suspect you're right. We'll see 'em another time."

Hickok jerked a thumb into the hallway. Richter obediently hobbled past, and Stanley, his eyes downcast, fell in behind. Cody and Hickok, with a last look at the children, followed them through the house. Omohundro and Phelan were waiting in the vestibule.

"All set?" Omohundro asked.

"All set," Cody replied. "Whereabouts is the jail in this town?"

"Twenty Second Street," Hickok said. "I know the man in charge. Clubber Williams."

"How'd he get a name like that?"

"Same way you got hung with Buffalo Bill."

They marched Otto Richter and Leland Stanley out of the front door.

"I want you tell me about Billy McGlory."

Richter stared straight ahead. "There's nothing to tell."

"How about you, Mr. Stanley?"

"Captain, I'm at a loss," Stanley said uneasily. "I don't know anyone by that name."

Captain Clubber Williams glowered at them a moment. They were standing before his desk, and Hickok and Cody were seated off to one side. He wagged his head with disgust.

"Mr. Cody. Mr. Hickok," he said. "I think we're getting nowhere fast. Would you agree?"

"Yessir," Cody agreed. "They're not too talkative."

Hickok nodded. "Looks like a case of lockjaw."

"Sergeant O'Hara." Williams bellowed. "Get yourself in here."

The door slammed open. Sergeant Alvin O'Hara was built like a tree stump, wide and square without an ounce of suet. He stamped to attention in front of the desk.

"You called, Cap'n?"

"I did indeed, Sergeant," Williams said. "These gentleman are being uncooperative. Any suggestions?"

"I could take'em down to the basement, Cap'n."

"Excellent idea, Sergeant. They're all yours."

O'Hara grabbed Richter and Stanley by the scruff of the neck. He waltzed them out of the office like marionettes on jiggling strings and closed the door. Cody glanced around at Williams.

"I'd just bet nobody wants to visit the basement."

"Not with O'Hara," Williams said wryly. "Of course, whatever the outcome, you gentlemen deserve the credit. I doubt we'd ever have solved the case on our own."

"Will you have any problems?" Hickok asked. "I recollect you told me it was political suicide to take on the Stanleys."

"Thanks to you, we have Richter as a songbird. There'll be no politics involved when we charge Stanley with murder."

"Well, Cap'n, it couldn't happen to a nicer feller."

Williams studied them at length. "Did you hear we found three dead men in Central Park last night? Billy McGlory's men, they were."

Hickok looked like a sphinx. "New York's a mighty dangerous town."

"And saints preserve us, we stumbled across a satchel filled with cash. Twenty thousand, it was."

"That's a powerful lot of money."

"Yes, it's all very strange," Williams said. "Then one of our patrolmen had his horse stolen. Some fine figure of a man jerked him clean out of the saddle."

Cody feigned innocence. "Sounds like a big night in the park."

"Indeed, one mystery after another. I've been wondering what to do about it."

"See what you mean." Hickok knuckled his mustache as though pondering the problem. "Don't you have a widows' fund?"

"I'm proud to say we do," Williams remarked. "Every nickel goes to assist the wives of slain officers."

"Why not toss in the twenty thousand? Found money ought to go to a worthy cause."

Williams stared across the desk. He knew Hickok and Cody were behind last night's ruckus in Central Park. Yet he was equally aware that they were responsible for solving a heinous double murder. One thing balanced another on *his* scales of justice.

"I admire a lawman with a generous spirit, Mr. Hickok. The widows' fund thanks you."

There was a rap at the door. Sergeant O'Hara marched in and snapped to attention. "Cap'n, sir," he barked. "I'm sorry to report the rascals won't talk."

"Perhaps you haven't reasoned with them sufficiently."

"We beat the livin' bejesus out of them, Cap'n. They

fear Billy McGlory more than they do hangin'. I suppose it's his reputation for butcherin' people."

"Yes, you're probably right," Williams said. "I'm sure you did your best, Sergeant. Thank you."

O'Hara quick-stepped out of the office. Hickok arched one eyebrow in question. "What'd he mean about 'butcherin' people'."

"McGlory's trademark," Williams explained. "Anybody who turns on him gets hacked to pieces with a meat cleaver. You can imagine it inspires loyalty—and silence."

Cody exhaled heavily. "I tend to doubt I'd talk, either."

"Well, look on the bright side," Williams said. "Our friends Richter and Stanley have a date with the hangman. Half a loaf is better than none."

"Don't forget the kids," Cody added. "What counted most was gettin' them home safe. I'll settle for half a loaf."

"You're right," Hickok said with a sly smile. "One way or another, McGlory's day will come. Ain't that so, Cap'n?"

Williams laughed. "Are you a prophet, Mr. Hickok?"

"I've been known to predict a thing or two."

"I believe you've done so again."

"How's that, Cap'n?"

"Doomsday is just around the corner."

Hickok thought Billy McGlory was as good as dead.

CHAPTER 24

DUSK SWIFTLY faded into nightfall. The lamplights along Broadway flickered to life like bright-capped sentinels routing the dark. Theater marquees glowed throughout The Rialto.

Hickok and Cody ambled along the street at a leisurely pace. The weather was brisk and invigorating, and they had decided to walk to the theater. For the first time in weeks, their time was their own. The fight was fought and won.

Neither of them felt any great sense of victory. Richter and Stanley were in jail, charged with murder, and they were satisfied justice would be served. Yet there was no feeling of triumph or jubilation. Their mood was oddly melancholy.

"Funny the way things work out," Cody said glumly. "Don't think I ever felt so low in my life."

Hickok grunted. "Maybe I'll get drunk tonight."

"You miss 'em, too, don't you?"

"Gus and Kate?"

"Who else we talkin' about?"

"Well hell, guess it's only natural. We got used to havin' them around."

"That's a fact," Cody said, thoughtful a moment. "You reckon they'll do awright with their grandma?"

"Don't see why not," Hickok allowed. "She'll give 'em what they need most. Grandmas are good at lovin' kids."

"Yeah, you're likely right. All the same, I'll still miss 'em."

"You ain't rowin' that boat by yourself."

For a time, they walked on in silence. The Rialto was stirring with the pulse of nightlife, and all along the street actors were hurrying toward theaters. They passed the Eaves Costume Company, the major supplier of wigs and beards, tights and swords for Broadway productions. A man rushed out the door with a Viking helmet, complete with horns.

A block farther down Cody stopped before the window of stage photographer Napoleon Sarony. A genius with a camera, Sarony was all the rage with the stars of Broadway shows. Over the years daguerreotype had been replaced by tintype, and Sarony was the master of a new wet plate process. In the window, handsomely framed, was a photograph of Edwin Booth.

"Look at that," Cody said. "Edwin Booth, the greatest stage actor alive. Not bad, huh?"

Hickok inspected the photograph. "Why's he holdin' that skull?"

Booth was attired in costume for *Hamlet*. He was posed in a dramatic stance, a human skull cradled in the crook of one arm. Cody studied on it a moment.

"Always heard Shakespeare writes some pretty rough stuff. Way it looks, he must've killed somebody."

"Just more of that stage tomfoolery. Wonder where they got the skull?"

"Beats me." Cody cocked his head, staring at the photograph. "Maybe I ought to let 'em take my picture. You know, buckskins and all the trappins."

Hickok glanced at him. "Why you want your picture took?"

"Told you I've got a notion about the show business. Might just turn into a regular thing."

"I still say it's not fit work for a man. Don't care how much it pays."

Cody frowned. "A man's got to play the cards he's dealt. Wasn't that what you always said?"

"Yeah," Hickok conceded. "So what?"

"Well, maybe I was cut out for the show business. Maybe that's the hand I got dealt."

"Know what I think?"

"What's that?"

"You got a crooked dealer."

A few minutes later they approached the Lyceum Theater. Hickok still got a mild headache every time he saw his name in lights. Cody, on the other hand, was mesmerized by the glitzy display on the marquee. As they turned into the alleyway beside the theater, the dim figures of several men stepped from the shadows. Billy McGlory and four of his thugs blocked their path.

"Far enough," McGlory said in a rough voice. "You broke your word to me, Hickok."

"Hell I did," Hickok said. "I told you Richter would leave the park alive and kickin'. That's just what happened."

"Don't gimme that horseshit! He's gonna hang."

"Why'd you expect anything else, McGlory? He killed them people."

"Well, boyo, you played me for a fool. So now I'm gonna kill you."

"No, you ain't," Hickok said with a tight smile. "I'll drill you before any of your men clear leather. You won't live to see me die."

"That goes double," Cody added. "You'll get my first shot too, McGlory. Guarantee it'll stop your ticker."

McGlory weighed the odds. Something deep and visceral told him they were telling the truth. They would kill him even though his men would kill them. He thought he'd have to commit suicide in order to commit murder. The price of revenge suddenly seemed too steep.

"There's always another time," he said. "You haven't seen the last of me."

"McGlory," Hickok said.

"What?"

"Don't let me catch you out of the Bowery again. I'll shoot you on sight."

"You don't scare me, Hickok."

"Yeah, I do," Hickok said quietly. "Quit while you're ahead. You'll live longer."

McGlory brushed past him. The four thugs fell in behind and followed their boss from the alley. Cody let out a low whistle.

"That was close," he said. "Why didn't you tell him about Richter?"

Hickok shrugged. "I expect he'll learn soon enough."

Richter had agreed to testify against Leland Stanley. A deal had been struck with the district attorney and Richter would serve life in prison, without parole. Hickok was not keen on the idea, but it ensured the safety of the children. The day Stanley was hanged the threat was removed forever.

"You're not foolin' anybody," Cody said. "You didn't tell McGlory because you wanted to kill him, right?"

"You always was able to see through me, Bill."

"Ever cross your mind you might've got us both killed?"

"Never happen," Hickok said lightly. "We're the Heroes of the Plains."

"You think that makes us bulletproof?"

"I just suspect we're gonna live forever."

Cody was forced to laugh. "You're full of beeswax."

"The show business does that to a man."

They walked off toward the stage door.

The theater was packed. Yet the show was oddly off, plodding along in fits and starts. For the first time since the production began, the children were not backstage that night. Everyone in the cast felt a strange sense of loss.

The audience nonetheless enjoyed themselves. A final curtain call brought a standing ovation for Cody and Hickok. When they walked offstage, they found Charlie Phelan waiting in the wings. He greeted them with a downturned smile.

"Funny thing," he said. "All through the show, I kept looking around for the kids. Doesn't seem the same."

"Guess it'll never be the same," Cody observed. "Gus and Kate got to be part of the family."

"Yeah, I'll miss them," Phelan said. "Things have a way of working out for the best, though. They're better off with their grandmother."

Hickok clapped him on the shoulder. "Charlie, it appears you're out of a job. Got any irons in the fire?"

"Never rains but it pours," Phelan said. "A man walked into the office this afternoon. Hired me to find his wife."

"What happened to her?"

"She ran off with a notions drummer."

"Hell, you'll find her," Hickok said confidently. "You're a prize detective, Charlie. Aces high."

Cody nodded. "We couldn't have done it without you."

"Honor's all mine," Phelan said. "How many detectives get to work with Wild Bill Hickok and Buffalo Bill Cody? Things will seem awful dull after this."

The plainsmen wrung his hand with genuine warmth. Phelan moved off with a cheery wave and went out the stage door. They started toward their dressing room only to be intercepted by Ned Buntline. He held out a telegram to Hickok.

"Western Union for you," he said. "Delivery boy brought it by just before the curtain came down."

Hickok tore open the envelope. His mustache arced in a broad smile as he read the message. He handed the telegram to Cody.

"I'll be jiggered," Cody said, scanning the contents. "Why didn't Sheridan wire me?"

Hickok grinned. "You're on leave of absence with the show business. Gen'rals want somebody they can depend on."

"What is it?" Buntline demanded "What are you talking about?"

"Sioux's on the warpath," Hickok said, reclaiming the telegram. "Sheridan's ordered me to report to Fort Laramie."

"Wyoming Territory!" Buntline screeched. "You can't leave the show."

"Why not? Sheridan needs a scout and there's nothin' here stoppin' me. Duty calls."

"But we need you! Your audience needs you!"

Omohundro and Giuseppina were drawn by Buntline's squalling cries. Cody gave them a troubled look, and Omohundro glanced from one to the other. "What's wrong?"

"Jack, I've been rescued," Hickok said, waving the telegram. "There's a Sioux uprising and Sheridan wired me to come running. I'm headed for Fort Laramie."

"Good God!" Buntline howled. "Will someone talk some sense into him!"

"Ned's right," Cody said. "For your own good, you ought to stick with the show till the season ends. What happens to that marshal's job in Kansas if you're off chasin' Injuns in Wyoming?"

"That don't worry me none," Hickok said. "Couple of months is plenty of time to corral them redsticks. I'll still be wearin' a badge come May."

"Guess I'd be wastin' my breath to argue otherwise."

"Yep, no two ways about it, my mind's made up. I'll catch a train in the mornin'."

"Oh, Beel," Giuseppina cooed softly. "We will miss you so. Must you go?"

"Dove Eye, you're the purtiest Injun gal I ever did see. I'm gonna miss you, too."

"This is madness!" Buntline snapped. "You're throwing away the career of a lifetime. I made you a star!"

"Look here, Ned," Hickok told him. "Jack's ten times the actor I'll ever be. Write him a better part."

Omohundro shook his head. "I'd sooner you stayed with the show, Bill. Wouldn't hardly be the same without you."

"Nope," Hickok declared. "Have Ned put your name in bigger lights. You deserve it."

"Why not sleep on it?" Cody temporized. "Maybe you'll see it different in the mornin'."

Hickok stared at him. "I come East to get them kids settled and the job's done. Time to head West."

Cody knew then it was a lost cause. He'd seen the determined look and that stubborn jawline all too often before. There was nothing more to be said.

Wild Bill Hickok was done with New York.

Grand Central Station was swarming with people. Trains were departing from every gate and passengers scurried to clamber aboard. The main terminal was chaos in motion.

Hickok paused for a last look at the ceiling. Shafts of sunlight from the stained-glass windows played off the azure dome and the celestial span of the zodiac. The sight reminded him of another morning, weeks past, when he'd first arrived in New York. He thought he would never return.

Cody walked beside him through the terminal. Outside, they descended the stairs to a platform beneath the vast iron-roofed railyard. Hickok's train was scheduled to depart at eight o'clock and they were a few minutes early. A cloak of silence enveloped them as they stood in the crush of people waiting to board. Neither of them wanted to be the first to say good-bye.

"Hate to see you go," Cody said, clearing his throat. "You still got time to change your mind."

"Guess not," Hickok said, his war bag clutched in one hand, "You and me both know I wasn't never cut out for the show business. Just ain't where I belong."

"Yeah, I know what you mean. There's times I get a hankerin' for the plains. But then—"

"You hear the applause and them crowds lookin' at you like you just rode in on a white horse. You always was a showboat."

"Goddarnit but it's true," Cody admitted. "Wish you was more that way yourself. No tellin' where it'd take us."

"Nowhere I'd want to go," Hickok said. "You're welcome to your show business and New York, too. The limelight's not for me, pardner."

Their past lives were a jumble of myths and realities, bits of illusion and shards of truth. Today they sensed a turning point, and a point of no return for all that lay ahead. One was destined to play it out on the stage and the other on the plains.

"Well, don't kill all the Sioux," Cody said with an exaggerated gesture. "Leave some for me on the summer campaign."

"There's likely enough to go around."

Hickok abruptly looked past him. Augustus and Katherine, led by a matronly woman, were moving through the crowd. Cody followed his gaze.

"I asked 'em to come," he said. "They'd never get over it if you left without seeing them. Just wouldn't understand."

"Bill, you know I ain't much on good-byes."

"Then now's a good time to start."

"Wild Bill!"

Augustus hurled himself into Hickok's arms. Katherine was only a step behind, clutching him around the waist, her eyes moonlike. He swallowed hard around a lump in his throat.

"Don't go!" Augustus pleaded. "We want you to stay."

"Yes, please do," Katherine insisted. "Buffalo Bill said you really didn't have to go."

Hickok laughed. "Buffalo Bill's been known to spin a yarn or two."

Elizabeth Stanley moved closer. "I understand you've been called to service by the army, Mr. Hickok. We want to wish you Godspeed and good fortune."

"Why thank you, ma'am," Hickok replied. "That's mighty kind of you to say so."

"Not at all," she said warmly. "Our most heartfelt gratitude goes with you."

"Wish I was going too!" Augustus exclaimed. "I want to see all the Wild West!"

Hickok ruffled his hair. "Gus, once you get growed up, you come on out West. I could use a deputy with your grit."

"All Aboard!"

The conductor's voice rang out over the station. People embraced loved ones and murmured their last good-byes, hurrying to board the train. Katherine pulled Hickok down and hugged him fiercely around the neck. Her voice was husky with emotion.

"I will love you forever and ever, Wild Bill. You will always by my Lancelot."

Hickok again swallowed hard. "Kate, I ain't never gonna forget you, either. Was I ever to marry, you'd be my gal."

"Will you wait for me to grow up? Will you, Wild Bill?"

"Cross my heart I will."

Katherine kissed him soundly, and Augustus snuffled loudly, his eyes wet with tears. Hickok disengaged himself from the children and nodded earnestly to Elizabeth Stanley. He stuck out his hand to Cody.

"We'll meet somewheres down the trail," he said gruffly. "The show business ain't got you yet."

Cody clasped his hand. "Look for me when you see me."

"I ain't never hard to find."

The train lurched forward with a toot from the engineer's whistle. Hickok swung aboard the observation deck on the last passenger coach. He stood tall, shoulders squared, and grandly waved his hat overhead. His mustache curled in a nutcracker grin.

"So long, Kate! So long, Gus!"

"So long, Wild Bill!"

"Soo long, New York!"